A Pepper McCallan Novel

By Alexi Venice

Copyright

Published by eBookIt.com

ISBN-13: 978-1-4566-2549-8

This book is dedicated to all of you who love to
read fiction as much as I do

The Pepper McCallan Series by Alexi Venice

Ebola Vaccine Wars – Introducing Pepper McCallan

Svea's Sins – A Pepper McCallan Novel

Victus – Margaret River Winery (Part I) – A Pepper McCallan Novel

Margaret River Winery (Part II) – A Pepper McCallan Novel

Table of Contents

PRINCIPLE CHARACTERS

Alistair Webb: Prime Minister of Great Britain

Allen Montgomery: Director of the Counterterrorism Unit in Boston

Bill McCallan: Physician and Pepper's husband

Blaire Starr: Jackie's younger sister

Bodil Stolt: First Swedish Minister for Foreign Affairs

Brent William Cahill: U.S. Counterterrorism Special Agent

Captain Linda: Captain of Ralph and Susan Tollefson's yacht

Carrie Ann: Pharmacy technician at Southview Hospital

Cecil Scott: President of the United States

Clive Von Steinland: Dana's partner from St. Martin

Dana de Wit: Mistress, spy and fixer from St. Martin

Felipe Malstrom: Swedish pharmacy intern at Philadelphia General Hospital

Gabriel Friedman: U.S. Secretary of State

Henrik Jensen: Svea Lovgren's stepfather

Jackie Margaret Starr: Trainer-owner of StarrFitness

Juergen Swanson: Svea's ex-husband

<u>Vicki</u>: PACU nurse at Southview Hospital in Minneapolis

<u>Weng Chee</u>: U.S. Counterterrorism agent in Bangkok, Thailand

PROLOGUE
Svea is Sworn

September 2018

Stockholm, Sweden

Svea Lovgren clasped her Queen Anne pearl necklace behind her neck and regarded her reflection in the mirror. Her long, light brown hair was swept into a French chignon that accentuated her patrician cheekbones and slender neck. Her porcelain skin was flawless, only nascent wrinkles around the outside edges of her eyes, the first sign that she was not immune to the aging process after unparalleled beauty for 36 years.

Among the stunning women of Stockholm, Svea still drew admiring stares from men, and envious glances from women. Her features were a rare combination of perfection and balance. Sculpted eyebrows framed Baltic-blue eyes. A slender nose lead to a button tip, accentuating her refined profile. Valentine-shaped lips, giving the impression of love, cleverly masked her Machiavellian core. She was a force of nature.

The pearl earrings resting in her seashell-shaped ears matched her necklace, which had been a graduation gift from her mother. She knew her stepfather, Henrik, had paid for them, but they were from her mother. She wouldn't accept a gift from Henrik, but she would benefit from him financing her mother's well-meaning intentions.

Unbeknownst to her mother, Svea had been relieved to leave home for university. She loved her mother, but her stepfather had a certain sleaziness about him that had made Svea's skin crawl throughout her adolescence. Leaving for university meant she no longer would have to endure his leering.

Svea attended Uppsala University with other wealthy Swedes, including Swedish royalty. She belonged to the elite class of Sweden, and chose to work in government rather than basking in her stepfather's wealth.

On this pivotal day in her career, Svea applied a small amount of makeup. She chose a subdued shade of rose lipstick since this was a governmental ceremony, not a social event. She wore a three-quarter length slip over her pale Swedish skin, which would be concealed by a conservative navy dress. While attractive, the dress was not revealing, because the new Minister for Foreign Affairs wasn't expected to look sexy during her installation ceremony. She was expected to look austere. After all, the Prime Minister of Sweden, Olaf Carlsson, had just appointed Svea to the post, a promotion from Deputy Minister, and he was personally presiding over her swearing-in ceremony.

Svea's appointment had come up unexpectedly for everyone, as her predecessor, Ms. Bodil Stolt, had offended the Arab states by raising the topic of women's rights during her speech in Dubai. Minister Stolt had been on official business in the Arab nations, and was asked to make some opening remarks at a dinner for the heads of state and royalty. Most of the Sheiks had walked out during former Minister Stolt's remarks, but King Abdullah, the most influential, had stayed and listened to the entirety of her cavalier comments. He was a calm man, waiting until the next day in a private meeting to tell her she was out of line by presuming to meddle in their social conventions. He informed her he no longer would take her meetings, and would be requesting Swedish Prime Minister Carlsson to fire her from office.

Stolt had been surprised but not upset, mistakenly believing the controversy would blow over. She had underestimated the King's convictions about a woman's place in society. King Abdullah not only followed through on his request for her termination, but also rallied the leaders from all other Arab states to put pressure on Prime Minister Carlsson for a variety of retaliatory actions.

The King showed Sweden he meant business by calling Carlsson personally and cancelling an order for $40 million in Saab missiles. That left the Swedes holding the inventory for missiles they didn't need, but revenue they did.

The Arabs proceeded to engage in a widespread cooling of business deals between Sweden and the Arab states, including much-needed petroleum products. This resulted in Swedish businessmen complaining to Prime Minister Carlsson to appease the Arabs, so the

Swedes could get back to manufacturing and commerce.

The final consequence of former Minister Stolt's faux pas was mostly diplomatic window dressing, but the Arabs' act of recalling all of their diplomats who were posted in Sweden had its intended effect. Prime Minister Carlsson capitulated, firing Ms. Stolt, which left her Deputy Minister, Ms. Svea Lovgren, to ascend to the position of Minister, at least on an interim basis.

Svea had been in politics her entire adult life, was fluent in Arabic, cultured and beautiful, so the Prime Minister had high hopes in her ability to re-establish diplomatic relations. And she knew how to keep her mouth shut in both politics and social situations, which is what he needed.

Svea knew what was expected of her and would not disappoint. She had trained for this moment her entire life. She had no aspirations to run for Prime Minister, but being in his cabinet would accomplish her domestic agenda, and, more importantly, provide a platform for her foreign agenda, which she hoped would be her legacy to the world.

She closed the door of her penthouse apartment and took the elevator to the first floor. She resided in an historic, sandstone building that had a flatiron footprint the size of a city block. Her Security Detail, Ulrik, had her government-issue Volvo waiting for her at the curb.

***

The installation ceremony was conducted in Prime Minister Carlsson's expansive office in Sager House at 11:15 a.m. sharp. Svea placed her hand on a Bible and swore to uphold the Swedish Constitution. Her fellow cabinet members, some dignitaries from the Swedish Riksdag, and specially-invited guests from the Social Democratic Party, were in attendance.

Afterward, there was a small lunch reception next door to Sager House in the Ministry of Foreign Affairs, known as Arvfurstens Palats, or the Prince's Palace. Since 1906, it had been the site of the Swedish Foreign Affairs offices. Svea's office was located in the austere building, which was originally built in the late 18th Century.

Absent from Svea's ceremony was Mr. Juergen Swanson, Svea's ex-husband of three years. He had moved out of their home at her request after eight years of marriage. She had insisted on the split, because he didn't support her career advancement at the expense of having a family. Even before they were married, she had told him children were out of the question, so if he wanted them, he would have to look for someone else. Perhaps he believed he could change her mind. When it became apparent that she was resolute in her stance, he had agreed there was nothing more to the marriage. She recently heard he had found someone. He was a nice- looking man, so she wasn't surprised. She wished him well, not giving their divorce a second thought.

As for Svea, she had a steady cadre of suitors in hot pursuit. She occasionally allowed a man the pleasure of her company overnight, but, unless he had a specific talent she needed, she moved on.

At her post-installation lunch, the seating arrangement placed her next to Prime Minister Carlsson, at his request, so they could talk business. After salads were consumed, the Prime Minister made it clear to Svea that foreign relations with the Arab States was at the top of his agenda. He ordered her to attend the Global Energy Summit in London, scheduled for the following week, seeking out as many Arab representatives as possible to make amends and sort out the situation. She readily agreed, and looked forward to the challenge.

She did not tell him, however, that she already had hatched a plan of her own that would restore Sweden to economic equilibrium, and leave her indelible mark in history, if she played her cards right in London.

***

CHAPTER 1
Svea Meets Volkov

London, England

Svea had been attending the Global Energy Summit in London for three days straight, and she was bored. She had a personal agenda for the summit, urgently needing to implement it.

The Russian President, Vadik Volkov, was central to her plan. She knew that Volkov meant "wolf" in Russian, and that Volkov had lived up to his name in both government and female affairs, but she was drawn to the wolf, and curious what he could do for her. With his resources and intellect, she was counting on him to accelerate her agenda for revenge against the United States.

In truth, Swedish politics provided little adventure or satisfaction for Svea. Volkov, on the other hand, could potentially add adventure to her personal life while simultaneously catapulting her onto a powerful world stage. Almost everyone who had interacted with Volkov over the years considered him pathological, viewing his methods and motives frightening. But Svea was intrigued.

She wanted to learn as much as possible from him while manipulating him for her own gain. Her female assets were essential to her plan. She assumed he wouldn't harm her with her security detail close by, and foreign relations with the Swedish sovereign at stake, so she connived a sexual relationship. After all, sex was Svea's most influential attribute, and she was accomplished at using it.

She seized her opportunity at Bodo's Schloss, a popular dance club in London that had been closed to the public, and reserved for the Global Energy Summit attendees and their numerous entourages. Bodo was a nickname for a young lady who was one of Prince Harry's classmates, and Schloss was German for castle, playfully similar to American slang for a fifth appendage. It was the perfect blend of ritzy and raunchy for the ultra-wealthy European crowd.

A fellow named Skippy, also Harry's classmate, had launched Bodo's Schloss in honor of his royal friend. Gaining popularity immediately, the who's who of London hung out there, hoping to bump into Prince Harry. Bodo's was conveniently located near Kensington Palace in the event Harry was in residence. This was a ludicrous notion, of course, because by the time Harry rolled out of any club, the sun would be up, and there'd be over a hundred middle-aged women in Kensington Park walking their dogs. He'd be spotted immediately, and barraged. By the women, not the dogs.

Bodo's exterior was Alpine ski chalet, the theme continuing inside. After paying an astronomical cover charge, a club-goer would be treated to model-like bar maids wearing blonde braids and seductive white blouses. It even had a red gondola with a working door and comfortable seats inside, flanked by drink cups.

Bodo's subscribed to the belief that everyone loved skiing, and they loved dancing after they skied. It offered a sizeable dance floor with a stage for live music.

Tonight, the global heads of state were a stiff crowd, so there wasn't a lot of dancing. Some of their younger attachés were swaying to a mix of modern music, but they were mindful of their bosses, keeping an eye out for disapproving nods or signals that it was time to leave.

Svea felt at home in the surroundings, having skied her entire life and spent a fair amount of time in clubs. She intended to enjoy herself, but had to dispense with her first order of business, making nice with the Arab Sheiks, as ordered by her boss. She knew they'd cut out soon because they weren't the partying types. All business. No alcohol. She wouldn't dare offend them by holding a drink herself when conversing with them.

Svea's Deputy Minister approached King Abdullah's attaché, and requested a moment of the King's time for a conversation with her. Svea pretended to look the other way, but saw the attaché survey her with a raised eyebrow. He nodded to her Deputy. The Deputy returned, and Svea took her time wrapping up her conversation with her counterpart from Belgium. Then, she walked over to King Abdullah, relishing his admiring gaze as she drew near.

The King's attaché introduced her with a feigned boredom. "King Abdullah, may I present the new Minister for Foreign Affairs for Sweden."

"Madame. It is a pleasure to meet you," lied the King in English.

"The pleasure is mine," lied Svea in Arabic.

The King raised his eyebrows, surprised at her Arabic. He switched to his native language.

"Are you advancing the same agenda as your predecessor?" he asked.

"Absolutely not," she said in Arabic. "And on behalf of Sweden, I apologize to you and your Kingdom for the offense. Ms. Stolt was presumptuous and brazen. She wasn't representing the sentiments of Prime Minister Carlsson or of the Swedish sovereignty. I intend to restore the restraint to the post that it historically had."

She's a smooth one, thought the King. "You have some mending to do. I can only speak for myself, but I'm sure the other Kings will be receptive to your message. It will take a while for the wounds to heal though. This type of insult cannot be so easily erased, no?"

They're going to milk it for all its worth, she thought. "Of course, and rightfully so, Your Majesty. I completely understand. I'm committed to you and the other Kings for the duration."

He kept his chin high, but lowered his eyelids so he could survey her face over his impressive proboscis. "I think you'll do quite well in this role."

"Thank you," she said.

They shook hands, and she took her cue to depart his company. Mission accomplished. At least the first step.

She dispatched her Deputy to fetch a Cosmo for her while she scanned the crowd for Vadik Volkov. Tonight was her last chance to talk to him.

Her Deputy returned with two cocktails. They clinked glasses and sipped. There was something about her exchange with King Abdullah that was reminiscent of Svea's stepfather, Henrik Jensen, the *American*. They didn't resemble each other physically, the King being dark with olive-colored skin, and Henrik being a fair skinned archetypical Nordic type. But they were about the same age, at least 30 years' Svea's senior, and they both had a lascivious look in their eyes. They were attracted to her, and would pounce on the opportunity for sex if given an invitation, *or leverage*. Svea had learned that cruel lesson the hard way with Jensen. At least the King wasn't an American like Jensen, she thought. Henrik's profile flashed through her mind and she felt sick. She'd prefer the Arab to an American. She recalibrated her mind, and took another sip of her Cosmo.

She eyed the crowd and, being taller than most, saw movement in the opposite corner of the dance floor. It was the unmistakable head of Volkov. He looked very Russian with his broad forehead and almond-shaped eyes. His sandy blonde hair was thinning, barely covering his head. He was trim and fit, always on the move. He never stood still, even when he was standing still.

She sipped her Cosmo, and continued making small talk with other diplomats while waiting for an opening with Volkov. Finally, she told her Deputy to approach Volkov's militaristic-looking adjutant to arrange an introduction. Her Deputy understood that, as soon as Svea was introduced to Volkov, the Deputy was to vamoose into the crowd. He made his move during a break in Volkov's nonstop parade of men from the southern hemisphere who wanted to compare notes on oil production.

During the Deputy's conversation with Volkov's adjutant, the adjutant conducted the obligatory recon of Svea, nodding his head in appreciation of her beauty. He whispered to Volkov, motioning in Svea's direction. Volkov glanced at Svea, gave a curt nod, followed by a tilt of his head, and approved her request.

Volkov was intrigued by the gorgeous, long haired woman. He never would have rebuffed such a creature, although he assumed it would be another boring diplomatic exchange.

He couldn't have been further from the truth. After her Deputy hastily departed, Svea spoke to Volkov in passable Russian.

"President Vadik Volkov, I'm Svea Lovgren. I hope we can be close friends."

He took her offered hand in his, noticing her delicate bone structure and supple skin. He also noticed that she let her hand linger in his for a moment.

He questioned whether she knew what she was actually saying in Russian, so he politely responded. "Congratulations on your new appointment, Minister, I'm always open to new friendships."

"I hope we're going to be more than friends," she said, again in Russian, training her piercing blue eyes on him. She sipped her drink and seductively swayed her hips to the club music, maintaining eye contact. Her message was received loud and clear. Volkov appreciated that she looked like a lady who always got her way.

"In that case, Ms. Lovgren, perhaps we should continue our dialogue in a more private setting," he suggested.

"You don't dance?" she asked.

"Absolutely not," he said. "Would now be a good time to leave together?"

"Yes," she said. "Let me notify my Deputy and security detail," which she did by giving them a look to return to her side.

After the logistics were conveyed to Svea's entourage, Volkov ushered her out the back to his idling black Mercedes, instructing his driver to bring them to One Aldywch Hotel. They spoke easily about the Summit sessions during their short ride.

This accomplishment was the first thrill for Svea.

***

CHAPTER 2

Brent's Stakeout

London, England

Brent Cahill ended his call with Jackie Starr. The only thing he missed about his old fashioned desk phone was that he could slam the handset in the cradle after a frustrating conversation. With a woman. Like Jackie Starr. She was an enigma. And she had him tied up in knots.

He didn't know what he had to do to crack her tough exterior. He'd been pursuing her for two months. At least he thought he'd been pursuing her. She didn't seem to appreciate him. While he was showering her with attention, she was pulling back. He couldn't stop himself. Her allure permeated his entire being. When they had been together in Minneapolis, where she lived, he had been passionate yet gentlemanly on the few dates they had managed.

He had been on assignment there, but had to return to his job in Boston, which took him on assignment all over the world. He thought she had felt the same way because they couldn't take their eyes or hands off each other, but now he wasn't sure. Maybe he had misread the entire situation. What is my next move? he wondered.

In actuality, Brent didn't have time to stew over a woman. He was one of the highest ranking U.S. Counterterrorism Agents in the field. Make no mistake, he was a field agent, not a desk agent. He had been active in the field since he had joined the United States clandestine agency after honorable discharge from the Navy's SWCC (Special Warfare Combatant-Craft Crewmen) force 12 years ago.

SWCC was code for fast boats and big guns. Brent had patrolled the waterways of North and South America, supporting the Navy Seals all over the world. He could handle himself on land, on the water in any boat, and under water in scuba gear. He knew he had been destined for the Navy, having had an affinity for water from a young age. He was scuba-certified at age 12, which was the youngest the instructors would teach. He surfed and dove throughout college at U.C. Santa Barbara, teaching multiple dive classes to put himself through college. He graduated from college with a degree in criminal justice, and a minor in Arabic languages.

Recently, Brent had been recognized and promoted for solving an international terror attack on a U.S. pharmaceutical company called Futuraceutical. The attack had taken place in London and had been perpetrated by a faction of an anti-Big Pharma group originating in Austria under the name of BodyTruth Worldwide. BodyTruth had planted a bomb outside the Lyceum Theatre in London that had exploded and killed 14 Futuraceutical employees, injuring 21 more. Brent had worked closely with his Counterterrorism counterpart in England, Manfred Kincaid, and the Futuraceutical Company Chief of Compliance, Pepper McCallan, to solve who had attacked her colleagues and family, and why. In fact, it was Pepper who had introduced Brent to Ms. Jackie Starr, the pretty puzzle preoccupying his thoughts.

Brent's first interaction with Jackie had been at her workout empire named StarrFitness, located in Minneapolis. Jackie had dazzled him while they had done a strenuous CrossFit workout, with Pepper McCallan tagging along.

Brent had crashed Pepper's regular workout with Jackie, and it had changed his life. Or so he had thought. After Pepper had excused herself for the night, the sparks had ignited between Jackie and Brent in her office. His senses had been overpowered by her mischievous brown eyes, sexy smile and sculpted 29-year-old body. He had kissed her until they were drunk with passion, but she had drawn a line in the sand. No sex. He couldn't blame her. Instead, they had ordered in Chinese food and eaten it on the sofa in her office, making out and laughing between bites. He had stayed until the middle of the night talking to her.

Jackie was a compact package of muscle and feminine curves, and she was now the object of Brent's sexual desires, including his conscious and subconscious thoughts. Jackie was perhaps too athletic and independent for some men, but he was drawn to her strength and independence. He wasn't interested in a vulnerable girl for whom he'd have to think. He'd been there and done that, and frankly, it had been a lot of work.

Now he was beginning to think it was a hopeless situation with Jackie, his career taking him all over the world, and her business grounding her in Minneapolis. Tonight's frustrating phone call had demonstrated how difficult it could be for a long distance relationship.

Jackie had made it clear she wasn't a wall flower who would wait for Brent to surface occasionally, wining and dining her between global assignments. She wanted a steady commitment.

He was sure she could find someone stable. She probably had men hitting on her routinely. A girl couldn't look like Jackie and not have men falling at her feet. She was surrounded by good looking men in her gym all day, and a girl could get lonely at night. She might cave to an invitation. The thought drove him so mad he wanted to put his fist through a wall.

Jackie was from New Castle England, on the Scottish border, her faint English-Scottish accent making his legs weak. He had picked up on her accent when she had been angry at him, intriguing him like no other woman's. Angry or not, it had a lilting quality that made him feel as if he were strolling along with her on the green bluffs in Scotland, overlooking the North Sea.

Brent had never daydreamed about a woman like this, envisioning himself in a long-term relationship with her. His daydreams usually included sexy themes, but dissipated before a relationship could emerge. He had always been straightforward with women, telling them he couldn't settle down due to his job. The reality had been that his job had been a convenient excuse to avoid commitment. With Jackie, he wanted to commit, and he was surprised to find himself doing mental gymnastics about how he could have a long-term relationship with her and still do his job. He didn't want to give up either.

Presently, Brent was stuck in London on a stakeout. He had been there for a week and ached for Jackie's touch. On their last date in Minneapolis, she had invited him to spend the night at her house, unfortunately offering up the sofa rather than her bed. They had wanted each other so much while kissing, he was sure he was destined for her bedroom, but she had made it clear she wasn't interested in a one-night stand. She wanted a real relationship before sex, and he had respected her wishes. Hell, the rejection had made her hotter. He needed to show her what she meant to him, hopefully convincing her he could be in a monogamous, meaningful relationship, regardless of distance.

He had suggested they spend a week with each other on vacation, and had talked about going to an island in the Caribbean. Unfortunately, he couldn't give her a firm date, so she seemed like she was losing interest. He felt like she was out of his league.

Shit. He was losing focus on his present assignment. He was supposed to be tailing the Russian President, Vadik Volkov, and photographing his dining and sleeping partners. It was a full-time job. There were 28 countries represented in London at the Global Energy Summit, a conference the President of the United States had organized, attended for opening ceremonies, and then ditched. The U.S. Secretary of State, Gabriel Friedman, had stayed in town, and was representing the U.S. at the table during the numerous meetings. Volkov seemed intent on dining with most of the attendees.

It was after 10 p.m. London time, and President Volkov was departing Bodo's Schloss with a ravishing beauty, legs as long as a gazelle's. She had her hand through Volkov's arm, surrounded by security detail. Brent was able to photograph their exit from the club in the alley, and their hasty entrance into the back seat of his chauffeured black Mercedes.

Brent was surprised Volkov had picked up a woman at the club. Had the hosts hired hookers? Was she Russian? She looked Russian to Brent. Brent wasn't surprised because Volkov was constantly proving his virility. The lady in a sequins dress definitely was not Volkov's new, young wife - the gymnast who Brent would have recognized.

Brent also knew Volkov was staying at One Aldwych Hotel, on the corner of Aldwych and Wellington Street. Volkov had recently started staying there, as it was commonly known in the intelligence community that he was acquaintances with the new owner. Volkov also liked that hotel because it had a chlorine-free lap swim pool with underwater music and mood lighting, swimming being Volkov's preferred form of exercise. The management indulged Volkov's private exercise at any time of the day. It also had a full spa, so Volkov had enjoyed a rub-down after swimming for the last three days.

Brent watched the Mercedes drive down the alley. Volkov's motorcade would have to drive on the main thoroughfares back to One Aldwych, so Brent stashed his camera and drove his government-owned BMW to the hotel by a shorter route, beating Volkov's motorcade by a few minutes.

Brent had observed over the last few days that Volkov entered through the front door and modern lobby of the hotel, rather than coming in through the service entrance in the back where the delivery trucks parked. Most heads of state took advantage of the added security, and protection from media, that a hotel service entrance provided. Not Volkov. He basked in the attention and limelight as he strode through the compact lobby. At this time of night, there were still plenty of media camped out on the sidewalk awaiting Volkov's return.

Brent parked on Exeter Street at the corner of Strand, which gave him a full view of the front and back entrances. He aimed his camera at the hotel entrance. He glanced to his right and saw the scaffolding still attached to the Lyceum Theatre where they were rebuilding the wall after the bomb blast four months prior. He shuddered to think how many people were killed and maimed when the anti-Big Pharma terrorist group retaliated against Futuraceutical company employees. He thought about Pepper McCallan, her husband Bill, and their son Jake, who had died in the blast. They were good people, and it had ruined their lives. The tragedy reminded him of the importance of his work, so he refocused on the Aldwych entrance.

Brent noticed that the leggy, brown haired beauty with the silver dress on was about six steps behind Volkov, buried in his entourage. Brent took more photos of them entering the hotel, then called to relay his report to his nightshift replacement. He'd type up his report when he returned to his hotel. Hopefully, he'd be able to sleep, but the time difference from Boston to London was upsetting his circadian rhythm. His body knew it was midafternoon back home, but he was physically exhausted from a day of work in London. He anticipated his mind would be racing as soon as he lay down. Maybe he'd grab a quick Carlsberg on tap in the hotel bar before he retired for the evening.

***

CHAPTER 3

Hamanasi Resort

Hopkins, Belize

Bill and Pepper McCallan sat on the veranda of Hamanasi Resort in Hopkins discussing their travel plans. They had been at Hamanasi almost a month to recuperate from the loss of their ten-year-old son, Jake, due to a terrorist attack on Pepper's previous employer, Futuraceutical Company. The attack had taken place in London and was perpetrated against Pepper's former employer because its Chief Operating Officer, David Arnout, had killed a village of Africans in his greedy quest to develop an Ebola vaccine. Jake had been caught in the notorious crossfire, destroying the McCallan family of three.

After Jake's funeral, Pepper had helped Brent Cahill and his English counterpart, Manfred Kincaid, Special Investigator for the United Kingdom Counterterrorism Agency, solve the mystery of who masterminded and implemented the attack. Brent and Pepper became friends throughout the three-month ordeal.

The investigation brought Brent and Pepper to Belize to inspect a bank account and safe-deposit box owned by David Arnout. They discovered incriminating evidence that resulted in his charges and ultimate plea agreement with the U.S. government. Bill had joined Brent and Pepper, and after Brent had returned to the United States, Pepper and Bill had decided to stay in Belize for a while.

Pepper and her friend-trainer, Jackie Starr, were keeping up with each other through texting, mostly about Jackie babysitting Pepper's disabled Duck Tolling Retriever named Daisy.

But Jackie had texted Pepper earlier in the day about Brent. He had invited Jackie to meet him on the Caribbean island of St. Martin for a romantic getaway. Jackie was expressing ambivalence about making the trip. She insisted it wasn't the travel or time away from running StarrFitness that was the issue. It was 'something else.' Pepper couldn't figure out what the issue really was. They texted:

Jackie, how is my little Toller doing?

Daisy is doing fine. She's easy to babysit. I think she loves me more than you now. She's sleeping in bed with me!

I really miss her. The resort cat isn't a substitute. She bites me! I'm anxious to get home to see Daisy.

Yeah, I want my friend back too.

Have you heard from Brent?

Yes.

And?

He invited me to meet him in St. Martin but I don't know what to do...

I thought you liked him.

I do, but a week together for our third date?

Ur both adults.

It's not that.

What then?

What if I can't stand him after the 3rd day?

Fly home!

It's not that easy.

Sure it is. You have to take a chance. He's a great guy. Getting away from work might be good for you.

What if we're not good together?

Did you feel a spark when he was in Mpls?

YES!

Well, there's your answer.

I wish you and Bill could double date with us. It would make me feel more comfortable.

Hmmm. Interesting thot. R u serious?

Yes. Would u consider meeting us in St. Martin?

Let me talk to Bill. What about Daisy?

Ur parents-in-law?

I'll text my parents-in-law.

Pepper sipped her key lime pie martini while she stroked Ginger, the Calico resort cat. She considered how best to spring this news on Bill, who wasn't prone to spontaneous travel plans. Ginger's personal kingdom included the entire sofa, but she made an exception for Pepper, tolerating Pepper's presence at the opposite end, as long as Pepper gently patted her back. Ginger had bitten Pepper's forearm when she initially sat down, but after a few scratches behind the ear, Pepper had ingratiated herself to the cat. Ginger did not care for Bill and would bite him if he came anywhere near her kingdom. Thus, Bill was relegated to a club chair a few feet away. He sipped his Belikan beer and watched the sun set over the bay, trying his best to ignore the feline but not his beautiful wife.

Pepper was the center of Bill's existence. She and Jake both had been, but they no longer had Jake. Pepper and Bill had met when she was in her last year of law school and Bill was in his last year of medical school. When Pepper had walked into a gathering at her friend's house, Bill's world had been turned upside down with attraction. She had a captivating personality, one that drew in both men and women. While Pepper was a head turner, women didn't feel threatened by her beauty because she was so disarmingly sincere. She genuinely wanted to know about other people's stories, and she didn't have an ounce of ego in her. Bill had noticed through the years that Pepper purposefully didn't talk about herself or her work to others. Instead, she asked them about their interests and accomplishments, and their hobbies and ideas, because she didn't consider herself that special.

In fact, part of Bill's attraction to Pepper was that she didn't know she was beautiful. She didn't work at it with products and curling irons or seductive clothing. She was simple and low maintenance, or as low maintenance as any woman could be while still being a woman. They were women after all. He knew he loved her from the moment she looked in his eyes and said his name. He hadn't thought of another woman since.

***

There were other couples enjoying cocktail hour on the Hamanasi veranda, talking softly, reading books and playing cards. Most of them were 20 years older than Pepper and Bill. The resort catered to retired and romantic couples. It was very quiet and low key, and the staff was beyond polite. Cocktail hour was from 4-6 p.m. every night, then dinner service started and went through 9 p.m. Most of the crowd were early bird diners. Pepper and Bill laughed in the privacy of their suite at the older-crowd culture in which they found themselves, eating dinner at 6 p.m. What were they becoming at the ages of 37 and 42?

"So Bill," inquired Pepper.

"Yes?" He held his gaze on the bay.

"Do you want to go to St. Martin next week?"

"Why?" he asked.

"Brent invited Jackie to meet him there, and she's chicken to go alone. She wants us to be there at the same time for a week-long double date."

"Oh." He watched a sailboat making its way to a buoy.

"So?" she prompted.

"Do you want to go to St. Martin?" he asked.

"Yes. I want to support Jackie because I think they"d be great together," she said.

"Okay." He watched the sailboat deckhand gaffe the mooring line from underwater at the buoy marker.

"I take it that's a 'yes'?" she asked.

"Is there a direct flight from Belize City?" he asked, watching the deckhand tie off the line on the bow cleat.

"I don't know. I wanted to talk to you before I checked," she said.

Pepper thought that was enough info for Bill to let him consider the proposal. They sipped their drinks and watched the bay.

There was a couple sitting in the two club chairs that flanked the sofa where Pepper and Ginger sat. They were in their mid-sixties and looked attractive in an understated fashion. They wore the typical attire for resort guests; he in lightweight tan pants with a polo shirt and she in a sedate sundress. They were both tanned and friendly looking, and very American in appearance.

The man addressed Pepper. "Excuse me, Miss, I didn't mean to eavesdrop, but did I hear you were considering going to St. Martin next week?"

"Yes, you heard correctly," said Pepper.

"I'm Ralph Tollefson and this is my wife, Susan."

Pepper stood and shook both of their hands. "I'm Pepper McCallan and this is my husband, Bill. Pleasure to meet you."

Ralph and Susan looked up at Pepper, who was tall, slim, and sporting long blonde hair with sad brown eyes. She was thinner than she had been in quite some time, not having eaten much since Jake had passed away. Susan immediately sensed the sadness in Pepper.

"We're planning to be in St. Martin one week from today ourselves," said Ralph.

"Oh, that's interesting. Are you flying out of Belize City?" asked Pepper.

"Well, no. We're traveling by sea. That's our yacht moored out in the bay," he said, motioning. There was only one motorized yacht moored in the bay, and it was ginormous.

Holy crap, thought Pepper. It was awe-inspiring. The Tollefsons had glided in silently last night after dusk, looking like a space ship had landed. Everyone at the resort had been conjecturing who it was. George Clooney? The President of a third world country? It was three stories high, over 100 feet long, and was a brushed silver in color, in stark contrast to other Caribbean yachts, which were mostly white. There was nothing like a multi-million-dollar yacht to get the resort goers gossiping. Ralph and Susan were high rollers. They must have decided to slum it for dinner at the resort. Pepper looked at the pier and saw their skiff tied there.

A tall black man was lounging on it. The skiff itself was at least 18 feet long and had two

150 horse Mercury outboards on it. Where Pepper came from, one 150 Merc was plenty enough for an 18-foot ski boat to pull a skier out of the water and buzz around the lake. This skiff was a work horse. If people were cheese, the Tollefsons would be a $180 round of Humboldt Fog from the northern California coast, thought Pepper.

"Very handsome yacht," said Pepper.

"Thank you. It's comfortable. In fact, it's too big for just Susan and myself. We have a crew of five, but it still feels empty without family or guests aboard."

"Yes, I suppose so." Pepper couldn't think of anything else to say in response to Ralph's lament. Seriously, how did a person respond to someone complaining that his private yacht was lonely?

"How long are you staying? Do you plan to engage in any of the activities the resort offers?" Pepper decided to talk to the Tollefsons like she would anyone else at the resort, despite their wealth.

"Just a few days, then we're off. We signed up for the kayak trip down the river tomorrow as a fresh water diversion from our saltwater life on the yacht," said Ralph.

"What a coincidence. Bill and I are signed up to go kayaking as well. We're hoping to spot some crocodiles. People also have said the bird watching from the kayaks is tremendous. And it's only about a two-hour trek, which means it's right up my alley," said Pepper.

"Terrific. Us, too. Judging by your accent, Pepper, I'm guessing you're from the Midwest. Michigan?" asked Susan.

"Ha. No, but close. Minnesota. I grew up in North Dakota and just can't seem to shake the accent." They laughed.

"And where are you from?" asked Pepper.

"Most recently, we reside in Florida. We've lived all over the world though," said Susan.

"Of course," said Pepper.

"I assume you're dining here tonight?" asked Ralph.

"Oh yes, the food is fabulous. We wouldn't consider eating off the resort," said Pepper.

"Would you like some company for dinner?" asked Susan.

"That would be delightful. Please join us. Right, honey?" Pepper asked Bill. Pepper thought it was a little quick for a dinner invite, but she was game.

"Yes, please join us," chimed in Bill unenthusiastically. Pepper cast him a look to behave.

***

The McCallans and Tollefsons talked easily over dinner about their lives and, in spite of himself, Bill enjoyed Ralph's company. They were a pleasant diversion for Bill and Pepper from the same old hum drum.

The Tollefsons motored back to their yacht after dinner, but were in full form early the next morning for the river kayak trip. The party constituted just the four of them with a resort guide. They chatted comfortably in the 30-minute van ride over to the river, and had an exciting time down the river, even seeing a crocodile up close.

Once they returned to the resort, the foursome ate lunch together and marveled at all the iguanas they had seen on the treetops along the river bank. Pepper felt she had known the Tollefsons for longer than a day because they were so easy to be around. They reminded her of her parents. Talk once again turned to the Tollefson's departure for St. Martin after they finished lunch.

"We should start thinking about making preparations to pull up anchor and motor across the Caribbean to St. Martin," said Ralph to Susan.

"Well, we wish you bon voyage, and maybe we'll bump into you in St. Martin next week, right?" asked Pepper.

"That's right. I'd forgotten. You mentioned last night that you were going to fly out of Belize City," said Ralph.

"Yes, that appears to be the best way to go," said Pepper.

"If you and Bill would like to join us, you're welcome to travel to St. Martin on our yacht. We have a spare stateroom and en suite bath for you. It usually takes us about a week from here, if that fits with your schedule," offered Susan with a smile.

"Good idea, Susan. Yes, please join us," said Ralph, making a point to look at Bill.

Pepper was stunned by the spontaneity and generosity of Susan and Ralph's offer. She looked over to Bill. His eyebrows were raised in surprise, too. He wasn't a man of quick comebacks, so he looked at her to respond on behalf of them both. He nodded imperceptibly, and she could tell by the look on his face that he was game.

After a bit of throat clearing and shifting in her chair, Pepper said, "Goodness Ralph and Susan, that's a generous offer, but you barely know us. What if we're really annoying travel companions?"

They both laughed. "How Midwestern of you. I'm sure you're not annoying. We've become acquainted enough over the last 24 hours to feel comfortable, if you are," said Susan.

"I feel very comfortable. Bill?" asked Pepper.

"It's a deal. Thank you for your generosity. I feel like we need to pay for something though. Like fuel or groceries. Maybe we can discuss it on board. When would you like to depart?" asked Bill.

"Does first thing tomorrow morning work for you?" asked Ralph.

"Absolutely. That'll give us time to settle up our bill with the resort and pack our things," said Bill.

***

Pepper texted Jackie later that afternoon:

Bill and I are boarding a yacht bound for St. Martin. We'll be there one week from today. Hope to see you and Brent!

What? Bill agreed? Did you buy a yacht?

Ha. No. Strangest thing. New friends. I'll explain when we get there. If you decide not to come, we'll fly home from St. Martin.

Okaaay. No pressure or anything. Guess I'll be there.

We're good either way. You should come tho.

Fine. I'll call him and tell him to book the flight for one week from today.

Yeah! I have a feeling about you two.

Did you text your parents-in-law? Can I drop Daisy there?

Yep. They look forward to seeing you.

I better go buy some sexy swimsuits!

***

CHAPTER 4

One Aldwych

London, England

When Svea and Volkov reached One Aldwych Hotel, Volkov instructed her to wait in the car a minute while he entered first. The hotel was in the heart of the London theatre district, the Lyceum Theatre being directly across the street from it. The Lyceum was currently closed for repair due to the car bomb that had blown out its entire side on Exeter Street. In the spirit of musicals, and the "show must go on," the Lion King cast had been replaced, and the show was currently running three nights a week in the Royal Opera House, which was just a few blocks away.

Svea watched as the One Aldwych bellman opened the glass door framed in wrought iron for Volkov, as he walked up the short set of stairs. Ulrik, Svea's security detail, exited the front passenger seat and opened her car door a few moments later. The bellman held the oversize glass door for Svea and she followed the entourage into the expansive lobby.

The floor was white tile and she noted floor-to-ceiling windows with dark wood trim. A piece of art caught her eye. It was a life-sized carving of a naked Caribbean man in a small vessel with 20-foot-long oars pointing into the air. It dominated the lobby. They ascended a short set of stairs and turned sharply to the right. Since the building was triangular in shape, the interior was designed in 35 degree angles. No hallway was perpendicular to another. A small elevator bank awaited them. Volkov was waiting at the back of the elevator, which was lit up like a disco, its walls backlit with a blue and yellow checkerboard pattern. Svea moved to the back to stand next to Volkov as their security piled in behind them.

The security detail entered a key card for the penthouse suite, and when they arrived on Volkov's floor, several Russian guards with Uzis were awaiting them. Volkov and Svea were shown to a double set of dark wood doors that also required use of the security card. Volkov and Svea entered the small living room with her two security guards in tow. To Svea's surprise, there were at least three more Russian security guards in the suite. Svea ignored them, walking in the direction of the sofa to get comfortable. Why the small army? she wondered. Was he paranoid or were people really trying to assassinate him? She selected the sofa because she wanted Volkov to sit next to her. She crossed her long legs and pushed up her dress a little to flaunt her toned thighs.

Volkov went to the handsome bar and removed a bottle of Stolichnaya from the freezer. He pulled two shot glasses from behind the bar, and walked over to the stylish living area where Svea was comfortably resting in the center of the sofa. He noticed she looked like she expected him to sit next to her, her legs crossed and her skimpy dress showcasing her flawless upper thighs. Volkov made no attempt to disguise his lustful stare or turn down her invitation. She was Swedish perfection and he had never had a Swede. It was not lost on him that Swedish and Russian relations had never been conducive to a mingling of the sexes. That fact excited him even more. He couldn't wait to conquer her.

He decided he would show no mercy during sex because she knew what she was getting into. She had made that clear back at the club when she had propositioned him.

Back at the club, he had expected her to engage in the customary dribble that heads of state spewed. "Nice to make your acquaintance President Volkov, I look forward to open communications and a productive working relationship, blah, blah..." He had been pleasantly surprised with her overtures.

Volkov poured them each a shot of vodka in the small glass with the name One Aldwych etched into it. He handed her the shot and prepared to make a toast. He didn't speak Swedish, but he knew some English and he didn't mind practicing, so he said in his heavy Russian accent, "To the most beautiful woman with whom I have ever had the pleasure of conducting state business."

They locked eyes and tossed back the vodka. He reached for the bottle to pour another, but she put her hand on his arm. She shook her soft brown tendrils, and he instinctively reached up to curl them around his finger. She smiled invitingly, so he leaned in and kissed her. She thought he was being gentle for a man of his reputation. Both contingents of their security detail looked the other way.

"Would you like to join me in my bedroom?" he asked.

"Yes."

"I don't allow security detail in my bedroom," he said.

"Neither do I," said Svea.

He rose and extended his hand. She took it, and he steered her to his bedroom. Ulrik searched her face for confirmation before she slipped behind the door. She shook her head softly, indicating no need to follow her. Ulrik paled in fear for his bos,s as he had heard of Volkov's reputation.

Volkov wasted no time. He turned on the music and tossed his suit coat on a chair. He advanced on Svea with a ravenous look, kissing her more aggressively than he had in the living room. She arched into him and not only accepted his tongue in her mouth, but sucked on it and swirled her own tongue around his. She felt him harden considerably through his grey wool slacks.

He unzipped her silver sequins dress and let it fall to the floor. She was, indeed, one of the most beautiful women he had ever seen. Regal, alluring and flawless. She stepped out of her dress and stood before him in her high heels, lacy black bra and thong. He kissed the tops of her breasts, then trailed kisses down her tummy to her personal hotspot. He pulled the thong aside, dropped to his knees on the thick carpet, and pleasured her until she screamed his name. He might have given her a sharp spanking somewhere along the way, but she was so lost in ecstasy that she didn't notice the slap or Ulrik's surprised expression when he opened the door in response to her scream. Ulrik had seen Svea's hands on Volkov's head, and her hips thrust into his face, so he had closed the door quietly. He hoped things would continue to go in her favor.

Volkov picked Svea up and lay her on the bed. He kicked off his shoes and ripped off his clothes while she watched. His eyes were dark with desire, and she was peaking with sexual curiosity. She noticed he was starting to grow man boobs in his middle-age, and his legs were knobby and unattractive, but he was well-endowed, which no doubt gave him the confidence he exhibited around other men.

He made no pretense of looking for a condom, instead landing on top of her and parting her legs with his knees. He unsnapped her bra and tore off her thong, then rubbed his hairless chest onto her breasts while he thrust into her. She screamed in pleasure again, which excited him. Volkov was a sporting man with a lot of energy. At one point, Ulrik entered the room again only to see Volkov spanking Svea as he rode her from behind. Svea took one hand off the headboard and waved Ulrik away. Volkov made a note to lock the door next time, as he would be damned if he allowed another man to see him having sex. Especially a Swede.

Afterward, they lay in bed while Volkov smoked a Cuban cigar. He liked it rough and she had delivered. He seemed quite pleased with himself as he made smoke rings and stared at the ceiling.

"So, I assume you didn't seduce me for the sole purpose of sex, Svea. What do you want from me?" inquired Volkov.

"To explore opportunities for mutual benefit." She pulled up the sheet and fluffed the pillows so she could join Volkov in leaning against the headboard.

"What can you offer me?" he asked.

"Aside from what I just gave? The chance to destabilize America if you give me some favors in return."

Volkov tried to mask his reaction, but his excitement was belied by a twitching eyelid. He momentarily held his breath, and rested his hand on his lap, letting the cigar burn.

"Go on," he urged.

"Before I tell you what I have in mind, I need to know if you're amenable to giving me what I want," she said.

"I might be. Continue," he said.

"I need a quick deliverable to fix something my imbecile predecessor fucked up," she confessed.

"Let me guess. You want me to take some missiles off your hands," he said.

"How did you know?" she asked.

Volkov looked at her and took a puff of his cigar. "Your feminist predecessor's insults to the Saudis were splashed all over the newspapers, Svea."

So far, she was boring him. Swedish women clearly hadn't learned their place in politics.

"Fair enough," she said. "I don't share her ideologies. Can you buy some inventory that the Saudi Arabians reneged on? It's only about $40 million in Saab missiles."

"If the price is right," he said.

"The price will be right. I need to unload them so I can deliver some money during my first month in office," she said.

"What else?" he asked.

"I need a better price from you on crude oil," she ventured.

"Not negotiable." Who does she think she is? he thought.

"Tell me you'll give me a better price...only a few cents per barrel, and I'll blow your mind," she promised.

"Okay, two cents," he said.

"Eighty."

He laughed. "Fifty or nothing."

"Deal." She smiled.

"Tell me your big secret." He took a puff.

"I'm going to deliver a nerve gas attack on three major United States cities while simultaneously disabling the largest hospitals in those cities from administering an antidote to the victims." She paused for his reaction.

While he considered her idea, Svea got out of bed and used the bathroom. When she came out, he was still thinking, so she threw on a robe and went out to the bar in the living room. She grabbed a beer from the fridge, popped the top, and returned to Volkov's bed. Ulrik watched her come and go. She dropped the robe and resumed her position beside Volkov. She offered him a drink, but he declined.

Svea took a healthy pull. "And?"

"Why? What do you have against the Americans?" he asked.

"Let's just say I had some repeated encounters with a certain arrogant American who thought he owned me." Jensen's face flashed in Svea's mind, but she controlled her expression as she looked directly at Volkov.

"Were your raped by an American man, Svea?" he asked.

"Yes," she said.

"Who?" he asked.

"Why does it matter? I don't want to tell you," she said.

"Maybe you'll find the courage to tell me in time. Back to your scheme. Is that the reason? To exact revenge on this American?" he asked.

"In part. I have no love for any American," she said.

"Why not just kill the man who raped you?" he asked. Women were so illogical.

"That really isn't possible," she said, thinking of her mother.

"I find that hard to believe in the face of what you just proposed to me, don't you?" he asked.

"You'd be surprised," she said. They were getting off track and she felt the need to refocus him. "The Americans are imperialistic pigs who think they own the world. It's about time their reign comes to an end, don't you think?"

"While an American crisis would benefit the Russian economy, I doubt your chances of success," he said.

"I have a team in place. I just need to cover a few logistics with you," she said.

"Like?" he asked.

"I need Sarin gas from you," she said.

"I knew there was a catch," he scoffed. Women!

"Oh, come on, it's not that difficult. I know you must have a little supply stashed somewhere..."

"Give me your phone," he ordered.

She handed it to him. As she expected, he removed the battery while he watched her closely. She held her disinterested look, taking another drink of her beer.

"My purse is out in the living room," she offered.

Volkov got out of bed and went to the door. He instructed one of his security guards in Russian to search her purse for microphones. He turned around and picked up her sequins dress and shoes, and threw them out into the living room. She watched in amusement.

"Aren't you going to ask me if I'm bugged?" she asked, the absurdity making her smile.

"In my experience, people rarely give a truthful answer to that question," he said. He surveyed the room and concluded it was safe to proceed.

He took up his spot in bed. "For the sake of indulging your little fantasy, let's assume I have a small supply of the nerve gas you're seeking. What's your plan for transporting it from my country to the United States?"

"I have connections with a cargo company in Bangkok that will ship it by both sea and air to the United States."

He looked skeptical. "You think you can accomplish what others have tried and failed to do?"

"Yes. I have a better plan and the contacts to execute it," she said.

"What are the specifics of your plan, Svea?" he asked.

"My stepfather's pharmaceutical manufacturing company in Thailand will deliver ampules, nebulizers, labels and boxes to your Sarin manufacturing plant in Russia. Your team will be responsible for filling the ampules and nebulizers, and packaging them with my materials, which look legit," she said.

"That's a lot to ask, but I think my plant can do it," he said.

"You'll transport the products back to the Old Bangkok Port known as the Khlong Toei Port, on the Chao Phraya River. It has much less traffic and governmental oversight than the new deep-sea port in Bangkok. You'll have to transport the packages on a small ship so it can navigate up the Chao Phraya River. It's important your ship isn't from Russia. Everyone knows Russia doesn't manufacture pharmaceuticals for global distribution. Use a Chinese ship."

"It's easy to repurpose a small ship with the appropriate markings," he said.

"You'll also need temperature-controlled containers to keep the sarin from rising above 70 degrees Fahrenheit. Install some refrigerated cargo containers on your Chinese ship. Your people in the industry will know what I'm referring to. You'll offload the cargo into refrigerated containers at the Khlong Toei Port, which will be provided by my Thai Cargo Shipping company."

"What's your connection to this Thai Cargo Shipping company again? Is it someone who can be trusted?" he asked.

"My stepfather owns it. I worked at his company for several years, traveling around to the different offices. The employees there can be trusted to be discreet," she said.

"Okay, go on," he said.

"That cargo will be divided. Two thirds of it will be shipped by air to the State of Pennsylvania, and one third shipped by sea to the Port of Los Angeles."

"What's your plan for clearing customs in the U.S.?" he asked.

"At the Port of Los Angeles, they have a program for high-volume shippers, like refrigerated pharmaceuticals, that expedites the unloading by peeling off those containers and bringing them to a nearby yard for processing. My sources tell me these pharmaceuticals are cleared with minimal inspection as long as the paperwork is clean."

"And by air?" he asked.

"My Thai Cargo jet will fly into Cargo City at Philadelphia International Airport, which handles a lot of cargo, and is strategically located on the east coast. Thai Cargo Shipping is a regular customer, and they have their own warehouse. It's within a one-day drive of almost half of the U.S. population. The U.S. Customs at the airport is used to dealing with Thai Cargo Shipping, and they have a smooth working relationship. They're also used to processing refrigerated pharmaceuticals, which are subject to an expedited clearance."

"Impressive plan, Svea. What's your ground distribution network?" he asked.

"I'm not at liberty to describe every detail of my plan once the sarin is on the ground. You can understand why I might want to keep some aspects of the operation secret," she said.

Beautiful and connected, he thought. "If I'm going to participate, I need to know your entire plan."

"Oh Vadik, don't pressure me. As with any sensitive operation, you know how important it is for only one person to know all the aspects of it. It's best if each team knows only its own role in the event of capture. You want deniability, don't you?" she asked, impatiently.

"I want to know what I'm signing on to. You will tell me," he said.

She clenched her jaw and stared at him with her frosty Swedish eyes. "I think not." She flipped her hair over her shoulder.

He set his cigar on the bedside table and rolled over to face her, slipping his hand under the sheet. He found her most sensitive spot and started massaging it with his thumb while his fingers slid into her. She moaned and bucked up involuntarily into his hand.

"Vadik, this is not going to work," she said.

"Of course it is." He kept moving his thumb in rhythmic circles, and she closed her eyes.

"I'm not going to talk... Oh, right there," she said.

"What's your distribution network?" he asked.

"Oh...yes...there. I'm not going...to...tell... you," she insisted.

He stopped rubbing. Her eyes flew open. "Vadik!"

"Tell me," he ordered.

"Okay, start again with your hand and I will," she said.

And she ultimately did.

***

CHAPTER 5

The Mythos Yacht

Hopkins, Belize

Pepper and Bill walked down to the pier with their bags and introduced themselves to Joe, the large Belizean man Pepper had seen on the skiff last night. He was intimidating, but polite. Pepper and Bill traveled light - each with a small roller and backpack. Pepper actually had purchased some swimsuits in Belize because they hadn't originally planned to stay more than a few days after the bank bust. Joe easily lifted their bags into the skiff and untied the lines from the pier.

Joe was at least six feet tall, tall for a Belizean, and had his long hair cornrowed and twisted up under a colorful hand-knit hat with a brim as long as a baseball cap. He had broad shoulders and was very muscular in a classic V-shape. He powered up the twin Mercury outboards and they sped away from the pier toward the Tollefson's silver yacht. As they approached it, Pepper noticed the model name of "Mythos" imprinted on the side with raised silver letters. When they pulled up to the stern of the Mythos, she could see that it had been named "The Hermit" in cursive writing on the back.

There was another Belizean man standing on the teak swim platform off the stern. Joe threw him a line and the shorter man tied it off on a cleat. He offered Pepper and Bill a hand onto the platform and introduced himself.

"I'm Catch," he said.

"We're Pepper and Bill." They shook hands.

"Leave your bags and we'll bring them up," said Catch in a heavy creole accent. Pepper could barely understand him. It's as if he had a mouthful of rocks and dropped the last syllable of each word. He must have been a smoker at some time because his voice was pretty hoarse.

They ascended the short stairway to the rear most deck, known as the aft deck. Neither Pepper nor Bill had a working knowledge of nautical terms so they'd have to be oriented to the locations on the boat.

Ralph and Susan greeted them with open arms. Behind Ralph and Susan stood three more crew members who Susan introduced as Captain Linda; Belinda – the cook; and Cheri – the housekeeper. Pepper and Bill learned that Joe was in charge of the skiff and fishing. Catch was in charge of fileting the fish, snorkeling and diving excursions. They both pulled security duty.

Cheri showed Bill and Pepper to the guest quarters, which was forward through the salon and past the galley on the main deck. Their stateroom was contemporary in design with chrome accents, a white lacquered ceiling, white washed oak floors, Canaletto walnut built-ins and recessed lighting. It had a queen-sized bed and a walk-in bathroom that included a shower and a double sink. The guestroom was designed for a king with a small sitting area and white leather sofas. There was a bank of windows on one wall of their room and a large screen T.V. at the foot of their bed. A few of the windows were cracked and a soft Caribbean breeze was filtering through, accompanied by the sound of the waves kissing the hull. It was more spacious than an executive suite at a hotel, and had first class décor. The interior of the yacht was more impressive inside than it had been from shore, if that was even possible.

Bill and Pepper stowed their gear and returned through the galley to the salon, which was the main living area in the center of the yacht, an expanse measuring the entire beam. There was an arrangement of sofas and swivel chairs, and a small dining area forward of the salon. They sat across from Ralph and Susan on the sofas and were served coffee and tea by Cheri, who also was a Belize native. She had a plump figure and a cheerful face.

Captain Linda entered to chat with Ralph.

"Hello Ralph. We're pulling up anchor, and making preparations to motor out straight east with the destination of St. Martin entered in the GPS. We plan a comfortable cruising speed today of about 11 knots. It's 750 nautical miles to Jamaica, so we need to keep the speed below 15 knots to conserve fuel. When we reach Jamaica, we plan to fuel up at the Errol Flynn Marina. They've been good to us in the past, and the harbor depth accommodates our draft."

"Sounds good," said Ralph.

"From Jamaica, it's about 420 nautical miles to the Dominican Republic. If it meets with your approval, we'll use the Casa de Campo Marina in the Dominican for refueling. Despite the crime, it has the best reputation in the sailing community in that region. We'll take better precautions this time than we did last time, and attempt to time our arrival and departure between 8:00 a.m. and 5:00 p.m. so we won't be stuck overnight. I might have to bribe them $200 or more in U.S. dollars, though," she said.

Linda stopped to let Ralph absorb what she had said. Defying the stereotypical salty male Captain with a long white beard, Linda was a pretty woman in her mid-forties. She had a short haircut and was very fit. She wore a cute khaki skirt and blue cotton blouse. What a classy Captain, thought Pepper. It was probably best to have a female because, in the past, Pepper had witnessed male captains insult Bill. It was a mystery to both Bill and her why male captains didn't like him. But in two out of two excursions, the insults had taken place. Maybe a female would be nicer to him.

"I approve of the gratuity to the harbor master, Linda. Your course sounds well charted," said Ralph.

Captain Linda smiled pleasantly. "Are we in the mood to make any stops for snorkeling today? Glover's atoll is about two hours away."

Ralph looked at the group. "Would you like to snorkel at Glover's atoll?"

Bill spoke for both Pepper and himself. "If you would, we would. We love to snorkel."

"To Glover's atoll then," said Ralph. Captain Linda nodded and disappeared in the direction of the helm.

Once they were underway, Susan suggested they enjoy the sun and fresh air, so they walked outside along the edge of the boat, holding the rail on the starboard side, until they reached the forward deck, which had a spacious booth-style seat that faced the bow. A sturdy table with a white top was bolted to the deck in front of the seat. When seated, Pepper felt like she was water skiing on the Caribbean, except she was about 20 feet above the surface. Nonetheless, they were at the bow so the ocean was right there.

"Susan, this is magnificent. Thank you so much for inviting us," said Pepper. She breathed in the salty air and let the sun warm her body. She could tell this trip was going to be all about hats and sunblock application. She was 37 years old and didn't want to advance the aging process by overexposure to the blazing Caribbean sun.

"It's our pleasure. Please make yourself at home and enjoy the cruise," said Susan. She patted Pepper's arm like only a mother could. Pepper appreciated the gesture.

And so they passed the day, stopping to snorkel at the pristine Glover's reef, mooring in the safe harbor of a small island for cover from potential weather for the night. They were close to hurricane season, so Captain Linda's job was to navigate all aspects of the voyage as well as dodge the weather, if needed. Linda didn't like to travel at night because there were too many unmarked boats running drugs, she said.

Each day on the Caribbean brought a new adventure. Spotted dolphins rode the undercurrent off the bow, jumping up to break the surface to the group's applause. The foursome snorkeled and Joe brought them to a few islands on the skiff to visit the local bars and beaches. The bar at Marisol had a sign that said, "If you're drinking to forget, please pay your tab in advance." The next island bar had a sign that said, "no shirt - no problem. No shoes - no problem. No money – BIG PROBLEM." Pepper was getting the impression that island bars were a cash-only business with iffy collections.

She noticed that Joe and Catch always motored the skiff to the island a few hours before the foursome toured it. Big Joe adopted an intimidating posture and scowled at the men hanging around the pier while Catch seemed to make friendly and joke around with the islanders. Having been a lobsterman for several years, Catch spoke their language, and try as she might, Pepper still couldn't understand a damn thing he said no matter how hard she concentrated. She guessed he probably derived his nickname from his successful fishing days.

When Joe and Catch returned after island recon, they gave report to Captain Linda, who then made a recommendation to Ralph about whether it was safe to visit. Pepper also noticed that Joe and Catch took turns keeping watch and staying up all night in shifts. They both took a two-hour nap after lunch each day to recover from their night watch. Well, everyone took a nap after lunch because Belinda's cooking was so delicious they overate. Pepper had fallen in love with Belinda's coconut cake. It was moist and the flavors popped. It was too hot to be on the deck in the midday sun anyway, so each couple retired to their staterooms to recline in the nice cross-breeze as the yacht motored toward Jamaica.

The Mythos had an impressive locked-down appearance at night due to its aerodynamic design. The stern stairway folded up into the body of the boat and the anodized aluminum exterior was so smooth it wouldn't allow for any type of foothold for a person to climb aboard. The hull was so high that it would be difficult for a person to climb aboard even if they pulled up alongside the yacht with a dinghy. The only vulnerability was the skiff, of course, which was attached by two lines that could be cut with a large knife. Piracy was pervasive and pernicious in the Caribbean, and a yacht like the Mythos was an obvious target. The Tollefsons were lucky the skiff hadn't been cut loose yet.

The 122-foot yacht was spacious enough that Pepper and Bill could have avoided Ralph and Susan if they'd desired, but they found their company relaxing and comfortable. The foursome passed the late afternoons on the aft deck in the shade, drinking lemonade and playing cards. Once Ralph and Susan discovered Bill was an orthopedic surgeon, they explained their daily joint pains and asked for his advice. They both were in excellent shape, however, so there wasn't much diagnosing for Bill to do, beyond a description of mild arthritis and some suggested stretching exercises.

Of course, there was the inevitable inquiry into whether Pepper worked, and what she did. As soon as she mentioned she had worked at Futuraceutical Company, Ralph's eyes lit up, and he indicated he had followed the Ebola vaccine story very closely in the media.

Inevitably, Ralph asked about the company deaths at the Lyceum. This led Pepper to sharing with them Jake's tragic death in the theatre bombing. While Ralph and Susan were shocked, they were also incredibly understanding. They had lived long enough to have experienced grief, and understood what Bill and Pepper were going through.

"Ralph, you seem quite knowledgeable about pharmaceutical companies, is that your background?" asked Pepper.

"No, my background is in finance," he said. "Specifically, investing in Russian companies. But since I divested from Russian petroleum, I've been active in the emerging Asian markets, and that includes the manufacture of pharmaceuticals by large conglomerates like

Futuraceutical. I'm trying to determine if what happened at Futuraceutical is the canary in the coal mine for the industry, or if it was an isolated incident."

"Honestly, Ralph, if you want my opinion," said Pepper, "I think it was isolated due to the extreme actions of David Arnout. His bribery of an official at the FDA, and multiple members of the FDA Advisory Council, was unprecedented. In fact, I think there will be an enormous backlash by the U.S. government in response to Arnout's actions that will result in more regulation. They most likely will clamp down on research protocols. In the short term, we'll see depressed stock prices, but over the long term, the profits will still be in a pipeline of new drugs, so pharmaceuticals are still a good investment."

"Interesting. I hope you're right. I might consult you in the future if you don't mind," said Ralph.

"It would be my pleasure, Ralph."

"What type of Russian investing were you involved in" asked Bill.

"It's a long story," said Ralph.

"Well, we happen to be on a cruise so we have lots of time. I'm quite interested," prompted Bill.

"Alright. You remember Gorbachev's push for 'glasnost' in the late 1980s?" asked Ralph.

"Of course," said Bill.

"As you recall, 'glasnost' means openness in Russian. Gorbachev had intended it to apply to the communist party and government management of assets, including Russian companies. Glasnost was paired with 'perestroika,' which means restructuring. Hence, Gorbachev was trying to open up and restructure state-owned companies, like oil, so that the Russian people could invest in them. It was generally known as a privatization of state-owned assets," said Ralph.

"Both Gorbachev and his successor, Boris Yeltsin, implemented these policies for economic restructuring. Neither of them totally trusted the free market, though, so they created an auctioning process for company shares that resulted in only a few extremely powerful and wealthy men owning almost all of Russia's profitable companies," said Ralph.

"The oligarchs," said Pepper.

"Yes. The oligarchs. I knew most of them on a first-name basis," said Ralph.

"How is that?" asked Pepper.

"Susan and I lived in Moscow when I managed an arbitrage fund that acquired as many shares of undervalued Russian companies as we could. I waited for the rest of the financial community to figure out the value of those companies, which had been sold at a discount to the oligarchs, then I sold my fund's shares when the Russian stock prices soared. I made millions for my clients and myself, sometimes in excess of hundred times what we invested. The trick was knowing when to walk away from the table."

"When did you know it was time?" inquired Pepper.

Ralph chuckled sarcastically. "When President Vadik Volkov arrested the CEO of Yukos Oil company, Mikhail Khodorkovsky in 2003. Volkov went after Khodorkovsky's family and business associates too, making arrests through 2005. Maybe you remember that Khodorkovsky was tried in open court, with T.V. cameras broadcasting his entire trial? Volkov wanted everyone to see the oligarch go to jail."

"Khodorkovsky was convicted and sentenced to 9 or 10 years in prison. I can't remember. Predictably, Volkov ended up privately owning a large percentage of shares in Yukos. It was the beginning of Volkov's power move against the oligarchs, and it was the decisive signal for me to pack up and leave."

"Why did Volkov move against the oligarchs?" asked Bill. "I thought he needed them on his side politically."

"That was the problem. Not all of them agreed with Volkov's politics, and once they expressed opposition, Volkov had to go after them. It's the Russian way. He made an example out of Khodorkovsky's imprisonment, so the remainder of the oligarchs bribed him in return for Volkov not arresting them. Some estimate that Volkov became the richest man in Russia overnight. A very powerful man, indeed."

"He looks like a former KGB thug to me," said Bill.

"He is," said Ralph. "If you've noticed, his political detractors and opponents seem to turn up poisoned or shot. The man is a criminal. He isn't a communist any more than you or I are communist. He's a tyrant who uses Russia's resources and assets for self-aggrandizement."

"Volkov certainly has his hands full now, with former soviet countries and neighboring countries constantly rebelling," observed Bill.

"If you understand Volkov, you'd know that he purposefully works to destabilize neighboring countries so they can't achieve independence from Russia. Yet, he won't go to the trouble of invading them and taking them over," said Ralph.

"How?" asked Pepper.

"Crimea is a good example," said Ralph. "Her citizenry rejected the corrupt Russian puppet- government, rebelling. Volkov sent in his thugs, making it appear publicly that the Crimean citizens had opposing views. In other words, were at civil war with each other. But that was subterfuge. The 'opponents' were Volkov's Russian thugs. He knew that if Crimea successfully installed a democratically-elected leader, it would make Russia look dysfunctional and, in turn, reflect poorly on Volkov. So politically, he couldn't afford Crimea becoming democratic because it would result in unrest in Russia."

"I see," said Bill.

"And economically speaking, if he keeps his neighbors destabilized, they'll need to buy everything from oil to food from him. They'll never be independently functional with their own commerce. He knocks them off balance just enough to generate economic *dependence*," explained Ralph.

"So, the old adage of 'if my grass is brown, yours has to be browner,' applies to Volkov," said Bill.

"Yes, with a heavy dose of Russian pride. Military experts will tell you that Crimea is a stronghold for Russia in the Black Sea, and it was predictable that Volkov would do what he did to keep control over it," said Ralph.

"Interesting," said Bill.

"That's my read on Russia and Volkov. Told you it was a long story. Bill, you'd expressed an interest in seeing the engine room. Would you like a tour?" asked Ralph.

"Yes. I'd like to see the engines," said Bill.

Bill and Ralph stood, making their way toward the stairway to the lower decks.

Pepper could hear Ralph explaining, "Two engines, actually. They're made by a company that's a division of Rolls Royce, but based in Germany. Each engine is the size of an American pickup truck—not just the truck engine, the entire truck. Each is a V12 with 93 liters of displacement. Each of my engines has 3500 horsepower."

"Wow," said Bill. He had offered to split the fuel costs with Ralph for the voyage, but now wondered how much that would set him back. They probably could have purchased several airline tickets for the cost of diesel fuel to power this high-tech luxury vessel.

Susan shook her head. "Ralph loves to talk engines."

"He's a typical man, then. In the mood for some fresh air on the upper deck?" suggested Pepper.

"And maybe a swim," said Susan. "I'll ask Captain Linda if we have time to stop. I don't even know what depth we are at. It could be over 1000 feet deep here!"

***

CHAPTER 6

Jackie in Minneapolis

Fall 2018

Minneapolis, Minnesota

Jackie walked Daisy through the wooded area on the dog path close to her home in Wayzata, a suburb of Minneapolis. It was a beautiful September day. The leaves had turned, and the air was crisp. Both Daisy and Jackie felt energized. Jackie's neighbors stopped to chat, asking Jackie what was wrong with Daisy's front left leg.

Jackie gave the same explanation she had heard Pepper give numerous times, that Daisy was born without a radial bone in her front left leg so it was bent at an angle. That paw never touched the ground. It was up and facing forward like a hand shake.

Daisy's left leg had atrophied, and was substantially smaller than her right front leg, but it was still had a normal paw. It didn't interfere with her ability to run, and she hobbled around the house on three legs just fine. In fact, if Jackie threw the tennis ball for the little Duck Toller, Daisy would sprint across the lawn and get it as fast as any other dog Jackie had seen. She actually ran smoother than she walked.

Daisy also was quite a swimmer. Jackie's house was in a development by a lake, so part of their new routine was a trip down to the lake where Daisy could retrieve the ball. Daisy rode lower in the water than other retrievers, but she swam gracefully and fast. She was born to be around water, splashing and dashing around the beach in true retriever form. Jackie had grown quite fond of the little Toller, and would miss her while in St. Martin.

St. Martin meant seeing Brent. Jackie felt butterflies in her stomach and tingles down to her fingertips every time she thought of him. He was such a hunk. She was around men all day who lifted weights and kept in shape, but Brent was in another league. She admired how he carried himself with confidence, constantly surveying his surroundings, anticipating something bad could go down at any minute. She felt safe when she was with him.

He was not only smart, but also ruggedly gorgeous, with kind brown eyes. She had tried to memorize the shade of his brown eyes with the little gold flecks in them, but she was having trouble envisioning them lately. She needed an in-person refresher.

She had been weak at the knees when they had made out in her house. It was a good thing he was strong, because he had sensed her wobbly legs and picked her up, setting her on the dining room table the last time they had been together. They both had wanted to take it all the way, but Jackie had put the brakes on out of self-respect.

She knew her feelings for him were stronger than just the physical satisfaction she would get from a one-night stand. If she gave herself to him, she knew she would lose a piece of her heart, and she didn't think she could stand the pain when he inevitably left. The feelings he evoked made her too vulnerable.

He was going to leave. That was the problem. He lived in Boston, and his counterterrorism job took him all over the world. There was no reason for him to swing by Minneapolis. No one swung by Minneapolis. It wasn't on the way to anywhere. It was an intentional destination or nothing at all. A beautiful one, but not a convenient one. So where did that leave them? She certainly didn't want to be his monthly booty call.

She wanted a real relationship, one like Bill and Pepper had. Jackie was 29, and she was ready to settle down and share her life with someone. She wanted kids and a stable home. The question was whether Brent wanted that too. She didn't have a good feel for where he was at in his life. He was 34 years old, and didn't give the impression that he was looking for a house in the suburbs, a minivan full of kids, and a day-job that required a shirt and tie.

Unfortunately, Jackie's career required her to be in Minneapolis. She owned a CrossFit workout empire called StarrFitness that employed over 50 people at a 30,000 square foot upscale club. She was the boss. While she didn't need to be there 24/7, she had to steer the ship, and she had many clients, both individuals and sports teams, who requested her personally as their trainer. She loved what she did, so selling the business wasn't an option. If anything, at her age, she was considering expanding.

She had a meeting scheduled later that week with her accountant to discuss whether she had enough capital to finance an expansion. She could tell he had a crush on her and wanted to ask her out, but the spark wasn't there. She was kind to him though. She had to face it, since she had met Brent, her interest in other men had evaporated. There was no comparison to the way Brent made her feel when they touched.

Maybe it had been a good thing that they hadn't seen each other for a few weeks. She'd see if she still felt the same way about him in St. Martin. She was also grateful for Pepper and Bill agreeing to leave Belize and motor to St. Martin to support Jackie on a weeklong double date. It's not that she needed a chaperone to keep Brent in line; just someone else to talk to so it didn't get awkward being alone with him all the time. Being alone with Brent might be too much pressure. Hmm, being alone with Brent might be too much fun.

***

CHAPTER 7
Thai Cargo Shipping

Bangkok, Thailand

That's strange, thought the Harbor Master for Khlong Toei Port, also known as the Old Bangkok Port in Thailand. Why would China Shipping Line want to unload cargo here instead of at the new deep-sea port, Laem Chabang? The new Bangkok port was more accessible and had wider berths with larger, faster cranes.

The Harbor Master's job was to control traffic in his harbor, not discourage ships from entering it. After confirming the ship's draft, length and displacement with her captain, the Harbor Master, Pu Yai Bahn, cleared the Chinese cargo ship for entrance, and arranged for a tug to portage her into a container berth, where she'd be unloaded. He peered beyond the black flies on his large office window, looking down the river. He couldn't see the Chinese ship yet because she hadn't made her turn up the Chao Phraya River from the Thai Gulf.

An hour later after the Chinese cargo ship had tied off, the dockyard crew guided the cranes to unload her shipping containers. Once the containers hit the dockyard concrete on Thai soil, Sarawut Leekpai, a Thai customs official dressed in his navy-blue uniform, carrying his clipboard of paperwork, walked up to one of the containers. He was ready to perform a routine inspection of the cargo to clear it through customs for further shipping destinations.

He ordered the shipping container opened so he could verify the contents according to the customs forms. Curious, he thought, that crewman aboard the ship is speaking Russian to another crewman. They looked Russian rather than Chinese. Sarawut looked at the cargo ship again just to be sure he wasn't confused. Yes China Shipping Line. Since when did CSL hire Russians?

It was none of his business as long as the crew stayed on the ship and didn't set foot on the dockyard. They weren't subject to his authority on the ship. The Thai customs employees helped Sarawut open the refrigerated cargo container so Sarawut could step inside. There was at least a 20-degree difference between the interior of the container and the humid dock air, which was 90 degrees Fahrenheit at nine o'clock in the morning.

Sarawut walked over to a wooden pallet, cutting the plastic wrap around the boxes with his box cutter. Next, he cut open one of the four cubic foot boxes and bent back the flaps. He pulled out a smaller brown box. He set it atop the larger box and opened it. When he peeled back the flap, he could see white boxes with blue print on them. They were wrapped in clear plastic.

They looked like the pharmaceuticals his paperwork indicated were in the shipment. The manufacturer name of Zortis was visible in large print on the boxes. He removed one. He opened it and removed the contents. There were small ampules of a clear medicine that was labelled in English. He looked at the shipping manifest and compared the English words to the label on the ampule: "FENTANYL citrate, injection USP."

The name was printed in bold red on the ampule with the strength printed in smaller black lettering. It matched. He placed his customs sticker on the white inner box and initialed it.

Sarawut put the product back in the brown box and placed another customs sticker on the exterior of the brown box. He scribbled on the customs form attached to his clipboard, and walked out of the refrigerated container into the salty heat on the concrete pier. It was the responsibility of the shipping company, Thai Cargo Shipping, to repack and re-tape the boxes.

The smell of oil and diesel hung in the hot, humid air. The cargo was now cleared for Thai Cargo Shipping Company to transport by sea or air, as it had been hired to do by a Cayman Islands corporation named Whale Shipping. The forklift and semi-trucks owned by Thai Cargo Shipping were standing by. Someone was anxious to get this shipment moved off the dock.

The boxes in the middle third of the container weren't opened by Sarawut. If they had been, he would have seen small, portable nebulizers that ran on batteries, delivering aerosolized medications to asthma patients via a tube that connected with a mouthpiece. The tube and mouthpiece wouldn't be needed for Svea's mission, but they were included for show. The battery- operated ultrasonic nebulizer was made by a company called Vibrant, located in Shanghai. The label had Shanghai Vibrant Company printed on it in both English and Chinese.

These handheld devices were about the size and shape of a Camelback plastic water bottle. They contained an 8 milliliter medicine cup that delivered a super-fine, nebulized particle mist over forty minutes. The nebulizers were designed to be turned on and ignored. They didn't need constant attention.

The compressor was advertised to run up to 60 minutes on a rechargeable lithium ion battery, but in reality, it ran at full strength for only about 40 minutes. This was more than enough time for Svea's purposes. The compressor for the nebulizer weighed only .90 pounds and the battery weighed .40 pounds. The eight milliliters of fluid weighed a quarter of an ounce. In total, the package weighed about 1.4 pounds.

Sarawut Leekpai would never know these details about the mini nebulizer, or its appearance, however, because he hadn't opened those boxes. In addition, he hadn't noticed that the Chinese crewman who had been hanging back at the edge of the cargo container was wearing a small earpiece and had microphone on the lapel of his grease-stained shirt. He had been giving a status report to the Russian crewman who had remained on the ship. All was well. The boxes had cleared.

The three palletized boxes in the refrigerated container would now be divided. One pallet would be loaded onto a Thai Cargo ship bound for Los Angeles, California, and the other two pallets would be loaded onto a Thai Cargo jet bound for Philadelphia, Pennsylvania, where they would be unloaded and stored in the Thai Cargo Shipping warehouse for inspection by a United States Customs official.

The Thai Cargo Shipping employee picked up the disposable cell phone that had been delivered by overnight air to him with an envelope containing $5,000 in United States dollars, highly coveted in Thailand. He pressed the speed dial button and a woman answered.

"The cargo was inspected, and cleared Thai Customs," he said.

"Good. Did it ship out yet?" she asked.

"Yes," he said.

"Thank you. Please throw away your phone," she instructed.

"Okay," he said.

"Bye."

They hung up, and he decided to keep the phone because people in his country didn't throw away perfectly good devices when they were in good working order. He didn't have a plan for it, but he put it in his desk as a valuable item that he might be able to use in bargaining with someone else if he needed something to trade.

***

CHAPTER 8

Dominican Maneuvers

Punta Cana, Dominican Republic

Pepper was changing out of her swimsuit after snorkeling on the reef. They had stopped a second time between Jamaica and the Dominican to swim in the pristine marine life that was untouched by tourists this far off shore.

In just 12 feet of water, they had seen vibrant purple coral, fire red branches of coral that would burn skin if touched, and elk horn coral that resembled elk antlers in both shape and color. While Pepper was content to see just small sea critters, like tiny blue iridescent fish with yellow piping, she was thrilled to see two varieties of sting rays, the eagle ray and the brown and white spotted ray.

The six-foot-wide rays glided through the water like stealth bombers, undulating their bodies and gracefully flapping their wings, which weren't actually wings, but were connected like a web to their bodies. The water was so warm that Pepper had spent a comfortable hour swimming along the reef without getting cold. She didn't use fins or a wetsuit, so she had to swim a bit stronger to move along the reef and countercurrent. The effort kept her warm.

When Pepper had been snorkeling in about four feet of water, she had noticed an old ship steering wheel that was imbedded in the coral. Its wooden spokes were faded and rotting, but its brass plate was still adhered to it. She couldn't make out the inscription. She had tugged on Bill's ankle to pull him over to look at it. They swam around the area looking for other signs of an historic wreckage, but couldn't see any. It made her wonder about the story of how that wheel had ended up on this reef and to what ship it had belonged. How long had it been there? Maybe in another lifetime, she'd dive for ship wrecks and treasures.

Back in their stateroom, as Pepper stepped into the shower, Bill was magically at her side, entering with her. The guestroom shower was as spacious as any hotel shower, so they enjoyed themselves under the hot water, then napped on their king-sized bed until lunch.

They needed each other so much in the wake of Jake's death. It had only been five months, but time felt so elastic to Pepper. She'd never thought about the relativity of time, and the linear calendar-approach humans had invented. She came to understand that time was more of three-dimensional existence than a linear concept. The finality of death had crept into her soul, and had caught up to what her brain had registered the night of the theatre bombing. It felt like it had happened only yesterday. On the other hand, it felt equally plausible that Jake's death had happened five years ago.

Bill and Pepper held each other for a long time after they awakened from their nap. Their touch healed without speaking. They just needed to feel – to let the grief move through them like the waves moving across the sea. It was so relaxing to lie in bed and feel the soft movement of the yacht through the calm water. The Mythos engines were so quiet they could barely hear the light hum from below deck.

Neither Pepper nor Bill was close to returning to work at one-hundred-percent capacity. They were still in a state of shock, and processing their new reality. They were no longer Jake McCallan's parents. Now, they were just Pepper and Bill McCallan. A new identity. They'd be empty-nesters when they returned home.

The arrangement sounded so quiet that Pepper found herself wanting to avoid it. They still had Daisy to make some noise around the house, but she wasn't a child. Jake had been their only child and would be their only child. Shortly after Jake's birth, Pepper had suffered a uterine hemorrhage and had needed an emergency hysterectomy. She wasn't able to have any more children. This chapter of their lives had come to a tragic end, and they simply had to accept it, and start writing new chapters for their life together.

They snuggled for a bit longer, then decided they were hungry enough to dress and make an appearance above deck. They found Ralph and Susan playing cards and eating snacks. They beckoned Pepper and Bill over to the table to play.

As the foursome was playing their standard afternoon card game of 500, Captain Linda approached the table to give report to Ralph.

Linda was wearing her sporty uniform of a golf skirt and a short sleeved white blouse. She had on small dangly earrings, and her eyes were as sharp as Catch's fish knife.

"Hello all. Hope the voyage is comfortable thus far," said Linda.

"Good afternoon, Captain," said Ralph. "Everything is terrific."

"We'll plan to fuel at the Casa de Campo Marina in the Dominican Republic, sir."

"Okay. It's late afternoon now, do you anticipate entering before 5 p.m.?" asked Ralph.

"Unfortunately not. And we don't want to get stuck mooring in that marina tonight. There's a lot of chatter on the radio about increased crime on yachts in the marina. Apparently, the locals are now swimming out to the yachts and cutting the skiff lines or climbing aboard. Joe, Catch and I discussed the situation, and we recommend against it."

"Thank you. I agree. Where should we anchor tonight, then?" he asked.

"We'll anchor off Punta Cana, just outside the surf. I've checked, and there are a few other yachts there. Then, at eight tomorrow, we'll make our way to Casa de Campo."

"Very good," said Ralph.

***

The next morning, when Captain Linda had passed the landmark of the striped lighthouse, marking the starboard entrance to the Chavon River that lead to the Dominican marina, she turned her marine radio to VHF channel 16 and raised the Harbor Master, Captain Frank Castillo.

"Casa de Campo Marina, this is Captain Linda on The Hermit from Hopkins, Belize, requesting passage and a pilot dinghy for guidance into the marina. Over."

"Copy that Hermit. This is Captain Castillo. Did you hail Customs and Immigration? Over."

"Yes. No response. Over."

"What's your draft and length, Hermit? Over."

"The Hermit draft is 8 feet, and length is 122 feet. Over."

"Copy that. What country is the Hermit registered in, and what is her call sign? Over."

"The Hermit is registered in Belize, and her call sign is 'Whiskey Charlie 546niner.' Over."

"Copy. Pilot dinghy dispatched. Will you be staying overnight, Hermit? Over."

"No. Just a fuel stop. Over."

"How many liters?" he asked.

"Estimated 18,000 liters. Over."

"Copy that. Will any passengers be coming ashore from the Hermit? Over."

"No passengers coming ashore from The Hermit. Just fuel and departure. Over."

"Copy that. Do you have your Despacho from the Marina Guerra (Coastguard) of your last port, Hermit?"

"Yes. Over."

"Your dock fee will be $200 U.S.. Over."

"Copy that. Over."

"How many people on board?"

"Five crew. Four passengers. Over."

"Ultimate destination, Hermit?"

"St. Martin, French West Indies. Over."

"I see your vessel now, Hermit. No boarding by the DEA will be necessary. However, I'll board your vessel for Despachos, passport check and fees."

"Copy that. Hermit out," said Linda.

The pilot dinghy brought them into the fuel docking area, and Captain Linda powered down the engines to moor stern against the concrete quay. Joe and Catch threw the lines to the harbor crew who tied them off on foot-long cleats. The ninety plus degree air smelled of salt and diesel fuel.

Ralph instructed Pepper and Bill not to disembark, or they would have to submit to customs officials and a paperwork nightmare. The fueling would take an hour or so, and they could enjoy the sights and sounds of the Dominican Harbor from the yacht.

Harbor Master Frank Castillo walked over to the Mythos with his clipboard and paperwork. Big Joe helped him aboard. They shook hands. Catch lingered in the background, and Captain Linda materialized on the aft deck to sign the Despachos.

"Good morning, Captain Castillo," she said.

"Good morning." He looked around and sized up the quality. He had been on quite a few yachts, but this one was higher tech than he had seen recently. Her aluminum exterior was imposing, and the interior was first class. He thought his days of being impressed were over, but today he was anew. He chided himself for not requesting more than $200 in fees. For this operation, he should've requested double that amount. Captain Linda smiled knowingly. He looked her in the eye, then inclined his head in respectful nod.

She signed the documents and gave him a silver credit card for the fuel charge. When he reappeared later with the total, Ralph would sign it.

"Do you want to inspect passports, Captain," asked Linda.

"Yes, please have the crew and passengers present with their passports when I return with the fuel bill. I won't stamp them, but I need to see them. No one is disembarking, right?"

"Right," she confirmed.

It was important for the Harbor Master to feel confident about to whom he was allowing passage in his country's bays without a DEA inspection or Customs clearance. Hence the passport check.

They cast off the lines two hours later because everything took longer than expected in the Dominican. The humidity had produced a few pop-up clouds as the Mythos was guided out of the marina by the pilot dinghy.

As soon as they cleared the green and red entrance buoys, Linda moved the throttles forward so the Mythos could stretch her legs. She responded like a rocket that wanted to leave the atmosphere, but Linda held her back until they cleared the other boat traffic. Linda sent Joe to confirm with the guests that they were prepared for a cruising speed of 20 knots as she sipped an iced tea in her tan leather Captain's chair, enjoying the view.

She was squinting her eyes through the tinted windshield when a small drone suddenly appeared over the bow. She estimated it was three feet in diameter with multiple rotors on its legs. It had a camera suspended from its midsection. It looked like a marine copter that was capable of falling into the water, and popping out again. Piracy had always been an issue in the Caribbean, but now the pirates were snooping on their targets with drones before they attacked them.

Captain Linda hit the intercom button and informed the crew of a "drone alert." This was the code for Big Joe to make preparations to launch the Mythos drone to follow the intruder drone. It wouldn't do any good to shoot down the intruder drone because the pirates would know who shot it and seek revenge.

Rather, the Mythos crew had developed a protocol for waiting until the intruder drone departed, then sending the Mythos drone after the intruder to see where it came from, and to let the pirates know the Mythos had a camera on them, including their identities and vessel registration. It had worked as a deterrent thus far.

Big Joe heard the drone alert and calmly walked to a white bin on the aft deck above the staircase. He looked up at the intruder drone, knowing they were watching his every move. He went about his business unlocking the white bin, then sat on it, waiting for the intruder to circle the Mythos. While the intruder was over the bow, Joe popped the lid on the bin and removed the Mythos drone. He set it on the deck and grabbed the transmitter. The intruder was completing its surveillance circle, making one last sweep over the aft deck of the Tollefson's yacht. When it came around, the intruder would see the Mythos drone on the deck. No matter, Joe had it powered up. As soon as the intruder spotted the Mythos drone, it took a sharp turn and flew off. Joe had the Mythos drone in the air, tailing the intruder in two seconds. Like everything on the Mythos, its drone was first class and fast.

Joe tailed the intruder drone to an aging cigar boat with "Rhum Runner" painted on the side. A crew of four punks were standing in the Rhum Runner with surprised expressions on their faces. Joe circled the Rhum Runner, but maintained a safe height so they couldn't shoot it down. He didn't linger because the longer he stayed, the more vulnerable to a gunshot the Mythos drone would be. He took photos of the Rhum Runner's registration tag on the starboard side, then flew off. Joe hoped this would deter their piracy intentions, as it had others in the past.

Captain Linda and Ralph watched the video coverage from the Mythos drone on the large screen at the helm. Once the Mythos drone had safely landed on the aft deck, and Joe had stored it back in the white bin, he continued with his original task of informing everyone

Linda was going to punch up the speed to 20 knots.

He went to the helm to find Linda and Ralph there.

"Nice work, Joe," said Ralph.

"Thank you, sir."

"Looks like the Rhum Runner is a fast boat. We won't be able to outrun her," observed Ralph.

"No sir, but if we maintain a fast cruising speed for over an hour, the Rhum Runner might get frustrated when they realize we're not going to remain in the area overnight," said Linda.

"I agree. Just for fun, let's make some speed, Linda. Do we have enough fuel to max out cruising speed for an hour then ratchet it back?" asked Ralph.

"Yes sir. St. Martin is only 420 nautical miles away, so we should be able to do that comfortably," said Linda.

"Then, hit it!" ordered Ralph. He wasn't in the mood to act like a wimp in the face of some Caribbean punks.

Linda hit the intercom button again and said, "Attention, this is the Captain. Please take your seats. We're going to power up to full cruising speed in one minute. Again, please take your seats."

Linda flipped some switches and checked her depth finder as well as radar screens. She double- checked the route she had plotted for reefs and points. After 30 seconds had passed, she put her hand on the duel throttles that powered both engines simultaneously. She couldn't help but feel excited as she slowly eased the chrome throttles forward to 90 percent of their maximum, or 24 knots. The engines came alive, the Mythos blasting out a huge wake as it rose out of the water. It took a few minutes, then the impressive yacht eventually planed out at 30 knots, speeding across the surface like a silver bullet.

The pirates' cigar boat was built for speed, so it easily kept pace for a short distance. However, the pirates had a territory to protect, and fuel was expensive, so after 20 minutes of running at 30 knots, they made obscene hand gestures toward the Mythos and peeled off to return from whence they came. Captain Linda let the massive engines burn off some more carbon before she eased back the throttles 30 minutes later to a comfortable cruising speed of 15 knots. Mission accomplished. In style.

***

CHAPTER 9

Sint Maarten

Sint Maarten, Dutch West Indies

Jackie was riding in first class at a cruising altitude of 34,000 feet, traveling 525 miles per hour on a Boeing 757 with two Pratt & Whitney turbofans, each generating 43,000 pounds of thrust. She didn't care about all that shit though. Despite the jet's thrust, she still had more than four hours on the plane to wait for her upcoming reunion with Brent.

She was excited out of her skin, which she had shaved and lubricated to the extent he might slide off her if she ever let the man get naked on top of her. She couldn't take it any longer, she had decided they were going to get naked together. She was an adult, and saving herself for something more permanent with Brent was starting to sound like shaky reasoning to her. Why had she thought that in the first place? She had lost touch with her initial attraction, needing to rekindle it.

She hadn't been seeking a chaste relationship, but had convinced herself she was trying to preserve her self-respect. Huh? How could self-deprivation translate into self-respect? She was confused. Was this what love was like? Confusion laced with the hots? If she was attracted to his gorgeous body and charisma, then why not take advantage of what he had to give? She was a red-blooded American female and her body ached for a man's touch.

Men gawked at her at her gym and she appreciated the attention. She knew what they were thinking. Sometimes, she was thinking the same thing. It was one thing to find release from doing overhead squats when you had 120 pounds above your head. It was another thing to find release when you had a 180- pound American male on top of you, his soft brown eyes with golden flecks staring into yours. Brent. And those full lips. She wanted to suck on them until he came inside her. Okay, she was getting a little hotter than she had intended. She was still alone on a plane, and had a few hours to go.

And, more importantly, Jackie still had to make Brent work a little when she got there. She was certain that a man like Brent enjoyed at least a token chase. With his good looks, he probably had women propositioning him constantly in those foreign, exotic countries he visited. He probably had accepted a few of those propositions, too. She didn't care. She didn't need to know about his sexual conquests as long as he didn't need to know about her submissions. She had shared her near-perfect body, belly button ring and all, with a few lucky males, but not many. She had to calm down. Play it cool. Make a plan. Enjoy each other's company for a day before they got tangled up. She took a deep breath.

***

Jackie's plane landed on the Dutch side of the island, known as Sint Maarten. When she interacted with the Customs and Immigration official in the glass booth, however, Jackie had to declare where she would be staying. She told him she'd be at the Grand Case Beach Club, the French side of the island, known as Saint Martin. Even though a person could travel around the island freely without the need for a passport, the Customs Officer, stamp in hand, had to know which country was the destination, The French West Indies or the Dutch West Indies. For purposes of government bureaucracy, Jackie was going to France. Only the French...

After that fantasy world of a conversation, she descended the stairway to baggage claim. As she proceeded with the other passengers to carousel number 3, she saw Brent waiting for her with a bouquet of flowers. He had a slightly lopsided grin – just enough to be sexy, not enough to look drunk.

He was wearing faded blue jeans, hanging low on his hips, and a white short sleeved shirt that was gauzy enough for her to appreciate his body underneath. The top buttons revealed a hairy chest. She smiled and walked to him. He held his arms out wide, still holding the bouquet, and she magnetically adhered to him. His arms came around her, and he lowered his head and kissed her. A magnificent kiss. Yes, those full lips were still full, and his mouth was warm with a trace of mint. She felt the tingles down to her toes, reminiscent of what she had felt in Minneapolis. The spark was still there!

She didn't know whether to be relieved or terrified, but she knew she wanted more of this. They were temporarily lost in the kiss, not hearing the commotion around them.

Brent was waiting by the carousal holding the flowers. He had never felt this nervous to see a girl, not even on his first prom date. He was as close as he could get to the departure area, outside security, at the bottom of the stairs by baggage claim. He was watching the arrivals from Minneapolis, German and Nordic looking people who were destined to become sunburned their first day on the island despite how much sun block they used.

Then Jackie magically appeared at the top of the stairs. He loved her brown, sassy haircut that swung at the nape of her neck when she turned her head. He lusted after her feminine curves on top of her hard body. She was wearing a blue and white flouncy skirt that danced above her knees. He would worship her legs for the rest of his life. She had on a yellow, ruffled tank under a light blue jacket that emphasized her curves. She was everything he wanted in a woman. He would remember this image of her for the rest of his life, hoping he was good enough for her. He would try.

They reluctantly broke off their kiss and he handed her the bouquet. She was delighted beyond belief, and lightheaded from his kiss. She pointed out her bag on the carousal, and he nabbed it. They quickly exited the small airport to a black car that was waiting at the curb. The driver took Jackie's bag from Brent, and tossed it in the trunk, while Jackie and Brent slid into the backseat.

Brent asked her how her flight was and then they were kissing again. She felt the familiar zing, waves of pleasure sweeping over her. She couldn't get enough of him. Her hands were moving around his neck and through his hair while his hands were under her blouse and on her back, gently squeezing and exploring. He mumbled things like "I've missed you so much," and "you're so beautiful," as he dropped kisses down her neck and around her ears. Jackie felt like she was on a drug. Her lids were half closed and she was practically crawling onto his lap. She was surprised to discover that her hands had moved under his shirt and were searing a path of heat across his lower back and ribs.

After making out deeply for nearly thirty minutes, Jackie noticed the car had slowed, and they were turning into a resort. The island was quite hilly, even though she had missed the sights on the ride, she had felt the steep ascents. The terrain went from sea level at the beach to 300 vertical feet at the peaks.

They pulled into Grand Case Beach Club (pronounced "Käs") on the west side of the island. There was a slim stretch of white sandy beach, and white villas with red terra cotta roofs snugged up to the hill. The driver handed Brent the bag from the trunk and winked. Brent gave him a tip and guided Jackie to a guest room door with glass window slats. He waved the keyless entry card at the electronic spot, and opened the kitchen door. It was late afternoon, and the sun was setting over the Bay. The view through the manicured Sea Grape trees was breathtaking. There were sailboats of all shapes and sizes moored, the hills protecting them from the winds over the leeward side of the island. The surf was undulating rather, than crashing, as it washed up to the sugar sand. The sounds and smells were intoxicating.

Jackie turned to Brent. Their eyes met. There was an awkward second of silence where neither knew what to say. Jackie decided to follow her heart.

"Take me to your bedroom," she said.

He swept her off her feet and carried her up an impossibly narrow staircase, knocking paintings off the wall on their way up. They giggled nervously as the paintings crashed down the stairs.

***

CHAPTER 10

Grand Case

Saint Martin, French West Indies

Jackie and Brent awoke sometime after six p.m. He was spooned up behind her, holding her tight, his left hand cupping her breast. It had been spectacular, as each of them knew it would be. They couldn't believe their good fortune, basking in the relief that they had found each other. There would be time later to conjecture about finding the perfect soul mate, and commitment talk, but for now, they enjoyed the elation of requited love.

"What hotel are we in again?" asked Jackie.

"Grand Case Beach Club," he said.

"It's very nice," she said. "You did a good job."

"A 'good job?' That's how you're grading my performance?" he asked.

She laughed. "On the hotel. You knew what I meant. On the other thing? Well, I give you an A."

"Just an A? Not an A-plus?"

"Someone's an overachiever! You need something to strive for Mr. Cahill. Maybe you can score an A-plus next time." She yawned and stretched.

He rolled her onto her back and pinned her down with a deep kiss that promised more. Reacting to his touch, she arched her back and pushed her hips into his, feeling him harden.

He groaned. "You know I'd like to, but I promised Pepper and Bill we'd meet them soon."

"What? Pepper and Bill? They're here?" she asked.

"Yes. Waiting for us to have cocktails and dinner with them," he said.

"Why didn't you say so? I'm so excited!"

"Because I was afraid I wouldn't get you to myself for the first hour. Trust me, they understand," he said.

"Oh my God, did they know what time my plane got in?" she asked.

He nodded.

"So they know what we've been doing?" she asked.

"Of course not. I'm sure they assume we've been talking," he said.

"Yeah, right," she said.

They laughed, and got out of bed, then showered together. A half hour later, they walked out the sliding door of their unit, strolling down the inlaid stone path that had been quarried from one of the hills on the island. The solar lights made a romantic glow on the mottled stones, showcasing the Sea Grape tress above them, which had been manicured with flat tops at the height of the second floor balconies to preserve the view. They were excellent shade trees in the afternoon sun.

Thirty seconds later, and ten units down the path, Brent turned onto a patio to find Pepper and Bill sitting at a small table, playing cards.

They stood and the women squealed with excitement when they saw each other. They hugged while the men shook hands. Pepper pulled Jackie inside the sliding screen door under the pretext of helping her carry out some cocktails that no one had ordered yet.

Once in the kitchen, Pepper opened the fridge, removed four beers, and set them on the counter. She looked at Jackie, and they both burst out laughing.

"Got a little whisker burn there, Sweetie," teased Pepper.

"What? I do?" Jackie felt her cheeks, blushing.

"No. I'm just teasing you! Are you glad you came?" asked Pepper.

"Ecstatic! He's fantastic!" said Jackie.

More embarrassed laughter.

"Hey girls, are you going to bring out the beers, or do I have to come in there and get them?" asked Bill through the screen door.

"You can tell me about it later," said Pepper.

They gathered up the beers and joined their men on the patio where Pepper had set out some light hors d' oeuvres. Everyone clinked bottles and drank.

"So, how was your fancy yacht trip?" asked Jackie.

"Ralph and Susan were very generous hosts," said Pepper.

"Tell us about it," said Jackie.

"Bill, tell them what Ralph did to you," said Pepper.

"Well, I offered to split the fuel costs from Belize to St. Martin, since they invited us as guests," explained Bill.

"We stopped for fuel first in Jamaica. Brent, what do you suppose marine diesel fuel costs per liter?" asked Bill.

"No clue. A dollar?" guessed Brent.

"Close. 1.20 Euros, which is about 1.30 U.S. dollars, at the current exchange rate," said Bill.

"And how many liters did their yacht take?" asked Brent.

Bill nodded. "Ralph played me pretty well. We filled up, and the Harbor Master brought the credit card reader to the yacht to slide someone's card through it. I was standing there, prepared to put half on my card. I took it out of my wallet, and suggested we split it. Ralph laughed, handed his card to the Harbor Master, and told him to put it all on his card. I was sort of offended. After the Harbor Master left, though, Ralph showed me the receipt. The Mythos has an 18,500 liter tank. His bill was $23,400!"

"Holy shit. What did he say to you?" asked Brent.

"He said, 'Bill, are you still sure you want to split the fuel? No sweat Buddy. Maybe just chip in for some food,'" said Bill, laughing.

"Not only do they cost a fortune, but they're expensive to run on top of that!" said Brent.

"I didn't realize," said Bill. "We could have made several round trip flights from Belize to St. Martin for that price!"

"Good story," said Brent.

"Another funny thing," said Pepper, "both Bill and I are having trouble walking on dry land. You know how you get used to the sway of a boat while you're on it all day?"

Brent and Jackie nodded.

"If you do that for a week," said Pepper, "when you come back to dry land and start walking around, you still sway, but you don't need to. It's like reverse sea sickness. I feel like I could fall out of my chair right now if I turned my head too fast."

"Drink more alcohol," suggested Brent.

"I'm sure it would help. Seriously, we were spoiled for a week. If you look out into the bay right now, you can see the Tollefson's yacht, The Hermit. She's in the center of those sailboats, all lit up like a Christmas tree," said Pepper.

The Hermit was moored at the furthest reaches of the bay, beyond the smaller catamarans and single-hulled boats, but she was still visible because of her size.

"I hope she's still there tomorrow morning, so you can see her in daylight," said Pepper.

***

They walked into the town of Grand Case, and Pepper was reminded of walking along the French Riviera. The Europeans had imprinted not only their language, but also their infrastructure and design on the landscape.

Unlike the Village of Hopkins in Belize, Grand Case's streets were actually paved, but they were narrow, European-style, allowing for only one-way traffic, parking on one side of the street only. And like many seafront villages in the Caribbean, there were dilapidated cinderblock buildings of bygone days, mixed in with the maintained shops and restaurants. It was clear there was no overarching development plan, just each property owner's personal choice on design and decoration. On the upside, the village was a dining paradise. There was one French restaurant after another, with a few Italian mixed in for diversity.

Pepper and Jackie picked out a restaurant on the waterfront called Le Tastevin, and were shown to a table on the deck overlooking the Bay. By this time, the sun had set, and the moored sailboats had their white anchor lights ablaze at the top of their masts. Beyond the bay, lay the island of Anguilla, only ten nautical miles to the northwest. Its shoreline was speckled with lights as well.

Le Tastevin offered a fine selection of champagne, and since everyone was in such a celebratory mood, Bill and Brent decided to order a bottle of Gosset Rosé Brut. They toasted their reunion in St. Martin, and ordered an appetizer of foie gras poêlé, which was seared foie gras in a mushroom sauce. They caught up on one another's lives, ensconced in the French-Caribbean ambiance. The restaurant had a nautical theme, dark wood floors and vaulted ceilings, teak trim and royal blue tieback curtains framing the views. Lantern-style lamps glowed on the inland side.

The water was lapping on the rocks below the deck, giving them all the sensation of being on a boat. Pepper ordered the filet de vivaneau, which was grilled red snapper with a French glaze, zucchini and mashed potatoes on the side, just like at home. Except everything tasted French. And cost a lot more. For dessert, they had espressos and tartes aux pommes maison, which was French for an apple fritter that resembled apple pie a la mode.

Contrary to rumor, the French wait staff were polite, providing exceptional service, respectfully addressing Bill as "Monsieur" throughout the dining experience, leaving him in a very agreeable mood. Pepper made a mental note to call Bill Monsieur in the future if she needed anything from him.

"So Brent, what have you been up to?" inquired Pepper.

"On assignment in London. Most boring thing I've ever done," he complained.

"Is that right?" she asked.

"Yes. But that's not exactly a recruiting tool if I'm going to use you as a consultant, is it Pepper?" he said.

"I could actually use 'boring' right now. It suits me. Besides, I love gathering intel and putting the pieces of the puzzle together," she said.

"Well, maybe you'd like to join me tomorrow in reviewing a couple hundred photos on my laptop that I took of President Vadik Volkov at the Global Energy Summit. I need to write a report of who met with him while he was in London," said Brent.

"I'd love to," said Pepper.

***

CHAPTER 11

The Swedish Intern

Philadelphia, Pennsylvania

United States of America

In furtherance of her plot, Svea had directed her counterfeiter, Hugo, to create the backstory and legend for the false identities for three twenty-something university students who were in her Social Democratic Party for Students.

Svea and Hugo had known each other since school days, when they had experimented with alcohol and marijuana together. Hugo's older brother had been a well-known dealer for the teenagers in Svea's circle, thus ingratiating Hugo to the wealthy, beautiful set. Hugo had pursued an underground life when Svea had gone off to Uppsala University, but she had made a point to stay in touch, sensing he would play a useful role in her life. They shared an easy friendship, Svea finding him quite useful for odd jobs. He was loyal, and she could trust him to be discrete. She had never judged his activities, and as far as she could tell, he hadn't judged her. Hugo had carved out a special skill in identity work, among other, darker trades.

The students, Felipe Malstrom, Valter Nylund and Max Björnsson, each needed to infiltrate a hospital pharmacy in America, so each needed a fake passport, university transcript and professor recommendations for a three-month internship. They needed to be believable and likable. And they were. All three were nice-looking young men who wanted more out of life than a university education and a routine job in Sweden. They had drunk Svea's radicalized Kool-Aid, and they wanted to aspire to the highest potential she saw in them. She had met with each of them individually to prepare him for this mission, telling each it would be a special favor to her.

Svea had known Felipe Malstrom the longest of the three. He had been in her underground club since he had started university four years ago. He had a crush on her, which had been his original reason for joining. Even though she was twenty years his senior, she was still the hottest woman with whom he had interacted while at the University of Stockholm. Svea's age and sophistication just made her that much more attractive to him.

He couldn't explain his need to please her or his love for her. Her club had initially been rooted in political activism for socialism, bordering on communism. They considered themselves activists, protesting and organizing constantly, spending a lot of time together. The club had become Felipe's surrogate family. He hadn't graduated from university yet because he enjoyed taking a wide variety of classes, so he had failed to narrow his studies enough to accomplish a major.

When Svea pointed him in a direction for a substantive field, he followed her direction, wanting to please her. If she suggested he pick up a few other classes, he did. He had taken a fair number of management classes, and had just completed some pharmacy classes to prepare him for this important assignment Svea had given him. She was finally taking an interest in him personally. This was his opportunity for a breakout moment from the rest of the men in the club, whom he suspected had joined and religiously attended the meetings for the same reason he did – a crush on Svea.

Felipe fantasized about Svea's body on top of his, teaching him what she liked. He had floated some inviting comments to her after club meetings, but she hadn't caught them or cared. Propositioning an older woman was beyond his skill set. He was a persistent 22-year-old man, however, so he'd keep after her. In the meantime, he would follow her anywhere, and now that she was in the Prime Minister's Cabinet, she was a magnet of power to which he was drawn. He'd prove himself to her sooner or later.

***

His assignment was to intern in an American hospital pharmacy, locate their antidotes for nerve gas poisoning, then report back to Svea for further instruction. He was in his third week of internship at Philadelphia General Hospital, which he learned was a certified trauma center, stroke center, burn center, mass casualty center and bioterrorism center. It was a strategic hub for all kinds of human disaster, which is why he supposed Svea had placed him there. It had a large and complex inpatient pharmacy department that supported 420 hospital beds.

Felipe liked his American boss and mentor, Mary Adams. She had been extremely generous with information and tips for him in the past few weeks, taking him to lunch in the cafeteria and giving him tours of every aspect of the pharmacy distribution she could think of. She reminded him of his mom - short, plump, brown hair about shoulder length, spectacles and lipstick that seemed to overflow the outline of her lips. She kept up with her lipstick application on an hourly basis so the ruby rose was ever present.

Mary had worked at Philadelphia General Hospital for 30 years, so she knew virtually every aspect of the pharmacy business, from supply chain to drug interactions. The woman was a walking drug-reference manual.

He had noticed that most employees at the hospital had similar longevity. It was rare to find someone who had worked there fewer than 10 years. He knew why. They had a friendly culture and good benefits. Of course, no company's benefits approximated the Swedish socialist government benefit scheme, but this hospital was generous. Mary would retire very comfortably to her lake house in northern Pennsylvania.

By week number three, he knew his way around the basement maze of pharmacy offices and inventory supply rooms. They were numerous and secure. His hospital identity badge that had his photo on it also had a magnetic strip on the back that swiped him into most locked areas. Most, but not all.

Svea had specifically instructed him a few days ago to learn about the hospital supply and storage of two medicines, atropine and pralidoxime chloride (also called II PAM chloride). Svea told him to say he was learning disaster planning procedures for Swedish hospitals, and that he wanted to study the American procedure for rapid deployment of these two medicines, which were widely known to be antidotes for nerve gas poisoning, or a duo dote. Bioterrorism was in the top ten list for planning and drilling at every hospital, whether it was located in America or Europe, so Svea told Felipe his American manager would understand and appreciate Felipe's curiosity.

Felipe had represented to Mary that he was training to be a hospital pharmacy manager after his internship, so he wanted to learn as broad a range as possible of all pharmacy operations. Mary had obliged. It probably hadn't hurt that he had charmed her like a school boy. Although he didn't look like a stereotypical Swede with blond hair and blue eyes, he nevertheless was handsome with dark hair, horn rimmed glasses, a slim build and a nice smile. He shamelessly sucked up to her, fetching her coffee and offering to do all sorts of tasks that she otherwise would have handed off to her secretary. He found a way to accompany her to as many meetings as he could, and to be by her side most of the day.

At lunch, Felipe asked Mary in a heavy Swedish accent, "I have been reviewing the hospital policies for mass casualty planning and I would like to know more about the pharmacy's role in disaster situations."

Mary nodded. "Good for you. Way to take initiative. Obviously, depending on the specific disaster, the pharmacy protocol will be unique. For example, a bus accident is quite a bit different than a toxic chemical spill in terms of pharmaceutical needs."

"In Sweden," he said, "we're very concerned about the bioterrorism risk since we're so close to Russia. We have a strong distrust of Russia and her methods in controlling her people, including humans residing near her borders. We fear that Russia will deploy a nerve gas and the prevailing winds will take it over Sweden, resulting in death of our citizens. We're developing governmental supplies and distribution networks to hospitals for the antidotes to such attacks, and we've realized what a complex task it is for our small country. How does a country the size of America do it?"

"Oh, a nerve gas attack," she said. "Fortunately, there are people in our government who get paid to anticipate just such a scenario, and they've developed a network of drug distribution through the Centers for Disease Control, or the CDC, a government agency. Being one of the largest hospitals in the region, Philadelphia General has been designated by the government as a strategic hub to treat nerve gas toxicity. We coordinate our designated inventory of antidotes with the CDC's assistance."

"Really? What does that mean? You have an inventory of antidotes that is readily available?" asked Felipe.

"Oh no," she said. "We have a locked and highly secure area where we store special antidotes. There are a variety of medicines in there for various scenarios, including atropine and II PAM chloride, a duo dote the military has used successfully in treating Sarin nerve gas poisoning. Do you want to see the room?"

"Of course," said Felipe.

"I'll take you. We just have to swing by my office, get the key, and notify the Security Department that we're entering it, so they don't see us on video and send a team to kill us," said Mary.

"They would do that?" he asked.

"No, just joking," she said. "They don't carry guns. They would call the police though."

Felipe logged this information. He also noted where she kept the key to the secure room when they stopped by her office to retrieve it.

The secure room was located in the basement, among the maze of hallways with white tiled floors and whitewashed cinder block walls. Mary and Felipe came to a nondescript wooden door. It was unmarked, and the only notable feature was that there were two security camera bubbles in the ceiling tiles outside the door. He hadn't noticed two security bubbles this close together anywhere else in the hospital. He made a note to himself to observe how many camera bubbles were concentrated in a certain location to determine how important the area was. More security obviously meant more important items.

Felipe watched as Mary turned a key in the door lock and punched in a security code in the door handle. He memorized her key pad entry because she did it so slowly, and whispered it out loud. It would have been impossible for him not to have picked it up.

They entered a large storage area with a concrete floor, white dry walls, and white ceiling tiles that had temperature probes that were 8 inches long hanging from them. Mary explained the room was maintained in a temperature range of 60 to 65 degrees Fahrenheit, and 25 to 30 percent humidity at all times. Some of these medicines had only a six-month shelf life, so CDC personnel came to the hospital every six months to swap out the expired medicines for new ones. It was expensive, but the American citizens paid for it so that emergency medicines would be available in an emergency.

Mary pointed out the security cameras in the room, the smoke detector and the fire sprinkler heads in the ceiling, indicating that if the sprinklers went off, they could ruin some of the medicines. Some medicines were in vials and ampules, and others in pill bottles. They weren't really considered water resistant, much less water proof. The medicines were stored in large steel cages the size of a deep filing cabinet. The cages had mesh doors with Plexiglas built into them. Mary pointed out the metal rope surrounding each cage that connected to a plastic padlock-device in the front of each cage.

"In order to open the cage," she explained, "you have to break this plastic padlock. Once broken, it will electronically notify the CDC that the lock has been compromised. They know the date, time and location of this lock, so they'd immediately call our security department to confirm purposeful entry and the nature of the disaster."

"And if security cannot confirm purposeful entry?" inquired Felipe.

"Then the CDC would notify the local police station to investigate," she said.

"Oh, brilliant planning. How many doses do you have stockpiled in this room? Like how many patients could you treat?" he asked.

"Good question," she said. "Depending on the potency of the nerve gas the patients were exposed to, we estimate we could treat over a thousand patients with this current stockpile, if, and this is a really big if, the patients got here in time. Nerve gas acts pretty quickly - like an hour or less for victims directly affected."

"Is that right?" he asked.

She nodded. "For victims with a secondary exposure, like who came in contact with the victims who were initially affected, the window of time for treatment might be longer - up to 10 hours in some rare circumstances."

"This has been quite helpful," he said. "The first thing I'll do in my new post in Sweden is to address the hospital preparedness for biologic agent warfare. I'll compare the Swedish system to the one you have here. May I take your hospital policies with me?

"Of course," she offered. "Print and take them. The hospital industry in America routinely shares policies with one another."

"So there is cooperation in your system even though the government doesn't own the hospitals?" he asked.

"Oh yes, it's in the best interests of patients. That's what motivates us. We don't need the government to tell us to do something. If it's in the best interest of patients, then we do it regardless," she said.

"Fascinating. Thank you again," said Felipe.

"You're welcome," she said as she switched off lights and locked the room as they left.

***

Felipe had a phone call with Svea that night, relaying everything he had learned. She congratulated him on a job well done, promising he would be rewarded for his hard work when he returned. Her voice was so sexy over the phone, he found himself playing with his junk while he talked to her.

"Felipe, I need you to be on my team. Can you be on standby for my direction on a few very specific tasks in the near future?" She said to him in a serious whisper.

"Of course," he mumbled.

"There will come a day in the next week or two when I contact you with more information, and secret duties to complete that are important to me personally. Can you promise me you will be ready to do as I say?" she asked.

"You know I'd do anything for you, Svea," he said. He was stroking lightly now.

"Good. You're important to me. You're one of the brightest members of the party I have," she said, as she was making herself breakfast in Sweden.

"Thank you," he said in a softer voice, still working it.

"Are you taking care of yourself?" she asked.

"I try, but I miss you, Svea," he ventured, his breathing becoming stronger.

He missed her? That was a bit overboard, and Svea could tell he was distracted during their conversation. She couldn't hear any background noise, but he sounded as though he might be walking.

"Hmm. Is that right, Felipe? I miss you too," she said.

"Yeah," he said in a husky voice, definitely breathing harder.

It suddenly dawned on Svea what he was doing. He's jacking off while talking to me! Her immediate reaction was repulsion, then she realized he was a male in his twenties, and she might be able to use it to her advantage. After all, she needed him. She was surprised at his audacity though.

"You know you mean a lot to me, right Felipe?" she asked, adopting a huskier tone.

"Yeah..." He pumped harder.

"I'm in my bath right now with a glass of wine, thinking about you, Felipe," she lied.

"Oh...yeah...," he said, his breath coming in short bursts now.

"Yes, and I'm touching my nipples where you would be sucking on them if you were here with me," she said softly.

"Ahhh...Oh...Oh...yeah," and the line went dead. She laughed, feeling a little excited. When he returned from America, she might have to spend some one-on-one time with him. That is, if he lived.

***

CHAPTER 12

Pepper Helps Brent

St. Martin, French West Indies

The morning after their French dinner out, Pepper and Bill were having breakfast at the resort café, sitting on the deck overlooking the bay, when Brent and Jackie joined them. The new couple was freshly showered and had smiles plastered on their faces. True love was impossible to suppress. Or true lust - whatever was going on there.

"Good morning, lovebirds," said Bill.

More smiles. Jackie blushed.

After croissants and strong French coffee served by a waiter who shrugged indifference at everything the foursome ordered, Brent asked Pepper if she still wanted to review photos. She enthusiastically agreed, so Bill and Jackie excused themselves and made plans to meet at the beach below their patios while Brent and Pepper worked.

Brent removed his laptop from his beat up brown satchel, and cleared a space at the small café table. The French waiter with the goatee snorted disapproval at their table monopoly, but didn't have the guts to challenge Brent's confident stare. Just to show him who was boss, Brent ordered a bottle of water.

Brent powered up the laptop and found his file of Volkov photos. He clicked through them, introducing Pepper to heads of state and Volkov's usual entourage.

Brent clicked on Svea Lovgren outside the London club called Bodo's Schloss, casually referring to her as "one of Volkov's many mistresses." Pepper made a mental note of Svea's profile while reviewing the shadowy photos of her outside Bodo's in the alleyway. The clearer shots of Volkov walking through the lobby at One Aldwych, with Svea trailing behind him in the entourage, however, offered Pepper a better image. She asked Brent to pause on a few.

"This woman went to Volkov's hotel and walked in with his security detail?" asked Pepper.

"Yes," said Brent.

"She's not a Russian mistress," said Pepper. "She looks like the new Minister for Foreign Affairs for Sweden. What's her name? Something Lovgren. I'm blanking on her first name. I read it in the Belizean newspaper a few weeks ago. Big flap in Sweden over the previous Minister for Foreign Affairs, also a woman, Something Stolt. I remember thinking it rhymed with dolt."

"Anyway, Stolt offended the Arab League by raising women's rights at a conference in Dubai. The headline was something like 'A Policy Puzzle of Swedish Goals in the Mideast.' As a result, the Saudis reneged on a purchase of Saab missiles from Sweden, and most Arab nations recalled their diplomats from Sweden. They put so much pressure on the Swedish business industry that Prime Minister Olaf Carlsson fired Stolt, and appointed the

Deputy Minister, Ms. Lovgren, to replace her," said Pepper.

Brent was taken aback. "You follow Swedish politics?"

"Not particularly. But it was in the international news because the Arabs were so offended." Pepper snapped her fingers. "That's it! Svea. Her first name is Svea. Svea Lovgren, new Minister for Foreign Affairs for Sweden. Quite a beauty."

"Awesome," said Brent. He exited the photo file and accessed the internet to log onto his work database of foreign heads of state. Sure enough, there was a photo and complete biography of Svea Lovgren in the database. They read it together.

Name: Svea Lovgren

Citizenship: Sweden

Passport Status: Diplomatic

Date of Birth: April 20, 1982

Title: Swedish Minister for Foreign Affairs

Education: Swedish Secondary School in Stockholm. Uppsala University in Uppsala, Sweden. Major focus was political science and international business. Fluent in Swedish, English, French and German. Schooled in Russian, Arabic and Thai.

Affiliations: Swedish Social Democratic Party. President of Student Social Democratic Party.

Minority Voters League. University Progressivists.

Employment History: Jensen Shipping, Inc. (age 16-20). Congressional Staffer to the Social Democratic Party Leader in the Riksdag, Björn Linde (age 20-22). Employee at the public relations firm of Kjelstad & Cohen (age 22-26). Social Democratic Party staffer (age 26-28). Manager in Social Democratic Party (age 28-30). Ministry of Foreign Affairs staffer (age 30-33). Ministry of Foreign Affairs Deputy Assistant (age 33-34). Deputy Minister of Foreign Affairs (age 34-36). Minister of Foreign Affairs (age 36 - present).

Marital Status: Married to Juergen Swanson at age 25. Divorced at age 33. Ms. Lovgren resides in their marital home and Mr. Swanson moved to Norrlandsgatan 312, Stockholm. Ms. Lovgren has been seen socializing with a variety of men, but does not appear to be in a long term relationship with any of them.

Biography: Born in Stockholm to Marta and Sven Lovgren. Father died in 1986. Svea was 4 years old. Mother remarried Henrik Jensen, an American shipping magnate when Svea was 6 years old. Jensen's business took the family all over the world. Svea worked for him in the summers until age 22. Mother and step-father have residences in America, Sweden, Thailand and Greece. Ms. Lovgren infrequently visits her parents.

***

"Seems like a profile of someone who sought a career in politics, no matter where she lived," said Pepper. "Her career trajectory reads like it was methodically planned. Look at her time in the political party, then the public relations firm, then back to the political party. She must have been considered smart and powerful to rise up the ranks so fast in the Foreign Ministry. And, it probably didn't hurt that her stepfather is mega wealthy. Of course, she's quite beautiful, being only 36 years old."

"Yeah. I would have taken her for 32 – tops," observed Brent.

"Maybe Volkov did too. Did she spend quite a bit of time at his hotel?" asked Pepper.

"Just that one night – all night. I came back on shift at seven the next morning, and got these photos of her leaving about 8:20 a.m.," he said.

Brent exited the data base and returned to his photo file. He clicked through until he found Svea doing the walk of shame through the Aldwych lobby, sporting wet hair and wearing a sweat suit.

"Looks like one of her security detail is carrying a small overnight bag for her," said Brent. "I assume she returned to her hotel to change out of the sweat suit before she attended the energy summit meetings for the day."

"What do you make of the tête-à-tête?" asked Pepper.

"What I initially took for a sexual liaison could be something more. Why would a seemingly innocent Swedish beauty want to sully herself with Volkov?" he asked.

"My guess? Despite her beauty, her bio reflects a fairly calculated individual. Why would we think she's satisfied in her current role? So far in life, she's demonstrated that she just keeps climbing the political ladder. Maybe Volkov is the next rung," said Pepper.

"What could he give her?" asked Brent.

"Pure speculation, but maybe he'll buy those Saab missiles from her that the Saudis reneged on. That would be a quick political win for her back home, and probably was a fair trade for a night in bed with her, from both their perspectives," said Pepper, raising her left eyebrow.

"I like the way you think," said Brent. "Which reminds me, I have a little something for you to look over."

Brent reached into his satchel and pulled out a document in a plastic sleeve. He set it on the table in front of Pepper.

"I don't expect you to read and sign it right now," he said. "Review it tonight, and let me know what you think tomorrow. It's our standard consulting contract. Pays well but no benefits. All your travel expenses will be reimbursed, and you can usually get away with traveling first class. Of course, food and lodging like this week at Grand Case would be reimbursed, if you sign it before we end this trip, that is."

"Let me read it. Does the Agency entertain any negotiation?" she asked.

"No. But you might feel better if you read it before you signed it," he said.

"Will do," she promised.

"You'll see that if you sign this," he said, "there will be extensive security application and confidentiality requirements. You'll also have to be oriented to Agency protocol in Boston. That'll be important. If you like consulting, I'd recommend that you take a few of our basic certification classes in field training with hand-to-hand combat and weaponry. There're some online classes on intelligence-gathering that you'll also want to take when you return to Minneapolis."

"All of that sounds interesting," she said. "I'm ready for a new challenge. Let me discuss it with Bill."

"Of course. As soon as you sign the contract, I'll orient you to a few policies and get you started with some of the online courses," he said.

They ended their morning meeting and went their separate ways.

***

CHAPTER 13
Pepper Signs the Contract

St. Martin, French West Indies

After changing into their swimsuits, Brent and Pepper caught up with Bill and Jackie on the beach. They were sitting in lawn chairs in six-inch-deep water, sipping tropical drinks. Their feet and ankles were wet, but the rest of their bodies were dry. It was so peaceful, the gentle surf lapping at the shore. Unbeknown to Bill, an iguana was sunning itself on the black rocks right behind his head. Pepper took a photo.

"This sugar sand is the softest I've ever stepped in," said Jackie.

"Isn't it beautiful? The water is so warm. Did you go swimming yet?" asked Pepper.

"Yeah, it's like bath water. Hey Pepper, I noticed some people wake boarding with a boat that says 'Eole de Wake' on the side. It came to the boat launch at the north end of the bay to pick up skiers. Do you wanna hook up with that deal?"

"Absolutely! I'm all in," she said.

A short time later, the foursome was standing at the end of the boat launch at the foot of the hill, waiting for the driver to pick them up. He rolled up in his tri-hull 20-foot speedboat with a 150 Merc outboard on the back. He had metal racks over the top of the boat, holding the wake boards and water skis. He was a very tan young man with reddish hair, a shaven chest and a tattoo arm sleeve, swirling with a mermaid and some other mysterious imagery. He introduced himself as Francois, and asked if they knew how to ski.

"A little," said Pepper.

"Technically, I don't," said Brent.

"We'll teach you," said Pepper.

"I'll watch," he insisted.

"Have you had anything to drink today?" she asked.

"No. I was with you all morning. Remember?" he said.

"Let's ask Francois if he has a beer for you," she said.

"Why?" he asked.

"Helps the confidence level for first timers," she said.

"Not gonna happen," he said.

"Oh come on, you're an athletic guy. You'll pick it up fast. Weren't you a big bad ass in the Navy?"

"Yes, I was in SWCC, but they didn't drag us behind the boats. It was more of driving the boats and shooting big guns from them," he said.

"Oh. Well, watch me. I won't get dragged so much as pulled," said Pepper. Bill shook his head and took the beer that Francois was offering.

Francois motored them out to the middle of the bay where all the sailboats were swinging to and fro with the tide on their moored buoys. The energy in the boat was palpable. The ladies were laughing and talking about who would go first. Pepper volunteered, so Francois handed her a wakeboard with a funky design on it. Pepper noticed the fin on the bottom wasn't as wide as her own at home, which meant it would ride more like a saucer, enabling the 180 degree turn easier. She'd have to adjust for that when she got up.

"Now Francois," said Pepper. "I do thumbs up for faster and thumbs down for slower, okay?"

He smiled knowingly, saying, "oui, oui."

"Then, when I'm ready to go, I'll yell 'hit it,'" she said.

"What? I do not understand this," said Francois. He looked at her for an explanation.

"You know, when I'm in the water and I want the boat to take off and go, I yell 'hit it.'" Pepper gestured with her hands and body.

Bill was shaking his head at this exchange.

"Oh, oui, oui, of course, Madam," said Francois.

"Time to get in the water, Pepper. I'll let him know what you mean when you say 'hit it,'" ordered Bill.

Pepper sat on the teak platform at the back of the boat, next to the propeller, and eased her feet into the black rubber booties on the wakeboard. Francois handed her the rope handle. She took it and nimbly pushed off the platform to ride the elevator down into the salt water. The wakeboard allowed her to descend slowly enough that it resembled an elevator descending. Her personal goal was not to get her hair wet.

Francois drove the boat forward to take the slack out of the rope, while Pepper positioned her feet and the board horizontally in front of her with the rope in the middle. When the rope was taught, she yelled "hit it," and the speedboat easily pulled her up. As soon as she was up, she turned sideways to the boat with her left foot forward. She hung onto the rope with her right hand while she adjusted her suit bottom with her left, just to assure there weren't any wardrobe malfunctions from the force of being yanked out of the water.

Pepper quickly scanned where they were going to see what her safe zone would be when she boarded outside the wake. There were sailboats on both sides. She couldn't believe she was wakeboarding off St. Martin, with the hilly terrain and white colored resorts in the background. The sun was beating down on them, and the water was a beautiful turquoise.

It all made her smile with delight. Then, she rocked back on her heels, pulling the rope handle toward her left hip. This motion, along with shifting her weight, pulled her outside the wake and into the rippling sea. She immediately noticed how different it was than boarding on a lake. In addition to the surface ripples, there were the swells, which were basically large pillows she had to navigate, similar to moguls when snow skiing. The entire bay heaved and retreated, in contrast to her calm lake back in Minnesota.

Jackie cheered from the boat, so Pepper went out as far as the rope would allow, then shifted her weight onto her toes to carry her back toward the wake at full speed. She jumped the wake, going into the air about two feet, pulling up her knees to bring the board up. She cleared the entire wake and landed on the other side, pulling hard on the rope handle to carry the momentum through the landing. Back and forth she went across the wake, jumping each side and hot doggin' it. When her hands became too tired to hold the handle any longer, she threw the rope high into the air, and kept her hands up as she glided to a stop, taking the elevator down until she was up to her neck in water. Her hair was still dry, which translated into a perfect run for her. No wipeouts.

Pepper quickly unfastened her feet from the booties, and had the wakeboard at the surface, ready to hand to Bill when they circled back around her.

As the boat came to Pepper's side, Francois asked, "how do you feel?"

"Fabulous, Francois! That was awesome!" she exclaimed.

He smiled, and Bill grabbed the board from her.

Pepper hoisted herself onto the teak platform at the back of the boat and Bill gave her a hand to leap over the seat.

"You looked beautiful, baby," he said.

"Thank you," she said. "You men are so visual, aren't you?"

"Maybe, but we're tactile too," said Bill, and he wrapped his arms around her.

Jackie was next, wasting no time in strapping on the wakeboard and jumping in. Jackie was a much more aggressive skier than Pepper, not only doing jumps over the wake, but also 180 degree spins while flying across it. This drew applause from Pepper, Bill and Brent, and also from the neighboring sailboats. Brent was awestruck. And a little humbled at what a hot shot jock she was.

When the boat pulled around to Jackie, Francois took the board and said, "Very impressive Mademoiselle."

Brent pulled her into the boat and unzipped her life vest so he could hug her skin-on-skin. He whispered something about a sexy bikini in her ear, and Jackie felt shivers go down to her toes. The air temp was so warm and the sun so hot, she didn't even need a towel, especially with Brent's big arms wrapped around her.

Bill asked Francois for a men's life vest. Francois reached under the driver's console and pulled out his largest French vest, which covered about half of Bill's broad shoulders. He couldn't even get the arm hole over his deltoid. Pepper laughed and asked Francois if he had anything bigger. He shook his head and threw up his hands in the common French gesture that included a shoulder shrug and a dismissive turn of the head. It was their signal that there was no more that could be said on the topic.

Bill was wearing his blue and grey O'Neill surf shirt, so decided to go without a life vest, not that it had any buoyancy like a wetsuit, but he figured he was more buoyant in sea water than Minnesota lake water. He grabbed the slalom ski off the top rack and jumped over the side with it. Francois tossed him the rope handle and Bill put on the ski in the water.

Francois took the slack out of the rope, and when it was taught, Bill yelled "hit it."

The speedboat had to struggle to pull his 240 pounds out of the water, but once he was up, it planed out quickly. Bill glided easily across the wake from one side to the other, sending up a rooster tail of a spray that rose 20 feet into the air. When the sun hit the spray just right, it made a mini-rainbow for a millisecond, delighting Pepper. Bill had learned to water ski in his thirties, but he was so athletic that he looked like he had been doing it his entire life. He skied like the football player he was.

When Bill finished, they asked Brent if he wanted to go. Rather than risk making a fool out of himself in front of his hot shot girl, he politely declined and mumbled something about next time.

Pepper came to his rescue and said it would be harder to learn on this ocean chop with swells than it would on her lake back in Minnesota, so she promised to teach him next time he visited Minnesota.

Francois took them on a brief tour of the bay, moving north along the coastline, pointing out coral reefs and nearby islands. Everyone cracked a beer and basked in the hot sun.

The coastline was so different from other Caribbean Islands Pepper had seen. There were palm trees and sea grape trees at water level along the beaches, but the lush greens quickly diminished with elevation. The tallest hill on the island was 424 meters, and that was close to the beach, creating a very steep slope. The hill behind Grand Case Resort was uncreatively named by the French explorers, First Stick Hill. Pepper wondered if it had been so named because it reflected the first French flag placement.

The hills rising out of the shoreline actually reminded Pepper of northern California. If St. Martin's green shrub trees were replaced by junipers, the hills could easily pass for the Marin headlands in the San Francisco Bay area.

It was cocktail hour by the time they tied up to the boat launch, so they agreed to shower and meet at Pepper and Bill's patio to make dinner plans. Brent told Bill quietly not to expect Jackie and himself for at least an hour.

While showering together, Bill asked Pepper if her morning work session with Brent had gone well.

"Yeah. I like the work, and the consulting role suits my tastes right now. I got burned by being a loyal employee of Futuraceutical Company so I kind of feel like I need to be on my own for a while. And I can get behind counterterrorism work. The money is pretty good, but there isn't a retirement plan or other benefits. I'll have to switch onto your benefit plan, I suppose. Brent said there might be travel involved, but I'd fly first class, and all food and lodging would be reimbursed. Not too bad," she said.

"If it's something you want to do, I'll support you," he said. "I just hope you don't spend too much time away from home."

***

When Brent and Jackie joined Pepper and Bill on their patio later, Pepper gave Brent the signed contract. She was officially a consultant to the United States Counterterrorism Agency. Brent said he'd get her some identification materials, a laptop, passwords and other standard-issue items after he returned to Boston.

He was very clear that she'd have to go through formal training in both the field and classroom, which would require some time in Boston. She said she understood, and looked forward to it.

They sipped their beers and listened to the doves calling across the resort grounds. There must have been a hundred doves in and around the resort, adding to the peaceful ambiance. They were small with brown mottling, constantly combing the grass for flower petals.

Brent told Pepper that he had requested the information analysts at his home office in Boston to research whether Sweden was, in fact, moving Saab missiles to Russia. They wouldn't have to rely on satellite reconnaissance alone, as the U.S. had plenty of intelligence gathering on the ground in Sweden. In fact, Brent learned there was even a Counterterrorism Agent in Stockholm named Louis Brown. If need be, Brent could call Mr. Brown and have him do some legwork. He hoped to hear back in the next few days from the analysts.

For dinner that night, the foursome decided to do the opposite of their fancy French dining experiences. They walked into the village of Grand Case, going to a highly recommended open-air barbecue market where the locals grilled pork ribs, chicken and lobster over huge half barrels, serving them with all the sides of rice, beans and coleslaw.

There were four restaurants in the open air market, distinguished by their different colored wooden booths. Each restaurant had a salesman standing on the common sidewalk to talk up the attributes of his restaurant – personal advertising. The blue-booth restaurant did brisk business early in the evening as it was closest to the road, and its salesman was quite good with the tourists. Bill had it on good authority from the resort staff, however, that the red-booth restaurant named Au Coin Des Amis was preferred by the locals as having the best dry rub and most meat on the rib.

They were shown to an expansive booth that could comfortably sit six people. Bill and

Brent had such wide shoulders that they each took up the space of two French men. Under the fluorescent lights, the group drank beer and ate ribs with rice and beans. It was a family-run business, each restaurant's employees and cooks chatting with one another and sharing supplies. The little kids were running among the booths and the teenagers waited tables. Everyone had a job.

Brent and Jackie were obviously head over heels in love as they couldn't keep their hands or eyes off each other. They shared bites of food as only lovers do, and kissed a thousand times during their meal. Their affection was infectious, resulting in Pepper and Bill sharing a modest smooch here and there. There was nothing like being in the presence of young love to rekindle a marriage.

***

CHAPTER 14

Volkov Watches

Werfen, Austria

Svea Lovgren had vast resources, both legitimate and black market, making her a formidable force in her new position with Volkov, her Russian ally. When she purposefully used her striking blue eyes, long brown hair and Swedish curves, she was capable of manipulating almost any male. After all, she had successfully brought Volkov to his knees with one evening's effort.

Now that she had conquered him, she felt invincible. The power of her own momentum was pushing her forward in her daily affairs, managing her simple cabinet duties while masterminding her attack on the United States. She didn't have anything against America per se, although it represented Henrik Jensen, and he had taught her how American men operate.

Like most Europeans, Svea considered America and its leaders to be arrogant muscle-flexors, despite America's lack of contribution to art, culture or architecture. She intended to leave a legacy on this Earth, and she wasn't discriminating enough to care whether her legacy was creative or destructive. The only thing that mattered at the moment was acquiring more resources, obtaining more power, and using those resources and power to implement her revengeful plan.

It was a simple recipe, really, one that had worked for men for centuries. Wars had been fought and rock concert tours staged through the basic male desire for power, sex and notoriety. She believed the 21st Century belonged to females, and their ultimate dominance of mankind, believing that she was at the top of the heap.

Her current challenge was that it was almost impossible to plan a clandestine meeting between President Volkov and herself. Whenever Volkov left Russia, the international press corps swarmed him. Svea had less attention on her, able to move freely throughout Europe, but if she were seen with Volkov outside a formal diplomatic assembly, it would be a front page story in Sweden, and most likely around the world. She had to avoid that type of exposure.

She had no reason to travel to Russia, and a trip of that magnitude would be planned months in advance, requiring the approval of Prime Minister Carlsson. Volkov wasn't prone to visiting Sweden for any reason, in large part because it would entail visiting with Prime Minister Carlsson. They didn't care for each other and had nothing to discuss.

Svea and Volkov had already been to London together, and while Svea regularly visited London, Volkov didn't want to raise speculation that he was hinting at a meeting with the English Prime Minister, whom he couldn't stand. It was widely known that Volkov considered the English PM to be an elitist gas bag. All of these obstacles for a triste presented a problem for Svea. She urgently needed more of Volkov's resources, but she couldn't discuss her plans over the phone with him. She had to see him person, alone, where she could convince him to increase his contribution to their venture.

They finally decided on a vacation destination in Austria, a small village named Werfen that was nestled in the Alps, about an hour south of Salzburg. The tourism season was coming to an end since it was October, so they'd have the town virtually to themselves before the ski season ushered in another onslaught people.

Svea first arranged a meeting with her Austrian counterpart in Vienna to make her Austrian visit look legit. After that meeting concluded, she traveled by train to Salzburg, then by private car along the Salzach River to Werfen. The river flowed bright green, being rich in mountain minerals. The countryside was thick with evergreen trees, and the Alps rose into the blue sky, in breathtaking, jagged peaks.

The plan was for Volkov to fly into Werfen on his Mi-8 helicopter, known in Russia as The Hip. It was his version of the U.S. Marine One. He was granted a visa by Austria without raising an eyebrow, as the stated purpose of his trip was to hike in the Alps, which he had never before visited. There was a strong tradition of Alpine hiking among the Austrians, traversing the mountainside from hut-to-hut for days. They could identify with Volkov's desire to hike.

Svea's black Mercedes rolled into Werfen first, and she checked into the exclusive Hotel Obauer, a boutique hotel owned by the brothers Karl and Rudolf, who were renowned chefs in Austria, consistently winning the Chef of the Year Award over a decade. They weren't strangers to celebrities or politicians dining at their restaurant or staying at their hotel.

Svea would wait for Volkov's arrival later that evening, and planned to occupy herself by touring around the resort town. The Obauer brothers were extremely generous to Svea, putting her in one of the two suites on the top floor of their small hotel. They provided her complimentary French champagne, Petitjean-Pienne, which came highly recommended by the restaurant sommelier. The wait staff arranged an assortment of cheeses, foie gras and rye bread slices on her buffet, accented by a vase of orchids.

Svea immediately noticed the undercover agents in the Russian Federal Security Service, a successor agency to the dissolved KGB, stationed outside a suite down the hall. She assumed Volkov would occupy that one. They kept a covert watch on her, and all who passed through the front doors prior to Volkov's arrival.

Neither she nor Ulrik were ruffled by the Russian agents. They would have been surprised if they hadn't seen them doing reconnaissance work ahead of Volkov. Russia had sent their most congenial agents, those who were civilized and could blend in modestly without upsetting the hotel staff, who always stood at attention when they were present. Karl Obauer welcomed the agent, being an effusive hotelier, paying attention to every detail for food and accommodation for his foreign guests.

Svea informed Ulrik she wanted some fresh air. They left on foot to enjoy a walk in the late afternoon sun. Both she and Ulrik could see their Soviet tail through the streets.

Svea was no stranger to the Austrian architecture. It was similar to Stockholm's in many respects. The difference was that Austria had suffered destruction in both World Wars, but the rebuilding was admirable and true to traditional design. The Obauer Hotel was located in the center of the small town, in a 12th Century building that Karl and Rudolph had renovated in 1987. Further up the hill, the residential homes were built into the side of the mountain base, having a distinct Swiss Chalet' flavor.

During her stroll through the quaint town, an attractive young couple caught Svea's eye. The young woman was average height, shorter than most Swedish women, and had gorgeous blonde tendrils and electric blue eyes. She was tanned and had a relaxed island look about her, with a dangerous undertone to her countenance. She was exquisite, perhaps even more so than Svea herself. And she was clearly out of place in Werfen.

The man accompanying her was handsome, too. He had longish, slicked black hair that curled around his ears. He was taller than the woman, with broad shoulders, narrow hips and muscular legs under tight fitting black jeans. His tight, black V-neck sweater revealed his strong build, and his day's growth of beard looked stylish. He, too, was tan for this time of year, indicating he was most likely not from Austria. He opened doors for his female companion, escorting her through the shops. They seemed to be on the same shopping circuit as Svea, which piqued her curiosity.

At one point, they almost bumped into one another in a small hat shop named Zapf. Svea made eye contact with the young woman first, and a spark arced between them. Then Svea purposefully looked at the young woman's companion, who smiled mischievously. There was silence among the three as they beheld one another. A song named Probably by Flunk was playing over the speakers of the shop. Svea felt like she was at a club, drinking and dancing with these two strangers. It was rhythmic yet detached. She admired their composure during this strangely intimate exchange, quickly realizing the attraction was mutual.

She blinked, shaking head slightly to break the spell. Her eyes darted momentarily for Ulrik and he was at her side, leading her out. When she hit the sidewalk, she breathed deeply and felt a chill run down her spine. She was filled with insatiable sexual need. Must be her anticipation of Volkov's arrival, she thought.

Speaking of Volkov, she heard the unmistakable rumble of several rotary blades on the largest helicopters in the Russian fleet. She turned to see three objects materializing in the sky over the jagged peaks. It had to be him. She watched as the three black helicopters made their way to the local airport. Her heartbeat picked up as she dashed back to the hotel.

She raced up the stairs to her room, and freshened up, trading her pants and sweater for a black dress. She was wearing a red, lacy thong and matching bra underneath. She looked at herself in the full length mirror, admiring her full breasts and long lines. Decided the younger blonde in the shop had nothing on Svea.

She tossed her hair back, and applied some lipstick. There was a forceful knock on her door. Ulrik opened it to one of Volkov's security men. The Russian asked to speak to Svea. She walked over, and he said that President Volkov sought the pleasure of her company. He offered her his arm and she took it. Ulrik squinted his eyes at the Russian, following close behind.

The Russian guided Svea to Volkov's suite, obviously built for exclusive guests like its present occupant. He knocked and Volkov opened the door. He stood back and admired Svea, then hugged her and kissed her in the traditional Russian fashion, a peck on each cheek. She wondered why the formality, but as he turned to bring her into the living area, she realized there were others there. The blonde Svea had seen in the village was on the sofa, and her handsome boyfriend was standing next to a club chair. The blonde had changed into a dark blue wrap-dress that accentuated her eyes and breasts. And legs. Very tanned legs. She didn't stand for the introduction, but smiled invitingly.

"Svea, I'd like you to meet some friends of mine. This is Dana de Wit," he said, motioning to the blonde, "and this is Clive Von Steinland. They're from St. Martin."

Svea extended her hand to Clive, who closed the gap between them, taking her hand in both of his. His hands felt strong, yet pampered. He had a sexually confident air about him.

Dana didn't stand, but reached up for Svea to take her hand. Svea did, and was surprised at the nature of her grip. The young woman caressed Svea's hand with her thumb as she shook it, then patted the seat next to her.

"Please, sit next to me, Svea," said Dana in a seductive voice.

"I think I will," said Svea.

Volkov clapped his hands in delight and pulled a bottle of champagne from a bucket of ice. He poured while Clive delivered the flutes.

Volkov toasted, "to new lovers."

Svea felt a shiver of excitement as they all drank.

Volkov and Clive took the club chairs facing the sofa.

There was mellow music playing in the background, and Svea noticed Volkov's men retreating to other rooms.

"Svea, you look especially lovely tonight," said Volkov.

"Thank you, Vadik." She sipped her champagne. It was the first time she had used his first name in front of others.

There was a silence while they surveyed one another, Svea again struck by how attractive and magnetic Dana was. She could feel the heat of her tanned body radiating across the sofa. Svea slowly turned her head to look at Dana. Yes, she was the same woman from the shop in the village. Svea wasn't disappointed. Dana was alluring, and held her gaze. She smiled slightly as she lay her hand on the cushion between them.

"How was your meeting with the Foreign Minister in Vienna?" asked Volkov of Svea.

Svea had to force her eyes away from Dana to look at Volkov. "It was nice... productive."

"I've missed you," said Volkov.

"And I you," lied Svea.

"You two women are so beautiful, sitting together on the sofa," said Volkov. "I'm sure Clive and I could sit here all evening watching you. Would you like to entertain us some?"

The double entendre was received by the two women. Svea looked from Volkov to the handsome Clive, whose lips were curled in a small grin. When she looked at Dana again, she was smiling and her eyes were alit with sexual energy. Dana gracefully set her empty champagne glass on the end-table next to her, and turned her attention to Svea.

She leaned in and caressed Svea's leg, reaching under the slit in her dress to run her fingers along Svea's inner thigh. Dana took her time, knowing Volkov was watching with intense pleasure. Svea's heart raced, blood rushing to where Dana's fingers hovered.

Dana took Svea's champagne glass from her, and drank half of it, leaving her fingers on Svea's inner thigh as she did. Dana held the glass to Svea's lips so she could drink the other half. Then, Dana set the flute on the end-table next to her empty one.

When Dana turned back, Svea reached for the nape of Dana's neck and ran her fingers through her hair. Dana leaned her head back and moaned with pleasure. Svea bent down and dropped kisses on Dana's throat, resulting in Volkov groaning with pleasure.

***

Later, as Svea dozed next to Volkov in his bed, he watched the news and smoked a cigar. Dana and Clive had taken the other bedroom across the living room.

"How do you know that couple?" asked Dana.

"Through a friend. I was on his yacht in the Caribbean last year, and they attended a party he hosted. Attractive, aren't they?"

"Quite. Are they a couple?" asked Svea.

"I assume so, but they have a very open relationship. Clive is very generous with Dana," he said.

"Is she likewise generous with him?" asked Svea.

"I've never asked. Russian men aren't interested in other men," said Vadik.

"Well, I don't have the energy for another man when I'm around you," she said.

He snorted in disbelief.

"Do you mind if I talk business?" she asked.

"I assumed you would. I'd like a status report on our little project," he said.

"We've made progress. I received word that the sarin cleared Thai Customs and one box of nebulizers was loaded onto a ship bound for Los Angeles. The other box of nebulizers, and a box of ampules, were flown by cargo plane from Bangkok to Philadelphia International Airport. They're currently resting in a Thai Cargo Shipping airport warehouse, awaiting Customs inspection and clearance," she said.

"Ah, the first significant hurdle. We'll see how convincing the packaging is, won't we?" he asked.

"Yes. I'm sure your team did a competent job. I have a problem though," she said.

"Which is?" he asked.

"I have a bunch of weakling students working for me," she admitted.

He shot her a look. "You represented to me that you had a vast and powerful network of employees."

"I do, Vadik. But for an operation this sensitive, you need skilled people who won't ask questions. The young people these days... they ask too many questions," she said.

"I see," he said, blowing smoke rings.

"And, they are spineless," she said.

"At least in Sweden" he observed.

"I need some men with military training who follow orders and who know how to operate drones," she declared.

"I have plenty of men," he said. "You know that. But this wasn't my idea, Svea. It was yours. I suppose you will now ask me to send my men to America to do your dirty work for you?"

"It's still my project, but I need your help," she insisted. "My young Swedish team has rented warehouses in Philadelphia, Minneapolis and Los Angeles, but none of them know how to work the drones. They think they're setting up a supply chain for the pharmaceutical industry. They haven't been trained with drones."

Volkov rolled his eyes in disgust.

"I was intending on training a small group in Sweden, then sending them over, but I'm having difficulty with too many inquisitive young people. They want to know what they'll be doing, and why they'll be doing it. They're young and idealistic, wanting to know how it fits into our democratic socialist agenda in Sweden. And, frankly, I don't have any good answers for them. Can you help me?" She traced her finger around his man boob.

"It's going to cost you," he growled.

"I'd think less of you if it didn't," she said.

"I'll see what I can do with a small number of men and tactical drones," he said.

"I knew you'd come to the rescue," she said.

"I'm going to punish you for putting me in this position," he announced.

"What kind of punishment?" she asked.

"Roll over and get on your hands and knees," he commanded.

Dana and Clive heard screams all the way across the living room. They looked at each other in surprise. It was obviously Svea, and they could tell the screams were not in pleasure.

Ulrik was in the kitchen, and immediately ran to Volkov's bedroom door. A Russian security guard blocked his entrance. Ulrik attempted to wave him away, but the Russian stood his ground. When they heard another yelp from Svea, Ulrik pulled his Glock out of his holster. He didn't feel the presence of the second Russian behind him, who knocked him cold with the butt of his own pistol.

***

CHAPTER 15

Nerve Gas Movement

St. Martin, French West Indies

One week stretched into two at Grand Case Resort for Brent, Jackie, Pepper and Bill. Brent and Jackie were falling in love, and Pepper and Bill were taking a much needed break from their lives in Minnesota. The magnetism of the turquoise water, and relaxed island life were too inviting to leave.

The foursome had settled into a daily routine on the island where Brent and Pepper met on her patio each morning to orient Pepper to Agency policy and review information gathered by Brent's research analysts in Boston, piecing together what it meant. Brent helped Pepper complete the security applications for the Agency so she could join the team. Fortunately, her secretary back at Futuraceutical was able to pull her attorney bar license number and other documents for her. The virtual on-boarding process took five mornings to complete.

They worked until Noon, went their separate ways for lunch, and met up in the early afternoon to do water sports as a group. They sea kayaked, paddle boarded, skied and swam. The resort lay claim to the nicest swimming bay on the island, roping off a small inlet. Pepper and Bill swam several laps per day together with diving masks on so they could watch the schools of fish.

Dinner found the foursome together again, although Pepper and Bill had insisted that Brent and Jackie go on a date night alone. They chose a romantic Italian restaurant on the beach called Il Nettuno.

Jackie had never been away from her CrossFit business, StarrFitness this long, but did some emailing in the mornings when Brent and Pepper worked. Jackie told Pepper privately that the trainers at StarrFitness were getting along just fine without her, and she felt like she was on a pre-honeymoon with Brent. She knew she loved him, but hadn't said the words yet. Neither had he. Jackie said she didn't know how they'd make their careers work with their relationship, but she was interested in trying.

Pepper told her that when a couple was in love, they found a way to make it work, and she was confident Brent and Jackie would.

Pepper was really starting to miss her dog, Daisy, as it had been five weeks since she had last seen the little Toller. There were so many dogs on the island that she was reminded of Daisy everywhere she turned. A local French artist had a boxer named Ben. He was so affectionate that Pepper got a temporary dog fix by scratching Ben's back and tousling his ears. She murmured the same words up close to him as she did Daisy, and he seemed to soak it up, thrashing his strong tail back and forth against a table in his owner's art gallery.

Ben's owner, Artist Sylvie Bellamy, painted beautiful portraits of lions and elephants. She had a thriving business in her upstairs gallery located in Grand Case village. Pepper was thinking she needed a portrait of elephants to hang on her lake cabin wall back in Minnesota. Sylvie had captured the intelligent gaze of her elephant subjects, one that Pepper had seen herself when looking into the eyes of an elephant at the San Francisco Zoo years ago. The painting just sang to Pepper, which was as good a reason as any to buy art. If it didn't *sing* to her, she didn't buy it.

Pepper listened as Sylvie called Ben to her side in French, "viens ici, Ben."

Once Ben was sitting beside her, Sylvia leaned down and scratched his ears, whispering in a universal dog loving voice, "c'est bien mon chien...bon toutou." Ben thrashed his tail against a chair and smiled up at her.

Pepper decided she'd need to teach Daisy some French dog commands because, well, in this day and age, it was important for a Duck Toller to be bilingual. You never knew when it might come in handy, she thought.

***

Late one afternoon, as the sun was dropping across the bay, Bill found a hammock with his iPad in hand. Pepper eased onto it, snuggling up to him, resting her head on his chest. She was thinking she'd doze while he read. He clicked open the latest medical journals that had been published online, and one of the articles caught Pepper's eye.

"Swedish Interns Visit U.S. Hospitals." It was a recently written article. Since she and Brent had so intensely reviewed Svea Lovgren's biography, Pepper was momentarily of a Swedish mindset. She nuzzled Bill to click it open so they both could read it.

The article explored the current novelty among hospitals in Los Angeles, Minneapolis and Philadelphia of hosting University of Stockholm interns for three months in their hospital pharmacies. Each intern was interviewed, giving similar answers about focusing his studies on supply chain management of pharmacy inventories in growing healthcare systems. The interns wanted to review the American system for efficiencies to see if they could import the American processes to Sweden.

It looked like the only hospital the reporter had physically visited was Philadelphia General Hospital in Philadelphia, which made sense since the reporter was located nearby, in New York City. The reporter must have had a photographer along because there was a photo of a young, brown-haired man with spectacles standing with his arm around a much shorter middle-aged woman, who was the pharmacy manager. The photo caption read: "Filipe Malstrom, Swedish Intern with Mary Adams, PGH Pharmacy Manager."

"Hmm. That's interesting," said Pepper.

"What about that is interesting?" asked Bill.

"Since when did Sweden send students over to America to intern in the healthcare industry?" she asked.

"I don't know. Guess I never thought about it much," he said.

"See? I've always thought of Sweden as having its contained little, government-run healthcare system that didn't interact much with American healthcare systems. Much less for training. Maybe their universities collaborate with American universities in research, but I've never heard you mention anything about Swedes training in our hospitals," she said.

"I guess that's true. Like I said, I've never thought about it much. One of these interns is at Southview Hospital in Minneapolis, though. That's where I do most of my surgeries," said Bill.

"I know. If we ever return to Minnesota, you'll have to be on the lookout," she said.

"For what? Swedish spies?" he asked.

"No. I'm just joking," she said.

"Or paranoid. The Swedes have never done anything to us. Or to the world for that matter," said Bill.

"Right. Norway, Sweden and Finland all kind of live an isolated existence up north. In peace and solitude," she said.

"Yes. A beautiful people who are peaceful," said Bill.

"It's the 'wudka' and saunas," said Pepper.

"And good breeding," finished Bill.

***

The next morning when Brent and Pepper met on her patio to work, Brent said, "Our intel forces on the ground in Sweden confirmed that Russia is, in fact, buying $40 million in Saab missiles from Sweden. No one is acknowledging that they're the missiles that were intended for the Saudis. They're making it look like it's an independent deal. You called that one, Pepper."

"Looks like Svea Lovgren scored a quick point in the first month of her new position. That night with Volkov in his hotel room paid off for her," said Pepper.

"You're telling me. It would have cost him a lot less to hire a Russian hooker," he said.

"Brent, he gets the missiles in return," she said.

"But they're Saab, Pepper, Saab. Have you ever driven a Saab?"

"Lord no," she said.

"I have, and they suck. Not even close to a BMW for performance," he said.

"I'll make a note," joked Pepper.

"In other news, I thought you might find this interesting. The analysts in the bioterrorism unit reported that our undercover Russian sources inside Russia reported that there was a Russian shipment of nerve gas aboard a Chinese ship, bound for the Bangkok Port in Thailand. We have tennis shoes on the ground in Thailand. His name is Weng Chee. He's going to investigate at the docks and call me," said Brent.

"From Russia to Thailand. That'd be a circuitous route for Russia to help out its Middle Eastern friends poison each other," observed Pepper.

"You're right," he said. "They wouldn't need a middleman to ship nerve gas to Syria. They already have. They just box it up, call it humanitarian supplies, and fly it in on a C-130 cargo plane."

"Which means that if it's true that Russian-manufactured nerve gas went through a Thai shipping port, then the nerve gas is destined for some other country that has more stringent customs inspections than any in the Middle East," said Pepper.

"Good point. Of course, the initial reports are unconfirmed at this time," said Brent.

"How would you confirm something like that?" she asked.

"A couple of ways. Satellite imagery that was good enough to track it from the source to the destination. Human sources along the way who reported the same details without knowing or talking to one another. Customs inspections by friendly government officials. Covert paramilitary inspections. Agents like Weng Chee who will talk to the locals. You can imagine this will get some attention by the top brass, so resources will be dedicated to confirming whether it's true or just rumor," he explained.

"How reliable have the Russian undercover sources inside Russia been in the past?" asked Pepper.

"Variable," he said.

"What does variable mean?" she asked.

"Sometimes the info is 100 percent. Sometimes it's false," he said.

"When do you expect to hear back from Weng Chee, the Thai agent?" she asked.

"For something as hot as this? Couple of days," he said.

"How will he gather the info in Thailand?" she asked.

"Most likely, it will involve personally visiting port authorities, which can be frustrating and painstaking," he said.

"Why?" she asked.

"They lie. They're away from the office so you have to keep stopping back. Their paperwork is a mess. They've been paid off. Any of the above," he said.

"I see," she mused.

"Russia is up to so many clandestine and illegal activities at any given time, that it takes an entire network of undercover agents to gather intel around the world, then analyze the dangerous tidbits. And the subject matter is so broad, it's everything from gold market manipulation to arms dealing. There just isn't an angle that Volkov doesn't play," he said.

"I can see the breadth of the information would lead to dead ends and false connections," said Pepper.

"Precisely," said Brent.

"So, as I work with you to stay ahead of what he and the Swede might be doing, I have to keep in mind that not everything is a solid lead or has a connection in a broader scheme," said Pepper.

"Right. In fact, Volkov and Minister Lovgren might have concluded their missile deal and never see each other again. Sometimes a fact, a very significant fact, lives in isolation and doesn't go anywhere for years. You tuck it away in the back of your mind. Then, when you're presented with new information, or unfolding world events, you access the facts you've stored away, and compare their relevance to the new information you've learned to see if there are any matches," he said.

"I'm definitely familiar with that technique," she said.

***

That night, Jackie and Pepper decided the group should dine at Ocean 82 by the Sea, on Boulevard de Grand Case, another French restaurant nestled above the surf on the sugar beach. They were steered to a table on the veranda overlooking the sunset, which was glorious as it backlit a new fleet of sailboats moored in the bay.

It was a popular harbor for yachts that were touring the islands around St. Bart's, Anguilla and St. Martin, all of which were within a day's reach. As a result, the resort goers were treated to a new variety of yachts each day to enhance their view of the bay. It was an added bonus that this bay had a row of restaurants along the pier, so the moored boaters could come in every evening on their dinghies to dine. They'd pay the local kids at the end of the concrete pier to watch their dinghies. If they didn't pay, their dinghy most likely wouldn't be there when they came out of the restaurant in the dark.

Brent and Jackie sat on one side of the table so they could hold hands and kiss, with Pepper and Bill on the other side.

Brent leaned in close to Jackie's ear, whispering something as he tickled her legs under the table. She giggled and brushed lips with a kiss. Pepper and Bill averted their eyes, looking out at the bay.

The waitress appeared, and they ordered cocktails.

As Pepper and Bill were admiring the sunset and Jackie and Brent were admiring each other, Pepper said, "Bill, look at that. Is that what I think it is?"

She pointed and they all followed her gaze. Sure enough, there was a white drone flying above the masts of the sailboats, dipping down and around the boats, then flying back up again. It was a sizeable quadcopter, which meant it had four propellers on top, with long white legs, making it easy to see from the restaurant, which was several hundred yards away. Since it was also quite noisy, they could easily hear its hum from the shore.

"Do you suppose the same thing is happening as we experienced on the Tollefson's yacht," asked Pepper.

"I'm sure it is," said Bill. "I can't believe the audacity of the pirates, coming into a harbor and taking stock of every boat to see which one they want to rip off. Drones are everywhere now. I was looking at them on YouTube, and they even have drones that can fall into the ocean, get wet, and fly right back out again. They're called mariner drones. It doesn't matter if salt water gets the propeller wet, it still works fine. That one looks exactly like what I saw on YouTube."

"Incredible. Anyone could be working this drone. It could be land-based. After dark, they could send the thieves out to the boats," said Pepper.

"How do you know about this stuff?" asked Jackie.

"When we were with the Tollefsons on our voyage over here, we learned how pirates use drones. A drone came close to the Tollefson's boat to scope out who and what was on board. That one was larger than this one," explained Pepper.

"Joe, the security man for the Tollefsons, told us the pirates would sometimes tail a yacht for several miles until they saw an opportunity to board it and steal electronics and valuables," said Bill.

"What did the Tollefsons do?" asked Jackie.

"They had a drill for dealing with these intrusions. And, of course they have money so they don't miss a trick," said Pepper, describing the Tollefson's fancy drone.

"It was just matter of time before the bad guys figured out how to use drones to do their dirty work," said Brent. "History has demonstrated that military technology usually translates into civilian technology. Drones are here to stay. We better get used to them," said Brent.

"Law enforcement will have to do what Joe did," said Bill.

"Can't you just shoot them down?" asked Jackie.

"Sure, but it depends on what the drone's mission is. Technically speaking, it isn't violating any laws. It's doing recon to see which boat has the most stuff on it to steal. It's no different than the pick-pockets on the street outside scoping us out as we walk by. It isn't a crime to look," said Brent.

"I think you're right," said Bill. "Local police forces will have to become more robust in having their own drone forces. From there, it's a small step to arming the drones so they can shoot each other," said Bill.

"Nice thought," added Pepper.

"I'm glad we have guys like you protecting us," said Jackie to Brent. She squeezed his bicep and kissed him.

Pepper looked at Bill and made a mock smooching gesture with her lips, then squeezed his sizeable tri-cep.

After Brent came up for air from their kiss, he squinted against the sun, glancing around the restaurant. His eyes momentarily met a woman's electric blue eyes, a few tables away.

She was spectacularly sexy and gave Brent a seductive smile, as if she were tempting him to cheat on Jackie. He had been the recipient of inviting looks like that before, but not since he had fallen in love with Jackie. He was momentarily knocked off balance. Not because a sexy woman was smiling at him from across a restaurant, but because it just occurred to him that he loved Jackie. The awakening shocked him. He felt a surge of anxiety; part of him scared as hell that he had fallen, the other part scared as hell that she might not feel the same way.

He started to freeze up, his heart pounding, palms sweating and mind was racing. He had seen this happen to guys in combat situations, where they lost touch with what was happening around them and couldn't move. He took a deep breath, steadying himself.

Jackie casually wrapped her hand around his forearm while talking to Pepper, sliding her hand down his arm to rest her hand in his. Her gesture was so natural, it was as if they'd been together for years.

Brent looked down at her, seemingly oblivious to Bill and Pepper's presence, and blurted, "Jackie Starr, I love you."

Tears sprang to Jackie's eyes. "Brent! I love you, too."

She put her hand on his swarthy neck, pulling him in for a passionate kiss.

Pepper and Bill were taken aback at Brent's declaration, especially that he made it in public. They didn't know what to do, so they kissed too. The waitress appeared at the table, thought better of it, and moved along.

Across the restaurant, the striking blonde woman with the electric blue eyes signaled to her dining companion, a handsome young man with slicked black hair, that it was time to leave. He stood, sliding her chair out for her. She elegantly rose, and they walked through the restaurant toward the exit.

She knew all the men were looking at her, her long blonde tendrils, her tanned legs, and her white dress with a v-cut in the back that revealed she wasn't wearing a bra. She was more than just another blonde beauty, she had an air that signaled danger.

As she walked past the maître d', he said, "Mademoiselle Dana, bonsoir."

***

CHAPTER 16

Philly Warehouse

Philadelphia, Pennsylvania, United States of America.

Philadelphia International Airport has one of the country's largest air cargo traffic terminals. It's known as Cargo City, and was created in 1966 when Philadelphia spent $50 million to develop 150 acres on the airport's northwest section.

Cargo City is surrounded by an eight-foot high fence capped with barbed wire. It has business operating hours that start in the evening and run through the night until dawn when the passenger side of the airport comes to life. In addition to several freight carriers, the U.S. mail service ships 200,000 pounds of mail every day in and out of Cargo City, and over 300 FedEx employees in Cargo City load and unload 8 to 10 aircraft per day with thousands of packages.

Over 400,000 tons of cargo move through Cargo City per year with 30 airlines making over 500 departures on a daily basis. Most of the cargo jets land and depart at night so they don't interfere with passenger jet traffic. Hence, there's an active nighttime business at Cargo City that thirty million airline passengers never see.

Cargo planes from all over the world fly into PIA and are cleared through U.S. Customs in the large warehouses. The volume is so high that the cargo shipping companies are constantly working with Customs to improve container expediting and paperwork processing so they can move their product out of the airport warehouses and onto cargo planes or semi-trucks for distribution across America. It's all about clearing customs fast, a business nightmare for any company to have its goods delayed in Customs.

Most of the large shipping companies have their own warehouses at the airport, making it easy for Customs officials to inspect shipments. The cargo companies also employ their own Customs brokers who interact with the government Customs agents to assure all the paperwork is in order, and the duties are assessed correctly. The managers of the warehouses have computer systems to monitor the status of each shipment, so they can provide tracking data to their company service department representatives who, in turn, notify the customers of package tracking status.

Being the sixth largest metropolitan area in America, over a third of the American population lived within a one-day drive of Philadelphia. Svea concluded it was a populous hub from which to launch a sarin gas attack.

***

Thai Cargo Shipping had its own warehouse in Cargo City, smaller than some, but still sizeable at 20,000 square feet. The entire warehouse was air conditioned to keep the inventory between 60 and 65 degrees Fahrenheit. The warehouse had eight managers who worked in shifts throughout the week. They oversaw a work force of 25 employees who moved cargo and processed the paperwork. They also had two Customs brokers on staff who managed the imported cargo under provisional consignment from the government, meeting with the U.S. government Customs officials.

Customs Officials came through the warehouses on a daily basis, performing random inspections of cargo, so Thai Cargo Shipping had to keep the uninspected cargo separate from other cargo. Trevon Jennings, a U.S. Customs Agent, walked through the door at Thai Cargo for his nightly routine of random inspections.

"Hi Trevon, how ya doin'?" asked Tony, one of the company Customs brokers.

"Life sucks, man. Did you watch the Eagles game last night? Lost to Tampa Bay. Never gonna win the Division if we can't beat Tampa Bay," said Trevon.

"It's early in the season. We still got 10 more games," said Tony.

"Yeah but five of those are away," said Trevon.

"I like our odds. Sam Bradford threw for almost as many yards as Aaron Rogers last season," said Tony.

"That shoulder injury could come back to haunt him again. I think he's got the injury curse, man," said Trevon.

"Waddya wanna inspect tonight?" asked Tony.

"How 'bout those two pallets over there? The Air Cargo Manifest says they're pharmaceuticals shipped from Bangkok," said Trevon, pointing to a pallet in the middle.

"Yeah. Both pallets. Let me get my clipboard," said Tony.

Tony returned with his clipboard, meeting Trevon at the first pallet of brown boxes, wrapped in plastic. The pallet was 40 x 48 inches, the standard shipping size. Tony watched as Trevon cut the plastic wrap with his box cutter, then opened one of the four cubic-foot brown boxes. Trevon flipped the lid, and Tony helped him pull out a smaller brown box, about two cubic-feet in size. Trevon cut that flap open, removing a white box about a cubic-foot in size.

The contents looked like the pharmaceuticals his manifest indicated were in the shipment. The manufacturer name of Zortis was visible in large print on the box. He slit the lid and removed one of the four boxes. He cut open that box and pulled out the contents. There were small ampules of a clear medicine that was labelled in English.

He looked at his paperwork, comparing the description to the label on the ampule. "FENTANYL citrate, injection USP" was printed in bold red on the ampule, with the strength printed in smaller black lettering. It matched. He placed his customs sticker on the white inner box and initialed it. He set that box inside the larger white box, then put that box in the brown box. He initialed the brown box and put his sticker on it. He left that box on top of the largest box, then initialed the largest box and placed a U.S. Customs Inspection label on it. He also initialed a sticker and slapped it on the second palletized cargo with plastic wrap all the way around it, the one he hadn't inspected, indicating it had cleared Customs as well. He checked off some items on a form on his clipboard and moved along the concrete floor to his next inspection.

Tony moved with Trevon to the next inspection area while another warehouse employee, Steve, came over to process the pallet Trevon had just inspected and cleared.

Steve re-taped and repacked the boxes into the larger boxes. When Steve had finished resealing the boxes, he used the roller of plastic wrap to rewrap the entire pallet.

Steve used his handheld device to scan the bar code on the first box on the pallet. He went over to the computer and looked for the shipping destination for that pallet. It indicated it was to be shipped by air to an address in Minneapolis, Minnesota. The street address was clear, but the name of the business was fragmented, as if whoever entered it didn't understand English.

Steve constantly encountered this problem with his counterparts in Thailand. It had "South...House..." typed in the field for business name. Steve looked up the past shipping history for pharmaceuticals that Thai

Cargo Shipping had sent to Minneapolis and "Southview Hospital" came up in the directory. He shook his head, cursing his Thai counterparts.

He entered Southview Hospital in the field for the business name. Seeing the address was also incorrect, he fixed that and printed out a new shipping label. He then clicked to another screen to signal that the pallet was ready to be loaded onto the cargo plane on the tarmac. A short time later, a forklift driver picked up the cargo pallet and drove it out to the cargo plane, gingerly resting it in the belly. After several more pallets were loaded, the plane was cleared for takeoff to Minneapolis.

Steve returned to the other pallet that had come in from Bangkok, the one Trevon hadn't inspected, but had nevertheless cleared. He scanned that bar code with his handheld device and went back to the computer at his station.

He looked for the shipping destination, and learned it was destined for an address in Philly. Steve recognized the area, but he didn't know the neighborhood. It was an industrial warehouse section of the city. He double checked the address then typed in the appropriate field that the shipment had been cleared by Customs. He printed out a label that indicated the pallet was ready to leave the warehouse, and walked over and slapped it on the large box.

He assumed there were probably pharmaceuticals in that box too, but he didn't give it much thought. There was no entertainment value in guessing what the contents were in the thousands of boxes that moved through the warehouse.

If the U.S. Customs Agent Trevon Jennings had opened this box, however, he would have seen the small portable nebulizers that delivered aerosolized medications to asthma patients. The inner boxes had labels that said Shanghai Vibrant Company printed on them in both English and Chinese.

The handheld nebulizers, about the size and shape of a Camelback plastic water bottle, were now cleared to be delivered to a warehouse in Philly. A short while later, a forklift drove in and picked up the pallet. The driver loaded the pallet onto the hydraulic platform of a van for city deliveries. It was the only pallet on the van, which had Philly Delivery written on the side with a toll free phone number printed beneath it.

***

CHAPTER 17
Svea's Frustration

Stockholm, Sweden

Svea paced the length of her historic office in the Arvfurstens Palats, still finding it painful to sit after the whips Volkov had delivered to her bum in Werfen. The first strikes were exciting, but the sadist had continued past her pain threshold. He hadn't been satisfied until she bled. She had begged him to stop, but he had ignored her.

Why did it always come back to sex and domination for powerful men like Volkov, she wondered. She was a powerful woman, yet she didn't have a desire to dominate her partners sexually. It was the stiff price she had paid to get his men to fly the drones in America, so it had been worth it. After all, she had survived worse sexual experiences and recovered.

Her office was on the Lilla Värtan River where most of the Swedish government buildings were clustered. She had a beautiful view of the water. It was a pristine fall day by any measure, one of those rare throwbacks to summertime as a last tribute to warmth before the cold, dark Swedish winter descended. Svea overlooked the massive roundabout named known as Gustav Adolfs Torg, and surveyed her kingdom. She loved Stockholm, all of its sophistication and history. She had been born in Stockholm and planned to live out her life there.

While her office had modern décor, it was steeped in history and had been occupied by only men for the first 200 hundred years of its existence. It even smelled like an historic building, the old oak floors and plaster walls that the retrofitted ventilation system simply couldn't refresh.

The steam-generated radiators smelled musty and either worked too well or not at all. It was a delicate balance between keeping a window open and setting the thermostat. Svea anticipated that the staff would begin lighting the fireplace in her sitting area next month when the icy wind blew right through the walls. At least a warm fire would add some ambiance to her stark surroundings.

Unfortunately, the old building reminded her of her stepfather's offices in southern Manhattan. She had worked there one summer between her junior and senior years of university. Having worked at Henrik's shipping company in both Stockholm and Thailand for a few years by that age, she was familiar with the cash handling side of the business.

The protocols were the same from office-to-office, and a ton of money flowed through the company. She had rotated through the business office, and could extrapolate from the revenue she saw on the books that her stepfather was a very rich man. Of course, that didn't mean he shared any of it with Svea when she was that age.

She felt as if she were on a tight leash that summer, having to run to Henrik every time she wanted a bit of spending money to go out clubbing in Manhattan. Svea was addicted to the clubs, being at the stage in life where young men were always hanging around, seeing if they had a chance. Svea relished the attention. It fed her soul. She had been aware of her beauty since adolescence, but was just beginning to appreciate her sexual power in her early twenties. It had been a time in her life for experimentation of how the opposite sex reacted to her. And to her delight, they reacted.

She had been thrilled to learn that men of all ages were drawn to her beauty and charisma. She had become accustomed to the stares, practicing her flirtatious banter and nonverbal cues. She discovered there was a fine line between playfulness and expectation, and one should be especially careful when alcohol was involved. She had ventured over the line a few times and found herself in situations where the man had expected something Svea wasn't prepared to deliver. Fortunately, she had been in public places where she could rely on the protection of her friends. She knew that wouldn't always be the case.

At the age of 21, she realized that with a seductive look and a few encouraging words, she could have just about any man at her feet. Her sexual prowess and position at the company emboldened her that summer. She wanted to fly independently of her stepfather, but he had financial control over her, so she had decided to try her skills at electronically skimming a bit of cash at her job.

She didn't reflect on why she thought it was a good idea, other than she felt rebellious and considered herself to be cunning. There was a thrill involved in getting away with something at Henrik's expense. Svea had made a few test transfers to her local bank account in small dollar amounts, waiting to see if anyone noticed. When they hadn't, she methodically transferred over $10,000 into her Manhattan bank account over the course of a month. She no longer needed to beg Henrik for money, so that limited her interactions with him.

It all came to a crashing halt one day when Henrik confronted her in his office. His accountants had noticed the embezzlement from multiple accounts even though she had attempted to mask her activity by stealing small amounts from each account. She had denied it at first, but his proof of her computer system activity was rock solid. He had printouts of every single transfer she had made, and they were lying on his desk. He towered over her while she sat in the chair facing the evidence.

She was teary, but didn't break down, in part because Henrik didn't appear angry. He had been very matter-of-fact about it, not raising his voice even once. He might have said he was disappointed in her, but she found it difficult to concentrate on what he was saying due to her embarrassment.

Henrik had insisted that they walk together to her bank where they could check her balance and deposits together. It had been located only a few blocks away, so he had firmly grasped her elbow and walked side-by-side with her. After they had reviewed her statements, Henrik had surprised her by telling her she could keep the money.

Once they had exited the bank, however, Henrik told her she was going to have to earn the money, and he had something very specific in mind. He walked her to an apartment near his office, which was not his prime residence in Manhattan. She had never visited this one-bedroom apartment, and hadn't realized it existed. He offered her a gin and tonic, and she accepted. He turned on some music and invited her to sit on the sofa in the well-appointed living room. She asked him about the apartment, and he said with a laugh that he used it for his more intimate meetings while he was in town.

The alcohol went straight to her head, making her mind swirl with emotions after the events of the day. Henrik joined her on the sofa and began playing with the curls at the end of her long hair. He calmly and affectionately told her that she would have sex with him that summer if she didn't want her mother to know about the embezzlement. He said he could report her to the Manhattan police if he wanted to, but he didn't think that would be necessary. His blackmail was firmly delivered in a friendly tone. He tempered it by telling her that he was a gentle lover, and he could teach her the intricacies of sex if she relaxed and enjoy him.

She initially submitted to him out of fear, but their relationship developed into one of giving and taking, sometimes laughing, and other times engaging in rough sex while he dominated her. It was a twisted relationship that toyed with her emotions and conscience. He was an attractive man in his 50s so she wasn't repulsed, at least not initially.

He quickly unearthed and nurtured her desires for some light masochism, heightening her awareness of sexual pleasure. Despite the release she had learned to enjoy in his company, the summer had left her irrevocably damaged. She told him she would never work for him again, and would visit her mother only when he wasn't there. He made her feel dirty when she was around him. She knew she would hate him forever, and she silently vowed never to return to America or see another American man.

Svea snapped out of her sordid reverie, willing herself to separate her current office space from Henrik Jensen's office space in Manhattan. She would be intentional about not drawing comparisons in the future.

She paced across the expanse of her office, the floor creaking under her high heels. No one on her youthful team could tell her where the Fentanyl ampule shipment intended for the Minneapolis warehouse was currently located. She had received confirmation from Thai Cargo Shipping that the two palletized shipments of ampules and nebulizers, one bound for Minneapolis, the other bound for a Philly warehouse, had cleared Customs in America at the Philadelphia International Airport, but she had no idea where those shipments were at the present time.

It was a glaring departure of Thai Cargo's efficient electronic tracking system. With their bar codes, scanners and software, they should have been able to tell her exactly where her cargo was hour-to-hour. She was stunned by the incompetence. If her operation hadn't been covert, she would have complained to Henrik herself about his business, demanding that those responsible be fired.

Svea's cell phone rang. She didn't recognize the number, but answered anyway because she was hopeful it was someone at Thai Cargo Shipping to give her a status update.

"Yes," she said in her iciest Swedish.

"Svea?" asked a woman.

"Yes. Who is this?" asked Svea.

"Dana de Wit."

"Oh." There was a long pause. Svea's mind racing. She felt a surge of emotion from her stomach to her heart.

"How are you?" asked Dana.

"Frustrated. You?" asked Svea.

"Sorry to hear that. I'm very good. Clive and I miss you, and we're in town," said Dana.

"Town? What town?" asked Svea.

"Stockholm," said Dana.

"Where are you staying?" asked Svea.

"The Hotel Diplomat on Strandvägen on the waterfront," said Dana.

"When did you get in?" asked Svea.

"Last night. Can you come over?" asked Dana.

"To your room? Hmm. No, I have a better idea," said Svea. "It's such a sunny day for this time of year, I don't want to be cooped up in a hotel room. Is your room facing the marina?"

"Yes," said Dana.

"Walk over to the window and tell me if you can see a large white passenger ferry with 'Strömmas Cinderella' written on its side," said Svea.

Svea waited while Dana looked out the window.

"Yes, I see it," said Dana.

"Good. That's berth number 20 or 21, I think. A few berths to your left, you should see a sailboat at berth number 18. Do you see it?" asked Svea.

"I see a large sailboat with a blue main sail twisted around the mast, but I can't make out any name on it because I'm looking at its bow from this angle," said Dana.

"Okay, you are looking at my yacht. I'll contact my skipper and meet you there in 20 minutes. It would be a shame to waste such a warm, fall day when we know it will probably be one of the last. Let's enjoy ourselves on the water, shall we?" asked Svea.

"Clive and I always like being on the water and this will be a welcome change from the Caribbean," said Dana.

"Wear a sweater and windbreaker, Dana. The water is quite a bit colder here," warned Svea.

"I don't plan on jumping in, Svea. Do you?"

"Of course not. The water temp makes the air cooler. You make me laugh!" said Svea.

"See you in 20 minutes," said Dana.

The women ended their call.

Svea was suspicious. Had Volkov sent Dana and Clive to spy on her? Sonofabitch. She didn't have time for this. She had cabinet duties to fulfill and an overseas clandestine operation to run. She would be a good hostess for the day, but she resented Volkov's meddling. She worked independently and answered to herself, not to these tanned lovers. However, she realized she was in a bind, so she had to cooperate. The wounds on her bum were a fresh reminder of that. She decided she'd please them, then send them on their way.

Svea called her skipper, Peder, and arranged for him to meet her on the dock right away. He ran a charter service, which included working for private individuals like herself to handle their yachts. His business would be slow on a weekday this time of year, so Svea assumed he'd be available. In the meantime, Svea tasked her assistant with running to a local food Co-op for snacks and beverages. She didn't have time to run back to her apartment, but she had a stash of warm boating clothes and deck shoes in her spacious office closet.

Ulrik brought Svea's government-issued Volvo around, and loaded the groceries into the trunk. He, too, was dressed in boating clothes, always prepared for Svea's whimsical pursuits. He'd accompany them on the yacht for security purposes, and be another pair of hands to help Peder with the voyage. It was a short drive from her office to Strandvägen, where her yacht was currently being prepared by Peder at kajplats 18, which was Swedish for berth 18.

Ulrik took the opportunity in the car to express his concerns to Svea. He still had a decent-sized bump on the back of his head where the Russian had clocked him. Svea was lying sideways on the backseat because her bum was too sore to sit on the hard leather seat.

"Ms. Lovgren, might I have a quick word with you about what transpired in Werfen?" asked Ulrik.

"If you must, Ulrik."

"I don't mind taking a beating for you, but I'm concerned about what will happen next in Volkov's company. I can't save you from him if you enter his locked bedroom," he said.

"I know, Ulrik. I understand what I'm doing. I'm really sorry about your head. That was most unfortunate. I don't foresee that happening again, okay?" she said, hoping this would be the last of it.

"Okay. Will there be any screaming on the boat today, Ms. Lovgren?"

"No. Absolutely not. No need to worry today, Ulrik. It's just Dana and Clive," she said.

"Very good," he said, satisfied.

***

CHAPTER 18

The Goodbye

St. Martin, French West Indies

Pepper swam over to Bill in the warm turquoise water, wrapping her legs around his waist. He stood firmly on the sandy bottom in the five-foot-deep water with his arms loosely around her back. She rubbed her neck against his whiskers, kissing him below his ear. They canoodled as the sea swells rocked them back and forth.

"Are you sure you're okay with my going to Boston with Brent?" she asked.

"Of course. It's Agency headquarters and you have orientation to do. There's no avoiding it," he said.

"Thanks for being so understanding," she said.

"I have to return to work anyway," he said.

"Will you be alright going home alone?" she asked.

"I'm a big boy. I think I can handle it," he said.

"Should Daisy stay at your parents' house?" she asked.

"Yeah. She gets more attention there. I'll be at work all day. I'll see her when they have me over to dinner," he said.

"Oh. What night are you going for dinner?" she asked.

"I don't know yet, but I'm sure Mom will call me as soon as I get back."

"We're lucky to have them in our lives," said Pepper.

They kissed, then broke apart and swam the length of the bay a few times to stretch out before their day of travel.

***

That afternoon, Brent and Jackie were fiercely making out at Gate 4A of Princess Julianna Airport in Sint Maarten, the Dutch side. Pepper and Bill were strolling through the brightly lit duty free shops so they didn't have to witness the love fest. Airports were generally considered to be an exception to the no-public-display- of-affection" rule, but Brent and Jackie were pushing the boundaries of decency. There were children nearby!

"You're so hot I can't stand it," whispered Brent.

"I'm going to miss you," murmured Jackie.

He had her pushed up against a wall in a corner for privacy but his legs were getting weak standing. He wanted to be lying down, back at the resort.

"Will you marry me?" he heard himself ask, not entirely sure where it came from.

They broke apart, foreheads resting against each other, panting.

"Brent, did you just mean to ask me to marry you for real, or are you as dizzy as I am after a sex-filled vacation?" she asked.

He laughed, realization dawning as much as his brain would allow when he was in

Jackie's presence. "I meant it. Will you marry me?" he asked again.

Tears sprang to her eyes. "Yes, Brent Cahill, I'll marry you."

They both had tears running down their cheeks as they renewed their kissing.

"Do you want me to surprise you with a ring, or do you want to go shopping together?" he asked.

"Surprise me!" she said.

"Deal. Are you an old fashioned girl or a modern girl?" he asked.

"I'm a simple girl, Brent. Something small with a compact setting. I'm going to wear it when I lift weights, so it has to be durable. I don't want the diamond to get knocked loose," she said.

"Right. Titanium band with a hard rubber casing over a diamond that's bolted down. Got it," he joked.

"I'm sure you'll be just fine. I can't wait to see what you come up with. I'll love it no matter what, because it will be from you," she said.

"I feel the pressure already," he said.

She laughed, kissing him some more as her flight was being called for boarding. Jackie and Bill were traveling together to Minneapolis, while Pepper and Brent were taking a nonstop to Boston. The Minneapolis flight left first. Pepper and Bill approached Jackie and Brent.

"We should probably board now," said Bill to the kissing couple.

Jackie broke free from Brent and came over to hug Pepper goodbye. Bill shook Brent's hand, and asked him to look after his wife while in Boston. Brent nodded solemnly knowing there would probably be more truth to that statement someday than Bill realized.

Pepper took one look at Jackie, and saw she was a heap of emotion. "I'm gonna miss you. I promise to come in and work out when I get back."

"Yeah, I'm gonna miss you too," said Jackie, crying again.

Pepper looked at Bill and Brent.

Brent put his arm around Jackie. "Jackie, honey, are you going to tell Pepper and Bill?"

"Do you want me to?" she sniffled, sliding her arm around his waist.

"Absolutely. If it's too much for you, I can," he said.

"Nooa...," The faucet of tears was running full strength now.

"Good Lord, what's going on?" asked Pepper.

"I asked Jackie to marry me and she said yes," said Brent.

Pepper squealed with delight and hugged Jackie. Bill shook Brent's hand again, congratulating him.

"I'm so happy for you guys. Thanks for springing this on her right before we board, Brent. Looks like I'm going to have my hands full on the plane," said Bill.

They all laughed as the final boarding call was announced. Pepper and Jackie promised to call each other as the group broke apart with one last hug between each couple. Brent and Pepper watched as Jackie and Bill had their tickets scanned by the gate agent, disappearing down the jet way.

"There goes the woman of your dreams, Brent. And to think I introduced you to her. Yay me!" said Pepper.

"I'll always be indebted to you, Pepper."

"And I reserve the right to remind you if I ever need to," said Pepper.

***

CHAPTER 19

Pepper Goes to Boston

Princess Julianna Airport

As Pepper and Brent were getting settled in their first class seats, the jet taxiing down the runway, Pepper felt overcome with emotion at separating from Bill. They had been with each other exclusively for the last five weeks, and she hadn't realized how attached she had become.

The separation was tangled up in grief for Jake as well. She felt like a wave of grief was going to overwhelm her, but there was no opportunity for privacy. She couldn't go to the bathroom because they were taxiing for takeoff. The tears began slipping over her lower lids, falling like rivers. Maybe if she looked out the window, and didn't wipe her eyes, Brent wouldn't notice.

The last thing she wanted Brent to think was that she was too weak to do this job. What had she been thinking? Maybe she was too weak to do the job. Maybe she should have gone home with Bill, stayed by his side, picked up Daisy from her parents-in-law's house, and...and. And then what? Stayed home and cried while Bill went to work? Being home alone for more than 24 hours would kill her right now. She'd sink into the black abyss of loneliness and loss, and never climb back out. No, she'd pray for strength. She knew she was on the right course. If she could just stop the current waterfall of tears running down her face.

She felt Brent's large hand cover hers. He gave it a light squeeze and retreated.

"Pepper, I understand," he said. "Saying goodbye to Bill must have triggered the feelings of loss again. Like I told you back in Minneapolis when we were working on the Futuraceutical project, I've been through the loss of an immediate family member, too. You can cry in front of me. I don't consider it a sign of weakness. When I was in SWCC, I saw macho men cry for days after losing a brother during an operation. It's part of the process. I wish I could fast forward it for you, but I can't. You just have to go through it. Feel the highs and the lows. Don't worry, in time, the lows won't be quite as low and they won't last quite as long. Your emotions will even out. But for now, cry it out. I'm here for you," he said.

"Oh, God Brent, it hurts so much. I miss him so much. Thank you," she sobbed. He scrounged up some napkins from the seatback and handed them to her.

As the plane took off from the tarmac, Pepper cried for about 20 more minutes, then fell into a deep sleep.

***

Boston, Massachusetts, United States of America

Pepper and Brent landed at Boston Logan International Airport late that night, and it was after midnight when they had cleared Customs and Immigration. Brent had arranged for a town car to pick them up. He planned to drop Pepper at her hotel before going to his apartment. She was booked at the Boston Marriott Copley Place in downtown, which was close to his headquarters. He hadn't invited her to stay at his two-bedroom apartment because, frankly, he didn't know how to host a platonic female guest, especially a business partner. Talk about awkward. He couldn't remember what type of shape his place was in, and didn't want to gross her out. In fact, he probably had to do some deep cleaning before Jackie visited him, or she'd back out of the engagement.

Brent accompanied Pepper to the hotel reception desk, and waited until she was checked in. They hugged lightly, and he told her he'd pick her up in the lobby at eight the next morning. His office was close by, so they'd walk.

Pepper had done some preplanning, and had contacted the downtown Talbot's by email from St. Martin to have them deliver three conservative pantsuits, five silk blouses, some knee high hose and shoes. She told them to throw in a trench coat with a wool liner as well because it was October in Boston, and it could be unpredictably chilly. The hotel receptionist indicated Pepper's garment bag had arrived from Talbot's, and she'd have the bellhop bring it up to Pepper's room with the rest of her luggage. Once in her room, Pepper tipped bellhop after he had unloaded her gear, and locked the door behind him.

After exchanging texts with Bill, who indicated Jackie remained on cloud nine for the duration of the six-hour plane ride from St. Martin, Pepper slept as well as anyone could in a hotel room.

***

The next morning, Pepper chose a navy blue pinstripe pantsuit with an ivory silk blouse, and wasn't disappointed. Talboring, as she referred to it, had never let her down. She knew her size in their suits, and it fit perfectly, if not a little loose given her recent weight loss. She was prepared for business. It actually felt strange to put on real shoes instead of flip flops. Her toes would have to reacquaint themselves to the confinement.

She met Brent in the lobby, and was glad for the lined trench coat as the fall chill was in the air. He had two lattes from his favorite coffee shop, and they walked together a few blocks to his office building.

Brent's office building was a nondescript 20-story building that was surrounded by other office buildings. The security in the lobby was typical for a big city building with a metal detector and two guards. Upon closer inspection, however, Pepper noticed these guards had not only military-issue Glocks on their waist band holsters, but also submachine guns slung over their backs.

After they had walked through the metal detector, they passed into a second lobby, and had to place their bags on a conveyor belt that took them through an x-ray machine. Brent chatted with the security guards, showing them his I.D. He brought Pepper to the lobby desk, and she was issued a guest I.D. badge with her photo on it, which they took on the spot. They also asked both of them for their cell phones. They held Pepper's phone next to a black device and told her they were copying everything on it, from her music library to her contacts list. Standard Agency procedure. She was surprised, but figured she'd have to become accustomed to the new level of intrusion and paranoia in the Agency.

Brent led her to the elevator bank, and pressed the button for the 26th floor. There wasn't a directory in the elevator indicating what was on any of the floors. He smiled at her. She raised an eyebrow, impressed.

The elevator opened and a male receptionist with shoulder length black hair who looked about 18 years old greeted Brent.

"Hi Devon, how's it goin'?" asked Brent.

"Good, good. You got a tan. Have a good time in the Caribbean?" he asked.

"I did some work too, you know. Why are you sitting up here?" asked Brent.

"Jo is on break. I'm covering for her because I'm such a nice guy," said Devon.

"I'll bet," said Brent.

"And this beautiful woman with you must be Pepper McCallan," said Devon as he stood, coming out to shake Pepper's hand.

"Yes. Pepper, this is Devon Blake. He's the director of the administrative assistants. He basically runs the floor and tries to run our lives," said Brent.

"Nice to meet you, "said Pepper.

"And you. I look forward to working with you," said Devon.

"Translation – trying to run your life too," teased Brent.

Brent led Pepper down the hall toward his office. It was a male-dominated environment, and they all had heard about Pepper, the female consultant who had helped Brent on the Futuraceutical case, and was currently helping him with some Russian information-gathering.

As Brent and Pepper walked down the hallway, cubicles on one side and offices on the other, all the men glanced up, then glanced up again with a double-take. Brent hadn't told them Pepper was a looker. She looked younger than 37, had a deep tan, and her blonde hair was currently tied back in a ponytail. And there was no mistaking her curves under the conservative suit.

They almost made it to Brent's office when a large black man with short, grey hair stepped out of his door jam, colliding with Brent. By sheer force of physics, Brent was knocked into a cubicle across the hallway. Pepper stopped and the man, who was at least 6'5", laughed at Brent, then turned to Pepper. Pepper guessed he was close to 50 years old, but still had a body like a rock. He was wearing charcoal dress pants and a snug black sweater. She noticed immediately that he smelled good. Masculine coupled with sandalwood. He extended a hand the size of a baseball mitt, and smiled. Her own hand disappeared in his warm hand. It felt really powerful, and a little dreamy.

"I'm Allen Montgomery. Nice to meet you," he said in a deep, sexy voice.

"I'm Pepper. Pepper McCallan," she said.

"Welcome aboard. I heard Brent recruited you, but I didn't expect a woman as lovely as you. How long are you in town?" he asked.

"As long as it takes to work through some information. This week at least," she said.

He smiled. "I'd like to take you to dinner. Show you around a bit. You like seafood?"

Pepper glanced at his left hand. No wedding ring. She felt a little self-conscious.

Brent stepped in. "Nice try, Allen. She's married. But if you're offering dinner, both Pepper and I would like to come. How does seven tonight sound?"

"I can see she's married, Brent. I don't hit on everyone in a skirt like you do. I'm civilized. Let's do seven. Where should I pick you up?"

"I'm at the Marriott a few blocks away," said Pepper.

"I'll be in the lobby at seven sharp. I have a car. Brent can meet us in the lobby there, too, so I don't have to drive over to his place."

Brent laughed. His place was only about 10 blocks from the Marriott.

They to Brent's office next. He shut the door.

"That was interesting," said Pepper.

"Yeah. He's a great guy. I was just giving him a hard time. He's the Director of our Unit. Head honcho. My boss' boss. I get along with him better than my boss, so I usually just deal with Allen. My boss hates it."

"Who's your boss?" she asked.

"Deputy Director Marty Cavanaugh," he said.

"When do I get to meet him?" she asked.

"In about an hour, when we're scheduled to meet with him," he said.

"Lovely," she replied.

"Oh he's quite lovely. He'll be impervious to your beauty, you know," said Brent.

"Okay. Thanks. Speaking of which, do I need to watch out for Allen?" she asked.

"Well, he's probably on the hunt right now because his second divorce was just finalized. Serious ladies' man. But no, as long as I've known him, he's had good boundaries at work. And he can take a hint," said Brent.

"That's a relief. I enjoy playfulness, but any more than that gets tiresome," she said.

"I wish I could say I understand, but I'm usually the guy on the other side of that equation. Rest assured, not anymore. But I used to be. By the way, the guys here don't know I'm engaged to Jackie yet," he said.

"No worries. I'm not monitoring your behavior to report back to Jackie," she said.

He smiled. "Let me show you to your temporary office where information security will set you up with a password for our system."

They left Brent's office and walked a short distance to an empty office that smacked of government. The technology was first class though. There were two computer screens and some serious central processing units being hooked up. A geeky looking guy was crawling around on the floor, hooking up cords. Brent introduced him to Pepper, and made a hasty exit.

While Pepper was waiting for the information tech to hook her up, she called Talboring, and asked them to deliver a couple of dinner dresses with hose and pumps to her hotel. She had sent her Caribbean dresses home in a suitcase with Bill because they were too revealing and light to wear to professional dinners in cold weather. She needed something for tonight.

***

A couple hours later, Brent and Pepper were sitting in Deputy Director Marty Cavanaugh's spacious office. He had a long rectangular conference table that he had sandwiched up against the front of his desk.

For their meeting, Marty came out from behind his desk and joined them at the conference table. Pepper noticed that Marty was more of a desk agent than a field agent. If men were egg products, Marty would be of the hard-boiled variety. His egg-like body began with a balding head that sat atop shoulders without much of a neck to support it. His chest morphed into a ski jump over a pot belly, accentuated by his tight white dress shirt, supporting a yellow tie that was clipped. The horizontal tie clip rested in the middle of the ski jump. If it had been clipped vertically, it would have been poised to get some serious air, thought Pepper. His navy suit pants were hiked up high enough to clear his love handles, which smartly dropped off into a wide bottom and legs that hadn't seen a treadmill in years, if ever.

Marty's handshake was noncommittal, and he appeared nervous to Pepper. It looked like he had psoriasis on his eyebrows and upper eyelids, giving the impression his eyebrows had been singed off with a blow torch. He couldn't make eye contact, instead moving his eyes in a circle around Pepper, looking at the wall above her, Brent to her left, the floor at his feet, his desk to Pepper's right, and back up to the wall behind her again. Round and round Marty's eyes went.

"Marty, how are things?" asked Brent.

"Fine. What do you have for me?" he asked.

"We're piecing together some fragmented info, and we have a few possibilities but nothing solid yet," said Brent.

"Let me see if I can help," said Marty.

"Okay. We know that Russian President Vadik Volkov started a relationship with the Swedish Minister of Foreign Affairs, Svea Lovgren," said Brent.

"When you say relationship…," ventured Marty.

"I mean intimate relationship. She stayed the night at his hotel in London a few weeks ago," said Brent.

"Oh," said Marty.

"She's new on the job, having just replaced the previous one who scuttled a missile deal with Saudi Arabia by bringing up women's rights at an Arab conference in Dubai," said Brent.

"I heard about that. Heh, heh. The Saudis reneged and left Sweden holding the missiles," said Marty.

"Right. Svea Lovgren curried favor with Volkov, and he took them off her hands. They've been shipped to Russia," said Brent.

"No kidding? He probably got them at a discount," said Marty.

"Agreed. Here's another piece of information. One of our intelligence gatherers in Russia reported the manufacture and shipment of the nerve gas sarin to Bangkok aboard a Chinese merchant ship. That was a significant report, so I'm working on crosschecking it for confirmation," said Brent.

Marty made a note on a yellow legal pad. "That's fairly significant. How are you crosschecking?"

"Tennis shoes on the ground in Bangkok. Our agent there, Weng Chee, spoke to the Bangkok Port Harbor Master. He said a Chinese ship unloaded a refrigerated container on the dock, then it was divided into two containers, one departed by sea, and the other left for the airport. The Harbor Master promised to find the paperwork for Weng, but he was called away while Weng was there, so Weng didn't get a chance to follow him to his office. He'll stop by tomorrow," said Brent.

"If it's true, and we don't know that for sure, that would be a dangerous development," said Marty.

"Agreed. We need to get the shipping manifests as soon as possible, but you know how things work over there," said Brent.

"Yes. Frustrating. What else do you have?" asked Marty.

"A fragmented piece of information that Pepper noticed. There are three Swedish interns at hospitals in the U.S. The hospitals are in L.A., Minneapolis and Philadelphia. Pepper saw it in an article in a medical journal. Very uncharacteristic. They don't usually send university students to America to intern in our hospitals. I'd like your permission to go to Stockholm to verify their backstories with the University of Stockholm, since they all supposedly attend there," said Brent.

Marty looked like he was going to vomit. He had the most distasteful look on his face – but not quite a sneer. His mouth was open and his lips were pulled back. He kept shaking his head to the right, but only to the right, as Brent was talking. It was obvious that Marty didn't agree with Brent's suggestion, not bothering to look at Pepper at all.

"You're right," said Marty. "That sounds really tangential. Just because Svea Lovgren is from Sweden doesn't mean we have to be suspicious of all-things-Swedish. Permission denied. Stay here and track the alleged sarin shipments. I thought you were going to request to go to Bangkok. That would have made more sense."

"No. Weng doesn't need me looking over his shoulder. He'll be fine," said Brent.

"Keep me apprised." Marty stood suddenly and started walking toward his desk. Meeting over.

Brent stood, signaling to Pepper to follow him out. There were no goodbyes.

"That was…interesting," said Pepper once they reached her office and closed the door.

"You probably noticed his social skills are as lacking as his imagination," laughed Brent.

"Struck me as the type of guy who plays it by the book, one step at a time," she said.

"That's as fair a characterization as any. The problem is, in this business, sometimes you have to play hunches. Marty hasn't had a hunch his entire career. He wouldn't recognize a burning bush if it blew up in his face," said Brent, frustrated.

"Tell me how you really feel," she said.

"I'm serious. We'll talk to Allen tonight at dinner. I never argue the point with Marty. I just nod and go do my own thing. He forgets what he signed off on anyway. He knows how to take credit for a job well done, though, when it's successfully completed," said Brent.

"Ah yes. I'm familiar with that model of boss," sighed Pepper.

***

Brent and Allen were standing in the Marriott lobby chatting when the elevator door opened and Pepper stepped out. She was positively striking. Her sun-streaked hair hung loosely over her shoulders in soft curls, and her black dinner dress accentuated her curves. It had a tasteful v-cut front and was long-sleeved. It was narrow at the waist with a thick belt, and the fabric melted over her hips, flowing to a hem just above her knees. Any living, breathing male within sight stopped what he was doing and watched her walk over to Allen and Brent. She had a new, black cashmere coat hanging over her arm, along with a cream-colored silk scarf.

"Stand down! She's married," whispered Brent to Allen.

"A man can still drool, can't he?" asked Allen.

"Hi guys. Hope you haven't been waiting long," said Pepper.

"Pepper, you're the most beautiful creature who's ever worked in our Agency," said Allen.

"Thank you, Allen. Will you help me with my coat?" she asked.

"It would be my pleasure." He held her coat as she slid her arms in.

Allen's chauffeured SUV brought them to his favorite Italian restaurant on Beacon Hill, Artú Trattoria. The food was just as good at Mother Anna's in the North End but Allen didn't feel as comfortable there. He didn't like being the only African American in the restaurant. At Artú, the maître d' knew Allen by name, showing them to his reserved table. They were a handsome threesome, and Pepper noticed both men and women glancing up to watch them walk by.

Once they were seated, and Allen had ordered a bottle of Chianti Classico Riserva, Brent gave Allen the same report as he had given Marty earlier in the day.

"Sounds to me like you should go to Sweden. What do you think, Pepper?" asked Allen.

"Since I was the one who planted this mysterious Swedish seed in Brent's head, I agree that we should go to Stockholm. Sometimes you find things out in person that you can't see from a distance," she said.

"Wise beyond your years, I see. I agree, something might catch your eye that you wouldn't have noticed from here. Good old fashioned detective work," said Allen.

"Glad you see it our way," said Brent.

"With the new relationship between the Swedish Foreign Minister and Volkov," said Allen, "I might get asked about it at our weekly situation report with the President. I want to be able to say we're on it, and that I have my Agency's assets on the ground in Stockholm investigating further."

"Ah, another important angle. Very thorough," said Brent.

They dined on pasta, and talked mostly about sports because Allen was an avid football fan and his beloved New England Patriots were having a phenomenal year, despite Tom Brady's injured knee. He took a hit to his left knee in the 2017 Super Bowl the previous season, and had surgery in the off-season. Some fans were calling for his retirement, but Allen was willing to give him the benefit of the doubt, despite deflate-gate.

***

CHAPTER 20

Clive's Suggestion

Fall 2018

Stockholm Archipelago, Sweden

Svea arrived at the marina with Ulrik, and he jumped out to hold the door while she exited the backseat of her car. She gazed up and down the docks but didn't see Dana or Clive, so she entered kajplats 18, while Ulrik carried the bags behind her. Captain Peder extended a hand to Svea as she stepped onto the 55-foot yacht. She disappeared below deck, and Ulrik handed the groceries down to her for stowing. She placed the champagne and duck liver pâté in the small fridge in the teak trimmed galley, then dropped her bag on the bed in her master stateroom.

Svea checked the master bath and noticed it was clean. Her crew had done a nice job tidying up after her last excursion. After hanging fresh towels, she joined Peder and Ulrik on the deck. Peder was running through his engine checklist and rigging lines to raise the sails. He was a tall, slim man with grey hair and calloused hands, tanned and worn from tying lines, pulling up anchors and working on boats.

"Ms. Svea, where would you like to sail today?" he asked.

"Out to Waxholm for lunch, Peder," said Svea.

"One of the last beautiful days before it turns chilly. We should turn back before two o'clock, so we have plenty of daylight to sail back to port," said Peder.

"We'll see," she said. "We might stay at the Waxholm Hotel for the night. Can you contact them, and inquire into a two-bedroom suite?"

"Of course. I'll do it before we depart," he said.

Svea glanced toward the kajplats and saw Clive and Dana entering. They descended the stairs and walked to Svea's yacht. She stayed onboard, but extended her hand to welcome them. Clive was the first to step aboard and greet her. It had been a few weeks since they had last seen each other in Werfen, Austria.

"Svea, how good to see you. You look lovely," he said smoothly. He smiled, and the ice around Svea's heart melted a bit.

Despite her suspicions, she allowed Clive to kiss her on both cheeks. She had forgotten how handsome he was. Of course, he was a few years younger than she was, but that didn't bother her. Dana boarded, and Svea immediately noticed that she looked radiant in the sunshine. Dana gripped Svea's hand as she stepped onto the aft deck, joining the group. The spark from Austria was still there.

The three of them moved to the open deck where Peder was warming up the engine. Ulrik jumped onto the dock and untied the lines from the black cleats. He threw them onto the yacht, and Peder expertly motored away from the dock. They were off.

Svea was struck by how ravishing Dana looked, and couldn't help but feel flattered by the presence of these two beautiful people for her benefit. The sun shone off Dana's hair and skin, making her glow. Perhaps Svea had reacted rashly to Dana's phone call, suspecting they here only to spy on her for Volkov. She could feel the sparkles of excitement building in her stomach.

Dana caught Svea staring at her, so took the lead, as she had in Werfen. She quickly closed the distance between them, resting her hand on the back of Svea's neck, gently guiding her face down to hers. Svea's long brown hair cascaded around Dana's face. Svea resisted slightly at first, self-conscious with Ulrik and Peder nearby, but as soon as Dana's lips touched hers, she melted. Dana's lips were much softer than a man's, and her mouth was smaller. It was a warm, wet kiss, filled with passion, but not possessive like a man's could be. Svea found her own tongue in Dana's mouth, exploring the silky softness, setting her body on fire.

Svea instinctively brought her hands to Dana's jaw, tilting her face upward. Svea was lost in the sensation of kissing. It was like swimming in chocolate pudding while taking in Dana's intoxicating fragrance - earthy with a hint of jasmine. Liquid desire emanated from her brain to her toes. She mashed against Dana's body, Svea's breasts slightly above Dana's due to her height. They melded together easily and the heat from Dana's body infiltrated Svea's cold Swedish disposition. Dana rested her hands at the small of Svea's back, and pressed her hips against her through their tights and sweaters. Electricity buzzed through Svea's body, and she no longer cared that Peder and Ulrik were witnessing her affection for Dana.

A few minutes passed as Ulrik and Clive watched. Peder pretended to be keeping a lookout for boat traffic. When Svea finally broke off the kiss, her eyes were dancing with lust. She glanced toward the stateroom below deck. Dana followed her gaze and took her by the hand. No stranger to boats, Dana led Svea down the stair. Svea reached back and grabbed Clive's hand, too. He readily followed. Ulrik was left out in the cold, again. At least Svea had promised there wouldn't be any screaming this time.

After the threesome had engaged in sinful pleasure, they lay tangled up in the sheets, bodies askew on the king-sized bed with the yacht tilting to port, catching the wind. They were in full sail. Svea was finally sated, but not in the depraved fashion Volkov insisted on. Her mind felt clear, and she realized being with Dana was exactly what she had needed. Clive was absent-mindedly rubbing her feet, which felt glorious. She was in a state of deep relaxation when she realized that Dana's hand was resting on her breast. It felt warm and soft. She could get used to this. She sighed, and Dana stirred.

"Umm. Svea, how are you?" asked Dana. "I hope we didn't hurt the lashes on your derriere."

"They're healing. You were very gentle. Thank you for that. I'll never forgive that bastard Volkov for whipping me. That was fucking painful," said Svea.

"I can only imagine. You know Clive and I aren't into that shit, right?" asked Dana.

"I know. I trust you," said Svea.

"I want to know how you are doing in your life," pressed Dana.

"I'm fantastic," she said, and rolled over to snuggle up closer to Dana.

Dana held Svea's body, stroking her hair while Svea sighed with contentment. Dana affectionately kissed the top of Svea's head as she held her. Svea had never known such gentle affection from a lover, and it filled her with peace. They drifted off to the sound of the yacht breaking through the cold water as they tacked toward Waxholm. It was a shame that Dana and Clive weren't enjoying the view of the majestic Swedish homes that lined the shoreline, being so much more colorful than the pastel homes in St. Martin, but the pleasure below deck had been worth it.

Much later, when Svea heard Peder start the boat engine again, she awoke to Dana snuggling her front side and Clive spooned up to her back. She was cradled between the two, who were both soundly asleep. The time difference must have caught up to them.

Svea decided she needed some champagne, so she scooted out the bottom of the bed, and opened the door to find Ulrik sitting at the galley table. She put on a robe and fumbled around until she found the champagne. She asked him how long it would be before they reached Waxholm and he reported it was only minutes away. Svea asked him to confirm both dinner reservations and a hotel room for the night at the Waxholm Hotel. She decided they'd sail back to Stockholm the following day.

When Svea entered the stateroom, Clive had awakened so he offered to open and pour. They clinked glasses and drank to one another. They sipped as they dressed for dinner, wearing casual attire when the yacht docked at the Waxholm marina next to colorful blue and red wooden boats that were used for zipping around the harbor. It was after four o'clock because Peder had taken the scenic route once they had disappeared below for their private activities. The setting sun shone off the old Waxholm Hotel, radiating stateliness and charm. It was painted a muted yellow, and had burgundy trim and a black tin roof with a dome in the center.

The suite reserved for Svea was at the edge of the peninsula, overlooking the channel and historic Waxholm Fortress that was built in 1544 to defend Stockholm against Russian invaders. While that strategy had been successful, it wasn't much help in stopping the recent parade of Russian submarines that crawled through the 100-foot-deep channel. The Waxholm Fortress was a small island unto itself and had been remodeled into a restaurant and conference center for leadership training. Svea was beginning to think the Swedish Navy should have retained ownership of the fortress, and outfitted it with the latest sub-detecting technology, including radar.

Svea led Dana and Clive up the dock and across the street to the hotel. The proprietor recognized her, greeting her warmly. The three of them ascended the stairs to Svea's suite. Once in the suite, Svea sat on the sofa and opened her briefcase to check her emails on her iPad. Nothing from Thai Cargo Shipping yet. The Fentanyl ampules were still missing, putting her entire operation in jeopardy.

Dana noticed the troubled look on Svea's face as she and Clive dropped their overnight bags and refreshed in the bathroom. She walked over and massaged Svea's shoulders gently, eliciting a relaxed sigh from Svea. Dana leaned down and kissed the top of Svea's head. Svea put her hand on Dana's and pulled her around so she could kiss her. Dana sat on the back of the sofa, then slowly slid over it, plopping down next to Svea. She rested her head on Svea's lap as they affectionately held each other.

Svea pushed Dana's hair back around her face, tracing her fingers along Dana's jawline, down her neck and back around her ear. They held each other's gaze and Svea felt an unfamiliar surge of warmth from her heart to her toes. She had never experienced such sincere emotion, not even in the early years of her marriage to Juergen. She slowly lowered her head, her hair making a tent around Dana's face, and kissed Dana's forehead. Svea's heart raced, her hands exploring Dana's tanned shoulders and arms. Dana couldn't restrain herself any longer, dragging Svea to her mouth, kissing her deeper than she had previously. More than sex was present in Dana' touch. She moaned with longing as their tongues swirled.

Svea was enraptured by Dana's kiss. She would have taken it further if she hadn't been famished - for food. They broke apart, each panting and popping with sexual energy.

"I've never felt this way about a woman before," rasped Dana.

"Me either," whispered Svea, relieved that Dana had said it first.

"I worry about you, Svea. This mission looks like it's weighing heavily on your mind," said Dana.

"I worry about me, too. It has turned into a challenge but I still have faith that I can pull it off," said Svea.

"It's not too late to drop it, you know. You have nothing to prove to anyone," said Dana. "You could come to my place in the Caribbean and relax. I could show you a good time, like as in a different life style, you know?" Dana's electric blue eyes looked convincing, but Svea was motivated by demons that Dana didn't understand.

"I'm sure you could, but my destiny lies here, Dana. I can't explain what drives me but I know I have to see it through," said Svea.

"As you wish. But, when all this is over, promise me you'll come to my island and spend time with me. I care about you, and I want to spend more time getting to know everything about you," said Dana.

Svea beheld Dana's eyes. There was no guile there. No one had ever spoken such kind words to her. Of course, Swedish men weren't renowned for sharing their feelings, so it wasn't a surprise. She felt a surge of warmth toward Dana, and vowed to herself that she'd follow through on Dana's offer when her mission was complete. If Dana would still have her. They kissed again and Clive came over and sat in the chair facing them. He waited patiently. He and Dana had never been in a relationship, so he wasn't jealous in the least. In fact, he was happy for both of them.

The three gathered themselves for dinner and descended the hotel stairs to enter the dining room. Ulrik and Peder were seated at a table in the bar, awaiting the threesome's arrival. They would dine at a table nearby so Ulrik could fulfill his security duties. It was a light crowd given the time of the week and year, and Svea couldn't remember the last time she had felt so content. They took their time over salmon gravlax appetizers served with white wine, and they all ordered an entré of arctic char over couscous and vegetables.

"How are things?" asked Clive.

"Better now that you two are here," said Svea.

"I'm glad. And the project you're working on with Volkov? That's going well?" pressed Clive.

There it was. Svea set down her fork and squinted at Clive. She had wondered how long it would take for it to become obvious that they were here on Volkov's errand. Should she tell them everything or withhold information? Her natural inclination was to be circumspect, but she needed Volkov's ongoing support and resources.

Clearly, Clive was just doing his job, and his disinterested expression impressed Svea. If Clive and Dana were the conduit through which Svea's information had to flow, then she would tell them the details. However, she didn't approve of Volkov's tactics because it widened the circle of people who knew what the operation was, increasing her personal risk of capture.

"Yes. The project is coming along. You can tell Volkov that I have things under control," she said.

"He'll want more detail than that, Svea. And he isn't a man to be denied," said Clive.

"I know," said Svea.

Clive stared at her with an expectant look.

"How much do you know?" she asked them, not wanting to jeopardize her scheme.

"Everything," answered Clive.

"Prove it," countered Svea.

Clive dropped his voice so it was barely audible. He leaned in close to Svea's face. "We know that you're planning a nerve gas attack on Americans in three cities. The delivery system is with both ampules and nebulizers, the nebulizers being carried by drones..."

"Okay, okay," she interrupted. "You know what's going on. Truth be told, I'm having some problems with confirming the two Sarin shipments from the Philadelphia International Airport. One was supposed to have gone to a Minneapolis warehouse, and the other to a Philadelphia warehouse. I've received confirmation of neither, so I'm troubled."

"Is there something we can do to help?" asked Dana.

"You two are available to help with operations?" asked Svea.

"Yes," confirmed Dana. "Volkov is paying us very well, and instructed us to help you in whatever fashion you deemed appropriate. We can stay as long as needed." Dana's statement took some of the shine off Svea's feelings toward her. Being paid well.

Svea surveyed Dana critically. Dana had an uncanny ability to absorb Svea's stare, from which most people shrunk. Svea respected Dana's temerity, giving her hope that both Dana and Clive were capable.

"What skills do you have?" asked Svea.

"We're quite versatile," said Dana.

"Well, as much as I'd like to send you to America to check on the shipments in person, I think your presence would alert too many people. You're an unforgettable couple, which is not necessarily a good thing for operations such as this."

"Is there something else we can do for you?" asked Clive.

"I might have a way in which you could help. I'll give you the address of an old friend I need you to visit. His name is Hugo von Ruden. He's an old school chum. Ulrik will arrange for someone to drive you in an untraceable car. Hugo lives outside of Stockholm and it's inconvenient for me to go there, but I have a hand- delivery for him. Are you busy tomorrow or the next day?"

"We're at your disposal, Svea," said Clive.

"Good. Then I'd like you to deliver a package to him. It's on the boat, securely stowed," she said.

"What's in it?" inquired Clive.

"Do you really need to know?" asked Svea.

"My personal policy is that I need to know what I'm carrying if I'm being used as a mule," he said.

"Fine. I suppose that's wise," said Svea. "There's a round trip ticket to Bangkok, and a piece of paper with the name and address of the Harbor Master for the Old Bangkok Port. Hugo needs to pay the Harbor Master's office a visit and recover some shipping manifests for me. All the information is in there. Can you instruct him accordingly?"

"Of course. Simple enough," said Clive.

"Do you have something a bit more challenging for us?" asked Dana.

"What are you doing the rest of tonight?" asked Svea.

"Making love to you," whispered Dana, so the other diners wouldn't overhear.

The thrill on Svea's face was not lost on Dana. Dana reached across her plate, entwining her fingers through Svea's, inducing a soft moan from Svea. Dana realized in that moment how vulnerable Svea really was.

"Why don't you two ladies retire to the room and I'll settle the bill," suggested Clive.

"Good idea," said Svea. Clive held each of their chairs and the two women walked out of the dining room and up the stairway. Both men and women alike admired their beauty as they walked arm-in-arm.

***

The next morning, Peder prepared the boat, and the threesome boarded in the face of chilly temperatures and a stiff sailing wind. The sky was a beautiful blue, reflecting off the choppy Baltic Sea. Yesterday had been summer's last hurrah, so Svea suggested they move below-deck to the galley once they were underway.

As they took their seats and Svea made tea, Clive asked, "Svea, have you thought about an insurance policy in your dealings with Volkov?"

His statement caught Svea off guard. She had no idea what he could be talking about. "No, Clive. What do you mean?"

"I'm talking about something that would shift the spotlight from you to Volkov if this ever came back on you. Dana and I were considering how events could play out, and we thought of a way for you to protect your downside. I'm happy to describe it to you but we'll expect payment. This type of consultation is how we make our living."

"I understand. How much?" she asked.

"I don't expect you to pay us as much as Volkov is, nor do we have a set dollar amount in mind. Why don't I tell you our idea, and you can decide what it's worth to you," he offered.

"Okay. I'm game." Svea looked at Dana, who nodded encouragingly.

"I propose we make a video of you on our way back to Stockholm," he said. "I can keep the video safe for you, and release it whenever and to whomever you designate in the future."

"Fabulous. I bet you have something in mind for me to say on the video, don't you?" she asked.

"Yes," they said in unison.

Svea poured the boiling water in their tea cups, and sat down to listen to Clive and Dana's idea.

***

CHAPTER 21

Southview Hospital

Fall 2018

Minneapolis, Minnesota

United States of America

Mike, the loading dock manager at Southview Hospital, signed the shipping receipt for the pharmaceutical delivery. Not a very big load, he thought. Just one pallet. He supposed the pharmacy must have needed a specific item for its inventory. He noted it was marked as a schedule II controlled substance, which translated into narcotics.

The delivery truck driver moved the hydraulic lift on the back of his truck up to the height of the loading dock. The hospital's forklift driver scooped up the pallet, driving it across the concrete platform, down the hallway, and unloading it against the wall, snugged up next to the other pharmaceutical pallets.

Inside Mike's office, which was a beat up work bench with computers on it, enclosed behind a floor-to-ceiling metal cage, Mike entered the shipping receipt into his software. Then, per protocol, he emailed the pharmacy manager to alert him that there were schedule II drugs at the loading dock. Hospital policy mandated that schedule II drugs be transported to the pharmacy immediately, including on weekends. Usually, Mike had enough personnel available to bring the drugs directly to the inpatient pharmacy inventory on a cart via the basement hallways but he was short-staffed today due to illnesses, so he made it clear in his email that the pharmacy needed to send a technician over to pick up the narcotics immediately, diminishing the likelihood of theft.

Pursuant to policy, a pharmacy tech came to the loading dock with a silver cart forty minutes later.

"Hey, Carrie Ann, long time no see," said Mike.

"Hey, Mike. Like your Packer sweatshirt. Did you go to the game Sunday?" she asked.

"Always. It was AWESOME. Aaron Rodgers really pulled that one out," he said.

"I think we're gonna have a good season, don't you?" she asked.

"Another Super Bowl win," he said.

"Have some people out sick, huh?" she asked.

"Yeah, something nasty is goin' around," he said.

"I know. In the pharmacy, too. Do you have P.O. for me to sign?" she asked.

"Over here," said Mike.

Carrie Ann entered Mike's cage, and they traded paperwork, including her signature on the shipping receipt that went on the top of a stack of receipts on Mike's workbench. Mike pointed her to the narcotics pallet, and she rolled her cart over to it.

Carrie Ann cut the plastic wrap with a box cutter, and loaded all of the brown boxes onto her cart, then took the service elevator down to the basement, pushing her cart through the white hallways for a quarter mile until she reached the intersection for the cafeteria. She pushed the cart to the side of the hallway to rest against the wall while she entered the cafeteria to get a snack. It was long past her break and she was starving. She hurried through the hot food section, getting a to-go container of breakfast food and a cup of coffee.

As Carrie Ann chatted with the cafeteria staff, the door for central supplies swung open next to her abandoned Fentanyl cart, and an employee pushed a metal cart with sterilized surgical trays through the opening, colliding with the Fentanyl cart. The top box of ampules teetered on the edge but didn't fall to the tile floor. The central supplies employee stopped and grabbed it, repositioning it atop the cart again. He cursed, pushing his cart by the Fentanyl cart, heading to the elevator so he could deliver the sterile trays to the operating room. After he pushed the elevator button, he thought better of leaving the Fentanyl cart in the hallway for someone else to hit, so he left his surgical tray cart for a second and returned to open the double door to central supplies, intending to push the Fentanyl cart back in, figuring it belonged there.

At that moment, Carrie Ann came out of the cafeteria with her food and coffee.

"Hey wait a minute. That's my cart," she said.

"Why did you leave it in the middle of the hallway? I ran into it!" he said.

"I just made a quick pit stop for food. I pushed it up against the wall," she said.

"Well, I hit it when I came through the doors with my cart," he said.

"Oh, sorry," said Carrie Ann.

"Yeah. No problem."

Carrie Ann put her food on top of the boxes, and sipped her coffee as she pushed her cart the remainder of the way to the pharmacy.

When Carrie Ann reached the pharmacy door, she swiped her badge, and the door clicked so she could open it, wheeling her cart into the receiving area. She brought the shipping receipt over to the computer and typed in the information, specifically the quantity so the hospital inventory could be electronically updated. She sat on a stool and set her food on the counter, deciding now was as good a time as any to eat as she watched the bustle around her.

After her snack, Carrie Ann unloaded the Fentanyl, counted the white boxes, and verified their amounts with the shipping receipt.

She moved the individual boxes into the secure storage area where there was a large safe with a computer entry system called a C2 machine. The C2 simply stood for schedule II controlled substances.

Carrie Ann scanned her I.D. badge and entered the information for the Fentanyl ampules into the computer to update the C2 machine inventory system. While she was standing in front of the C2 machine, she was on the inside of a piece of red duct tape on the floor that marked a square around the machine. For safety purposes, people were not allowed to talk to an employee who was on the inside of the red tape at the machine, because distraction might cause an error not only in the selection of the drug, but also in the amount removed.

Carrie Ann removed all of the Fentanyl ampules from the boxes, storing each individual ampule in its correct plastic bin in the C2 machine. She completed her shipment, logged out of the computer, grabbed all the boxes, and brought them over to the recycling bin to toss. As she tossed them, she noted the Customs stickers on them from both Thailand and the United States. That's kinda cool, she thought.

***

The next day, the electronic inventory system in the pharmacy indicated that the Pyxis machine in the Post Anesthesia Care Unit ("PACU"), which was in the same area of the hospital as the operating rooms, was low on Fentanyl medication, so a pharmacy tech had to bring more up to the machine and stock it. The Pyxis machine was about the size of an ATM, with a computer for scanning and entering the medication and dose, and locked drawers that only opened when proper access was gained.

Carrie Ann was tasked with bringing Fentanyl ampules from the pharmacy C2 machine up to the PACU Pyxis machine for restocking. She retrieved six Fentanyl ampules that she had loaded into the C2 machine the previous day, and put them in a plastic transport box.

She walked up the stairs to the PACU and swiped her badge to enter. Once inside, she scanned her badge at the Pyxis machine, entered her password into the computer, and typed in the amount of individual ampules that she was restocking. A drawer popped open, and a plastic lid automatically lifted to reveal an empty tray for the ampules to be stored. She opened the lid on her plastic transport box, transferring the ampules into the Pyxis tray, then firmly closed the drawer. She logged off the computer and returned to the pharmacy. The ampules were now ready to be used by any nurse who was ordered to administer Fentanyl to a patient in the PACU, which was where patients awoke after surgeries.

***

Thirty feet away from the PACU, and behind a double set of metal doors with a red sign on them that said "STOP - Proper attire must be worn beyond this point," Dr. Bill McCallan completed his third orthopedic surgery for the day, a hip replacement. After Bill finished talking to the husband of his patient, he went into the perioperative suite and dictated his operative note. Then, he went to the surgeon's locker room and shed his scrubs, took a shower, and changed into street clothes. He took his cell phone from the top shelf in his locker and noticed Pepper had texted him while he had been in surgery.

Hi Honey. Brent and I r going to Sweden. Leave tmrw. Luv u.

Bill thought about the message for a moment. He hoped she wasn't following up on that Swedish pharmacy intern thing. He thought she was barking up the wrong tree on that suspicion.

Luv u too. Dinner tonight w parents. Daisy is good. Stay safe.

He was ambivalent about this new job of hers. He missed her.

***

Meanwhile, at a warehouse located on 6th Avenue and North Washington Street in downtown Minneapolis, a bored Swedish twenty-something waited for a pharmaceutical shipment of Fentanyl ampules in vain. There was nothing for him to do except surf social media on the laptop that Svea Lovgren had purchased for his assignment. He finally decided to send an email to his boss. He hated to disappoint her, but several days had passed and she deserved to know.

Svea,

I have been waiting for deliveries but nothing has arrived. What do you want me to do?

Johann.

His answer came about three hours later.

Johann,

Stay put.

Svea.

Johann knew there wouldn't be any more deliveries after 5 p.m. that day, so he put on his leather jacket, stuffed the laptop into his man bag, and slung it over his chest crosswise. He walked the short distance to Cuzzy's Bar on 5th and Washington. Hopefully, he'd find an American hookup after he stuffed himself with a burger and fries. It was only a two-block walk from Cuzzy's to Target Field, which was part of Svea's original plan.

***

CHAPTER 22
Volkov's Drone Team

Krasnoyarsk, Siberia, Russia

It was a beautiful fall day, warmer than average, at 51 degrees Fahrenheit in the subarctic zone at the 56th parallel in the center of the great land mass known as Siberia. Since 2013, the region had been setting temperature, wild fire and carbon emission records from thawing permafrost. Global climate change was evident in Russia, even to a Tea Party Republican.

Krasnoyarsk, the third largest city in Siberia, was accessible by the Trans-Siberian railway, which is how the group of 12 young soldiers in Volkov's army had arrived. The young men were several miles outside the city and its suburbs, which had a population of about a million people. They were on the edge of the Stolby Nature Reserve, which featured giant granite rock formations over 300 feet high. The granite rose from the mountains of the southern bank of the Yenisei River, and were a popular attraction for adventurous young people.

The most popular granite formation was known as The Feathers, because it looked like upright feathers, not unlike turkey feathers stuck into the ground. It was an ideal destination for Russian hotshots called solo climbers to show off their skills by climbing without ropes. In fact, there was a bronze plaque placed in the granite at the base of The

Feathers to memorialize the solo climbers who had died here. The first Feather rock was 162 feet tall.

Many of the city people from Krasnoyarsk came to the Stolby Nature Reserve for the weekend to walk in the wilderness and breathe the fresh air. The kids savored the sense of freedom that climbing the granite cliffs gave them, reaching the peaks, where they were even with the tops of the pine trees. The views were spectacular from the top, overlooking the river valley below. They frequently videotaped themselves, posting their videos on YouTube.

The rock formations also provided obstacles for Volkov's soldiers to use for practicing their drone flying skills. They didn't know where they'd ultimately have to fly the drones on their secret mission, but they knew there'd be obstacles involved, so they swooped in and around the rock formations, only occasionally smashing into the granite. While crashing a drone was frowned upon by their Army General Commander, the soldiers were well-supplied with a few drones to spare.

After practicing with the drones, some of the young soldiers would test their rock climbing skills on the granite formations, going solo themselves. They were getting bored flying drones, having been at it for two weeks already. The climbing was a healthy outlet, much preferred to drinking vodka from their commander's perspective.

The soldiers were practicing with a new class of quadcopter drones that had transmitters on a large wrist band that fit on the operator's arm. When the operator flexed his forearm and moved his arm up, the drone moved up. When he moved his arm to the right, the drone moved to the right, etcetera. Wearing a wrist band instead of holding a transmitter freed up the operator's hands from having to use joysticks. This enabled the operator to watch the live video feed on the iPad that Volkov had issued to each of them, holding the iPad in the opposite hand as the wrist band was worn.

This technology had been piloted in Silicon Valley, but Volkov's tech department had stolen it through cyber warfare and improved it to the operational level for the soldiers to use on their upcoming mission.

They also were practicing with the small canister that each drone had to carry. They filled them with water to approximate the weight of 1.5 pounds per drone. They were experiencing slipping problems with the plastic canisters, and had remedied that by taping the canisters to the drone talons with duct tape. The tape was light enough not to compromise the drone's ability to fly, even to sore quickly to over 100 feet, which is what they were told would be needed.

Their flight plan involved an explosive take off to 100 feet, then running several laps around a 15-acre air space at three different elevations, without running into one another. With 12 drones, the plan was to fly a formation of four drones at three elevations, one about

30 seconds behind the other in a clockwise motion. They were to continue the laps for at least five minutes, or until they had circled the airspace twice. They had mastered the flying formation in a matter of days.

Volkov had promised the group's commander, an Army General in the Russian Army, that Volkov would visit the soldiers to check on their progress. The General was the second highest rank in the Russian Army, the Marshal being the highest. Of course, President Volkov was the Supreme Commander-in-Chief of the Armed Forces of the Russian Federation, a role he cherished over any other title he held.

The twelve-man drone team was standing around debriefing their afternoon flying session when the Army General heard the unmistakable sound of a Russian Ka-52 double engine attack helicopter. There was no tail rotor in the newly designed helicopter. Rather, it had a double coaxial rotor, or two blades mounted one on top of the other. The sound was uniquely thundering. Two of them were deafening. The two Ka-52s flanked the Hip, Volkov's helicopter. The Hip wasn't as capable as Marine One, but with a Ka-52 on each side, Volkov was well-protected.

Volkov exited the helicopter once it had landed, and walked with full command authority to the group. The Army General saluted him, as did the soldiers. Volkov returned their salute, ordering them to stand at ease.

"These are the drones?" asked Volkov. He surveyed them on the ground.

"Yes, sir," replied the General.

"How is the team doing?" asked Volkov.

"They've mastered their training exercises, sir," said the General.

Volkov started walking among the drones, inspecting them. The duct tape was visible.

He pointed to the duct tape with his toe. "What is this?"

"We had trouble with the drone talons holding the canisters, sir. We improvised with duct tape, and discovered it secured the canister nicely and didn't affect the aerial acrobatics."

"I see. I'd like to see the full demonstration now," ordered Volkov.

"Very well," said the General.

The General ordered the twelve soldiers to put their transmitting wristbands back on and power up the drones. Each of the drones still had a canister full of water taped to it.

On the General's command, the first set of three drones exploded into the air, going 100 feet up, and flew north about 100 yards. Then, they assumed a clockwise flight pattern about 15 acres in diameter. Each drone was at a different elevation, in a tiered formation. Thirty seconds later, the second set of three drones flew up and did the same thing, taking up a rear position, followed by the third, and finally, the fourth set. They flew in formation for five minutes, going around the 15-acre diameter twice. It was a fast trip. One by one, they flew back to the operators, and landed safely on the ground.

Volkov applauded their work, allowing a rare smile. He spontaneously shook each soldier's hand.

When he had finished saying "well done" to the last soldier, he told the General that they could scale back the 15-acre diameter to just five acres for their future drills. He said they'd have to adapt to the size of their target when they received more information.

"We'll continue practicing, sir," promised the General.

"You have two more days, General. Then be ready for pick up and transport with the drones. During air transport, the soldiers will be provided with more information and planning."

"Yes, sir."

"Good work, General. You will be rewarded for your efforts," said Volkov.

They saluted, and Volkov walked to his Hip and got in. Volkov flew off as loudly as he had flown in. The soldiers had to hold the drones on the ground so they weren't blown around from the heavy rotor wash.

***

CHAPTER 23

Thai Harbor Master

Bangkok, Thailand

Pu Yai Bahn meant big man about town in Thai. And tonight, the Harbor Master for the Old Bangkok Port was indeed the big man about town. It was his 50th birthday, and a small group of captains and dock workers had insisted on taking him out for drinks.

He was a worn man, having labored hard on the docks since the age of 12, then at sea for 20 years, and now back on the docks as the Harbor Master. The miles and sweat were reflected in his wrinkled skin and rolled shoulders. But his skinny body was still wiry and fit.

He had grey unwashed hair and a few missing teeth, which meant he looked like every other Thai captain. His piercing brown eyes missed nothing, radiating energy and intellect. He was sharper than the other captains, which is why he had risen through the ranks to become Harbor Master.

He wore his trademark blue polyester stocking cap that he folded above his ears, so his unkempt hair popped out around the edges. The stocking cap was a throwback to his fishing boat days when he was a crew member of a shrimper, and later the captain of a cargo boat that ran a route down to Singapore and back. He wore navy blue chinos, a western style dress shirt, and a windbreaker with grease stains on it.

In his office job of eight years, he had a reputation for being competent and conservative. Unlike many Harbor Masters, he didn't insist on exorbitant bribes, just reasonable amounts to run his operation. He was paid a small wage by the Port Authority, but his superiors assumed he would exact bribes from the cargo carriers to make ends meet. It was a common industry practice. Pu Yai was clean-shaven most days, but tonight he had uneven bits of stubble around his jaw due to the late hour.

He and the boys were at their favorite watering hole down the street from the dockyard. They all referred to it as Captain's, because the bar owner was a retired tugboat captain. Pu Yai liked this bar, and had encouraged his old friend to buy it due to its ornate carvings of ships, mermaids and anchors in the antique wood above the bar.

There weren't any flashy neon signs or dancers in this bar. The tourist scene was up the street, clustered around the hotels, far away from the docks and slums. The port had become overrun with hookers and drug dealers that the hard working dock laborers avoided. First, the dock workers couldn't afford hookers. Second, they couldn't afford the antibiotics they'd need to treat the sexually transmitted diseases they'd pick up from the hookers. Pu Yai had a wife and six children. He didn't have the time or energy to become involved with hookers or drugs.

The celebrating men drank late into the night, both rice whiskey shots and Pu Yai's favorite lager, Singha. It was well past midnight when Pu Yai pushed back from the table, announcing he had to leave. He yelled goodbyes through the revelry, accepting more slaps on the back, then he left alone, stumbling down the street toward the dockyard. He decided not to go home because he might wake his wife and children, some of whom might be sleeping with her. Through his drunken fog, he decided it would be better if he stumbled back to his office, and slept on the small sofa covered in office junk.

The yard was still limping along with men going about their work when he returned. They ignored Pu Yai as he walked toward his Harbor Master office. When he was about 20 feet from his office, he noticed a light move through the office window. It came from within, and looked like a small flashlight.

Pu Yai figured that someone was in his office rummaging for money or valuables. Slums surrounded the port, so he wasn't surprised. The workers kicked kids out of the boatyard on a daily basis. Just in case the intruder was someone larger than a hungry kid, Pu Yai looked around for something to use as a weapon. He grabbed an iron bar from a junk heap, and walked up the wooden steps to his office door.

He felt a rush of adrenaline as he turned the door knob. He held the iron bar above his head, more to threaten the kid than anything.

The door swung wide and Pu Yai stepped inside the dark office. He felt a searing pain to his right elbow, and heard a cracking sound. His right arm fell limp to his side.

Being a scrappy deckhand for years, Pu Yai knew how to fight. He disregarded the pain and spun on his right front toe, raising his left hand toward the attacker. His fingers found the attacker's throat, and he squeezed hard. He could hear the attacker gasping for air when he felt a blow to his left chest. There was a sharp popping sound, just one, but it was enough to incapacitate him.

Pu Yai went limp immediately as his heart pumped its last beats. Blood began oozing out of his chest wound as he fell face-first onto the floor.

The attacker shoved his gun in his waistband, closed the office door and dragged Pu Yai's body into the corner. Then, he stuffed the shipping manifests he was tasked to retrieve into his waistband, stepped over Pu Yai's body, and quietly shut the door behind him.

Once outside, the attacker shook off his nerves and readjusted his shabby sweatshirt. He pulled his worn baseball cap low and walked off casually, not too fast, not too slow. He exited the dockyard without anyone noticing him. When he was well away from the dockyard lights, he removed his 9 millimeter Beretta with the silencer on it from his waistband, and chucked it into the Chao Phraya River. He rolled off his latex gloves, put a small rock in each of them and threw those into the river as well.

He walked for at least 30 minutes through the run-down Khlong Toei District to his hotel, The Imperial Queen's Park Hotel. He had checked in 24 hours earlier under the name of Hugo von Ruden, which matched his Swedish passport. Once Hugo was in his room, he shed his clothes and showered, washing out the temporary black hair dye he had put in before he left Stockholm.

He had only a few hours before he had to be at the airport for his flight back to Stockholm, with a layover in Frankfurt. It was a grueling 15 hours of plane travel, but he was being compensated well. He'd have to meet with Svea in person tomorrow to explain what had happened.

While he had managed to retrieve the shipping manifests she sought, he hadn't intended on killing anyone. The death would be a wrinkle he hoped didn't cause her too much complication. After all, who would care about a Bangkok Port dock worker? He had killed men with higher profiles and never been apprehended, or even suspected. Hugo felt lucky that a stream of workers hadn't followed their buddy into the office to back him up.

Svea would understand the predicament in which he had found himself, being attacked in the dark. He reacted out of instinct more than anything else. If he hadn't killed the dock worker, he would have risked exposing his true identity and relationship to Svea.

***

"What the fuck were you thinking, Hugo?!" Svea was beside herself with anger at Hugo for killing the Harbor Master.

They were having drinks at the Trattorian Italian bar and restaurant on the waterfront of the Riddarfjärden, not far from her apartment building.

It was a trendy place that was overrun with beautiful young professionals at happy hour. There was scarcely a place to squeeze in two people, every inch of the establishment being crammed with eclectic furnishings. Svea and Hugo were huddled in a corner, sitting low in wicker chairs with a candle resting on the coffee table between them. They were speaking in hushed voices, and there was plenty of noise among the crowd to cover their conversation. She was sipping a Cosmopolitan and he was guzzling a Carlsberg beer.

"Jesus, Svea. Cut me a break. He had his hand around my throat and was going to kill me if I didn't kill him. Was I supposed to die for you in Thailand?" he asked.

"No, of course not, Hugo," she said. "It's just that I didn't think he'd end up dead, you know? That will result in an investigation by the police. People will start asking questions."

"It's Bangkok. Nasty shit happens there all the time, and it takes weeks for the police to follow up on it. I made a mess of the office so I'm sure they'll assume it was a robbery in progress," he said.

"I hope so. Don't get me wrong. I value your work. You know that. Thank you for retrieving the shipping manifest. Let's drink to your successful trip." She raised her glass and they clinked.

Svea decided it was best to depart Hugo's company before she was recognized by someone in the packed bar. She thanked him again, and walked out into the chilly evening air. The river was still flowing without ice on it, and there were people strolling along the bike path. The hearty Swedes would be outdoors running and biking until the snow prevented them from doing so.

Despite the snag with Hugo's mission, her project was reaching its final stages, and the end was in sight. She needed to double-check logistics with Volkov, and time the operations with her Swedish interns. Communication was the key at this point. She might be able to use Dana and Clive to help.

Rather than return to her apartment, she hailed a taxi and instructed him to bring her to Hotel Diplomat. She had walked to the Trattorian so as not to draw attention to herself in her government car.

On the taxi ride, she could feel affection stirring in the bottom of her stomach as she drew closer to Dana's hotel. Svea couldn't believe the feelings she had for Dana, having never experienced them for a man. She didn't know whether she was in love or in lust. She paid the taxi driver, and went up to the top floor suite, where Volkov was paying for them to stay.

She knocked, and Clive answered the door. He welcomed her with a kiss.

"Svea, how nice of you to drop by. Would you like some hot tea? It's a chilly night out," he said.

"Maybe later. Is Dana here?" she asked.

"Yes, she's in the shower at the moment," he said.

"Perfect. A hot shower would feel good." Svea patted him on the shoulder, and walked in the direction of Dana's bathroom.

***

CHAPTER 24
Stockholm University

Stockholm, Sweden

Brent and Pepper's plane touched down at Arlanda Airport in Stockholm, Sweden. It was nighttime and Pepper was exhausted. They cleared Customs and went to their waiting car, a Saab four-door driven by a U.S. Counterterrorism Field Agent who was their local contact, Mr. Louis Brown. Pepper smiled at Brent.

"Now you'll get to experience firsthand the inferiority of a Saab," he said.

"Unlike some people I know, I have an open mind," she replied.

"They're not too bad. I'm Louis Brown, your host while you're here."

"I'm Brent Cahill and this is Pepper McCallan. Nice to meet you."

They all shook hands and Brent volunteered to sit in the back, offering Pepper the front passenger seat.

Louis told them it would be a 40-minute drive to Hotel Clarion Amaranten, where they were staying. It was dark, so they wouldn't get to appreciate the wooded view on the drive into Stockholm.

"Thank you for picking us up, Louis. How long have you lived here?" asked Pepper.

"Two years. It's very relaxing compared to my previous overseas assignments," he said

Pepper studied Louis' profile while he drove. He had handsome silver hair with a stylish cut. He wore trendy spectacles and had a clean shaven face. She could tell he exercised regularly because his skin and face looked healthy. He had olive-colored skin with a beautiful complexion, and was a good looking man in his mid-sixties.

As soon as they were on the highway, Brent turned on his cell phone. It blew up with text and phone messages. He had an international cellular plan, so he got texts and phone calls wherever he was in the world.

"What's going on back there?" asked Pepper.

"Weng Chee has been trying to get ahold of me. I'll call him back and see what the issue is," said Brent.

Brent dialed the field agent in Bangkok.

"Weng Chee speaking."

"Weng, it's Brent Cahill. How are things?"

"Not good. I went back to visit the Harbor Master, Pu Yai Bahn, and he had been murdered the night before," said Weng.

"Murdered? How do you know?" asked Brent.

"The dock workers told me. He celebrated his 50th birthday out drinking with his friends, then returned to his office after midnight. He was shot in the chest and left to die on his office floor," said Weng.

"Do you think he interrupted a robbery?" asked Brent.

"Doubt it. The police tell me it was a point blank shot to the chest. No one heard anything so a silencer must have been used. They don't have those in the slums around here. Looks professional to me," said Weng.

"Ballistics?" asked Brent.

"This is Thailand. It could take weeks," said Weng.

"Did you get the shipping manifests?" asked Brent.

"That's the other thing. The murderer rifled through the papers on the Harbor Master's desk, and stole the manifests for the dates you mentioned. The police let me search his office after I explained this could be part of an international nerve gas shipment. I looked through all the papers, and the only ones missing were the date ranges you and I discussed. Gone," said Weng.

"You know what this means," said Brent.

"Yes. First, we probably have an international shipment of nerve gas. Second, I have to find some other way of getting the information. I spoke to the dock workers, and they told me that Thai Cargo Shipping handles most of the freight out of here, especially refrigerated cargo. I plan to follow up with Thai Cargo later today," said Weng.

"Thank you," said Brent. "I think you're right. If someone got murdered over shipping manifests, we must be dealing with a nerve gas shipment. I'm thinking the Harbor Master must have surprised whoever was looking for the manifests, and he got shot. Is there any video footage?"

"Ha. No. It's not like in America. There are no security cameras here," said Weng.

"Okay, I thought I'd try. Thanks for all your work, Weng. Keep me apprised," said Brent.

"Will do. Bye," said Weng.

"Bye."

Brent ended the call.

"Is that what it sounded like? The Thai Harbor Master was murdered?" asked Pepper.

"Yes. This is significant. In my mind, it confirms that nerve gas was shipped out of Bangkok by sea or air to another destination. Or by both. Or maybe to more than one destination. Weng will check with Thai Cargo Shipping Company to see what he can find out. It's a long shot but we need him to continue trying," said Brent.

"Should we tell Allen?" asked Pepper.

"Yes. I'm going to send him an email right now," said Brent.

Brent emailed Allen about Pu Yai Bahn's death, and his working theory that Russian-manufactured nerve gas actually made it through Bangkok Port in Thailand, and was shipped by sea or air, or both, to unknown further destinations.

Allen told Brent he'd devote additional resources to help Weng Chee get information directly from Thai Cargo Shipping. He'd bring Marty Cavanaugh, the Deputy Director, up to speed and ask him to assist Brent.

Louis brought them to the front entrance of the Amaranten on Kungsholmsgatan Street. It was located in a mixed residential and restaurant district, only six blocks from the waterfront. It was a nice hotel, but not a luxury property, since the government was picking up the tab. Ironically, it was only a block from Svea's apartment building, but neither Brent nor Pepper knew that. Many of the government officials and high society lived in the area. Louis accompanied them into the lobby and waited until they were checked in.

Since it was late, Pepper and Brent said goodbye to Louis, and Pepper went to her room. She connected to WIFI and emailed Bill to tell him how much she loved him. It was close to 6 p.m. in Minneapolis, so she got a reply right away.

He missed her, too, saying the house was lonely without her. She felt the heaviness of being lonely as well, which made her vulnerable to grief. It sounded like it was the same for Bill. It used to be that when they worked hard, they'd just be tired and grumpy at the end of the day. Now, after a long day, they were tired, grumpy and sad. The sadness baseline was always present but it seemed to spike with sleep deprivation, separation from each other or exhaustion. Or all three, which is what she was experiencing now.

Pepper brushed her teeth and put on one of Bill's extra-large t-shirts to sleep in. She thought about their lives a year ago. She never would have dreamed she'd be in Sweden on assignment with a new colleague she barely knew.

Their family life had been so perfect. Jake was the apple of their eyes, and they had been so consumed with attending his ball games and piano recitals. Their social life had been built around Jake's activities, and being with the families who likewise had children in those activities. It had all came to an abrupt halt after Jake had died. Her identity was no longer Jake's mom. She had to reinvent herself, resurrecting what she had been like before she had had a child.

She had loved being Jake's mom. She wanted that back. She wanted to hug him, serve him breakfast, wash his clothes, tuck him in at night and watch him throw pitches. When Jake's face lit up with excitement, her world had been complete. Now, she didn't have any idea what would make her world complete. It felt empty and directionless. At least Brent presented her with important problems to solve – find the terrorist before he kills people. It seemed so easy compared to the confusing world of loss, and living a meaningful life after loss.

Unfortunately, Pepper didn't have the mental capacity to process her new set of problems like she used to at Futuraceutical. She used to mull them over. Sleep on them. Let her subconscious do some of the heavy lifting. Now, she was distracted by grief - processing that her son had left Earth for Heaven.

She felt like she couldn't concentrate on solving a problem unless she was talking to someone about it. Verbally processing it. After lying awake for several hours in her hotel room, crying, feeling lonely and thinking,

Pepper finally drifted off. It was an unrestful sleep, filled with dreams about nerve gas attacks and Brent fighting a shadowy figure who was pointing a gun at them. Somewhere in there, there was an explosion like she had experienced at the Lyceum Theatre in London where Jake had died. It was a miserable nightmarish scene, similar to the reality she had experienced.

She was actually relieved when her phone rang with the wakeup call at seven. She was scheduled to meet Brent and Louis Brown in the lobby at eight for breakfast and investigative planning. She showered and did the best she could with the newly formed dark circles under her eyes. A light layer of makeup helped.

She pulled on a soft amber cashmere sweater and some grey dress slacks. Black boots that insulated her from the nippy Swedish October air completed her outfit.

She joined the men, who were having coffee but waiting for her before they went through the buffet line. They both stood when she arrived.

Brent gave her a reassuring smile in his lopsided kind of way, and Louis made easy conversation with them both. Brent asked Louis how he had ended up in Stockholm, and Louis indicated he had requested it because he considered it a plum assignment.

Louis had worked in the CIA for over twenty years, serving in the Middle East and India, where he had engaged in both spying and diplomacy. He was as experienced as they came. This was his reward for many years of service, an easy assignment in Sweden before official retirement from the government. Sweden was considered a low activity destination by any measure, and there was little, if any, movement of terrorists through it. Louis was a softspoken gentleman, and Pepper liked him immediately.

"The biggest excitement we've had around here is over Russian submarines," said Louis.

"Really. Volkov has set his sights on Sweden?" asked Pepper.

"I doubt it. But Sweden is obsessed with worrying about a Russian invasion. A few years ago, a Swedish fisherman thought he spotted a Russian submarine in the bay, about five miles from the coast. That got everyone's attention!" said Louis.

"Really? Do you think it was true?" asked Pepper.

"Yes, even though the Swedish military couldn't confirm it after extensive searching. They've had strained relations with Russia for years so it's likely that it happened," he said.

"But it's unconfirmed," said Pepper.

"It was. About a year later, though, a salvage crew pulled the wreckage of a Russian sub from the bay," said Louis

"No kidding! I didn't hear about that!" said Brent.

"That's because the sub was over a hundred years old," said Louis. "It was vintage 1916, but still fueled the paranoia that Russia is poised to attack at any moment. Of course, Volkov hasn't done anything to allay Sweden's fears. He just keeps doing bigger and crazier things. There's more attention in the Swedish media now on being wary of strangers because they might be 'sophisticated Russian spies.' That's nonsense, of course. I've never met a sophisticated Russian!" Louis laughed at his own joke.

Pepper laughed too. Mostly because the comment had tickled Louis so much.

"I suppose it's appropriate for Sweden to take Russia seriously as a threat. Sweden is largely a pacifist country filled with beautiful people who are consumed with themselves," said Louis. "But Russia wants the military stronghold around the Baltic, so Sweden can't afford to be complacent. Over the last few years, Sweden has increased her defense budget and refurbished her navy and radar capabilities."

"Probably a good idea anyway, but we all know it won't be enough," said Brent.

"There is the 'peaceful route,' which some Swedes insist will work," said Louis.

"What's that?" asked Pepper.

"A few years ago, a group of pacifists made a sign of a gay man, and lowered it into the bay where they thought a Russian sub would enter," Louis explained. "It has the capability to send out Morse code signals, and the message it's currently sending is: 'Welcome to Sweden. Gay since 1944.'"

"What the hell?! I don't get it," said Brent.

"The pacifists think it will send the Russians running because they're homophobes," said Louis.

"That's just wishful thinking. Volkov will probably launch a missile strike on Sweden because he considers them weak and in need of being conquered for that hair-brained idea!" said Pepper. "It's too ridiculous to be true. First the dig on the Arabs, and now attempting to scare off Russian by proclaiming they embrace LGBT?"

"They're an opinionated culture, that's for certain," said Louis.

After they'd eaten a good portion of their breakfast, Louis inquired, "where would you like to go today, Brent?"

"We need to visit Stockholm University," he said.

"It's a sizeable campus. Any special building or department?" asked Louis.

"Yes. The student registrar. I need to see if three students are currently enrolled in pharmacy programs that provide internships in the United States," said Brent.

"I see. We can leave as soon as you like," said Louis.

They emerged from the hotel onto the street where Louis' Saab was parked. Pepper looked around the neighborhood, and immediately was drawn to a flatiron building to her right. They were her favorite architecture, so she had to take a few pics.

"Hey guys, do we have five minutes for me to walk a block and scope out that flatiron building?" she asked.

"What?" asked Brent.

"They're my favorite architecture, and this one is so beautiful. It will only take a minute," she said.

"Oh, Stockholm is filled with wedge-shaped buildings," said Louis. "I didn't know you were an architectural buff."

"I'm not actually. I just like these buildings." As they approached it, Pepper took out her cell phone and took some pics.

The building was made of sandstone, and had a sizeable circular front, reminiscent of a domed turret, with circular rooms that opened onto 180 degree balconies, black wrought-iron railings matching the black slate roof. The wooden doors onto the turreted balconies were dark mahogany with old fashioned transoms. Unbeknown to the group, Svea Lovgren occupied a penthouse apartment of the building.

Brent looked at his watch, and Pepper turned around and walked back to Louis' car. They all piled in. During the drive to the University, Louis gave Pepper a quick history lesson on the ancient architecture of Stockholm, including Old Town. Stockholm had been spared the widespread destruction suffered by Europe during both World Wars, so her 500-year-old buildings were still in relatively good shape.

***

Louis spoke excellent Swedish, so he was a huge help when they arrived to the Registrars' Office at the University. Louis introduced Brent immediately, who displayed his credentials and a letter from the U.S. Embassy requesting cooperation in confirming the student registration of three individuals: Felipe Malstrom (currently at Philadelphia General Hospital); Valter Nylund (currently at Southview Hospital in Minneapolis); and Max Björnsson (currently at Cedarbrook Hospital in Los Angeles).

The receptionist took the names with the letter, and disappeared down a hallway to their right. She came back all smiles, holding three newly printed sheets of paper.

"Yes, all three of these students are currently registered at the University, but they each are taking a trimester off. We run on trimesters and they all appear to be gone. They're senior students, so we assume they are either doing internships or working. They all three have indicated they will return next trimester."

She handed the printouts to Louis. Louis was all smiles in return, and politely asked her if they had a department that coordinated internships. She gave him directions. He kindly requested her to call the department in advance of their arrival, requesting cooperation. She said she would.

"Hmm. Good for them that they're enrolled in the University," said Pepper.

"Now, let's see if they're doing University-sponsored internships," said Brent.

Louis led them outside, and read the Swedish signs that brought them to the next building, which he indicated housed the career planning and internship services.

As promised, the Registrar receptionist had called ahead, so they were met by a friendly person who already had the three names of the students. She said that none of them had arranged for internships through the University office.

Louis asked if there was some other association they might have used. She indicated that she didn't know of any, and that 99.9% of the students who wanted an internship arranged it through the University office.

Brent dug around in his beat-up satchel, producing a letter on University letterhead from the "Stockholm University Pharmacy Department" to the Philadelphia General Hospital Pharmacy Department Manager, setting up an internship for Felipe Malstrom.

The lady looked at it quizzically, and said she would call over to the Pharmacy Department and ask if they had arranged for it themselves. She returned with a troubled look on her face. She said she had spoken directly to the Department Chair, whose name was at the bottom of the letter, and he confirmed he definitely had NOT arranged for any pharmacy internships in the United States.

Louis turned to Brent for direction.

"We need to go see the Pharmacy Department Chair in person. Can you get directions?" asked Brent.

Louis worked his charm, and they were off to the Pharmacy Department. Their worst suspicions were confirmed fifteen minutes later. Brent showed the Department Chair all three letters, and he denied writing any of them. They were forged. The Chair wanted to contact each of the hospitals, but Brent told him he'd take care of it because it was a sensitive matter. He also told him the students needed to be interviewed before they left America.

The Chair indicated he also wanted to call the Stockholm University Dean to expel the students, but Brent asked him to hold on that action due to a police investigation. The Chair reluctantly agreed.

They all thanked the Chair, and departed his building into the crisp fall air. Pepper noticed what a beautiful campus Stockholm University was as they walked across the quadrangle.

As they were piling into Louis' Saab, Brent glanced to his left at a young couple getting into the back seat of a grey Toyota. They were only about a block away. The woman looked like the tan woman in a white dress he had seen at the French restaurant in St. Martin. He never forgot a face, especially when it was attached to a body like hers. He knew he was right when he saw she was with the same man with the slicked black hair.

"Excuse me for a minute. I'll catch up to you," said Brent. He sprinted down the sidewalk toward their car, but they slammed their doors and sped off. He missed them by twenty seconds. Who were they? Why did he keep running into them? Were they following him? There had to be some connection. It couldn't have been coincidence.

Brent walked back to Louis' car.

"What was that all about?" asked Pepper.

"I recognized that couple. I saw them in St. Martin and now they turned up here. Something isn't right," he said.

"Do you think they're following you?" she asked.

"Maybe. Or I'm following them, and I don't realize it," he said.

"I'll keep a lookout for them as well," said Pepper.

***

CHAPTER 25

L.A. Child

Los Angeles, California

It was Saturday and Kennisha Turner had the afternoon to herself. Her single-working mom kept Kennisha on a tight schedule of school, tennis lessons, basketball camps, piano lessons and girl scouts. This afternoon, however, she had some time to herself, and she was planning to get out of the house and explore her familiar neighborhood. Her mom was cleaning, so it was a good time to leave, or Kennisha would be recruited to help.

At the age of 12, she already made meals, packed lunches for her two brothers for school, and did the laundry. She didn't want to add cleaning toilets to her duties as well. She worked up the courage to tell her mom she was leaving the house.

"Mama, I'm goin' over to Jacy's to play outside," hollered Kennisha over the sound of the vacuum.

The vacuum turned off. This meant mom was giving Kennisha her full attention. "To Jacy's?"

"Yes, Mama."

"When are you gonna be back?" asked mom.

"Couple of hours?" suggested Kennisha.

"Okay. You got your new phone on you?" asked mom.

"Yes, Mama. I'll text you every hour like you told me to," said Kennisha.

"Good. You can go. Don't forget to text me, Sweet Baby," said mom.

"I won't. Love you," said Kennisha.

"Love you, too," said mom.

Kennisha burst through the back door, bounced down the steps, and skipped down the alley toward her best friend, Jacy's, house. It was only a block away. She watched for traffic at the cross-street, then ran down the alley and hopped up the steps to Jacy's back door. She knocked. Jacy's gorgeous older brother answered the door. He was in high school.

"What do you want?" he asked.

"Is Jacy home?" asked Kennisha.

"No." He had no time for cornrowed braids, innocent faces and flat chests.

"Oh. Where is she?" asked Kennisha.

"Don't know," he said.

"Oh. When is she gonna be back?" asked Kennisha.

"Don't know," he said.

"Will you tell her I came by?" asked Kennisha.

"If I remember," he said.

"Okay. Bye," said Kennisha.

"Bye," he said, and shut the door.

Kennisha was at a momentary loss for what to do. She kicked a Coke can across the alley, and continued walking because there was no way she was going home to get roped into cleaning. It was a pretty day, and she could see most people were out in their small back yards playing, grilling and chilling.

Some people had fences up in their yards, so she couldn't see what they were doing, but that just made her more curious, so she'd try to peak through slits or holes in the fence. She was very quiet, so they never knew she was there.

She and Jacy did it together when they were bored. They had their favorite fences in the neighborhood, with knotholes that were eye level and something entertaining to watch on the other side of the fence. Once, they saw a friend of Jacy's older brother making out with a girl. They watched them kissing for a good twenty minutes, covering up their giggles so they wouldn't get caught.

It felt good to walk and greet her neighbors so she kept going, waving to people and snooping on how they were spending their time. She pet the alley cats that rubbed up against her legs and followed her for a few feet. She didn't bother to keep track of how many blocks she had gone, but at least thirty minutes had passed.

The neighborhood transitioned from fewer houses to more storage units, empty garages and businesses. Not inviting businesses that were shops and cafes, but car transmission shops, parts stores and distribution centers.

Kennisha heard several men's voices behind an old wooden fence to her left. She and Jacy hadn't snooped through this fence before. She didn't recognize the language they were speaking, but there were obviously several of them. She stopped in the middle of the alley and listened for a few minutes. They were definitely grownups. They didn't sound like boys, and she couldn't hear any women's voices – just men's.

They weren't speaking Spanish because she had already taken a Spanish class, and she was familiar with some Mexican and Puerto Rican phrases from the neighborhood. They were talking in a harsh language that made the men sound angry when they spoke it. It was gruff, coming out in fits and grunts. It made her curious what they were going on about, and what they looked like, but the fence was much too tall for her to see over. She would find a way to see through it, like she always did.

Kennisha cautiously approached the fence, sensing this would not be one of her ordinary backyard snooping operations. As she quietly tiptoed through the weeds next to the fence, she searched for a knothole or crack large enough to see through. She located one but it was about six inches above her eye level. She needed something to stand on.

She searched the ground along the edge of the fence and alleyway for anything. She saw a broken milk crate on the other side of the alley, but when she picked it up, she could see it was pretty busted up. Maybe she could stand on the corner of it, balancing on just one foot.

She worked it into the weeds, careful not to let it knock the fence, and placed her left foot on the corner of it. It was a bit wobbly, but it held. She transferred her weight onto it, gently placing her palms on the fence to peer through the peep hole.

She was surprised at what she saw. There were three men who looked like they were homeless - scruffy beards, long hair and outdated jeans and shirts. But they weren't dirty like the homeless, just wearing really strange clothes. One of them had on a black captain's hat, which she had only seen in movies because nobody wore those. They were gathered around a drone on the ground and were arguing about how to connect something to it, a plastic thing that looked like a water bottle. They were so freaky that she decided to video them to show Jacy later.

Still balancing on the broken crate, she nimbly removed her cell phone from her right front pocket. First, she turned off the sound, then, like only a tween-age girl could do, she turned it on with one hand and clicked open the camera app, sliding it to video.

She held it up to the peephole and recorded for a full two minutes. Since she couldn't make any sense of what they were saying, and all they were doing was arguing about the water bottle, she decided it was time to leave. Besides, her left leg was getting tired. She clicked off her phone and stepped off the crate without making a peep. She sprang back into the alleyway as soft as a ballerina, and began walking back to her neighborhood.

Once she thought she was a safe distance away from the strange men, a few blocks at least, she pulled out her cell phone and watched the video. Jacy would be proud. Kennisha had been at a good angle to pick up the drone, water bottle and men. She could clearly hear everything they were saying. Maybe Jacy would know what language they were speaking. She was smart like that.

***

CHAPTER 26
The Royal Ball

Stockholm, Sweden

Louis, Brent and Pepper piled into Louis' Agency Saab and drove about thirty minutes to his office space. He had WIFI at his office, so Brent could send an encrypted email to Allen Montgomery right away. Once they were at Louis' offices, he showed them to a spare office, so Brent and Pepper could set up shop. They dropped their briefcases and opened their laptops.

Brent typed an email to Allen.

> Allen,
> Trouble. We confirmed that the 3 Swedish students who are interning at the hospitals in L.A., Mpls. and Philly are NOT on a University-sponsored internship program. The letters they sent to the hospitals were forged. Someone from the Agency needs to interview those interns ASAP.
> Brent

Allen must have been at his desk because he replied right away.

> Brent,
> Good work. Or should I say, Pepper, good work? I'll be in Philly on Sunday, so I'll interview the Philly intern myself on Monday morning. I'll task agents in

L.A. and Mpls. to interview the other two interns ASAP.

Allen

Any word on Thai Cargo Shipping from Marty Cavanaugh?

Not yet.

Thanks. Let me know when Marty learns something. Brent

"I sure would like to interview Svea Lovgren," said Brent.

"Yeah, me too. I have a feeling she's behind this Swedish intern business. What if it's linked to the nerve gas shipments?" asked Pepper.

"That's my concern, too," he said.

Louis appeared in the spare office door jam, and asked if he could be of service. Brent decided to read him in on all of their information because Louis was not only smart, but also had the highest Agency clearance. Maybe his years of experience would result in him pointing out some angles, thought Brent.

Louis pondered the intelligence they had gathered for a moment, and said, "I think you should meet Svea Lovgren."

"We'd love to, Louis, but under what pretense could we arrange a formal visit with her on such short notice?" asked Brent.

"Ah, the best kind. A social event to which I'm formally invited tonight. I'll have my assistant add your names to the invitee list as my guests," said Louis.

"What sort of social event," asked Pepper.

"It's called the Royal Colloquium Ball. King Felix XV Gustaf hosts it each October. It concludes a week of international scientists meeting in Stockholm to collaborate on a variety of international issues. It's pretty high profile, and I know for a fact that the Minister for Foreign Affairs, Ms. Svea Lovgren, will be in attendance," said Louis.

"That sounds pretty formal," said Pepper. "Where will it be held?"

"It'll be at the Royal Palace in Stockholm's Old Town. It has a modest sized ballroom that they decorate beautifully. It's black tie," said Louis.

"I take it 'black tie' means I need a tux?" asked Brent.

"Yes, indeed. Did you bring anything?" asked Louis.

"Of course not," said Brent.

"Then we need to go shopping, don't you think?" asked Louis.

"Sure. Pepper, are you up for this?" asked Brent.

"Oh yeah. We get to meet Svea Lovgren AND I get to go to a royal ball? All of my girl fantasies have come true," she said.

Louis brought them to an elite shopping district where he knew he could rent a tux for Brent and find a proper royal gala gown for Pepper. Louis could shuttle back and forth between the two shops, if needed. He suspected that Brent probably wouldn't have a good feel for elegance, so he would require Louis' trained eye.

First, Louis brought Pepper to an exclusive dress shop named Elaine's. Louis knew the proprietor would give him the Agency discount, so they didn't have to spend a fortune. He planned on using his Agency operational supplies budget for the expenditure for both the tux and gown. Truth be told, they barely used their budget in Sweden because the country was so dull. A demur woman in her fifties approached them, and she and Louis hugged and kissed. Pepper raised an eyebrow. Louis is a smooth operator, thought Pepper.

"Pepper, this is my wife, Barbara," he said by way of introduction.

"Oh, Barbara, it's my pleasure to meet you," said Pepper.

"I have to confess, I texted her in advance of our arrival, Pepper. She's ready to show you some gowns for this evening. Barbara will be attending with us, of course," said Louis.

"I'm so relieved. I thought it would be just another night out with the boys, and that gets so tiresome, you know," said Pepper.

"Follow me, Pepper. Louis, do you want to walk across the square and check in on your male colleague?" asked his wife.

"Yes, Dear. I can take a hint," he said.

"Pepper, with your height and lean lines, this should be easy. I'm guessing about a size 10, is that right?" asked Barbara.

"That's right," said Pepper. "I didn't bring any jewelry, shoes or a clutch with me either, so I'll need those, too."

"I have some things in mind," said Barbara.

Pepper exited the dressing room looking striking in a floor length royal-blue lace evening gown. It had a Juliet neckline with cap sleeves that accentuated her slim, yet shapely upper arms. The satin lining was also blue, so it added depth behind the lace pattern. The dress hugged Pepper's figure to the top of her thighs, where there was a small pleat over the left thigh that draped nicely to an irregular-cut hem, the left side falling just above the ankle, and the right tapering back to rest at her heels. It was easy to walk in, and swayed with her hips.

"This is your dress, dear," said Barbara with a wide grin.

"Are you sure? It's the first one I've tried on," exclaimed Pepper.

"Oh yes. There's no need to look further. We'll put you in black sandals. There's really no need for you to wear hose since your legs are so tan. Will you be okay with that?" asked Barbara.

"Ah, sure. If you tell me it meets social mores," said Pepper.

"I've attended a thousand of these over the years in several different countries," said Barbara. "You'll be stunning."

"I'll do whatever you think is best," said Pepper.

Barbara selected Swarovski butterfly teardrop earrings with delicate diamond studded wings on top, and a blue sapphire drop at the bottom for Pepper. They had a matching necklace with sapphires and diamonds, and the same butterfly pendant set in the center that fell to the top of the neckline of the dress. It radiated elegance. Since they were real diamonds, Elaine agreed to release them on loan for tonight's ball only. Barbara promised to bring them into work with her tomorrow morning.

The boys strolled into the shop a short while later to collect Pepper. Louis introduced Barbara to Brent. Barbara had the same reaction to Brent as most women. She was charmed. After Louis slapped down his Agency plastic on the counter to pay for the gown, Pepper hugged Barbara goodbye, and the two men walked with Pepper to the Saab.

Louis dropped Pepper and Brent off at their hotel, and told them he and Barbara would be back to collect them in a limousine at seven that evening.

Brent suggested the two of them meet in the lobby bar in twenty minutes to go over their plan. Once in her room, Pepper hung up her gown, texted Bill and called the hotel Salon to make a hair appointment for an updo later. She wanted a loose chignon du cou.

Pepper and Brent dined on a late lunch, going through a variety of conversational scenarios of how they would approach Svea. Brent would be wired for sound and video with a small lapel camera tucked into a rose. Louis had promised to arrange for that handy bit of technology.

***

At precisely 6:50 p.m., there was a knock on Pepper's hotel room door. She confirmed it was Brent through the peephole, and grabbed her chic black wrap and clutch. When she opened the door, she was momentarily taken aback at how handsome Brent was. She hadn't looked at him that way previously, but felt a rush of pride that she had introduced him to Jackie. She felt so happy for them both.

"Brent, I have to take a quick pic of you and text it to Jackie. You look so handsome!" she said.

"Pepper, we don't do pics or selfies on assignment. I don't want pics of me on your phone. It's way outside our protocol," he said.

"Fine, then let me take a pic of you on your own phone and you can send it to Jackie," she said.

"Because that wouldn't look like I was full of myself or anything, would it?" he asked.

"Okay, then I'm taking it. Here, step inside my room – now!" she said.

Pepper snapped the pic and texted it to Jackie with the message, "Look at this handsome man of yours!"

"This is ridiculous. Give me your phone and I'll take a pic for you to send to Bill," he said.

She smiled and he took her pic. She texted it to Bill immediately.

"Can we leave now?" He asked impatiently.

They were met in the lobby a few minutes later by Louis, who escorted them to his waiting limo. Barbara was sitting in the back seat, looking elegant.

***

They drove across the river and waited in line for the other expensive cars to drop guests at the front entrance. When the foursome entered the ballroom of the Royal Palace, Pepper felt like she had stepped into a Disney production of *Cinderella*. It was beautifully decorated in a mystic blue and white. Louis led them to the King's receiving line.

King Felix and his wife, Frederica, were flanked by his oldest daughter, the Crown Princess Helena, and her husband Timothy. Brent had read that Timothy had been Helena's personal trainer, and owned a successful workout club in Stockholm. His royal status didn't allow for him to continue to work at the club, but he hadn't given up ownership. He still looked fit, then again, all the Swedes looked fit.

Pepper followed Louis and Barbara's example as they moved through the receiving line, greeting the Royals. Brent did his own thing, as per usual, disarming the women with his rugged charm. When he reached Helena and Timothy, he shook their hands, told her she looked more beautiful than she did in the media, and turned his attention to Timothy.

"You used to be a trainer and you own a fitness club?" asked Brent.

"Yes, that's true," said Timothy.

"I've learned never to underestimate a personal trainer, and especially one who owns his own business. What's the name of your club?" asked Brent.

"Tim's Fitness. I have several chains. Fitness is very popular in Sweden," said Timothy.

"So I've noticed," said Brent.

"You're ex-military?" asked Timothy.

"See, I was right. Never underestimate a trainer," said Brent.

They laughed, and Brent moved along to join Louis, Barbara and Pepper in the bar area. They were served champagne from a silver tray. They air-toasted and sipped. A string quartet was playing in a corner, which provided the perfect level of background music. They all kept an eye out for Svea and her coterie.

Louis spotted her first. "There she is. All legs and sequins," he observed.

Svea was, indeed, one of the most attractive women at the ball. She didn't have a date, so Ulrik stood close by as she shook hands and chatted with dignitaries. Her Deputy Minister was also in tow, presumably whispering names in her ear as people greeted her. It was part of the Deputy's role.

"Ready when you are," said Pepper.

"Let's make our strike early in the evening. Catch her off balance," said Brent.

"As you wish. I'll make the introductions," said Louis.

Pepper was impressed at how relaxed and polished Louis and Barbara were. Barbara had auburn hair that was swept up in a bun. She looked stately in a deep emerald gown, complementing Louis' suave air. They were a handsome couple.

Louis lead the foursome, as he had met Svea on a few occasions. He nodded at both the Deputy and Ulrik, then shook hands with Svea, politely reintroducing himself and Barbara.

"Oh yes, of course, the American and his wife. Mr. and Mrs. Brown, how are you?" asked Svea, concealing her disgust.

"We are well. Thank you, Minister Lovgren. Congratulations on your new post," said Louis.

"Thank you. I'm enjoying the role. Did you bring some American colleagues with you tonight?" Svea cast a hooded glance at both Brent and Pepper, eyeing them suspiciously.

"Yes, we did," said Louis. "Let me introduce Pepper McCann and Brent Connolly. Pepper is a freelance journalist doing a piece on healthcare education in America and Sweden, and Brent works in the insurance industry." Louis' intro was Pepper's opening to drop the bait.

"Nice to meet you," Svea said. She ignored Pepper and directed her attention toward Brent, glancing at his ring finger. Brent didn't miss the glance. He gave Svea his dimpled, crooked smile and she softened.

"Yes, there was an article recently in *American Contemporary Healthcare* that covered three Swedish pharmacy interns working at hospitals in L.A., Minneapolis and Philadelphia. That sparked my interest," said Pepper, pausing for effect.

Svea didn't flinch. She gave Pepper an icy look that indicated she couldn't be less interested. Any other person would have been scared off, but Pepper plowed ahead.

"Is your Ministry encouraging any educational internships in American hospitals?" asked Pepper with a fake smile.

Svea regarded Pepper slowly while there was a pregnant pause in the conversation, which was revealing in itself. "No, of course not. The Ministry has more important things on our global agenda."

This lady is capable of deception, thought Pepper. Unruffled, Pepper continued, "I thought you might know the pharmacy interns since they all are in your Social Democratic Club for Students. Have you met them?"

"If I have, I don't recall," said Svea. Pepper had her attention now. Svea did a mental double-take.

The next part was a fib, but Brent had insisted Pepper say it. "Well, you must have had a big impact on Felipe Malstrom, because you were all he could talk about when I interviewed him," said Pepper.

Bingo. Svea's face cracked momentarily and her eyes darted to Brent, who feigning attraction. She narrowed her eyes, lasering a stare to Pepper. It was possible she was beginning to realize they weren't a journalist and insurance man.

"Really, what did he say?" asked Svea.

"That you were a generous leader and that he hoped to work for you someday...or something to that effect," lied Pepper.

"Ha. Students. They all say that. I don't have enough positions in my Ministry to employ them all," said Svea. "You people enjoy yourselves tonight. I must greet the other guests." Conversation over.

With that, she turned on her heel and walked away. Pepper looked at Brent, raising the corner of her mouth in a small smile. The remainder of the evening was uneventful from Pepper's perspective. There was a nice dinner, King Felix made a few remarks about collaboration in the scientific fields, and when the dancing started, the foursome decided it was time to leave.

***

CHAPTER 27

The Pick Up

Stockholm, Sweden

On the way back to the hotel, Brent removed the camera from the rose in his lapel and the digital recorder from his interior suit pocket. He handed it to Louis, asking him to email the video clip to Allen Montgomery right away. Louis promised he would.

When the limo pulled up to the driveway of the Hotel Amaranten at 11 p.m., Louis told Brent he would be back in thirty minutes.

"See you then," said Brent as he hopped out and held the door for Pepper.

"What was that about?" asked Pepper.

"I'll tell you when we're in the elevator," said Brent.

Pepper suppressed a yawn as they walked through the desolate lobby. Brent noticed a gentleman in a black tuxedo had followed them in, then veered off toward the bar.

"To the elevator," directed Brent.

He and Pepper got on. Brent pushed the button for every floor.

"Really?"

"That guy who came in right behind us is part of Svea's security. I think he tailed us. Be ready to go in thirty minutes. Jeans and a sweatshirt. Layer. As warm as you have. It will get cold tonight. Louis said he would bring each of us a jacket. Do not go back down to the lobby because that guy will see you. I'll pick you up. We'll take the stairs down to the parking garage and meet Louis there."

"Do you mean I should be packed and ready to leave the country?" she asked.

"No, not that. We're going on a stakeout. It will be fun," he said.

"Okay."

He practically pushed her out at her floor, not entertaining any further questions. Brent walked Pepper to her door and stepped inside to have a look around her room before he left. She was surprised at his new precautions. Good thing she hadn't left any undies on the floor. She changed out of her gown and put the earrings and necklace in her pocket to give to Louis. She grabbed a bottle of Ramlösa water from the mini-fridge and sent Bill a text while she waited. It felt good to put her feet up on the bed for a few minutes.

As promised, there was a soft knock on her door thirty minutes later. She opened it to Brent, wearing a pair of black jeans and a black sweatshirt. He even had on a black knit cap.

"Have a cap for me too?" she joked.

He produced one from his sweatshirt pocket. This guy takes his stakeouts seriously, she thought, pulling it on.

They ran down several flights of stairs to the basement garage. A beat up silver Hyundai was waiting for them. Louis waved them in. Despite its exterior, Pepper noticed the interior was fairly new and immaculate. There were three steaming coffee cups in a to-go container on the console. Pepper had the backseat to herself, and saw a blanket and jacket on it, too. She put on the black jacket. It felt good, as the temp had dropped.

They entered the expressway and drove west out of downtown Stockholm for about five miles. Pepper watched the signs and it looked like they were headed to an airport, but not Arlanda International Airport.

"Did you enjoy the Royal gala tonight, Pepper?" asked Louis.

"Yes. It was quite entertaining. I would say Svea looked a bit startled when I dropped Felipe Malstrom's name on her. Did she look surprised to you, Brent?" asked Pepper.

"Very. I got it on video," he said. "She actually blanched when you said his name. I'm sure anyone else would have been intimidated by her standoffish manner, overlooking her twitching and eye widening. It was pretty obvious on video, though."

"Yeah. I got under her skin. Not a good poker face," said Pepper.

"Did Brent brief you on our stakeout, Pepper?" asked Louis.

"As a matter of fact, no," said Pepper, hitting the back of Brent's seat.

"We're on our way to Bromma Airport outside of Stockholm. It's where most private jets arrive and depart, especially to Russia and the Middle East. It has a runway of about 5400 feet, so it can accommodate small and medium-sized jets, not the big luxury liners that commercial airlines use. If you wanted to keep a low profile, Bromma would be the airport you would use," explained Louis.

"And who are we hoping to see?" asked Pepper.

"Three guesses and the first two don't count," said Brent.

"You think Svea is going to make a run for it tonight?" asked Pepper.

"If you did your job, and she's truly behind the nerve gas shipments, she will," said Brent.

"Nice. I can't wait," said Pepper.

"I told you it'd be fun," he said.

Louis drove them to the back of the hangars on a service road that gave them plenty of sight lines without being noticeable. He parked next to a few other vehicles, cut the engine and tilted open the moon roof to cut down on fogging the windows. Brent removed a high powered camera from his sweatshirt, and Louis opened his coffee and sipped.

Having sat in a deer stand for many hours when she was a teenager, Pepper thought this stakeout was pretty cushy in comparison. She didn't know whether stakeout etiquette required silence like a deer stand, or if they were allowed to chat. She decided to remain quiet and follow the lead of her mentors.

The place was dead. The hangars were dark and there weren't any lights on in the front offices of the charter companies. After all, it was past Midnight. With the six-hour time difference from Boston, however, it felt like early evening to Pepper. She was buzzed from the trip and the mission. Brent started taking a few photos for lighting and settings.

"Have you and Barbara decided where you want to retire?" asked Brent.

"There are so many beautiful places around the world," said Louis. "All three of our children live in the States though, and Barbara wants to be close to the seven grandchildren, so my guess is we'll move back there. We haven't lived in the States for over twenty years, so returning there will take some adjustment."

"Where are the kids located?" asked Brent.

"Mostly in the southeast. We're thinking about Savannah, Georgia. You ever been?" asked Louis.

"Sure. Quite a few years ago. Quaint city. Friendly people. Took a river boat ride on the Savannah River. Easy town to get around in. Wait a minute. Louis, are you noticing what I'm noticing? I think that jet is in a landing pattern. What do you think?" asked Brent.

"I agree." Louis looked out the moon roof, which provided an excellent observational point for air traffic.

They watched as a medium-sized jet made an approach and landed at the far end of the runway. Lights blinking, it slowly taxied to one of the hangars. A fuel truck materialized, driving up next to the jet once it was stopped. A light flipped on in the front office of the hangar, and a disheveled man came outside. He waited for the jet door to open and the stairs to unfold automatically.

"That's a Learjet 70/75," said Brent.

"Yep. Bombardier. Are you getting a photo of the registration number on the aft fuselage? Looks Russian to me," said Louis.

"Yes. RA-2361G. The prefix indicates Russian registration. That model of Bombardier is popular with the Russian oligarchs," said Brent.

They all saw headlights from a large SUV approaching the entrance to the tarmac where the hangar was located. Brent took photos. The black SUV drove right up to the jet, and the front passenger hopped out to open the back door. It was Ulrik. Brent was at a perfect angle to photograph whoever exited the back seat of the vehicle, guessing it would be Svea. Even with black pants, a black trench coat, and her hair tucked up under a black fedora, Svea was unmistakable.

"That's Svea," whispered Pepper.

"I agree," said Louis.

"She's getting on a Russian plane. Do you think Volkov sent it for her?" asked Pepper.

"Either Volkov or an oligarch," said Brent, taking photos of her.

"I'm sure no one is going to exit the plane," observed Louis. "That would subject them to Customs and Immigration, and I think the sleepy looking man standing on the tarmac is a Swedish Customs Agent."

While the plane was fueling, Ulrik brought Svea's luggage to the top of the jet staircase and handed it inside, then returned to the bottom of the staircase and escorted Svea up. Once they were inside, the staircase folded up behind them. It took another few minutes to finish the fueling process, then the jet turned on its lights, fired up its engines, and taxied out to the end of the runway. It was cleared for takeoff and sped down the runway, becoming airborne well before the runway ran out.

"I'll run this registration number through our system as soon as we get back to the hotel to see if I can get an owner," said Brent.

"I bet money it belongs to one of Volkov's rich friends," said Louis.

"You have any contacts in the control tower for a flight plan?" asked Brent.

"Don't need any contacts. I can track it online with Flightracker.com. Read back the call sign to me, and I'll look up the flight plan they filed as soon as I get home," said Louis.

"Thanks," said Brent.

Louis waited until the fuel truck drove off, and all the interior lights in the hangar were shut off before starting the car. He drove out of the lot with his lights off. Once they were on the service road, he flipped the headlights back on, and they headed for Stockholm.

***

They made it back to the hotel service entrance by 1:40 a.m.. Pepper remembered to give Louis the Swarovski earrings and necklace, and made him promise to give them to Barbara. They agreed Louis would meet them for breakfast at 7 a.m. with the flight plan details. After breakfast, Brent and Pepper would make arrangements to fly back to Boston.

Brent walked Pepper to her room, then returned to his own to file a report that Svea Lovgren had left the country on a private Russian jet. He indicated he would supplement his report within six hours with the jet's owner and flight plan. He texted Jackie that he loved her, and looked forward to buying her a ring soon. She replied that she missed him and hoped she could see him soon. Brent removed his jeans and sweatshirt and crashed until his alarm went off at 6:30 a.m.

***

Sunday, October 21, 2018

When they met up with Louis at 7 a.m. for breakfast, he reported that the private jet that had collected Svea that night had filed flight plans to land at Sochi International Airport in Sochi, Russia. Sochi was a four-hour drive south of the palace at Cape Idokopas, also known as Volkov's Palace on the Black Sea.

Even though Volkov denied it, there were extensive media reports that he had built a large Italian- style palace and entertainment complex on the Black Sea, near the village of Praskoveevka.

There were journalistic investigative stories digging into who owned it, corporations or the men who owned the corporations, who were all under Volkov's thumb. A Cayman shell corporation in which Volkov's friends were stockholders retained most of the construction contractors, at an estimated cost of one billion dollars.

The photos surreptitiously taken by courageous paparazzi (and American spy satellites) revealed an ornate and sizeable palace that was reminiscent of 18th Century Italian architecture. It had three helicopter landing pads, two for Volkov's Ka-52 attack helicopters with the double blades, and one for the Presidential Hip.

Volkov had been photographed going to and from the palace multiple times, not only during the International Olympics that were held in Sochi in 2014, but also in the four years since then. It was obvious in the intelligence-gathering world that this was Volkov's Palace. U.S. spy satellites with surprising resolution had captured images of Volkov and his entourage, and various guests, moving about the grounds.

Brent would have to crosscheck with American intelligence to see if Volkov was seen in the last few days traveling to his palace to meet Svea there. Louis had already confirmed that the Bombardier Learjet belonged to one of Volkov's friends, one of the multi-billionaire oligarchs by the name of Dmitry Melnichenko.

Louis, Brent and Pepper ordered pancakes, eggs and coffee in the hotel dining room.

"Looks to me like Volkov and Svea Lovgren have hatched some type of plan together," said Louis.

"Us too," said Brent.

"The problem is that we have these fragments of information that don't all fit nicely together," said Pepper.

"Let's go over what you have so far," suggested Louis.

"Here's what we know." Brent began clicking off his points with his fingers.

"Number 1, Svea spent the night with Volkov in London.

Number 2, Svea sold Saab missiles to Volkov.

Number 3, our intel indicates Russian-manufactured nerve gas was shipped to the Bangkok Port then picked up by Thai Cargo Shipping Company for destinations unknown.

Number 4, the Harbor Master was murdered and the shipping manifests are gone, thereby confirming our suspicion of contraband.

Number 5, Svea probably placed Swedish interns at U.S. hospitals in the pharmacy departments," Brent concluded.

Louis thought about the points for a minute. "Has your agent in Bangkok visited Thai Cargo Shipping to get the documents directly from the company?" asked Louis.

"Weng Chee. He's working on that as we speak," said Brent.

"It might be a long shot, but have you investigated the ownership of Thai Cargo Shipping?" Suggested Louis.

"That might be a good idea. Wasn't Svea Lovgren's stepfather in the shipping industry, Pepper?" asked Brent.

"Yes. Remember when we looked at her bio in St. Martin?" said Peper.

"Okay, we need to do that today," said Brent.

"This might be way out there, just brainstorming the worst case scenario here. Maybe there's a connection between the Swedish pharmacy interns and the sarin gas. If I were going to plan a nerve gas attack on a city, I might try to sabotage the antidotes for treatment of nerve gas poisoning at the main hospital in the city I planned to attack," postulated Louis.

Brent and Pepper looked at each other. Chills went up Pepper's spine, and not the good kind.

"Allen Montgomery is going to interview the Swedish intern at Philadelphia General Hospital tomorrow," said Brent. "Or, a day and a half from now. On Monday anyway. It's Sunday morning here, which means it's Saturday night back in Boston. I guess he's going to a football game in Philly on Sunday, then staying overnight, and going to the hospital first thing Monday morning. I'll email him the information tonight. We need to get Agents to the hospitals in L.A. and Minneapolis as well."

"Have you thought about having President Scott contact Prime Minister Carlsson directly?" asked Louis.

"And say what?" asked Brent. "My intelligence team thinks your Minister is hatching a plot with President Volkov to poison America?"

"Sounds pretty out there," agreed Louis. "Unless you had a specific task for him, maybe it'd be best not to disturb him. After all, Svea is no longer in Sweden."

"Right," said Brent.

"We need to fly home today, so we can pick up the trail tomorrow morning at the Boston office," said Pepper. "There's nothing more for us to do in Sweden."

"Let's make our flight arrangements and leave as soon as we can," said Brent.

"I have my laptop open. Let me check. To Boston, right? For both of you?" asked Louis.

"Yes," said Pepper.

"There's a 12:30 p.m. nonstop from London Heathrow to Boston today. If we can get you from Stockholm to London to make that flight, you'd land in Boston on Sunday afternoon. Will that work for you?"

"Yes," said Brent.

"If you grab your stuff from your rooms and check out, I can look for the next flight from Stockholm to London. It'll be close. If you're back down here in 15 minutes, I can get you to the airport by 8:30 a.m. It's Sunday, so traffic should be light," said Louis

"That's sounds great. Thanks, Louis," said Brent.

"Louis, thank you for your suggestions. It's clear you've been in the information analysis business for a long time," said Pepper.

"My pleasure. I hope my brainstorming is way off base. I can check into the ownership of Thai Cargo Shipping company myself today while you two are in the air back to the States," he said.

***

CHAPTER 28

Svea's Arrival

Praskoveevka, Russia

Volkov, Dana and Clive were having tea and scones in Volkov's expansive library on the first floor of the palace. Dana and Clive had stayed the night and given him a full report on their observations of Svea and her operations in Sweden. Their report was favorable.

There was no reason for Volkov to be worried that Svea would reveal herself, or Volkov, as behind the attacks, which was his primary concern. Tomorrow (American time) was the scheduled day of the attack at the American football game, and they reported that Svea had her plans in order. They believed her people were in line, and ready to perform, based on their observations in Sweden.

There was just one problem. Volkov didn't believe them. He was polite, and believed that they were telling him the truth. He just knew that Svea was capable of masking many aspects of her operation from Dana and Clive. He fully anticipated that the United States would learn that Svea was behind the attack. The question for Volkov was whether Svea would rat him out, and whether he wanted to take that chance.

He had ordered Svea to come to his palace to watch the attacks on T.V. as a group, and she was en route. He had wanted to talk to Dana and Clive before Svea arrived to get a report from them. After all, he was paying them a princely fee to spy on Svea, looking out for his interests.

Volkov had decided it was best to have the core team together during the attack, so he could gauge their individual reactions, controlling information. Both their verbal and nonverbal cues would tell him a lot about whether they felt guilty enough to snitch if confronted. Some people just couldn't contain secrets of this magnitude, needing to get them off their chest by confessing to others. He was a good read of people, so would watch all three as the drama unfolded. If anyone cried at the images, he would have to deal with that person harshly. Frankly, he questioned whether Dana had the stomach for what was about to unfold.

They all heard commotion in the grand entrance of Volkov's guest wing, so they assumed Svea had arrived. Volkov knew that Dana and Clive had told Svea they were flying to Volkov's palace when they left Stockholm. It would be interesting to see if she was surprised that they were still here.

The three of them made their way from the library to the front entrance to meet Svea, who was just getting out of the car with Ulrik. Volkov walked outside, but Dana and Clive preferred to stay hidden inside so snoops with cameras and satellites wouldn't see them. They had business identities to protect. Volkov pecked Svea on both cheeks and led her into the palace. Ulrik followed with her bags.

"Dana, you're here!" exclaimed Svea. "And Clive, too. What a lovely surprise." Svea gave them each a polite peck on the cheek. Nothing more.

"How was your flight? Did you get any sleep?" asked Dana.

"It was smooth. I dozed, but I'm quite tired. Vadik, do we still have a few hours before the American football game?"

"Yes. You have time for a nap, Svea," he said.

Since Volkov was observing them very closely, and they knew he was paranoid, Dana and Svea decided not to make a scene. Svea begged off to her room, and Dana and Clive asked Volkov if they could swim laps in his pool. Volkov readily agreed, and told them all to reconvene in six hours in his entertainment center. He said the staff would show them where it was.

They all assembled in his entertainment center at approximately 11:00 a.m. East Coast time in the United States. Volkov had a hot buffet prepared with beer and other alcoholic beverages. They were watching the standard Sunday pregame show where the ex-football players in expensive suits over-analyzed game strategy, making their predictions about which team would win. Clive hit the bar, pouring himself a stiff vodka over ice with plenty of lemon slices. He decided he would let that numb his brain before he ate anything.

Volkov offered to open an expensive bottle of champagne for the ladies, and they accepted. He poured himself a scotch, and made a toast in his thick Russian accent.

"To the most beautiful team I've ever worked with. May your efforts pay off today at the American stadium. Cheers," he said.

They all drank. Clive drained his glass, so he went over to the bar and poured another. He noticed that Volkov's entertainment center was as upscale as the rest of his palace. There were several big screens, sofas, reclining chairs and pool tables. It was basically a small sports bar with top shelf electronics and booze. Volkov looked comfortable in these surroundings. He was munching on snacks and watching the pregame coverage.

It wasn't long before the cameras switched to Al Michaels and Troy Aikman in the press booth at Lincoln Financial Field in Philadelphia. They all watched as the American National Anthem was performed by an Army band. Everyone was nervous with anticipation, no one more so than Svea. She sat on a sofa, glued to the screen.

***

CHAPTER 29

Philadelphia Eagles Game

Philadelphia, Pennsylvania, United States of America

Sunday, October 21, 2018

Allen Montgomery parked his car and walked into a white illuminated hangar where several of the Counterterrorism Agency's light jets, the Eclipse 500, were stored. One was being prepared for Allen's 5:30 a.m. flight to Philly.

The Agency had picked up a small fleet of these private jets, built with a small cockpit and comfortable seating for 4-6 passengers. Its maximum take-off weight was fewer than ten thousand pounds, thus earning it the moniker "very light jet" in the early 2000s. There wasn't much of a market for commercial flights on it, however, so both the manufacturer and the airline that purchased them, DayJet, went out of business in 2008.

The federal government bought a dozen of them at a discount for low key operations where military equipment wasn't needed. The Agency had several at its disposal for short hops around the U.S., such as Allen's trip to Philly today.

He had scheduled his interview of a Swedish pharmacy intern at Philadelphia General Hospital on Monday morning, so he needed to stay over Sunday night. Allen had given the intern, Felipe Malstrom, a false cover story that he was a professor of public health at Harvard and he wanted to interview Malstrom about his American experience.

Allen also had convinced his superiors that the Agency needed to have a presence at the Eagles game due to increased chatter among Middle East terror groups about a call to arms for any solo jihadist to execute a terror strike against "the Western infidels on their homeland." All large gatherings, especially sports arenas, had heightened security. In fact, there was an Agency presence at almost every NFL game that day.

***

Roughly sixty-nine thousand fans were making their way to Lincoln Financial Field in Philadelphia, locally known as The Linc. For tailgaters, it was best to get there early in the morning, because the twenty-thousand-plus spots in the parking lots next to the modern stadium filled up quickly.

It was a beautiful October day for a noon game, 42 degrees Fahrenheit, sunny and no wind. The Eagles would battle the New England Patriots. Sam Bradford versus Tom Brady, two quarterbacks who had suffered injuries, but kept coming back to the gridiron. Of course, Brady had won four Super Bowl titles with deflated balls and Bradford had yet to make it to a Super Bowl, so it was a toss-up.

Kickoff was scheduled for 12:05 p.m., after the Star Spangled Banner was performed by the U.S. Army Concert Band while a live eagle flew from a trainer on an upper deck to second trainer's arm down on the field at the 50-yard line. Its flight would be televised on the high definition video boards behind the goal posts that provided twenty-two thousand square feet of video for the crowd to watch close ups and replays.

***

Allen had a few lucky men designated as his security detail who were accompanying him. He would be sitting in one of the 172 luxury suites, by invitation from a college friend who had made millions in the financial services industry in Philadelphia, Paul Black. Mr. Black was the sole owner of his own bond fund, Black Funds. His Linc suite held a dozen people and cost Mr. Black $100,000 per year.

The suite had several leather barstools at a counter overlooking the field through floor-to-ceiling glass. Behind that, there was a small sitting area with a sofa, club chairs and coffee table. There was a full buffet, bar, sink and stocked fridge that stadium staff refreshed throughout the game. Since Mr. Black entertained high roller clients, he enjoyed the quieter experience so he wouldn't have to shout in order to discuss financial matters.

There was a big screen on the wall in the sitting area, and smaller screens in every corner so the occupants wouldn't miss a play while they were talking business or eating. Despite the outdoor temperature, the suite was always comfortable at 72 degrees, made possible by the superior heating and ventilation system of the stadium. And it had its own bathroom, which meant the high rollers didn't have to mingle with the masses outside. The suite door locked for security purposes, but also was off the main concourse through a hallway that connected a number of suites.

***

Out in the parking lots adjacent to the stadium, the smell of charcoal briquettes permeated the air around the stadium by nine in the morning. The sacred status of the brat for Wisconsin fans was rivaled by the Philly cheesesteak for Eagles' fans. Fried onions and cheese dripped out of the steak hoagies, every tailgater having a grill with food to share.

There were all styles of green hair, body paint and Eagles jerseys on men, in addition to the elaborate homemade costumes. A rock band played classic rock that inspired dancing by midmorning when the tailgaters had their first buzz on.

Allen Montgomery's motorcade, consisting of a black Agency SUV, escorted by a Philly police car and tailed by another, bypassed the fan congestion as they sped down a service road entrance. Allen and his detail disgorged at the West Stadium Club and Suites entrance for VIPs, where they were met by a young man in an Eagles polo shirt who presented them with ID badges and lanyards. The young man showed Allen and his detail to the upper deck, where Paul Black's suite was located. It was after nine in the morning, and Paul had promised Allen a breakfast buffet. Allen was looking forward to some serious eggs and bacon as he never ate before air travel.

"Paul, how are ya, man?" asked Allen when he opened the door.

"Good! You?" asked Paul, and they shook hands.

Allen introduced Paul to his three-member security team, Bobby, Mason and Carlos. They were all large men, and readily accepted when Paul invited them to dig into the breakfast buffet.

"Glad you could make it today with your busy schedule saving America from foreign terrorists," joked Paul.

"Don't forget the domestic ones," quipped Allen.

"The only domestic terrorist I know is my ex-wife!" said Paul.

"Tell me about it. I gave up half of my assets twice in two divorces. Two halves is a whole! I lost an entire whole!" said Allen.

"Let me run your money and I'll grow it back for you," said Paul.

"Money? I don't have any money! I'm a government man whose wages are being garnished!" said Allen.

They laughed, and brought their plates to the snack bar overlooking the field. Paul got them settled, and excused himself to greet the other half of his guests for the game. The other guests were three couples who invested with Paul, and knew one another socially. Paul was currently without a female companion, which suited him just fine. No maintenance on game day. He could watch the game and chat with whomever he wanted without having to check on how his date was doing.

One of the couples was self-made millionaires in the shoe industry. He had started with a single shoe store in downtown Philly, and expanded throughout the region then in online sales. Now he had an empire that he was thinking about selling, so he could retire and enjoy rotating among his three homes in Florida, Colorado and Pennsylvania. After Paul made the introductions, Allen immediately concluded he liked this couple best. They seemed genuine and real, unlike the others, one of whom owned several car dealerships and the other who was an appliance sales king. His T.V. commercials were outrageous, which actually reflected his over-the-top personality. Allen made a note to avoid him for the next three hours.

***

After revving up the crowd with a video montage of spectacular Eagles' plays mixed with footage of Rocky Balboa running around Philadelphia in his grey sweat suit, the announcer invited the fans to remove their hats for a rendition of the Star Spangled Banner by the U.S. Army Concert Band, which was in formation on the 50- yard line.

Midway through the Anthem, three F-15s flew over the stadium, shaking the collective crowd to its core. After the jets had passed, the live eagle was released from the second deck and flew to its trainer's arm on the 30-yard line, a few feet from the band. The soaring eagle was displayed on the mega video boards at each end of the stadium, increasing the sense of nationalism among the hyped up fans. At the end of the National Anthem, both the visiting and home crowds went wild with applause.

Philadelphia won the coin toss and decided to receive the ball. On the Eagles' first drive, they marched to the Patriot end zone. Stafford was four for five in passing for 42 yards. On the scoring play at first and goal from the five-yard line, Stafford handed the ball off to DeMarco Murray, who ran it up the middle for a touchdown. Weather conditions were perfect so the extra point was easily made from the new extra point line, a rule enacted a few years prior.

The ball was snapped from the 15-yard line to the placeholder at the 22-yard line for a 32-yard kick, including the distance in the end zone to the goal post. The video boards replayed the kick and red laser-like lights circled the stadium on the LED ribbon boards. Since it was daytime, smoke jets shot fifty feet into the air from the cantilevered canopy above the third deck on both the home and visitors' sides.

Unphased by the home crowd euphoria, Tom Brady led the Patriots to a touchdown on their first possession, tying the game.

During the Eagles' second drive, one of Stafford's passes was intercepted by the

Patriots' cornerback, Malcolm Butler, for a 33-yard run down to the 35-yard line in Eagles' territory. With less than a minute remaining in the first quarter, the Patriots' placekicker, Stephen Gostkowski, kicked a field goal to make the score Patriots: 10; Eagles: 7. Allen Montgomery had to control his celebration for the Patriots in his Eagles' host's box.

***

No one paid any attention to the three white vans with red logos and the blue lettering of *Oromack* painted on the sides. They were food service vans, commonplace in Philly, the site of the company's headquarters, as well as at the Linc. The standard delivery vans were larger than a passenger van, with a full-sized rolling door at the back that could be opened to the top to allow for movement of bulky items. Hundreds of Oromack trucks made deliveries to the stadium for game day to supply the food counters in the concourse, as well as the more exclusive club-style eateries located in private areas for season ticket holders.

The first of the three vans approached the electric gate at the service road entrance. A vendor I.D. badge was needed to make the gate pop up. The Russian driver hopped out and waited for the next vendor van to arrive, a local Philly barbecue van. He told the driver he had lost his I.D. badge, and asked if he could use the BBQ driver's badge. The driver readily complied and handed the Russian his badge. The Russian scanned it, and all three Russian drivers proceeded through. The first driver pulled over to the side of the road and the other two kept going. The Russian returned the badge to the BBQ van behind him and caught up to his comrades' vans, where they parked next to one another a good distance from the actual service entrance, which was momentarily congested with other trucks. It was commonplace for vans to park, waiting to be called in for unloading throughout the game. Sometimes a van driver would wait an entire quarter to be called in to the service entrance door.

The Russian drivers remained in their seats for a few minutes to survey their surroundings. All was calm. It was business as usual in the parking lot. The next part of their plan was crucial if they were to be successful. The key was getting the drones unloaded and into the air as quickly as possible before anyone noticed. If they were caught during drone set up, they had planned to say that they were part of the half-time entertainment, which wouldn't make sense because they were in food trucks.

However, the Russians hadn't done any research on half-time entertainment companies, and they had concluded that a newly marked nonfood service van would have to show I.D. at the security gate, where there might be questions and inspections. Only one of them spoke passable English, so close scrutiny could bust the entire operation. Thus, they had taken food truck route, which would get them next to the stadium easily. The only catch was that they would have drones spilling out the back of their trucks. This meant they had to do it quickly. The drones needed to be in the air and over the stadium walls before anyone noticed the Russians wearing hazmat suits.

***

Filipe Malstrom was at Mary Adam's house, watching the Eagles' game with a bunch of hospital employees who knew Mary. They were all drinking beer, eating Philly cheesesteaks, and generally having a good time. He liked this American tradition. He didn't know much about football, so hoped to figure it out as he watched. He was just getting to know Mary Adams' niece, a cute little twenty-year old who attended Temple University, when his cell phone rang. It was Svea Lovgren. He excused himself, stepping outside onto the front porch.

"Svea?"

"Yes. Is this Felipe?"

"Yes. What can I do for you?" he asked, in Swedish.

"Remember I said I would need you to do something very sensitive?" she asked.

"Yes, I remember. What is it?" he asked.

"I need you to go to the hospital right now and destroy the medicines in the secret room you told me about," she said. "They're the antidotes for nerve gas, atropine and II PAM chloride, remember?"

"Okay. Why?" he asked.

"You don't need to know why, Felipe. Just promise me you will do it right now," she said.

"How? How am I supposed to destroy them?" asked Felipe.

"Use your imagination! Axe. Gun. Smash them with a rock. I don't know. Anything that will break glass. Open them and pour them out on the floor for all I care," she said, exasperated at the unimaginative young man.

"Do I have to do it right now? Can I go later tonight?" he asked.

"No, you Idiot. I'm calling you now so you go do it now," she exclaimed.

"Okay," he said.

They ended the call, and he stepped back inside the house to talk to the girl and finish his Philly cheesesteak. He intended to be only a few more minutes.

***

The game was in the second quarter, which was the Russians' window of opportunity to douse as many people as possible, before the crowd dispersed into the concourse for food and refreshments during half time.

There were four drones carefully loaded in each van, with one Russian operator for each drone. Since they had to turn on the nebulizers at takeoff, each man wore a hazmat suit with a full mask and impermeable white fabric. They would stand on the side of the vans that faced away from the stadium, still appearing highly suspicious. If anyone approached the group when the nebulizers were operating, the person would die almost immediately from the aerosolized sarin. However, anything was possible because no operation went exactly as planned.

Every man in the van was responsible for operating a drone. It wasn't possible for one man to operate two drones in a mission this critical. While the operators had trained at Stolby Reserve in Russia, the stadium presented tricky obstacles with which the operators were unfamiliar. They had to concentrate on their flight patterns and routes they had mapped while studying the stadium map online.

They planned to fly the drones into the stadium at the northeast corner where there was an opening. It was too difficult to fly them up over the end zone because there were 7 wind turbines, each 15 feet tall and weighing a thousand pounds, mounted above the stands. The sides of the stadium were 12 stories high, jets of smoke shooting into the air at unpredictable times, so the break in architecture at the northeast corner provided the best entry point.

After securing their gas masks to their faces, on a hand signal through the driver and passenger windows of the vans, all three back doors rolled up simultaneously, and the first man with the first drone stepped off the back of each van. They powered up the drones with their wristband transmitters, turned on the nebulizers, which efficiently spewed forth aerosolized sarin, and took off in the direction of the stadium corner. As the aerosolized particles of sarin drifted down into the parking lot, the human effects were immediate.

The Russians had added a small amount of oil as an emulsion agent to the nerve gas, so it wouldn't evaporate as quickly, ensuring the dispersed particulates would sink with gravity. Within five minutes, passersby and service workers dropped to their knees, gasping for breath that wouldn't come to them. Their diaphragm, a muscle responsible for making the lungs inhale and exhale, was rendered useless by the nerve gas. Due to the toxin, human nerves couldn't send signals to ignite any muscle, asphyxia being the first visible sign of poisoning.

All other muscles shut down within twenty minutes. People began drooling and foaming at the mouth, losing control of their bladder and bowels, then twitching and jerking until death overtook them. The medical officers in the military had designed a mnemonic tool for the lethal symptoms of nerve gas poisoning – SLUDGE. It stood for:

- Salivation – stimulation of the salivary glands

- Lacrimation – stimulation of the lacrimal glands (tear glands in the eye)

- Urination – relaxation of the internal sphincter muscle of the urethra

- Defecation – relaxation of the internal anal sphincter

- Gastrointestinal upset – diarrhea

- Emesis – vomiting

By the time a victim demonstrated the full constellation of SLUDGE, it was too late. Death was inevitable. The key to survival was decontamination and administration of the antidotes before all of the symptoms of SLUDGE took hold.

The second set of Russians stepped off the vans and deployed their drones and nebulizers, the third and fourth sets following suit. In total, there were 12 drones in the air with 12 operators on the ground, behind the vans, looking at their iPads for the video feed from the cameras mounted on the bottom of the drones.

The operators followed their preplanned flight patterns by flexing their forearms and waving their arms to adjust for altitude and speed. This allowed each man to hold an iPad in his left hand to watch the video. The plan was to circle the stadium with four drones flying single file, approximately 30 seconds behind each other, over each of the 3 decks, flying in a clockwise route. They hoped to circle the stadium twice for their five-minute flight time, crash the drones, and leave.

As the drones flew in and swooped over the crowd, the first set released the aerosolized nerve gas on each deck. The fans looked up and saw the large circular drones with the sarin spraying, but incorrectly assumed it was part of the entertainment for the game. The gas was odorless and usually colorless.

However, as the nebulizer released a mist, in the 42-degree air temp, it created a three-foot trail like a fogger would. The crowd mistakenly thought the drones would be spelling words or making designs in the air with fog.

Almost immediately, the symptoms of nerve gas poisoning manifested in the crowd like the wave going around the stadium.

There was widespread confusion. It wasn't even fathomable to the human mind what was taking place. As a person seized up and choked in front of another, it was so far out of context that others didn't know what to think or do. No one ran, because they didn't know what they were running from, and it was only a matter of minutes, seconds for some, before they convulsed, twitched and died.

One of the drones flying over the lower deck veered enough off course when it hit the field skycam wire for live footage. The drone spun around the wire and spiraled onto the field in the middle of the players. The Patriots offense was on the scrimmage line, and Tom Brady was calling the play when the drone dropped right into them, bouncing off several players on impact, then rolling to a stop in front of Brady. He looked over to the referee, who was doubled over choking, then began choking himself. The nebulizer kept spewing forth gaseous particles so the players coughed and choked to death in a matter of minutes.

The drones made it around the stadium in less than five minutes, then assumed flight patterns behind the last set of drones that had entered the stadium, circling the stadium again. The goal was to poison every last fan in attendance that day, or 68,193 people. Some of the lucky fans were in enclosed suites, the food concourses and bathroom facilities. At least 60,000 people would die within 20 minutes, however, due to direct exposure to the gas. Additional people would die due to secondary exposure, touching the clothing of the primary victims. It would be America's greatest civilian loss due to a single terrorist strike.

***

Allen Montgomery was the first person in the stadium to recognize what was happening, having studied nerve gas attacks and trained for them. In a dispassionate automatic mode, he dialed 911 and reported the situation, stressing it was a nerve gas attack so first responders needed to wear hazmat suits.

His 911 call was made at precisely 1:26 p.m. He instructed the guests in the suite not to open the door. Their only chance of survival was to seal themselves off from outside air, including stopping the ventilation system. To open the door and exit to the concourse was to guarantee death, possibly for all the occupants of the suite if poisoned air came in. Allen ordered one of his men, Bobby, to stand guard at the door and not to let anyone in or out.

Allen instructed Mason and Carlos to search the cupboards and drawers for tape, any kind of tape. While the guests watched in shock, Allen and his men found duct tape and began taping any visible crack to the outside air, like the split between the floor-to-ceiling windows overlooking the stadium.

They taped the suite door and made sure it was locked. Allen asked Paul where the thermostat settings were, and completely shut down the heating system. He saw an air return vent on the wall above the sofa, and removed his pocket knife and began unscrewing it. After he had it off, he ran to the buffet and removed the plastic wrap from the baked bean dish, covering the front of the vent. He did it a second time over the back of the vent with the plastic wrap that had covered the barbequed pork dish.

He raced back up to the vent shaft and screwed the cover back in place, this time with plastic wrap covering both its front and back. Allen asked one of his men to hand him the tape and he quickly taped the edges of the vent. He asked Mason to continue looking for any cracks to the outside air, taping a second and third time.

Once he felt they were sealed off, Allen called the Counterterrorism hotline to report the attack, which would alert Homeland Security, who he hoped would enact their disaster protocol to alert NORAD, the North American Aerospace Defense Command. In turn, NORAD was supposed to assess the threat, and alert appropriate military. Allen was hoping that, within minutes, an Air Force presence would be mobilized to Lincoln Financial Field to reconnoiter the situation and intercept the drone threat. He hoped. He noted his call to the Counterterrorism hotline was made at 1:37 p.m.

***

CHAPTER 30

First Response

United States of America

Every American watching the Eagles game on television was in disbelief or shock, or both. One minute Al Michaels and Troy Aikman were calling the game. The next minute, Al's commentary changed altogether.

"There appear to be some drones over all three decks of the stadium spraying a fog-like substance. What do you make of it, Troy?" asked Al.

"I wonder if there wasn't a miscommunication, and if this isn't intended for half time entertainment, Al. Look, one of the drones actually hit the skycam wire and is now plowing into the players on the field," exclaimed Troy.

The press box was at the top of the second deck, at an angle from where the drones had entered, so it was just a matter of seconds before the first drone flew right in front of the windows.

"Here comes a drone now," said Al.

"What kind of halftime entertainment could this even be?" asked Troy.

"More importantly," said Al, "look at the players on the field. They're coughing and choking and dropping to their knees. Do you suppose the fog from the drone is affecting them?"

The cameramen on the field had begun to suffer the same effects, some knocking their cameras as they fell to the ground, resulting in the camera pointing up in the air or at a wall. The other cameras were still operational, even though their handlers weren't. One was focused on the field, one on the crowd and one on the end zone. Any available image showed the same thing, people and players choking, foaming at the mouth, twitching, jerking, coughing and dying.

The announcers began to appreciate what was happening when the fourth set of three drones circled the stadium.

"Ladies and gentlemen, I think we're witnessing a poisonous gas attack on this stadium. People are choking and dying right in front of us. I hope the cameras are picking this up. I'd like to make a distress call on the airway for emergency help to Lincoln Financial Field in Philadelphia. This is Al Michaels and I am not joking. There is an attack of some sort of poisonous gas on this stadium. We need help here," said Al.

Troy Aikman was stunned and speechless. Al looked at him and decided to keep talking.

"I imagine it's a matter of time before those of us in the press box follow the same fate as the fans outside our windows. I can only request emergency help to the stadium to stop these drones. There must be 10 to 15 of them, circling the stadium and dispersing gas. Everyone is dropping to their knees and choking. Ladies and gentlemen, it looks like everyone is dying. We need help. This is a mayday call from Lincoln Financial Field in Philadelphia," said Al.

He listened for sirens but didn't hear any.

The nerve gas made its way into the press box within 5 minutes, not as potent as the outdoors, but enough to paralyze its inhabitants. Some had panicked and opened the door to the concourse, resulting in poisoned air coming in from that side of the box as well. The airwaves picked up the choking and coughing, then went dead with silence.

Anyone in America who had been watching the game was witnessing a genocide. The control room for all the video boards and camera angles was also located above ground, so it wasn't long before its inhabitants were poisoned through the door, ventilation system and seams in the glass windows.

***

At Mary Adams' house, Felipe Malstrom was glued to the T.V. like the other 25 people in her living room. He asked her if this was some kind of American humor, and they all yelled "no," then shushed him. Mary's training clicked into gear, and she announced to her husband that she had to go to the hospital immediately to prepare for the incoming mass disaster. He offered to drive her.

She asked Felipe if he wanted to come, and he said yes. During the trip to the hospital, Felipe thought about Svea's call to him. She had wanted him to destroy the antidotes for those poor people at the game who obviously were poisoned. Svea was behind the poisoning? He couldn't believe it. He didn't want any part of it. He suddenly felt sick to his stomach.

Mary was in the front seat crying, and her husband was going through a list of everyone he knew who was at the game that day. He assumed they were now dead. He kept saying it was an act of war against America. Felipe was dumbfounded. He would not destroy any medicines, but instead would go to the hospital with Mary to help in any way he could. Mary's husband offered to volunteer, too. As they sped down a stretch of freeway, Felipe opened his window and dropped his cell phone out. He saw the car behind them run over it.

***

With the visual confirmation of the televised victims and Al Michaels' distress call, the operators at NORAD didn't have a tough time confirming the veracity of the call from Homeland Security. At 1:40 p.m., an order went out from NORAD to the First Fighter Wing, an Air Force Unit assigned to the Air Combat Command Ninth Air Force, stationed at Langley Air Force Base in Virginia, to scramble two fighter jets to patrol the airspace above Philadelphia, specifically to search and shoot down any drones over the Linc.

The scrambling process would take about six minutes for the pilots to get into their cockpits and power up the engines. Simultaneously, NORAD notified the FAA to cease all air traffic over Pennsylvania and alert all control towers immediately. They had to get all air traffic on the ground immediately to help the fighter jets to do their jobs.

By 1:50 p.m., two Air Force F-22 Raptors were airborne and headed to Philly from Langley, about 150 miles away. Each was armed with six AIM – 120C advanced medium-range air-to-air missiles. In addition, each housed two sidewinder missiles on its side bay. The F-22 also had an internal Gatling gun, mounted just above the right wing, concealed until an inward opening door uncovered the muzzle for firing, which was capable of firing 100, twenty millimeter rounds per second.

At an altitude of 3,000 feet, the F-22s kicked in their afterburners, flying 1400 miles per hour to reach the Linc in less than seven minutes. The noise was deafening for people on the ground, rattling windows and scaring dogs. The F-22 Raptors descended into a tactical formation to search and confront any enemy aircraft or military threat from the ground. They buzzed the stadium and its 40 plus acre environs several times, giving radio report back to Langley that they weren't encountering any airborne threats.

They confirmed there was no human activity in the stadium, and sent back live video to the control center at Langley. It was grim. Over 60,000 people lay dead, heaped over one another, over chairs, in the aisles and on the field. The pilots also reported street traffic moving normally outside the parking lots on Pattison Avenue and on I-95. There weren't any speeding cars or suspicious looking vehicles.

At 2:11 p.m., the Air Command at Langley contacted the Philadelphia Police Department and ordered them to seal off all traffic going to and from the stadium. They also inquired about the Philly drone force. Like any major city, Philly had a sizeable tactical drone force for recon, as well as firepower. They were clearly marked with the Philly Police Emblem on the sides, so there would be no mistaking them for enemy drones. They agreed the Philly Police Department would send all available drones, upwards of 20, to the stadium immediately to gather video and shoot at any threats. It would take less than 15 minutes for them to arrive to the stadium. They estimated a PPD drone arrival by 2:30 p.m.

The NorthCom Commander notified the Joint Chiefs of Staff, whose job it was to notify the National Security Advisor, who was to notify the Secretary of Defense, who would notify the President. At precisely 2:14 p.m., President Cecil Scott was receiving the report in the White House underground Situation Room.

The Chairman of the Joint Chiefs of Staff, General Stewart, told the President that the F-22 Raptors in the area had encountered no visible airborne threats. Their working theory was that the drones that were currently crashed into the Linc stadium had dispersed a nerve gas, and that their operators had most likely fled the scene.

General Stewart also informed the President that 10 Predator Drones with hellfire missiles had taken off from Langley and would be circling the stadium in about 30 minutes' time. Their operators were aware of the Philly Police Department Drones, so wouldn't shoot them down. They'd gather video and take out any confirmed threats, which might be difficult without boots on the ground. Working with the Philly drones could aid in that mission.

"Survivors?" asked President Scott.

"Our estimate is that there will be very few, if any. Their only chance would have been in rooms under the stadium, or if they were in sealed off suites. We aren't hopeful though, sir. Curiosity is part of human nature, so opening doors and seeking to look, or maybe even attempting to flee the scene would result in death, if we think this is what it looks like," said General Stewart.

"And your preliminary report of what you think this was?" asked the President.

"Nerve gas poisoning, dispersed from canisters mounted on drones that circled over the stadium. Actually, the video replay from the game, with Al Michaels' narrating, is the best video we have so far. Would you like to see it?"

"Yes. Put it up on the screen," said President Scott.

The entire room watched as the drones circled the fan decks, dispersing the gas, while Al Michaels made his distress call. General Stewart paused the video in several spots to get a close up of the drones and nebulizers.

He also paused on the victims, who were suffering the classic symptoms of nerve gas poisoning, he reported.

"Is there a treatment if any of these people aren't dead?" asked President Scott.

"Yes," said General Stewart. "The military has found that if a combination of atropine and pralidoxime chloride (known as II PAM chloride) are administered within minutes, there can be a full recovery, depending on the potency of the exposure. In the military, we call it a duo dote. It's all about time management, sir. For people who absorb a non-lethal dose, maybe from exposure due to diluted airborne particles on the wind, they have more time to receive the duo dote, perhaps up to an hour. They still might suffer permanent neurological damage though."

"Is the local hospital on notice and equipped to handle an influx of patients?" asked the President.

"Yes, we put Philadelphia General Hospital on notice. It's a Level I disaster center, and has the antidotes on hand through a program administered by the CDC. They have enough duo dotes to treat about 200 patients. We're looking at shipping more medicines and alerting the National Guard to set up tents outside the hospital for decontamination of the victims."

"Good. I want to talk to the president of the Hospital as soon as you can establish a contact," said the President.

"Yes, sir," said the General.

"How do we dispatch emergency responders to the scene, General Stewart?" asked the President.

"Anyone approaching that scene on foot needs the highest level of hazmat suit on. We don't want to send the local ambulance companies in because they probably don't have them. We're mobilizing forces from the U.S. Army Reserve Command at Fort Dix, New Jersey. It's less than an hour away. We should have 1,000 trained troops on the ground, prepared to don JSLST suits and M17 protective masks inside of two hours."

"These suits and masks will protect the Army Reservists from sarin gas?" asked the President.

"Yes, they're rated for nerve gas. They consist of a fully encapsulated chemical suit with a face piece that has a self-contained breathing apparatus. They also have a two-way radio in the suit with voice-operated microphones and an earpiece. The gloves are sealed into the suit and are chemical-resistant," explained the General.

"Thank you." President Scott turned to his Chief of Staff, Charlie, and told him to make notes for the speech he intended deliver to the nation in a few minutes.

Assistants in the corner of the room scrambled to get the president of the Philadelphia General Hospital on the phone. While they were waiting, the Chairman of the Joint Chiefs of Staff received word that the Philly Police Department drones were sending video. The electronics technician switched the screen to the live video feed.

There was a collective gasp in the room. The video revealed thousands of dead bodies, with evidence that the people died in extremis and panic. As one of the drones circled the enclosed suites, however, it picked up a white sign in the window that said "Allen Montgomery – here. Suite number 132. 11 people alive. Phone number 617-547-1123." There were men waiving to the drone from the suite. The President asked the drone to hover so his staff could get the phone number.

"Get Montgomery on the phone," ordered the President.

"He's actually the Boston Director of the U.S. Counterterrorism Agency. He was the first to call 911 when the attack started. Our people have been talking to him."

"I remember him. Get him on the phone for me. Now."

A minute later, the Sit Room operator indicated she had Allen on the phone. They put him on speaker phone and the operator said, "Mr. President, I have Allen Montgomery on the phone."

"Hello?" said Allen.

"Mr. Montgomery, this is Cecil Scott, President of the United States. How are you?"

"We're alive, sir. We taped the windows and doors, and turned off the heat. It's getting cold in here, but we have jackets, and food and water. This is a full scale disaster, sir. Nerve gas poisoning as best I can tell," said Allen.

"I heard you were the first to call 911," said President Scott.

"Then I called the Counterterrorism hotline after I sealed the room. There are 11 of us in here," said Allen.

"Stay put. Do you hear me?" ordered the President. "We'll send Army troops with hazmat suits in an hour. Don't attempt to leave before that time."

"Confirmed. Is there anything you'd like to know?" asked Allen.

"Did you see where the drones came from?" asked General Stewart.

"They entered the stadium from the northeast bridge. All 12 of them. They came in sets of 3, four deep. They flew each set over a deck with these aerosolized canisters dispersing gas out the back," said Allen.

"Did you see anyone operating the drones?" asked the General.

"No, we kept looking for anyone in a hazmat suit with a transmitter, but we didn't see anyone. They must have been in the parking lot. That's our guess," said Allen.

"Okay. Sit tight. We might call you later. Do you have a phone charger?" asked the General.

"Yes. There's something else, Mr. President," said Allen.

"What's that, Director Montgomery?"

"Our Agency intelligence gathered over the last few days makes us suspicious that there will be two more attacks, sir. One in Los Angeles and the other in Minneapolis."

"Whoa. Wait a minute! How do you know that?" asked the President.

"We just pieced it together this morning that there was a nerve gas shipment through Bangkok, Thailand. The nerve gas was manufactured in Russia. We also know that Svea Lovgren, the Swedish Minister for Foreign Affairs, is having an affair with Russian President Vadik Volkov. We think Minister Lovgren was responsible for placing interns in the pharmacy departments of three hospitals, one in each city. We believe their job is to destroy the antidotes for nerve gas poisoning before victims arrive to the hospitals. It's what my team has gathered so far. We were planning to interview the Swedish interns tomorrow. I spoke to my team and they're working with the FBI to arrest and interrogate these Swedish interns tonight," said Allen.

"Holy shit, Montgomery. You're predicting a nerve gas attack in both L.A. and Minneapolis too?

"Yes, sir," said Allen.

"Okay. I'll order the appropriate follow up. Thank you," said the President.

"Goodbye," said Allen.

It was already 2:40 p.m. The President felt he needed to deliver a message to the citizens of the United States, and soon. He told the Chief of Staff to pull together a speech for delivery in 10 minutes from the Sit Room.

The staff informed President Scott that they had the President of Philadelphia General

Hospital on the line. He asked them to put him on speaker phone.

"Mr. President, I have Mr. Markus O'Malley on the phone from Philadelphia General Hospital," said the White House Operator.

"Mr. O'Malley, this is President Scott. How are you?"

"Been better, sir. What can I do for you?" he asked.

"Is your hospital prepared for a disaster of nerve gas poisoning?" asked President Scott.

"Yes, sir. We implemented our disaster plan, which includes incident command procedures for streamlined rapid decision-making. Will we be getting any government assistance by way of troops, tents and medicines?" asked O'Malley.

"Yes. NorthCom assures me they have a chemical response unit on a high level of readiness to respond. In addition, the Army Reserve at Fort Dix has been ordered to set up tents around your emergency room for the decontamination of victims before they are brought into your hospital. You should clear your parking lot," said General Stewart.

"We will. Do we know how many survivors there are?" asked O'Malley.

"No. It doesn't look good," said President Scott.

"Are we correct in assuming it's a nerve gas poisoning?" asked O'Malley.

"Yes, but we don't know exactly what type yet. The CDC should be at your site within the hour and they'll assist," said General Stewart.

"May I make a suggestion?" asked O'Malley.

"Of course. I don't have much time," said the President.

"Could you order people to stay in their homes? We're getting reports that people are driving to the Stadium to look for loved ones. My people tell me that nerve gas can travel on the wind and permeate the surrounding neighborhoods. I think we should quarantine the City, Mr. President. Just a suggestion," said O'Malley.

"And a very good one. I'll go live with a televised address in a few minutes, and that will be the first order of business. Goodbye, Mr. O'Malley and thank you for your service," said the President.

"Goodbye," said O'Malley.

It was 2:45 p.m., and President Scott felt like time was slipping away from him. The more time that went by, the less likely lives could be saved. The more time that went by, the less likely the terrorists would be caught.

***

CHAPTER 31

The Escape

Teterboro New Jersey

At 1:30 p.m., the Russian terrorists dropped their wristband transmitters on the ground, brought their iPads into the trucks, and rolled down the back doors. Still wearing their hazmat suits, they calmly drove out the service entrance, off the football stadium grounds, merged into traffic on I-95, and headed for New Jersey. After driving for an hour, the Russians pulled off the New Jersey Turnpike into the Woodrow Wilson Service Area, a rest stop with gas stations and restaurants.

They parked in the truck section, next to two Chevy Malibu four-door sedans they had rented from Avis, and left at the rest stop earlier that morning on their way to the game. They quickly doffed their hazmat suits in the back of the trucks, grabbed a small bag and exited through the passenger doors. Once they were in the cars, as a prophylactic measure, each one of the twelve men shot himself in the thigh with a preloaded auto-injector of the duo dote of atropine and II PAM chloride. They started the Chevys, passed out their fake passports with Ukrainian citizenship, and pulled back onto the New Jersey Turnpike, headed for the Teterboro Airport.

Traffic was light, so at approximately 3:15 p.m., they turned right onto Moonachie Avenue, then took a left onto Charles Lindbergh Boulevard, bringing them to a private charter section of Teterboro with several hangars. They drove to a silver hangar where a Gulfstream 650 was fueled and awaiting their arrival. The pilot and co-pilot were walking around the jet, checking it over and chatting.

When the pilots saw their 12 passengers, they walked over and introduced themselves. The Russians nodded and walked up the short steps into the cabin. The only Russian who spoke passable English lingered at the bottom of the stairs.

"All is good?" he asked.

"Yes. We've spoken to the control tower and we'll be allowed to fly despite the no-fly order issued over Pennsylvania," said the captain.

"Oh really?" asked the Russian.

"Didn't you see the news? Big terrorist attack in Philadelphia. Thought it might ground us, but they've cleared air traffic out of Teterboro. We'd better get going before they change their minds," said the pilot.

"Yes. Let us not delay," said the Russian as he hustled up the steps.

The Pilot filed his flight plan to Cayman with the tower, and was cleared once he taxied out to the runway. At 3:43 p.m., The Gulfstream's wheels left the runway and it was airborne for the Cayman Islands. The Russian soldiers breathed a sigh of relief.

After they leveled off at a cruising altitude of 30,000 feet, the Captain said over the PA system that their flight plan was being modified to push them out over the Atlantic in a bow-type fashion to avoid congestion and military flights over the east coast. They would rejoin their flight pattern over the tip of Florida, then pass over the Bahamas and Cuba before descending into Cayman. The detour added about an hour onto the flight time, he reported, putting them in Cayman by 8 p.m.

***

The Gulfstream landed uneventfully at Georgetown International Airport in the Cayman Islands at 8:10 p.m.. Customs and Immigration met the Russians as they walked down the stairway. Their Ukrainian passports were stamped, and they were cleared.

The men walked into another charter hangar, and met the receptionist to check in for their late night flight to Kiev, Ukraine. They boarded another Gulfstream 650 and the new pilot and co-pilot looked refreshed and ready to go. The distance was over 6,000 miles, so it would be at least a 12-hour flight. As soon as they were airborne, the men toasted one another with a bottle of Stolichnaya. A flight attendant served sandwiches and chips with more vodka. One by one, they drifted off to sleep. The plan was that once they landed in Kiev, a Russian military plane would carry them back to Siberia. Mission accomplished.

***

CHAPTER 32

The President

Washington, D.C., United States of America

The White House Situation Room

2:52 p.m.

The President was seated at the head of the table in the Sit Room with the United States flag over his right shoulder, and the Great Seal of the United States with the eagle in the center pictured on the video screen behind him. President Scott was wearing his black military jacket with his name and the Seal embroidered on its left breast. He looked somber, like he had aged 20 years in the last hour. His gray hair was combed back, his piercing grey eyes staring straight into the camera.

The cameraman gave him the cue.

"Ladies and Gentlemen, my name is Cecil Scott and I'm the President of the United States of America. I'm speaking to you live from the White House Situation Room located in Washington, D.C.

Today at approximately 1:25 p.m. Eastern Time, terrorists launched a nerve gas attack on American citizens attending the Philadelphia Eagles Game at Lincoln Financial Field in Philadelphia, Pennsylvania. The attack was fatal. There are very few survivors. The attack was carried out by drones carrying canisters of aerosolized nerve gas. The impact on the fans, players, teams, staff, concession workers, and all who were in the open air areas of the stadium was immediate death.

Today, we lost husbands, wives, children, grandchildren, friends and neighbors. Our nation is grieving. I'm grieving. I'm so sorry for our collective loss. We pray to a higher power for afterlife for our loved ones. We pray for strength and resolve for those who have survived." President Scott stopped to catch his breath, a tear rolling down his right cheek. He didn't wipe it off.

"I've ordered the United States military to conduct reconnaissance and threat assessment flights over the stadium, and all of Pennsylvania. We have a mighty military force that has been mobilized and will respond to any threat. Make no mistake, the United States military is prepared to defend our nation.

The highways have been closed to and from the Philadelphia Stadium. I've issued a Presidential Quarantine for the City of Philadelphia, which includes prohibiting cars from going to the stadium. I've ordered mass transit in Philadelphia suspended. I'm told that nerve gas can travel on the wind and permeate the neighborhoods, so I'm hereby ordering people to stay inside their homes. The military has been sent to the stadium and they'll wear special hazmat suits for protection. The military will render aid to any survivors and begin the work of identifying those who have died.

Stay in your homes until further notice. Do not go to the grocery store, work, school or anywhere else. Call your family members and tell them to stay inside wherever they are. Anyone seen outside their homes will be detained and placed in military quarantine.

I realize this will cause a great inconvenience, but it's for your safety. Nerve gas is deadly. We need to take immediate measures to protect all U.S. citizens from further harm. This quarantine is a vital step toward doing that.

I've spoken to the president of Philadelphia General Hospital, and that hospital is prepared to treat victims of nerve gas poisoning. The United States military has been sent to that hospital to assist.

As President of the United States, I hereby declare war on whoever perpetrated this heinous genocide on American citizens. I thank my colleagues in Congress who stand with me. I pledge to find who did it, including any nation who harbors them, and bring them to justice. We will not distinguish between the terrorists and anyone or any nation who harbors them. This murder will not go unavenged. The United States will make a proportionate response.

Homeland Security has raised the threat assessment level to "active." This means we are currently under threat. If you see anyone or anything suspicious, please report it immediately to local law enforcement. To defeat terror, we must work together as a nation, and the best way to do that is to stay alert and work with law enforcement and the military. This act of terror will not dampen the resolve of America. Our citizens, you, have built the strongest country on Earth with the greatest freedoms. I'm calling on you now to help law enforcement and the military protect what we've built.

I'll give you periodic updates when we learn more, and if the threat assessment level changes, Homeland Security, or I, will notify you by television broadcast.

Thank you for your help. God be with you, and God Bless America."

The President stared down the camera until it was off. It was now 2:57 p.m.

***

The phone in the center of the table rang, and Charlie answered it on behalf of the President.

"Mr. President, I have Mr. Alistair Webb, the Prime Minister of Great Britain, on the line," said the White House Operator.

"Put him on speaker, please," ordered President Scott.

"Alistair, thank you for calling. How are you?" asked Cecil.

"I'm horrible," said Alistair. "I've seen the news, and I feel awful for you and your country. Please accept my condolences. What can I do to help?"

"Assist with intelligence," said Cecil. "We'll need all the help we can get to apprehend these terrorists."

"I have MI6 working on it already," said Alistair.

"Very good. Let us know if you learn anything," said Cecil.

"Good day. I wish you well," said Alistair.

***

The President turned to the Chairman of the Joint Chiefs of Staff. "General Stewart, I want a full threat assessment in one hour on the cities of L.A. and Minneapolis."

"Already working on it, sir," said the General.

"I want a briefing on whether I should issue a Presidential Order prohibiting people from attending large gatherings, like events in stadiums."

"Yes, sir," said Charlie Duncan, the Chief of Staff.

The President rubbed his eyes and temples for the first time that day. He pushed away from the Sit Room conference table, and walked down the hallway to get something to eat and drink.

***

CHAPTER 33

The Atlantic

Somewhere Over the Atlantic Ocean

Pepper was napping, and Brent was fully powered up on his laptop. They were sitting in First Class on the British Airways flight from London to Boston, having spent a scant 40 minutes at London Heathrow to get their passports stamped and run to the gate. They made it onto the flight at the last call for boarding. It was an eight-and-a-half-hour flight, and they still had an hour of flight time remaining.

"Jesus, I can't believe it!" Brent exclaimed under his breath.

"What?" Pepper awoke with a start. Brent was ashen.

"Look at this," he said, turning his laptop so she could see the CNN news feed.

"Oh my God, Brent. It happened. And we're stuck on a plane over the Atlantic. I can't believe it," she said.

They were trying to keep their voices down, but the flight attendant noticed their horrified looks, and came over to ask what was going on. Brent showed her the news, then warned her that if other passengers saw it, they might start to freak out. He showed her his Agency credentials and asked her if the pilots knew. She said she'd ask and report back. She moved to her phone and dialed the cockpit. After she hung it up on the wall, she nodded to Brent. He waved her over.

"If you notice that other passengers are starting to learn about the attack, and there's panic, please tell the Captain to make an announcement," said Brent.

"I will. I'll tell the other flight attendants, and we'll watch," she said.

"If you have a problem with any passenger, you come and get me right away," said Brent.

"You can bet on it," she said. She walked back to the main cabin area to see what the passengers were doing.

"I wonder if we'll be able to land in Boston," said Brent.

"Good point. They might divert all air traffic in the area," said Pepper.

Brent looked at his laptop. "Look at these emails taking place between Allen Montgomery and Marty Cavanaugh in the Boston Office," he said. "They copied us on them. Thank God, Allen is alive. He's emailing from his cell phone at Lincoln Stadium. He was at the game, you know."

"It looks like he's ordering someone to take Felipe Malstrom at Philadelphia General Hospital into custody right away," said Pepper. "What if Malstrom's job is to sabotage the antidote supply for nerve gas poisoning?"

"They're also sending agents and extra backup to arrest Max Björnsson at Cedarbrook Hospital in L.A. and Valter Nylund at Southview Hospital in Minneapolis," said Brent. "If we can visibly interrupt the terrorist plan, even at the fringes, they might abandon their next nerve gas attack."

"Should we email Bill and warn him? Maybe he could help us from inside Southview Hospital?" asked Pepper.

"No," said Brent. "We don't want to get him involved. The hospital will be swarmed with agents and military. Bill will know to keep his eyes and ears open after he sees this on T.V."

"I feel so helpless!" cried Pepper. "Shouldn't we at least warn Bill and Jackie to stay inside, and not go to any large events where there are a lot of people? Not everyone knows that L.A. and Minneapolis are targets, too."

"That's a good idea," said Brent.

After they sent emails to Bill and Jackie, Brent received an email from Louis Brown sending his condolences. He said he felt horrible having had the discussion at breakfast, now watching the terror plot play out. He said he sent an email to both Director Allen Montgomery and Deputy Director Marty Cavanaugh in Boston with the information that Thai Cargo Shipping was owned by a corporation called Whale Shipping. Whale Shipping was a Cayman shell corporation with one stockholder – Henrik Jenssen, Svea's stepfather. Louis' conclusion was that Svea probably could control whatever shipping method she needed. It was his guess that she was involved in shipping the nerve gas with Thai Cargo Shipping, and that it was she who had it shipped to America.

Brent agreed with Louis' email. "So, Svea used her father's shipping company to transfer the nerve gas from Bangkok to the United

States. That's pretty obvious now. Since we already know that it's in Philadelphia, we have to assume the nerve gas has arrived in L.A. and Minneapolis as well. It'd be useless at this point to hold all containers at the ports to inspect them. We're one step behind Svea's team. Those containers have most likely been unloaded and the nerve gas transported. We have to leapfrog forward somehow," he said.

"We have the hospital-side addressed," said Pepper, "but that's only half the equation – sabotage of antidotes. If I were Svea Lovgren, I wouldn't tell the Swedish interns the other half of the plan - the details of the nerve gas attack - for fear of this very scenario. She wouldn't want them to spill the details under interrogation if they were caught, which they have been."

"Hopefully, the interns will all confess that Svea hired them to sabotage the hospital antidote inventory. That would incriminate her, giving us a reason to track her down and take her out," said Brent.

"We'll need a laboratory analysis of the nerve gas used at the Linc to see if we can tell if it was, in fact, manufactured in Russia," said Pepper.

"And the drones. We might be able to trace their technology to Russia as well," said Brent. "If we can tie Russia with Svea, then we know Volkov was in on it because he's spent so much time with Svea lately. Wait, I'm getting another email."

Brent read the email then turned to Pepper.

"Marty wants us to brief the President in person as soon as we land. There'll be a Marine chopper waiting for us at Logan International to bring us to the White House," said Brent.

"The President?" asked Pepper.

"The one and only," said Brent.

"We're not sure of anything. How can we be of help?" she asked.

"He has a lot of intelligence sources. I'm sure Marty and Allen have told the Director of the NSA about our efforts on the ground. It's a lot of vital information that needs to be pieced together with all the people gathered in one room. The Directors of the CIA and FBI will be there too, so we can have the benefit of sharing information. That's the beauty of the Sit Room," he said.

"I'm really nervous," said Pepper. "This seems so surreal. I wish I'd worn my other suit. At least I have a clean blouse in my carryon. I'll put it on right before we land."

Brent laughed. "Don't worry about it. I felt the same way the first time I went to the White House. And look at me now. I'm in a sweater and dress pants, and I don't care. Pepper, he doesn't care who we are or what we look like. He just wants to know what we've seen, heard and figured out. He needs our help to protect our nation."

"Yeah. You're right," she said.

Their conversation was interrupted by an announcement from the Captain. "Ladies and Gentlemen, this is the Captain speaking. I have some important information to tell you and I would ask that you remain calm after I tell you this. First, everything is fine on our plane. We're flying smoothly at 33,000 feet, having begun our descent into American air space. Our landing has been diverted from Logan International Airport to Washington Dulles International Airport. There's quite a bit of congestion on the East Coast, so they're diverting air traffic in a number of cities. I'm sorry for your inconvenience. British Airways representatives will be on the ground to assist you with both air and ground transportation options when we land."

There was a lot of groaning, and even some sneering by the passengers until they heard what the Captain had to say next.

"The second part of my message is this. Some of you with WIFI on board may have already seen the news. There was a terrorist attack at Lincoln Financial Football Field in Philadelphia today at a professional football game. Most of those in attendance were apparently killed by a nerve gas that was released in the stadium. I'm sorry for your loss if you had family members there." The Pilot's voice caught and he had to pause for a minute.

"As a result, the United States of America is on military alert and our flight plan will be monitored closely as we approach. We'll most likely be accompanied by United States fighter jets, so don't be alarmed if you see them outside your windows. We'll go ahead and turn the T.V. monitors to CNN news and confirm you all have ear phones so you can stay up to date with the breaking news. I'll provide another message when we get closer. As you can imagine, we've been busy up here in the cockpit. Thank you."

There was a collective gasp on the plane as the monitors sprang to life with CNN coverage of the stadium. People began crying.

"Guess we won't need the Marine chopper after all," said Pepper.

"It's not a coincidence that we're landing at Dulles. The President must really want to talk to us. Here's another email from Marty," said Brent.

"He says that the President redirected our flight so we could get to the White House sooner, and that hopefully Allen will be evacuated from the Linc by then to meet us there." Brent and Pepper read the details about Allen being in a suite and securing himself and his friends to survive the attack.

Brent and Pepper were kept in the informational loop for the next hour as agents rounded up Max Björnsson at Cedarbrook Hospital in L.A. and Valter Nylund at Southview Hospital in Minneapolis. They both immediately fingered Svea Lovgren for placing them in the hospitals under false pretenses, but neither of them knew how his internship was related to a broader plan. Svea had told them she'd be asking them to do something important in the future. She just hadn't told them what yet. They were young, shaken and naïve. Now, they were incarcerated.

Felipe Malstrom in Philly was a different story. He was cuffed and stuffed in a conference room at the hospital as soon as he arrived to the pharmacy with Mary and her husband. The curious thing to the agents was that Felipe didn't seem surprised to be arrested.

He sang like a bird, telling them that Svea Lovgren called him while he was at Mary's house, and asked him to return to the hospital to destroy the antidote supply. He couldn't believe what she had requested, and he had no intention of returning to the hospital to carry out her orders. Instead, he had gone back in the house to watch the game with everyone else, and watched in horror when he saw the nerve gas attack at the stadium.

The Agents asked for his phone, and he told them he had panicked and thrown it out the window on the way to the hospital because he didn't want to be called by Svea again. He actually pleaded with the agents for amnesty in return for testifying against Svea. He appeared genuinely remorseful for his conspiratorial role. Even though he hadn't harmed any property or people, he nevertheless had interned at the hospital under false pretenses with the intent to carry out a terrorist act against America. The Agents told him they'd talk to him soon. In the meantime, he would be flown to Langley 'for his own safety.'

***

When the pilot flying Brent and Pepper announced they were thirty minutes out from Washington Dulles, Pepper went into the bathroom and changed out of her blue blouse and put on a clean, white blouse. She hoped she looked presentable to the President after sleep deprivation and travel.

After the plane taxied up to the jet way, Pepper and Brent were allowed off the plane first, and were met by two Marines who walked them through the airport at a fast clip. They exited the building and were put into a black Suburban with their luggage. It was late evening by the time they got in the Suburban. They were part of a three-vehicle convoy that took about 30 minutes to get to the White House, where they were subjected to a search at the gate and provided with visitor I.D. badges. Pepper saw dozens of Marines surrounding the White House. All were wearing gas masks.

Once inside the White House, they were shown to the West Wing where the elevator to the Sit Room was located. One of the Marines swiped a card in a slot in the elevator bank, then inserted and turned a key. He pressed a button that said "SR," and the elevator descended a couple of floors. It opened into a foyer that required more badge swiping and a retinal scan. They walked down a long hallway, and the Marine knocked on a heavy wooden door at the end of it.

He was asked to identify himself, then was admitted. They entered a huge conference room that resembled any modern, high tech corporate boardroom, except it had the top military brass of the United States sitting around it, advising the President. There was a wall of monitors at each end of the table that currently had several split screens displaying various places and events.

The Marine whispered in the ear of Charlie, the President's Chief of Staff, who rose from his chair and walked over to shake Pepper and Brent's hands. When there was a pause in the current conversation, Charlie announced, "Mr. President, Counterterrorism Agents Pepper McCallan and Brent Cahill have joined us."

"Thank you, Charlie. Good to meet. I'm President Scott." He shook both of their hands and waved over Allen Montgomery from the other end of the room, so he could join Brent and Pepper at the table next to the President. Allen had arrived about 10 minutes before Brent and Pepper, and they were relieved to see him.

Pepper's stomach did summersaults as she glanced around the room.

"Brent and Pepper, I have a few questions for you," said the President.

"We hope we can answer them," said Brent.

"Have you personally seen the Swedish Minister for Foreign Affairs, Ms. Svea Lovgren, in the company of the Russian Prime Minister, Vadik Volkov?"

"Yes. I photographed them in London walking into the lobby of One Aldwych Hotel. She accompanied Mr. Volkov into the elevator at night. She left the next morning," reported Brent.

"I understand you met Minister Lovgren a few days ago in Stockholm, and asked her if she knew these Swedish students in U.S. hospitals?" asked the President.

"Yes. She denied any knowledge, but visibly blanched when I told her that Felipe Malstrom, the student at Philadelphia General Hospital, spoke highly of her. We have video of that," said Pepper.

Allen pulled up the video file on his laptop and the Sit Room tech projected the image of Svea on the large screen on the wall. They watched Pepper ask her questions and saw Svea's surprised reactions when she responded.

"Do you believe Lovgren assisted with the transport of Russian-manufactured nerve gas?" asked the President.

"Yes," said Brent and explained Weng Chee's findings and Svea's use of her stepfather's company Thai Cargo Shipping. He also told them about the murder of Pu Yai Bahn, the Bangkok Harbor Master.

"Did you witness Lovgren departing Sweden on a Russian jet?" asked the President.

"Yes, she left last night on a Learjet with a Russian registration after King Gustaf's royal ball. The jet is owned by one of Volkov's friends, an oligarch named Dmitry Melnichenko," said Brent.

"Do you believe she is with Volkov now?" ventured the President.

"It's my understanding that Melnichenko's jet brought Lovgren to Sochi, sir. Volkov has a palace four hours north of Sochi on the Black Sea. So, probably," said Brent.

"Would it surprise you to know that our military investigation has revealed that the nerve gas and drones used at the Linc were most likely manufactured in Russia?" asked the President.

"No, sir. That wouldn't surprise me, given what we know," said Brent.

"Would it surprise you to know that the Swedish intern, Felipe Malstrom said Lovgren ordered him to destroy the antidotes for nerve gas poisoning at Philadelphia General Hospital?" asked the President.

"As we suspected, but didn't have any proof. Did he have any information about potential attacks in L.A. or Minneapolis?" asked Pepper.

"Unfortunately not," said the President. He sat and thought for a minute, looking intently at Brent and Pepper.

"Did you want to tell them about the jet that left from Teterboro airport after the gas attack, Mr. President," prompted Charlie.

"Thanks, Charlie. Yes. Our military intelligence learned that a jet bound for the Cayman Islands departed Teterboro approximately two hours and twenty minutes after the nerve gas attack. It had 12 men on board with Ukraine passports. The pilot said one of them had a Russian accent. The jet landed in Cayman, and the 12 men boarded another jet that had filed a flight plan for Kiev, Ukraine," said the President.

He turned to General Stewart. "Bring up the satellite imagery of Lovgren's car and image at Volkov's palace again. Brent and Pepper, please look at this and tell me if you think it's Svea Lovgren."

The video came on and everyone watched as a motorcade pulled into the driveway at Volkov's palace. Several soldiers formed a perimeter facing outward around the three vehicles. Security exited both the lead and tail vehicles. In the middle vehicle, a man exited the front passenger seat, then stood to open the rear door for a passenger in the backseat. Brent asked if they could pause the video on that man, and perhaps zoom in. The video tech did.

"Does that look like Ulrik to you?" Brent asked of Pepper.

"Yes," she confirmed.

"We believe that man is the head security detail for Ms. Lovgren, Mr. President," said Brent.

"Okay, please carry on," ordered the President.

The video rolled, and Svea unmistakably exited the backseat. She was still wearing the black trench coat, but the hat had come off, and her hair was down around her shoulders. The tech paused and zoomed in as well as the satellite imagery would allow.

Brent and Pepper looked at one another and nodded.

"Yes, that's her," said Brent.

"Good to see you confirmed our intelligence," said the President.

"Thank you. In fact, I took photos of her wearing that same outfit in Sweden when she boarded Melnichenko's jet," said Brent.

The President looked at General Stewart again. Their eyes met, and the General knew what President Scott was about to ask.

"General Stewart, how confident do you feel that both President Vadik Volkov and the Minister for Foreign Affairs for Sweden, Svea Lovgren, are currently at Volkov's Russian palace on the Black Sea?"

"I'm ninety-nine percent confident Volkov is at his palace, Mr. President. Our spy satellites have confirmed that in the last couple of hours. With respect to Ms. Lovgren, I'll rely on the visual confirmation provided by Agents Cahill and McCallan to bring my confidence level to ninety-nine percent as well, sir."

"Do you ever say you're one hundred percent confident, General?" asked the President.

"Not unless they're standing in front of me, sir," said the General.

"Very well. General Stewart, please give me the best option for a military strike on Volkov's palace to kill both him and Lovgren. If possible, I want an option that won't trigger a military alert, and response by the Russian military. A covert, under-the-radar option. Understand?" asked the President.

"Understood, sir. How long do we have?" asked General Stewart.

"How long do you need?" asked Charlie Duncan.

"Less than an hour, but at least thirty minutes," said General Stewart.

"Very well. Meet back here in thirty minutes. Meeting adjourned," said the President.

The military brass exited the room quickly, and moved as a group down the hallway to convene a joint conference about resources. Everyone else used the opportunity to get something to eat and drink in the small cafeteria. Or simply to stretch and walk off the stress.

Allen told both Brent and Pepper they had done an exemplary job. His compliment put Pepper at ease enough to allow herself to drink some water.

***

CHAPTER 34

Bill

Minneapolis, Minnesota

It was after 8 p.m., Central Standard Time, after the football game disaster. Bill was still at Southview Hospital. He was on call, and had just finished operating on a teenager who had been in a car accident. The seatbelt had prevented the teen from hitting the windshield, but the frontal collision had pushed the engine into the front passenger compartment, resulting in two broken femurs for the teen. Bill spoke to the shaken parents in the waiting room. They both openly sobbed, thanking him for his help, then hugging him. Everyone was so emotional after what had transpired at the Linc Stadium in Philly.

He returned to the peri-operative area next to the PACU to dictate his operative note and enter some post-operative pain management orders into the electronic medical record for his teenage patient. The teen would remain intubated for another half hour, the ventilator breathing for her.

After Bill finished his op note, he walked through the hospital lobby and took the elevator to the fifth floor, which was the surgical recovery unit. He would make rounds on the 11 patients who were currently there, fulfilling the on-call surgeon's duty for his partners, rounding on their patients in addition to his own.

As Bill walked through the main concourse in his green scrubs with his I.D. badge securely fastened to his pocket, he nodded to the Marines in military fatigues with AR-15s slung over their shoulders. They were guarding the front doors. That was a first, working in a hospital with military guards.

He had heard from the OR staff that a pharmacy intern had been arrested by 'special agents' in dark suits with six Marines standing guard. He shook his head. Pepper had been right after all. He had thought her theory about the Swedish interns had been farfetched, but now that an intern had been arrested at Southview, it escalated the terror threat level in the entire city. He knew it also increased the likelihood of something bad happening at the hospital. He just didn't know what.

He was relieved that Pepper was back on U.S. soil although, as he thought about it, that was an irrational belief since America was under attack. She probably would have been safer staying in Europe. He hoped he would actually get to hear her voice tonight. She had texted when she landed at Dulles that she hoped to call him later, much later. He'd probably be at the hospital until midnight anyway, so he'd stay busy until he heard from her. He was amazed at the way her brain worked, and how smart she was about connecting the dots.

He wanted her to succeed at her new job, but he missed her. He couldn't believe that his wife was at the center of figuring out who had launched the largest terrorist attack ever against the United States on American soil.

Earlier, Bill had been watching the Eagles' football game in the doctor's lounge between surgeries when Al Michaels had announced the drones and nerve poison. Like every American, Bill's heart had ached for those at the stadium, and their loved ones who were grieving their loss. He and a few physicians in the lounge had watched the events, talked about treating sarin gas poisoning, and Southview's capability in the ED to handle a mass disaster of poisoned victims. They were all working with a heavy heart on this Sunday night, but they soldiered on.

***

The PACU nurse in charge of heart surgery patients, Vicki, looked up her patient's order set in the electronic medical record. The heart surgeon had ordered pain medication to be given in half hour increments once the patient woke up from anesthesia, and the endotracheal tube was pulled. The patient had awakened and the tube had been withdrawn, so the patient could breathe on his own. The heart surgeon had written for 50 micrograms of Fentanyl by IV push every 30 minutes.

Vicki logged off the electronic medical record and walked over to the Pyxis machine, where the Fentanyl was stored in the PACU. She swiped her I.D. badge and entered her password. The screen came to life and she entered the removal of a Fentanyl ampule, so she could pull it into a syringe and give it to the patient through the IV line. The drawer latch released, and she opened the drawer for the Fentanyl container.

The plastic lid popped open in the drawer and she removed one ampule of Fentanyl. She closed the drawer and logged off the Pyxis machine, which had recorded the time, Vicki's identification, and the removal of one Fentanyl ampule.

Vicki walked over to a prep counter next to her patient's bed. She opened a sealed pack for a sterile filter needle, and screwed it onto the tip of the syringe. Once she broke the glass top off the tip of the ampule, she'd have to use the filter needle to pull the clear liquid into the syringe, so no glass particles would be sucked up into the syringe. After pulling the Fentanyl into the syringe with the filter needle, she intended to unscrew the needle, discard it in the hazardous waste container on the wall, then use the Leur tip screw to connect the syringe with the IV tubing on the patient. The Luer-Lok on the patient's IV tube enabled a leak-free connection for the administration of medications.

Vicki never made it that far in her process though. As soon as she broke the glass tip off the small ampule, the vapor released into the air, right under her nostrils. The colorless and odorless fluid mimicked many of the medicines used in the hospital, but it was the deadly sarin that had been manufactured in Russia, and packaged as Fentanyl.

Her eyes stung and began watering immediately. She seized up, and started coughing. She was gripped with panic. She had never experienced a spasm like this. Her eyes bulged out, and her brain felt like it was about to explode. She couldn't take a breath to get enough air. Her diaphragm wouldn't contract. Her heart was racing, and she felt like someone had put a plastic bag over her head.

She dropped the glass ampule on the tile floor as her fingers became limp. The ampule shattered and the liquid inside splattered her shoes and the cupboards of the prep counter. The vapor dispersed into the airspace in an exponential fashion. Vicki fell to the floor, choking and drooling. Her body was beginning to convulse uncontrollably and her brain was on overdrive, sending signals to her nerves to stimulate her diaphragm so her lungs could suck in air. However, her nerves couldn't pass the message along to the muscles. They were paralyzed by the sarin vapors from the ampule.

A nurse nearby ran over to assess Vicki, and attempted to perform the Heimlich maneuver on her, thinking she had a candy or piece of food lodged in her throat. That nurse started coughing and choking too, falling to her knees beside Vicki, experiencing the same symptoms.

Within five minutes, everyone in the 500-square- foot PACU area was coughing and choking, except for a few post-operative patients who still had an endotracheal tube in their mouths that breathed for them through a ventilator, including the teenager on whom Bill had just operated. An anesthesiologist ran from the PACU to a phone on the wall in the hallway, and dialed the hospital's emergency response number. He was able to talk to the operator for a few minutes before he, too, collapsed. The double doors to the PACU closed automatically behind him, but not before some vapor was released into the hallway. It was like an airborne serpent that slithered down the hallway and around corners, floating on the air flow direction, paralyzing everyone in its path.

Bill was in a patient room on the fifth floor surgical inpatient unit, chatting with the family of a post-operative patient, when he heard the overhead page by the hospital operator.

"Emergency response team, hazardous waste spill, to Post Anesthesia Care Unit. Repeat: emergency response team, hazardous waste spill, to the Post Anesthesia Care Unit." The operator would wait two minutes then repeat the exact same message on the overhead pager for the entire hospital to hear again.

Bill calmly said goodbye to the family, and exited the patient's room. He went to the nurse's station where a few nurses and the unit coordinator were talking.

"What's going on?" Bill asked of no one in particular.

"We don't know," a nurse said.

"Dr. McCallan, we haven't heard that overhead page before. Are we under a terrorist attack?" another nurse asked.

"Let's not overreact. I don't know. If it's a hazardous waste spill, it could be a few things, couldn't it? Like chemotherapy drugs. Do we have a policy on hazardous waste spills? Can you pull it up on the computer?" he asked.

Bill had a bad feeling about what was happening. They didn't have chemotherapy drugs in the PACU. He knew nurses performed well under pressure, especially if they had a job to do, but this was unprecedented. The worst case scenario would be for staff to conjecture, panic and become distracted from doing their jobs. Maybe the policy would provide some structure and direction.

Bill wasn't part of the emergency response team, so he had no reason or business to walk down to the PACU to help. In fact, if every provider in the hospital responded to overhead pages for codes, there would be chaos at the site of the code. It was best to let the emergency team take care of it. Nevertheless, he felt his legs propelling him out of the surgical unit to the elevator bank, and down to the first floor lobby in the direction of the PACU, where his post-operative teenager was still recovering.

When he arrived in the lobby, he could see several people walking very fast toward the PACU, which was through a few connecting hallways in the next building. The emergency responders weren't wearing any hazardous waste protective equipment. Bill walked over to where the two marines in fatigues were standing with their machine guns.

"Hello Doctor," one of them said.

"Hi. How many people have you seen walking by in response to the overhead page so far?" Bill asked.

"At least a dozen, why?" one of them asked.

"Hmm," said Bill.

The three men watched in horror as a physician in scrubs came running from the PACU hallway, coughing and choking. He was trying to speak, but was having trouble with his airway.

"Bill...gas...air...," was all he could sputter before collapsing at Bill's feet.

Bill wanted to kneel down and assess him, provide mouth-to-mouth resuscitation, or do anything to treat his colleague, but he fought his instinct to do so. He knew that if sarin was on his colleague's scrubs, he'd be exposed to the gas himself. It was imperative to get the victim out of his clothes before rendering help. Fortunately, Bill had several pair of latex gloves in his white lab coat, which he was still wearing. He donned them and reached down and tore the scrub shirt off his colleague.

He looked up at the two Marines. "This is a nerve gas poisoning in our hospital. This is nerve gas, do you understand me? Alert your commanders. You need hazmat suits on. We need to seal off the corridors and call the operator. We need help!"

The two men looked at him, taking a moment to absorb what he said. One of them got on his two-way radio and relayed the message. Bill dragged his unconscious colleague over to the elevator bank and hit the button for the fifth floor. When they arrived, Bill dragged him off and laid him carefully in the waiting area, well away from any patient rooms. He ran to the nurse's station and asked for a nurse to open the Pyxis machine for atropine and II PAM chloride if they had it. He guessed they didn't supply the latter on the floor. The nurse flew into action and drew up a syringe of atropine for Bill.

He put on a protective mask and ran to the waiting area and kneeled down next to his colleague. He gave him the shot of atropine. Slowly, the drug took hold and the anesthesiologist began to cough. He vomited, so Bill rolled him on his side. The anesthesiologist was disoriented, but breathing. Bill told him he needed to get him in the shower to wash off the vapor that might be remaining on his skin. He helped him to an empty patient room and turned on the shower for him. He called to a nurse to help and instructed her to put him to bed once he was out of the shower. She looked at him quizzically, and Bill told her it was an emergency.

Where's a fire alarm, thought Bill. It would be the quickest way to seal off corridors to prevent the gas from continuing to move throughout the hospital. He ran down the 5 flights of stairs and pulled the nearest fire alarm to the lobby, since the emergency response would be triggered by location. Several automatic doors that were wired into the fire alarm system began closing. Bill ran back up to the fifth floor nurse's station. He picked up the phone at the unit coordinator's desk and called the operator. He identified himself, then told her to broadcast the following overhead page: "Hazardous waste spill in the PACU area and adjoining hallways. Evacuate entire first floor of main hospital. Do not come down to the first floor lobby area. Close doors to units and seal off areas. Close doors to patient rooms. This is an airborne hazardous waste." He told her to repeat it at least 4 times every two minutes for the next few minutes.

He also called 911 from the nurses' station. He explained to the operator that the hospital was under a nerve gas attack on the first floor, and they needed help from responders who were wearing hazardous waste protective gear. He gave her his cell phone number in case any emergency response personnel, including the military, had any questions. He called the operator at the switchboard again, and asked her to page the president of the hospital and the administrator on-call to advise them of the situation, and gave his cell phone number.

Then, he called both the Emergency Department lead physician and the pharmacy, advising them that he thought it was sarin. He said he administered atropine to a victim and it worked. The pharmacy manager confirmed they had a large supply in stock of the duo dote of atropine and II PAM chloride. He told Bill the CDC supplied it, and as soon as he broke the seal on the containers, the CDC would be electronically notified and would send help, in addition to informing other branches of government. Bill encouraged him to do so, preparing to get multiple orders for its use.

He was beginning to feel the effects of sarin vapor himself, having run down to the lobby a second time. He must have breathed in some of the vapor. He asked the same nurse who had drawn up the atropine for his colleague to draw up a quarter of that dose for himself. She did, and she administered it to him. As soon as it was onboard, he felt the symptoms dissipate. He obviously had experienced a mild exposure.

He helped the nursing staff seal off the floor and the patient rooms. For the 26 patients on that floor, he ordered the nurses to put an oxygen mask on every single one of them, plugging the mask into the special Oxygen outlet on the wall in each room. At least, they'd be insulated from breathing air that came through the ventilation system.

After about 10 minutes, Bill began receiving calls on his cell phone from the military commander, the fire department chief, the hospital president and the administrator on call. He advised all of them that he believed there was a nerve gas poisoning currently underway. He relayed that it started in the PACU because that's where the first page came from. t must have spread on the air through the hallway. He asked the administrator on call to talk to facilities about shutting off the air circulation system in the hospital, so poisoned air didn't move throughout the complex.

The military commander told Bill that they already had men in hazmat suits bringing victims out of the PACU to the Emergency Department, where they were being undressed and showered while simultaneously receiving the duo dote. For the patients in beds with endotracheal tubes, like the teenager Bill had just operated on, the trained emergency personnel in the hazmat suits simply administered more muscle relaxants to the patients so the ventilator could continue breathing for them. They administered auto-injectors that contained the duo dote, and wheeled them toward the ED with the ventilators in tow.

Other emergency personnel in hazmat suits located the broken ampule and cleaned up the liquid on the floor. They saved one piece of the glass ampule with the labeling on it in a clear, sealed container as evidence. They proceeded to clean up the floor, which would at least stop producing the vapor.

In the facilities department, the men reversed the heating and ventilation airflow to create a negative pressure environment in the PACU so the air wouldn't flow out into other parts of the hospital.

Bill was prepared to stay on the fifth floor of the hospital, providing reassurance to his patients and the staff throughout the night. They were all on lockdown and quarantine anyway. It was imperative that people not open doors and move through the hospital until given the all clear. It would be a long night, but he was hopeful that they had contained the disaster as best they could. He wondered how in the hell sarin had been deployed in his hospital. He hoped the forensics team in the military would figure it out.

Bill texted Pepper what had just happened, but didn't get a reply.

***

CHAPTER 35
Mission Igor

Washington, D.C.

White House Situation Room

The 30-minute break in the Situation Room was interrupted by everyone's pagers beeping. In a matter of minutes, they were convened again, and had the General of the Army Reserve headquartered at Fort Snelling in Minnesota giving them a report about a sarin exposure at Southview Hospital in Minneapolis.

Pepper gasped, and Brent grabbed her hand. Another attack, she thought. My Bill is there! Please tell me this isn't happening.

Pepper searched in her briefcase for her cell phone, and saw a text from Bill sent about ten minutes ago saying he was okay. She breathed a sigh of relief, listening to the rest of the report about how they had contained the disaster at the hospital. Two people had died, the nurse who had initially opened the ampule and the nurse who had come to her aid. Everyone else responded favorably to the administration of the duo dote, but not without nerve damage.

The military forensics team had identified the Fentanyl ampule in the PACU as the culprit, and was working on confiscating the drug from all Pyxis and C2 machines in the hospital on a systematic basis so as not to co-mingle the ampules from each location. All ampules from the PACU Pyxis machine were collected in one evidence box and labelled as such, as were the ampules from the C2 safe in the inpatient pharmacy. It wouldn't take long to test them at the military lab at Fort Snelling.

The government sent out a safety bulletin to all hospitals through a CDC notification system to confiscate and set aside all Fentanyl to prevent it from happening at another hospital.

President Scott turned to the Secretary of Defense, Donald Weaver. "How long before we can determine where the sarin in the broken Fentanyl ampule was manufactured?"

"I don't know, but I can find out," he said.

"Do that. I want to see if it was made in Russia."

"My team is working on that as we speak," said the Joint Chief for the Army.

"How long?" asked the President.

"We can compare its chemical composition with the sarin samples collected at the Eagles' game, so it should be less than an hour," said the General.

"Okay, good. 'd like the report on military options against Volkov's Palace while we wait for the forensics report on the sarin ampule from Ft. Snelling," said the President.

"Yes, sir," said General Stewart.

General Stewart stood and walked to the end of the table beside the video screen. On his signal, the screen showed a satellite map of the Black Sea, with Turkey to the south, Georgia to the southeast, and Russia on its east shore. Volkov's Palace was on the east coast.

"Mr. President, Volkov's Palace is located near the village of Praskoveevka in the Krasnodar Krai District. Here," he said, using his laser pointer to highlight a spot on the map.

"Our nearest military base from which we could launch a hunt and kill attack is in Merzifon, Turkey, on the southern shore of the Black Sea. Here," he said, pointing.

"Why do we need a land base? Can't we use the USS Donald Cook to launch missiles? I thought it was a destroyer that patrolled the Black Sea," asked President Scott.

"Yes, sir, it does. However, the USS Donald Cook is in port in Rota, Spain because it just finished a three-week patrol. Pursuant to the 1936 Montreux Convention Regarding the Regime of the Straits, warships from countries without a coast along the Black Sea must depart after 21 days. Turkey has control over the Bosporus and Dardanelles Straits, which connect the Mediterranean Sea to the Black Sea, and has been lenient with this rule for the U.S., especially when Russia reasserted control over Crimea. But since that time, we've adhered to the rule. At its present location in Spain, the USS Donald Cook is too far away to mobilize for an immediate mission."

"Okay. Please continue," said President Scott.

"We propose that we launch a hunt and kill unmanned aerial vehicle attack over both sea and land," said General Stewart.

"A drone attack?" asked the President.

"Yes. We already have a dozen drones in flight to Merzifon Air Force Base. They should arrive within the hour. They'll be refueled when they land, and some will need to be outfitted with more armaments."

"Where are they coming from?" asked the President.

"Multiple locations. Installations from Incirlik Air Force Base in Turkey, Qatar and Italy, as well as from the Carrier George H.W. Bush, which is currently patrolling the Mediterranean."

"Good," said the President.

"The drones are the MQ-9 Reapers, which are larger and faster than the Predator Drone," said the General. "The Reaper can go three times faster than a Predator, reaching a cruising speed of about 275 miles per hour, and they have a range of 1000 nautical miles. It's 300 nautical miles from Merzifon to Volkov's Palace as the crow flies over the Black Sea."

"For the other six drones that will travel over land along the coastline," he continued, "it will take about three times longer, so they'll arrive later than the squadron that travels by Sea. If the sea squadron successfully completes the mission, then we'll have the land-based drones fly back. On the other hand, if the sea squadron is shot down by Russian naval vessels, then the land squadron will have to complete the mission. Once they reach Volkov's Palace, the land squadron will run out of fuel before they can return, so we plan to crash them into the Black Sea."

The General paused for questions. The President nodded, so the General continued.

"Each Reaper will be armed with four AGM-114 Hellfire II missiles that'll be capable of destroying Volkov's Palace, which is the size of any respectable hotel. However, we want redundancy for this mission, so it's our goal to have at least four missiles, and maybe more, hit the target. Once again, each drone will carry four missiles," said the General.

"Where will the drone operators be stationed?" asked the President.

"Creech Air Force Base outside of Las Vegas, sir," said the General.

"Won't the Russians pick up the Reapers on Radar? Don't they have an extensive naval fleet on the Black Sea with Aegis radar?"

"Yes, they do," said the General. "Sevastopol is the center of Russia's Black Sea fleet, and it's located about 200 miles north of Volkov's Palace. At any given time, there could be Russian naval vessels patrolling the eastern coastline with Aegis radar. Our plan, however, is to have both squadrons of drones fly below the radar. The sea squadron will engage in 'sea skimming,' or flying lower than 20 feet above sea level, depending on weather conditions. Likewise, the land squadron will fly just above the tree tops, which is flying nap-of-the-earth."

"Do you think that will work?" asked the President.

"There's a high percentage it will. Each squadron will be aided by a high flying radar jamming plane. We'll have an EA-18G Growler Electronic Attack Aircraft flying above both squadrons at an altitude of about 35,000 feet. The Growler will take off from Merzifon AFB as well."

"I'm not familiar with the Growler. It jams radar?" asked the President.

"It's basically a redesigned F/A-18 Super Hornet fighter jet that now has radar jamming pods in place of armaments in its gun bays. It has what we refer to as 'high radiated power jamming transmitters' that suppress the enemy's radar systems. It still has a few missiles aboard, but its purpose is electronic warfare," he said.

"So, are you going to use the jammer even though our drones are flying under the radar?" asked the President.

"The Growler will first assess whether there are radar systems in the vicinity that would detect the drones. If there are, then it'll jam them. If not, it won't need to," said General Stewart.

"Alright," said the President.

"We've had a high success rate with this tactic in the Middle East, including over Libya. Russia is more sophisticated, of course, so there are no guarantees. That's why we're sending in six drones in each squadron, flying about five minutes behind one another," explained the general.

"So there will be 48 Hellfire missiles in total," said the President.

"Yes. The pilots operating the drones will be authorized to fire on the target, which is Volkov's Palace, as soon as they're within range. The sea squadron should have a travel time of only an hour. You can see a satellite photo of Volkov's Palace here, on the Idokopas Cape. The geographic coordinates are listed under the photo. They are 44 degrees North and 38 degrees East, plus the minutes, of course. The land squadron has a three-hour travel time. We're sending them up first, so the lead land drone will have a half-hour jump on the sea squadron," said General Stewar.

"And when do the Reapers depart Merzifon?" asked the President.

"We estimate they'll be refueled and ready to take off from Merzifon AFB within an hour and thirty minutes, at the outside, sir."

"So, in about two and a half hours, we could be sending Hellfire missiles into Volkov's Palace?" asked the President.

"Yes, sir," said General Stewart.

"What's the military name for the mission?" asked Charlie Duncan.

"Mission Igor," replied General Stewart.

"Very well. Is anyone at this table opposed to Mission Igor?" asked the president.

Gabriel Friedman, the Secretary of State raised her hand.

"Go ahead, Gabriel," urged the President.

She cleared her throat. "Mr. President, with all due respect, I don't feel like we have enough evidence that President Volkov is behind the attack. We know he's been cavorting with Svea Lovgren, who I agree is behind the attack, but anyone in Russia could have manufactured the sarin. Just because it's Russian-made doesn't mean Volkov knew about it. So, I'd propose that we gather more intelligence over the course of the next few days, and maybe weeks, before we fly into Russia to assassinate the Russian President."

"Thank you, Gabriel," said President Scott. "You've made a solid point. Does anyone want to add to Ms. Friedman's point?"

No one responded.

"Does anyone have any misgivings that Volkov is conspiring with Svea Lovgren?" asked the President.

No one responded.

"Does anyone other than Ms. Friedman have an objection to the immediate implementation of Mission Igor?"

Donald Weaver, the Secretary of Defense, raised his hand.

"Yes, Donald."

"Mr. President, I want to go on record of supporting the immediate implementation of Mission Igor. Today, we lost over 60,000 Americans at a football stadium to a nerve gas attack perpetrated by Volkov and Lovgren. The evidence is as clear as it's going to get. Frankly, I don't know how we could have better evidence from this distance. If we wait, Volkov and Lovgren will just go into hiding or ramp up military security. They'll learn we're onto them.

Right now, we have the element of surprise, because they don't realize that we know yet. I believe the mission is designed well, and will not instigate an attack from Russia. I say it's a go, Mr. President."

"Thank you, Donald. Anyone else?" asked the President.

No one responded.

The President spoke. "I authorize immediate implementation of Mission Igor. Let's reassemble in an hour, ladies and gentlemen. Meeting adjourned."

Everyone stood and waited for the President to leave the room before they began to mingle.

***

CHAPTER 36
The Lesson

Praskoveevka, Russia

Volkov successfully kept his guests cloistered away in a separate wing of his palace, so his expectant wife wouldn't realize who they were. She was under strict instruction not to venture into the guest wing of the palace when he was entertaining business associates. Nor did she want to. She had met some of the men with whom Volkov did business, and they scared her to the core of her being. She'd rather stick to her half of the palace, living in her fantasy world of expensive clothes and lavish furnishings, than see his dark world.

It had been several hours since the football stadium attack, and Dana and Clive had managed to sleep in their separate, but adjoining, rooms in their spacious suite that was decorated Old World Russia.

To Dana's delight, Svea had joined Dana in the middle of the night and ravished her. Svea was drunk with power over her successful attack, and wanted sex until they both were limp with exhaustion. Dana had offered to bring Clive in if Svea wasn't satisfied, but she had declined. Instead, Svea had surprised Dana with a gift of emotional commitment, a small ring with a ruby set in the middle. She said it was a sign of her love. She also said she wanted to come to Dana's island in the Caribbean to spend more time with her. Svea planned to return to her cabinet ministry post in

Stockholm, of course, so no one would be suspicious of a sudden departure. After that, she promised she would clear her calendar for the entire month of January to be with Dana.

Dana squealed with delight, snuggling with Svea until they both fell into a deep sleep. The sun rose before either of them was ready to leave the bed, but they showered and met Volkov and Clive for breakfast in the formal dining room of their guest wing.

Volkov had watched their bedtime romp by video last night so knew how close they were. He worked through the ramifications of their relationship in his mind. He couldn't decide whether Dana was continuing to fulfill her assignment or whether she had formed a loyal bond with Svea. He didn't understand women, which meant he didn't trust either one of them. His paranoia was alleviated somewhat when Dana passed behind him, giving his shoulder a squeeze. She could send a message with just one touch.

He knew it was time for Dana and Clive to depart, as there was nothing more for them to do at his palace. He was deciding if he could trust them to be discreet, and fade away back to their island life, or if he had to physically silence them. He decided he'd give them a chance because they were so good at their profession, he wanted to keep them on the payroll for future assignments.

However, he needed to teach them a lesson before they departed, since he was paying them handsomely. Being the smart operators they were, he trusted fear and money would keep them quiet. He was killing time with them over breakfast until his Army General informed him the lesson was fully prepared. He'd include Svea in the lesson as well. It'd be good for her.

They talked for a few more minutes until the Army General walked into the dining room and saluted Volkov.

"Mr. President, may I speak to you in private?" he asked.

"Go ahead and be candid in front of my friends, General. Say what you came to say," prompted Volkov.

"Sir, we have the Gulfstream jet on radar over the Ukraine with the twelve soldiers on board." The jet had been delayed out of Kiev due to refueling problems.

"Very good," said Volkov. "Let's go to the conference room with audio and visual. Svea, Dana and Clive, I'd like you to accompany the General and myself."

Dana looked at Svea with a jolt of fear. She attempted to cover it up, but Volkov caught it. Interesting that she looked at Svea rather than Clive. Overall, however, the fact that she was showing fear was good.

The group walked to an elevator and rode to the basement level, where badges and access codes were required. They walked down a hallway, one soldier leading and two bringing up the rear. Dana and Clive were beginning to feel a bit like prisoners. Svea was confident in her position, as per usual. She always stood straight, thrusting her chest out as she walked.

They followed as the soldiers turned into a modern military conference room with video screens and electronics. The Army General nodded to the lesser ranking man to pull up the radar feed on the video screen. Volkov sat at the head of the twenty-foot-long table, and the Army General sat to Volkov's right. Volkov motioned for Svea, Dana and Clive to sit next to him on the other side. They tentatively took their seats and sat like school children who had been summoned to the principal's office.

There was a blip on the radar making its way across Ukrainian airspace, obviously an airplane of some sort. On the split screen, the camera from one of the Russian MiG fighter jets filmed the chartered Gulfstream's flashing lights and jet engine fire in the night sky.

"Are we sure it's the 12 soldiers on board the Gulfstream?" asked Volkov.

"Yes, sir," answered his Army General.

"Svea, Dana and Clive, this is the team that flew the drones into the American football stadium and poisoned the fans. They ran a successful mission and should be commended for it. However, they know what they did, and soldiers have a reputation for drinking and talking. I don't like it when my confidants or soldiers talk. Do you understand?" asked Volkov.

Clive was the only one who had the guts to speak. "Of course, President Volkov. You can count on both Dana and me to be absolutely confidential about our dealings with you, including anything we've seen. It's how we make our living. We don't want to jeopardize our relationship with you because we're looking forward to more projects," said Clive. He stared straight into Volkov's eyes without flinching.

"Good. I'm glad you understand what that means to me. The soldiers have no such incentive, Clive. So I have no choice." Volkov turned to his Army General and ordered, "Destroy it."

The Army General turned and transmitted the order to one of the men at a control console wearing both a microphone and headphones. The soldier relayed the command to the pilots of the MiGs.

The soldiers on the Gulfstream hadn't even noticed the two Russian MiGs tailing their small jet. On the order from the officer over the radio, one of the MiGs fired an air-to-air short range missile into the fuselage of the Gulfstream, setting it ablaze and obliterating its occupants. The two MiGs flew off and began their return to the nearest Russian air force base.

Dana jumped a few inches out of her chair, covering her mouth with her hand. Clive stared at the screen, clenching his jaw. They were too scared to look at Volkov. Svea, an icicle of emotion, stared at Volkov and nodded her head.

"Well played," she said in a flat tone.

"Thank you." Volkov smiled. Mission accomplished on both fronts. He nodded to his Army General for a job well done.

"Now you know how I deal with unpredictable loose ends," said Volkov. He looked pointedly at Dana and Clive.

Dana and Clive both looked at him and nodded. Dana found her voice and spoke. "You can be absolutely certain of our secrecy, President Volkov. We've never met you."

"Very good," said Volkov, standing. Everyone else jumped up and followed him out.

There being no further business to conduct, Volkov told Dana and Clive there would be a car waiting to take them to the Sochi airport in 20 minutes. He instructed them to gather their things and meet him in the foyer.

Svea followed Dana and Clive to their room. She and Dana hugged for quite a while, then kissed.

"I promise I'll see you soon, okay?" said Svea.

"I'm going to miss you. I'm kind of worried about you staying here. Why don't you come with us?" asked Dana.

"There's no need, and Volkov hasn't given me permission to leave. I think he wants me to stay and make plans," said Svea. They all correctly assumed the room was bugged.

Clive hugged Svea, too, and she accompanied them down to the foyer to say goodbye to Volkov. They proceeded outside to their waiting car on the crushed white granite by the fountain. Their shoes made a crunching sound as they walked in silence. It was a cold sound that Dana would forever associate with Volkov, his palace, and what she had just witnessed.

Volkov glanced around the manicured grounds, seeing at least eight armed guards dressed in cammo fatigues patrolling the woods. He squinted as he looked up at the roof tops. He spotted three more. Of course, his plain clothes detail was swarming the interior of the palace and surrounding him at this moment. He was comfortable with the security today, in case the Americans suspected him of the terror act.

He had already kissed Dana goodbye and shaken Clive's hand inside the palace, as he didn't like the prospect of spy satellites catching him kissing her outside. He had gone through one divorce and had remarried a much younger woman. They had a baby on the way, and there was no need to unduly upset his young wife in case the photos became public. And then there were the Russian people who respected his youth and virility, but didn't want to see the sleazy side of him. He had a public image to uphold, after all.

He nodded to a man with a bull neck and boxer's nose. The man gave Clive a silver briefcase with $250,000 in cash inside. It was payment in full for all their services. They had done well for Volkov, and he'd keep them on his short list for projects in the future.

The chauffeur held the rear door open for Dana as she slipped into the backseat. Clive joined her on the other side. They were headed to Sochi for a commercial flight to Amsterdam, then ultimately back to St. Martin. They figured they might lay low in Amsterdam for a few days. Maybe make a large deposit in a trusted bank.

They would travel by car for four hours on Highway E97 that ran along the Black Sea Coast from Volkov's Palace to the Sochi airport. Their chauffeur got behind the wheel and pulled out of Volkov's driveway.

Dana and Clive breathed a sigh of relief once they were in the backseat with the door closed. They knew they were proverbial loose ends in Volkov's eyes, so he might decide to take them out despite his earlier assurances. In fact, he hadn't reassured them; he had only threatened them. There was nothing they could do about it now, however, unless they arranged for alternative transport, which was out of the question.

They sat in silence because they assumed the car was bugged. About an hour into their drive, Dana became genuinely fearful for Svea's safety back at the palace as she played with the ring Svea had given her. Her intuition told her something was brewing. She was too scared to say it out loud for fear of Volkov overhearing, so she decided to text Svea, hoping she would get reception in this area.

Svea, it's Dana.

Dana hit 'send' and her text appeared to go, making her hopeful for cell service. She kept checking her phone. At least 10 minutes passed without a reply from Svea. At last, a message popped up on her screen.

Miss me already?

Yes. I'm concerned about you. When can you leave?

Don't be. We're celebrating and making plans.

Just say the word and we could turn around. U could come with us.

Don't be silly. I'll plan to visit you in the next few weeks. Stay safe, my Sweet.

U too. Thank u for the beautiful ring.

Dana didn't like the feel of how this was wrapping up. On the one hand, she was glad to be leaving Volkov. On the other hand, was the ring that represented Svea's love, a love that might never be experienced again.

***

CHAPTER 37

Final Drone Act

Washington, D.C.

White House Situation Room

The group was on break until Mission Igor was ready to roll.

"Are we invited back in for the mission completion, Allen?" asked Pepper.

"As far as I'm concerned, you are. The President's Chief of Staff, Charlie, controls who's in the room for the benefit of the President. If he doesn't approach you between now and when we reconvene, you're welcome back. You two are responsible for figuring out most of this puzzle, so you're entitled to know how it turns out."

"Thanks. Allen, it had to be traumatic being at the Eagles' game. How are you?" asked Pepper.

"It was a battlefield. I knew what was happening right away because I did a tour in Iraq. My training kicked into gear, and I went into survival autopilot. We're actually lucky that Paul Black had duct tape in his stadium suite. If he hadn't, I'm not so sure we would have survived," said Allen.

"Were there any other survivors?" asked Brent.

"Actually, yes. A handful," said Allen. "The Russians used an oil emulsion to weigh down the aerosolized gas, so it would be heavier than air and sink onto the crowd. That weight also kept it from evaporating as fast, though, so it didn't carry in the wind as much as a nonoil gas mixture would have. Anyone who was underground at the stadium lived. In fact, the groundskeeper who paints the lines and end zones had an OSHA mask in his work area. He saw what was going on by watching T.V. in the underground break room. He put on his mask right away and had three other masks that he told his coworkers to wear. They stayed down there until military personnel safely evacuated them."

"Wow. Fast thinking and the right equipment," said Pepper.

"I'm not so sure those painting masks would have been effective if they had walked upstairs into the stadium proper," said Allen, "but they were smart to wear them down there. And more importantly, to stay put and lock the doors. Which they did."

"Glad you're alright, Old Man," said Brent.

"It'll take more than that to kill me off," said Allen.

"What's our plan for L.A.?" asked Pepper.

"We currently have military stationed at every hospital in Orange County. So, the treatment side of the equation is secure. The Sarin deployment side of the equation is still being investigated. We've requested the Mayor to broadcast on T.V. for people not to go to large gatherings in stadiums, etcetera. It isn't a tough sell, considering what just happened. We have both local and federal law enforcement following every lead on where nerve gas and potential terrorists could be located. It's a needle-in-the-haystack type of situation. After this second episode at Southview Hospital, we don't know whether we're looking for drones carrying nebulizers or Fentanyl ampules. That makes it even harder," said Allen.

"We need a lead or tip," said Brent.

"I agree. I never cease to be amazed at the observation powers of the American public though. Someone might see something that looks suspicious and call it in," said Allen.

"That would help," said Brent.

"Let's get some water and food, then return to the Sit Room. Activity will start now. Pepper, this will be an important learning opportunity for you," said Allen.

Pepper managed to steal a few minutes to text Bill that she loved him and wanted to see him soon.

***

After everyone returned to the Sit Room from their break, the President called the meeting to order. "General Stewart, it's your show, tell us what's happening."

"We've divided up the video boards at each end of the table. The sea-based squadron of drones will be at this end. The land-based squadron of drones will be at that end. We've split the screens at each end into six squares so you can see the footage from each individual drone. As you can see, the sea-based squadron is currently black because they aren't ready for takeoff yet. On the far screen, the land-based squadron footage has begun because they're just getting ready for takeoff. We're going to send them ahead of the sea-based squadron since it will take them two hours longer to reach Volkov's Palace. This will result in the lead land-based drone reaching the target one and a half hours after the sea-based squadron rather than two hours later."

They all watched as each individual land-based Reaper was cleared for takeoff and flew into the air. Since they were scheduled to fly out five minutes behind each other, it took thirty minutes for the entire squadron to become airborne.

Once the land-based squadron was in the air, the sea-based squadron began its takeoff pattern. After thirty minutes, they were airborne as well.

It was nighttime in Turkey, so the video images were dark, save for a few sporadic house lights from the land-based squadron. The sea-based squadron was practically black. The wind was calm, so the Reapers didn't have to contend with choppy sea swells, they were flying so low.

When the sea-based squadron was thirty minutes into its flight, the lead drone sent back live video coverage of Russian naval vessel, the SKR – Storozhevoy Korabl. It was patrolling the east coast, heading due south. It was roughly the equivalent of an American frigate, and had enough firepower on board to shoot several drones. It also was equipped with radar.

The lead drone was on target to pass in front of the frigate if it held its current flight path. With a 66-foot wingspan and a 950 horsepower turboprop engine, the lead drone would be vulnerable to either visual or audio detection by the deckhands on the frigate, in addition to radar detection. The Sit Room was silent while the Chief of Staff for the Air Force spoke to the Lieutenant General in charge of the mission on the ground at Creech AFB.

The Lieutenant General in the operator's office confirmed a new flight plan that would take each drone behind, or north of, the moving frigate. The lead drone made as quick of a turn to the north as it could at low altitude to create as much distance between itself the frigate. The drone's maneuverability was limited by its proximity to the surface of the sea and its long wing span. Fortunately, the frigate was traveling at a decent rate of speed, which widened the distance considerably between the drone, which had turned to the north, and the frigate, which was heading due south.

Pepper and the assembled brass watched as the lead Reaper passed abaft of the frigate by about 500 yards, the camera on the Reaper picking up the choppy wake from the frigate.

Onboard the frigate, no one was looking or listening for drones. Most of the crew was lingering down below in the mess deck after dinner. Their east coast patrol in the Black Sea was routine and generally uneventful, so one of the men had grabbed his guitar and was playing every Russian folk song he knew. He was a large man with a full, wiry beard and a big baritone voice. He smiled when he sang, and his eyebrows had a mischievous arch to them, sometimes hiding under his big mop of curly hair.

He was leading the men in a rousing version of "Polyushko-Polye," a Russian military song that had been passed down for a hundred years. Another Russian, Ivan Rebroff, had recorded it and made it famous for the general public. While it was quite lyrical and rhymed when sung in Russian, its English translation was a bit dull. All the men in the mess deck sang:

Field, my field, my wide field,
The heroes ride over the field,
Hey, the heroes of the Red Army.

The girls are crying,
The girls are sorrowful today,
Their sweethearts went away for a long time,
Hey, their sweethearts went away to the army.

You girls, cast a glance,
Cast a glance in our direction,
Wave far down the road,
Ey, the happy road.

We only see
We see grey mist,
The hate of the enemy behind the forest,
Hey, the enemy's hate, like a mist.

Hey, girls, look,
We are ready to engage the enemy,
Our horses are fleet-footed,
Our tanks are fast-driving.

Hey, while on the collective farms,
The work is efficiently progressing,
Today we are watchmen,
Today we are keeping watch.

Lyrics by Viktor Gusev, 1933

The chorus from the mess deck wafted up to the main deck, so the men on watch were listening to their patriotic song when the first drone flew by 500 yards abaft of the frigate. No one noticed it, and it was flying below the radar, so the radar operator didn't pick it up either. As the frigate continued south, the remaining five Reapers passed over the frigate's wake easily. By the last drone, there wasn't even a ripple in the black water from the frigate.

As predicted by General Stewart, the sea-based squadron made good time, and after one hour of flight, the video feed indicated the lead Reaper had made landfall. In a matter of seconds, the video showed a huge palace, the size of a hotel. The perimeter was well-lighted, but the interior lights were sporadic.

"We've locked on the target. Permission to fire," asked the Reaper flight operator from Creech AFB.

"Permission granted. Fire," ordered General Stewart.

Everyone in the Sit Room was glued to the video screen. There was a blast of red fire, then blinding white light. Debris came flying at the cameras. Small mushroom clouds appeared.

***

Svea and Volkov were swimming laps in his Olympic pool in the lower level of the palace. Svea said she needed to stretch out from her recent travels (and night of sex with Dana), and Volkov regularly swam three to four miles per day, so they hit the pool together.

Volkov told his military adjutant, who was also his valet, to alert the spa staff that he and Svea would need a massage and meal after their swim. It was a challenge keeping his affair with Svea private from his pregnant wife, who was currently in their bedroom suite three floors above the pool level. He had told his wife long ago that she was not allowed in the pool level while he swam his laps because he needed to clear his mind. His men kept guard at the door, and wouldn't let her enter if she appeared.

Svea swam up to Volkov, both of them being naked, and wrapped her legs around his waist and her arms around his neck. He became aroused immediately and she guided him into her. He stood in the middle of the pool and pounded into her. She was crazed with the power of having attacked the United States, and couldn't imagine a more satisfying victory lap than going at it with Volkov in his pool.

She threw her head back and screamed as he drove into her. That was the last thing she ever said or did in her twisted lifetime on Earth as the Hellfire missiles lived up to their names, obliterating both of them in a nanosecond. The explosions were thunderous, and could be seen for miles as one drone after another released its missiles into the palace, setting it aflame in brilliant blues and oranges, while pieces of bricks and mortar flew high into the air, dropping into the Black Sea.

All six sea drones fired their payloads into the palace, essentially eliminating it from the map. By the last of the 24 hellfire missiles, the Russian military radar was also exploding in color. The command alerts were being electronically transmitted to the nearest base, which was a few hours to the north. It wouldn't be long before the fighter jets were scrambled at Sevastopol and sent to Volkov's Palace, which was now a burning pile of rubble.

The land-based drones had already flown past the half way point, and the U.S. didn't want the Russians to identify them as U.S. enemy aircraft, so the order was given to crash them into the Black Sea. It was accomplished in short order, long before Russia's fighter jets even started their warm up protocol at Sevastopol.

At some point during a forensic investigation, it would become apparent that the Hellfire missiles were U.S. manufactured, but they hadn't carried any U.S. insignia, so the U.S. would still have deniability when the Russians confronted President Scott. That was the plan anyway. The Russians would be infuriated, and it was their nature to seek revenge, so the U.S. was on high alert for an intercontinental ballistic missile launch. The team remained in the Sit Room long after Volkov's Palace was destroyed.

***

CHAPTER 38

The Videos

Minneapolis, Minnesota

Allen Montgomery was in town for Brent's wedding, so he arranged a meeting with Brent and Pepper to debrief, and make a plan for Pepper's career with the Agency.

Pepper suggested they meet at her house rather than rent a conference room at a hotel, so they were seated at Pepper's dining room table. Bill was at the hospital. Daisy wasn't used to all the commotion, but she was happy to see Brent again, having met him at Jackie's house. She snuggled up to his legs and flopped herself down on his feet under the table. He would occasionally reach down and scratch her behind the ears, eliciting a moan and stretch.

Pepper prepared some sandwiches and salad, and they drank iced tea while they discussed the events that had transpired in such a short amount of time. It was still somewhat surreal that a nerve gas attack had been successfully carried out on a football stadium full of Americans. The nation was reeling in sorrow and shock.

Unfortunately, Allen would probably have to go to Capitol Hill to testify to a Senate Committee about why the Agency hadn't prevented the attack. He would probably take a beating.

It was also predictable that the Senate Committee would use parts of his testimony to begin drafting new regulations with respect to drones. Pepper pointed out that the current airspace laws didn't address drones, so they needed to write some - fast.

"Seriously, I'm surprised we haven't had any type of regulation yet, and not just by the FAA. I'm talking about state laws, similar to driving cars and boats," said Pepper. "Maybe drones should be registered like cars and boats. Maybe operators should have licenses after they've passed both a written and driving exam."

"Those are logical," said Allen. "Whatever Congress does enact, you can be sure it will miss the mark on preventing what happened at the Linc."

"Well, how about not allowing drones above the premises of big events at stadiums, for starters," said Pepper.

"I'd like to see a chip in drones that couldn't be removed. It'd be similar to the chip in your cell phone that would make it detectable by GPS," said Brent.

"Very good idea," said Pepper. "We need something, but my experience is that Congress usually overreacts after a catastrophic event, then we suffer under that for a while before we can scale back the regulations at a later date."

"All good points. You've just prepped me for my hearing testimony," said Allen. He cleared his throat, indicating he was going to take the conversation in a different direction. "Pepper, you were instrumental in solving this terrorism plot with Brent. I was skeptical at first about

Brent's recommendation to bring a consultant on board who didn't have a military or police background, but the way your mind works compensates for Brent's dull abilities, so you two make a good team."

"Too bad the suite had duct tape," said Brent.

"Thank you," said Pepper. "I had misgivings about my role as well, but having been through two investigations and two major terror plots, I'm developing a taste for this work. An addiction, really. It's purposeful work. To be honest, I feel that I'm not at my best right now because I'm still grieving my son's loss, and that takes away from my cognitive abilities. My grief therapist assures me my full intellectual capacity will return, though. I just hope it's sooner rather than later."

"Thanks for being honest with me. We'll train that honesty out of you at the Agency," he joked. "Seriously, we've all lost buddies in the field. Obviously, that loss isn't the same as yours by a long shot, but I understand what you're going through. I agree with your therapist that you'll get your full capacity back some day. The timing is different for everyone. In the meantime, we'd like to run you through some formal training – in both the field and the classroom. Are you up for that?" asked Allen.

"Of course. I look forward to it! Where would this take place?" she asked.

"Well, Brent is working on getting StarrFitness certified for the field training. Both hand-to-hand combat and weapons training require a pretty high level of expertise and certification, so I'm not sure if Brent will be able to pull it off. If he does, though, you could do some training there. Some of your classroom work can be done online. I'm happy to say you're a candidate for some high level training about information-gathering and subtle interrogation techniques, but you would have to come to Boston for that," said Allen.

"I fully intend to spend my share of time in Boston. I'm committed and want to do what's necessary. Like I said, I've sort of become addicted to fighting terrorists," said Pepper.

"Good. I'll get the paperwork going. Once you complete the training, it'll mean a bump in pay, too." That prospect made Pepper smile.

"Tell Pepper about the President's intention to send a letter to Bill," suggested Brent.

"What?" she asked.

"Yes, President Scott is up to his ears right now, but he's planning to send a formal letter of commendation to Bill for his quick thinking at Southview Hospital. Bill saved lives, and prevented a major disaster from happening, and that was not lost on the White House."

"No kidding? Bill will be embarrassed, but thrilled," said Pepper. "Actually, I have a question about the Fentanyl at Southview Hospital. Bill and I have been wondering if Svea and Volkov intentionally placed the sarin in the hospital pharmacy inventory to create the situation that happened, or was Fentanyl mistakenly shipped there?"

"Good question. It was mistakenly shipped to the hospital. You can tell Bill what I'm about to tell you, but don't make a habit of it in the future. He doesn't have any security clearance," said Allen.

"Understood," said Pepper.

"We traced the shipping documents from Southview's loading dock to Cargo City in Philadelphia where Thai Cargo Shipping is located. When we interviewed the warehouse employee, Steve, he showed us that the address for the Fentanyl was originally a fragmented sentence in the destination field of "South... House...," explained Allen.

He continued, "We now believe that the intended destination was a warehouse because the original address that accompanied it was a warehouse. And when we stormed the warehouse at that address in Minneapolis, it was vacant. Steve in Philly, however, was focusing on just the fragmented name so he looked up the past shipping history for pharmaceuticals that Thai Cargo Shipping had sent to Minneapolis, and Southview Hospital came up in the directory. He pulled up the address for Southview Hospital and typed it in, redirecting the shipment from the address to a warehouse in downtown Minneapolis to the hospital. The terrorists didn't intend for the Fentanyl shipment to go to the hospital. It ended up there by mistake."

"Fascinating. Were you able to track any other addresses from the Philadelphia warehouse?" asked Pepper.

"Only the shipment to the warehouse in Philly. The L.A. shipment of nebulizers never went through the Philadelphia airport because they were shipped by sea from the Bangkok Port. We found those nebulizers and drones in a house in L.A. based on an anonymous tip."

"Oh really? An anonymous tip? How did that go down?" asked Pepper.

"Turns out a curious little 12-year-old girl shot a video of the Russians from an alley. They were at a small house, and she was snooping. She was intrigued by the language they were speaking, and that they were playing with drones. She kept her video a secret from her parents until the President's television message for everyone to be on the lookout for suspicious behavior. When she showed her mom the video a few days after the President's message, her mom freaked out and called 911 immediately!" said Allen.

"As well she should have! That little girl is lucky she didn't get caught by the Russians. That would not have ended well for her," observed Brent.

"Agreed. Dodged a bullet there," said Allen. "Instead, she got a free trip to Washington, D.C., to meet the President. He gave her a medal for courage and bravery in a small ceremony at the White House. Her mom wanted to keep her anonymous, for good reason, but it was the sweetest thing I've ever seen. I had the privilege of attending."

"That gives me goose bumps, Allen. Did your L.A. team capture the Russian men that the little girl videotaped?" asked Pepper.

"Absolutely. We confiscated not only their drones, but also the sarin nebulizers," said Allen. "They're currently in custody, but they're not talkin'. The only phrase they keep repeating is 'back to Russia.' Yeah, right. Those guys aren't going back to the mother land. They'll be charged and tried. I predict they'll receive the death penalty. I'm sure they'll never finger Volkov. They probably don't even know he's dead."

"I agree," said Brent. "The Russian loyalty is amazing."

They ate and drank in silence for a few minutes, Daisy gazing longingly at Brent's plate.

"On another topic, do you feel confident we got both Volkov and Svea Lovgren? Meaning that they were in the palace at the time of the explosions?" asked Pepper.

"Oh yeah. All the satellite photos from the next several days after that confirmed no one could have survived that blast. We haven't seen any photographic evidence of either one of them," said Allen.

"Good. I have this recurring nightmare that they somehow made it out," said Pepper.

"You can rest easy from now on, Pepper. There's no way," said Allen.

"I actually feel sorry for Sweden in all of this, don't you guys?"

Both men laughed.

"Poor Sweden," said Allen. "They've never done anything to anyone. They've been one of the most peaceful countries on the face of the earth."

"Well, that probably started because they couldn't even sail a ship out of their harbor without it sinking. When you're that lame, you had better pursue peace," said Brent.

"Okay, I think you're being a bit harsh, Brent. You're obviously referring to the Vasa warship that sailed in 1628 and sank about 1000 yards into her maiden voyage," said Pepper.

"Did you two visit museums while you were in Stockholm?" asked Allen.

"No," said Pepper. "Louis Brown loves history and he told us all about Sweden because it tickled him. Brent was a good listener. The tragedy in all this is that Svea Lovgren completely ruined Sweden's pacifist reputation. This is obviously the first time in history that Sweden produced a terrorist."

"Yeah, well that's something I wanted to tell you as well. After the dust settled, President Scott got a call from Prime Minister Olaf Carlsson. He was so devastated that Svea Lovgren had been implicated in the terrorist attack, he apologized profusely. The President asked Carlsson how he knew Svea had been implicated, and Carlsson said he had a video that President Scott might want to watch."

"A video? Of what?" asked Pepper.

"Turns out that Svea Lovgren made a video while she was on a boat in the Stockholm archipelago. At the beginning of the video, she explains the date and where she is. After the President watched it, he sent it to our office to analyze for authenticity. I have Marty Cavanaugh and his tech team working on it right now," said Allen.

"Have you seen it? What does she say?" asked Pepper.

"Yes," said Allen. "Bottom line – she blames Volkov for blackmailing her into helping him carry out the terrorist attack. She takes her time in telling a story that she approached him about buying the Saab missiles that the Arabs reneged on, and that Volkov agreed, only if she agreed in return to help him with a nerve gas attack. She hastily accepted his deal, not knowing what he had in mind. She elaborates on how she and Volkov met periodically, and that he insisted she provide resources and use her shipping connections to get the sarin delivered to America. She says he threatened to kill her and her family if she didn't cooperate. It's quite compelling, really."

"Do you believe it? Because I don't," said Brent. "I met that icy bitch at the Royal Ball, and she was capable of deception."

"I think it's a long shot that there's any truth to it. I suspect she made it because she anticipated getting caught and wanted a scape goat. She knew Carlsson and others would probably believe her over Volkov because they hate Volkov that much. I doubt any of what she said is true," said Allen.

"I agree," said Pepper. "The woman I met at the Royal Ball was cold and cunning. Bigger question, though. Where did the video come from? Who sent it to Prime Minister Carlsson?"

"Ah yes. That, indeed, is the question, isn't it? It was hand-delivered by a bicyclist service to Sager House for the PM. The bicyclist rode off before anyone could talk to him. Sweden is so trusting that their security requirements aren't the same as in the U.S. The envelope was nondescript, and didn't have any writing on it. The DVD was off-the-shelf so could have been purchased anywhere. It's basically untraceable. I've concluded that there's someone out there who knew what Svea was up to in real time, but couldn't come forward for one reason or another."

"How about her staff? Brent and I noticed she had the same security detail while we watched her. Has Sweden interrogated them?" asked Pepper.

"Yes. Her staff didn't have any idea what she was up to, not surprisingly. Her security guard, Ulrik, was with her at Volkov's Palace when we sent the Hellfire missiles into it, so he went down in flames with her," explained Allen.

"I see," said Pepper.

Brent's phone started vibrating on the table and a text appeared on the screen. He picked it up and read it.

"Looks like it's time for me to go," he said. "Jackie wants me front and center at the church for the dress rehearsal. I want to keep my bride happy, you know. Are we wrapped up here?"

"Of course," said Allen. "You go. Do whatever Jackie tells you to. Don't make the same mistakes I did, Man."

"Thanks. Catch you guys later," said Brent. He brought his dishes to the kitchen, put on his parka and left.

Allen helped Pepper clean up the dishes while they chatted about the wedding, which was in two days. Tonight was the groom's dinner, to which they both were invited.

***

EPILOGUE

The Wedding

Minneapolis, Minnesota

It was a bitterly cold day in early December in Minneapolis, but Brent and Jackie were surrounded by family and friends in Jackie's Lutheran church. They faced the pastor at the top of the altar steps, in the same church Jackie had been baptized as a baby. Jackie had never felt more complete. The man she loved stood beside her and the man she considered to be her spiritual leader was about to join Brent and her in marriage.

Jackie wore an ivory silk shantung dress with lace accents and beautiful hand sewn pearls down the center seam in the back, making it difficult to decide which was prettier, the front of the dress or the back. It was a full length gown with a figure-fitting bodice through her hips, tapering to a short train that was beautiful, yet manageable.

It was strapless so her perfectly sculpted English-Scottish body carried it with grace and femininity. Jackie's sister, Blaire, a tall auburn-haired girl who emitted effervescent energy, was her maid of honor. She and Brent had decided to have only one person stand up for each of them.

Brent had been both physically and emotionally exhausted as a result of the intense work he and Pepper had done. Nevertheless, as soon as he had landed in Boston, he had gone to a jeweler near his office building and bought Jackie the most dazzling diamond ring he could afford.

He knew he loved her and he didn't want to be without her. The terrorist attack had reinforced that life was too short to delay being with the woman he loved. After cleaning up a mountain of paperwork at the office, he flew to Minneapolis and proposed again, this time with a ring.

They set the date as soon as they could reserve the church and a reception venue on a weekend. They kept the guest list small. Brent didn't much care how or where they were married, as long as he was the groom. Being a Catholic himself, he was fine with the liberal Lutheran approach to the pre-wedding counseling and the vows they were about to undertake. He had the most beautiful lady he had ever known by his side, and was filled with a happiness he hadn't experienced since childhood.

Brent was wearing a traditional black tuxedo with his lopsided grin and brown messy hair. From the guests' perspective in the pews, his broad shoulders dwarfed Jackie's small frame. Brent was a big man, and immediately to his right stood his younger brother, Reed, as his best man. Reed was as big as Brent, but a blonde-haired version. He currently resided in Australia, and Pepper heard that he ran a winery on the west coast somewhere. Brent and Jackie planned to stay with him on their honeymoon.

The Lutheran Pastor, Kevin Harris, addressed the guests and Brent and Jackie.

"Dearly beloved, we are gathered here today in the presence of God to witness the marriage of Jackie Margaret Starr and Brent William Cahill, to surround them with our prayers, and to share in their joy."

The small number of guests, about forty, sat in the pews looking at the backs of Jackie and Brent. Pepper and Bill were in the third row, right behind Jackie's family. Pepper wriggled her hand inside of Bill's as the ceremony started.

Witnessing Jackie and Brent's vows made her think about her own wedding, and how elated and nervous she had been when standing next to her big man, Bill. She looked at the ceremony bulletin and noticed on the back that there were two names under the caption of: In Memory of: Darin Cahill and Jake McCallan. It was so touching, Pepper pointed it out to Bill. Pepper wondered if Darin was Brent's father or brother. He had told her he lost someone close to him. Her heart swelled in her chest.

Pastor Kevin continued, "The scriptures teach us that the bond and covenant of marriage is a gift of God, a holy mystery in which two become one flesh, an image of the union of Christ and the church. As Jackie and Brent give themselves to each other today, we remember that at Cana in Galilee our Lord Jesus Christ made the wedding feast a sign of God's reign of love."

This was a special day for Pastor Kevin as well. He had known Jackie since she was in middle school. She had gone through his confirmation class and asked insightful and genuine questions, never too shy to question beliefs and probe deeper. Pastor Kevin had a special spot in his heart for Jackie, and he had been honored that she had asked him to perform their wedding ceremony. Having spent some time with Brent in the last few weeks, he was impressed with Brent's calm nature, especially given his work. It was clear to Pastor Kevin that Jackie and Brent were soul mates and blessed by God.

"Let us enter into this celebration confident that, through the Holy Spirit, Christ is present with us now also. We pray that this couple may fulfill God's purpose for the whole of their lives.

Pastor Kevin whispered to Jackie and Brent to face each other. As soon as their eyes met, they both teared up. Brent reached out and Jackie placed her trembling hands in his. Brent's hands were warm and steady.

"Jackie, will you have Brent to be your husband, to live together in the covenant of marriage? Will you love him, comfort him and honor and keep him, in sickness and in health, and, forsaking all others, be faithful to him as long as you both shall live?"

Jackie responded, "I will." Her sister handed her Brent's large gold band and Jackie guided it onto his finger. He smiled at her.

"Brent, will you have Jackie to be your wife, to live together in the covenant of marriage? Will you love her, comfort her and honor and keep her, in sickness and in health, and, forsaking all others, be faithful to her as long as you both shall live?"

Brent responded in his deepest baritone voice, "I will." Reed handed Brent Jackie's wedding band, and he smoothly slipped it on her finger to rest next to the engagement ring. She looked at him, tears welling up.

Pastor Kevin addressed the first few pews on both the bride and groom sides.

"Will you, the families of Jackie and Brent, give your love and blessing to this marriage?"

There was an enthusiastic mumbling of "we will," from both families.

Pastor Kevin looked up and addressed the entire congregation.

"Will all of you, by God's grace, do everything in your power to uphold and care for these two persons in their life together?"

A second enthusiastic mumbling of "we will" emanated from the guests.

"Let us pray," said Pastor Kevin.

"Eternal God, our creator and redeemer, as you gladdened the wedding at Cana in Galilee by the presence of your Son, so bring your joy to this wedding by his presence now. Look in favor upon Jackie and Brent and grant that they, rejoicing in all your gifts, may at length celebrate the unending marriage feast with Christ our Lord, who lives, and reigns with you and the Holy Spirit, one God, now and forever. Amen."

Pastor Kevin looked at Brent and smiled.

"Brent, you may kiss your bride."

Brent carefully raised Jackie's veil to reveal her bright brown eyes and trembling lips. He leaned down and gave her a reassuring kiss. She wrapped her fingers around his neck and gave him everything she had in that moment to convey her love. They broke apart and faced the guests.

"Ladies and Gentlemen, I give you Mr. and Mrs. Brent Cahill."

Applause erupted for the beautiful young couple. After the emotions the entire nation had been through from October, people needed some good news in their lives, and Jackie and Brent's love for one another demonstrated that America could heal and love again.

Jackie and Brent walked down the aisle to music and exited the sanctuary to wait outside with their siblings, Reed and Blaire, who were arm-in-arm behind them. They would form a receiving line with their parents. The wedding party had posed for photos before the wedding, so they could devote all of their attention to their guests after the ceremony during the reception festivities.

***

The reception was at the Minikahda Club on Lake Calhoun in Minneapolis. The Club was a bit dark and stuffy for Jackie's taste, but it had been available, so they had booked it. Pepper and Bill were excited to meet both sides of Jackie and Brent's families. In fact, Jackie and Brent's families were excited to meet one another!

After Bill delivered a glass of champagne to Pepper, he sought out Allen Montgomery, whom he had never met. He wanted to talk to his wife's new boss to get a feel for who he was, and, more importantly, make his own opinions known. He spotted Allen a few feet away and walked over.

"Allen, my name is Bill McCallan. Nice to meet you," said Bill.

"Bill, the pleasure is all mine," said Allen. "This is a great opportunity for me to tell you that the Agency and the Country thank you for your fast thinking at Southview Hospital. Without you recognizing what was going on and taking immediate action, that sarin spill could have been a lot worse."

"Thank you," said Bill. "I had the benefit of knowing sarin had been used at the Linc, so I put the pieces together. You, on the other hand, were at the epicenter of the first attack. I heard you recognized what was going on before anyone else. Your fast decision-making saved lives."

"I wish I could have done more, man. What I did do, I attribute to training and being in combat in the sandbox in the Middle East. And maybe a little divine intervention," said Allen.

"Well said. Cheers," said Bill. They clinked and drank.

"I want to thank you for keeping a lookout for Pepper. This new job of hers is scary business. It's quite a bit different than her previous corporate job," said Bill.

"No doubt about it," said Allen. "But she's got solid skills. The Agency needs people like Pepper. She approaches things in a creative way. Most of us are ex-military and ex-police, so we're pretty rigid in our investigative work. Pepper comes at things from a different angle. Did she tell you I asked her to go through some formal training?"

"Yes. The hand-to-hand combat should be fun to watch. I don't know whether to be happy or scared," said Bill.

Just then, Jackie's beautiful sister, Blaire, walked by, and Allen stared at her and smiled. She cast him a quick glance and smiled pleasantly.

"She's about 25 years old, Allen. Too young for you," said Bill.

"There's always a chance," said Allen.

Bill laughed and made a note to tell Pepper that Allen was a ladies' man, and she had better watch out.

"Back to Pepper, Allen. I think this mission took a lot out of her," said Bill.

"It took a lot out of all of us," said Allen.

"Yeah. The whole thing is unbelievable, isn't it? The Swedish Minister for Foreign Affairs conspiring with the Russian President to drop nerve gas on United States citizens at a football game?! If you had told me this would have happened five years ago, I never would have believed you," said Bill.

"Well, thanks to the hard work of Pepper and Brent, Lovgren and Volkov no longer inhabit the Earth," said Allen.

"Unfortunately, someone else is most likely waiting in the wings to take their places. When

Pepper gets involved in another case, I'd like your word that you'll look out for her," said Bill.

"You have my word," said Allen. "She's partnering with Brent, and I'd trust him with my life in the field, if it provides you any comfort."

"It does. He's a good guy," said Bill.

A young man who obviously was inebriated came walking by with an extra chair for his crowded table and said, "Here's a chair that isn't broken!"

Bill replied as only an orthopedic surgeon would, "Then don't fix it."

Allen laughed.

***

Pepper and Jackie were in the ladies' room, Pepper holding Jackie's train so she could tinkle. It was a laughable affair with hopeless logistics. When Jackie had finally righted herself in front of the mirror and washed her hands, they hugged.

"I'm so happy for you two," said Pepper.

"Thank you. I can't believe you introduced us, Pepper," said Jackie.

"I knew that night at StarrFitness that you two were destined to be with each other. You completely ignored me once Brent said 'nice to meet you.' You were a goner, girl!" said Pepper.

"Happily so. I just hope we can figure out how to live together with his job headquartered in Boston. It will take some work," said Jackie.

"Everything worthwhile takes some work. I'm confident you two will figure it out. You have something too good to let go," said Pepper.

"Well, you're sort of in the same boat. I guess you're going to work with Brent long distance from Minneapolis?" asked Jackie.

"I'm going to try anyway," said Pepper.

"You have to make it work, Pepper. You're my eyes and ears in the field with Brent," she laughed.

"Oh yeah, I've got your back, Sister. I'll beat the women off with a stick if I have to!"

"Now that we have that settled, I can rest easy," said Jackie.

"Are you excited for your adventurous honeymoon? Are you packed?" asked Pepper.

"I think I am. It's weird to pack shorts and stuff in December for a three-week trip, but I'm not complaining. I've never been to Australia," said Jackie.

"I'm jealous. I hear it's beautiful on the west coast. You'll have the most romantic time, swimming and walking the beach. How perfect," said Pepper.

"And we're going to spend a week at Reed's winery. He's so excited to show Brent what he's built, being the younger brother and all. He's a cutie patootie, isn't he?" asked Jackie.

"He is. There isn't a woman here under the age of 60 who hasn't noticed him. I'm sure he'll have plenty of dance partners," said Pepper.

"I just hope my sister Blaire isn't one of them. She collects men and tosses them aside three months later. I told her Reed is off limits because it would be too weird. Don't you agree?" asked Jackie.

"Yes, wholeheartedly. That would be weird if they got together and she dropped him," said Pepper. "It would sour the family gatherings forever. There are plenty of fish in the sea. She can look for someone else.

***

When Jackie and Pepper came out of the ladies' room, Brent was there to scoop up Jackie for their first dance together. Pepper found Bill and held his hand as they watched Jackie and Brent dance to *I Left My Heart in San Francisco.*

After that, the parents and wedding party were invited to dance as well. Blaire and Reed made an undeniably handsome couple, she with her long auburn hair and slim body. He, with his sandy blonde mess that needed a pair of scissors taken to it. He was surprisingly light on his feet, moving Blaire around the dance floor so her dress flowed like a swan. Pepper guessed there had been some dance lessons for both of them in their youth.

Bill leaned down to Pepper and gave her a kiss on her temple. He whispered in her ear. "I wrote something for you when I was sitting in the hospital the night of the sarin attack."

"Oh? What could it be?" she asked.

He pulled a folded piece of paper from his breast pocket and handed it to her. It was a poem.

<u>Dance</u>

Minds touch intertwined
Thoughts shared undefined
Ideas perceived in a glance
An interconnected soulful dance.

The essence of one
Dissolved in another
Shared through ideas
That bind each other.

No active thought is required
Truer love being desired
Those precious problems once acquired
So mindfully solved and admired.

Minds touch intertwined
Thoughts shared undefined
Ideas perceived in a glance
An interconnected soulful dance.

Pepper started crying after she read it. She wrapped her arms around Bill's neck and kissed him deeply. "Thank you, Honey. I love you."

"I love you too," he said.

***

THE END

ACKNOWLEDGEMENTS

For

Svea's Sins

I thank Jackie Barstad and Dana Schroeder for the continued fictitious use of their first names and hope that I have made them proud with the characters' trajectories. In return, they have graciously donated money to their favorite charities.

Thank you to Michelle Burgraff, Linda Pophal, Erin Skold and Dana Schroeder for their brave undertaking of reviewing the first draft, and providing me with candid feedback.

A shout out to Rochelle Gietman for showing me numerous Word functions and commands, and for patiently listening to my ideas for plot lines in my novels.

I am grateful to Ron Hitzke and Leanne Grangaard for certain pharmaceutical information. I am grateful to other professionals at my work who wish to remain anonymous and I don't blame them! You know who you are and I appreciate your insights and support.

Thank you to Keith for correcting my military terminology.

Finally, I am indebted to the love and patience of my family, Todd and Sarah Wright. They indulged my excursions and side trips in St. Martin, London, Stockholm, Salzburg and Werfen to set the scenes for much of this book.

The poem is by Todd Wright.

***

ABOUT THE AUTHOR

Alexi Venice writes thriller-terrorist novels featuring Pepper McCallan. The Pepper McCallan series includes Ebola Vaccine Wars, Svea's Sins, Victus and Margaret River Winery. Venice's thrillers extrapolate on current events, weaving relationships into nail-biting action. Venice's heroine, Pepper McCallan, travels the world on counter-terrorism assignments with her hunky agent partner, Brent Cahill. Venice draws on her own experience as a practicing attorney and avid adventurist. She makes it a point to attempt the same activities as Pepper McCallan, including flying the Eclipse jet and boxing in the ring. She is married and lives in Wisconsin. See her website at www.alexivenice.com.

Read on for a sneak peek at Alexi Venice's
third book in the Pepper McCallan series,
VICTUS, Part I of MARGARET RIVER WINERY

CHAPTER 1

The Sharpshooters

December 2018

Temecula Valley, California

Day One

The Mexican men walked among the grapevines in the greenhouses collecting the tiny sharpshooters, an ugly little insect similar to any number of miniscule flying bugs. The sharpshooters were as long as a pinky fingernail and skinny as a pencil lead. The workers scooped up the glassy-winged sharpshooters with hand held nets and shook them into their burlap gunny sacks and quart-sized jars. They also threw in some grape vine leaves for bedding for the sharpshooters because they would be in the gunny sacks and jars for about eight hours.

The glassy-winged sharpshooters' shortened wings allowed them to fly short distances to reach the tops of citrus and olive trees, so they were tricky to catch, being skittish little buggers. The workers had to swing their nets gently through the air and along the grapevines in a wave like fashion, scooping as many as one hundred sharpshooters with one sweep. If the sharpshooters sensed a threat, they flew, displaying their brown-black mottled bodies and burnt gold jaws.

The sharpshooters were native to the southwestern United States and northern Mexico. They fed predominantly on orchards before turning their attention to grapevines. The bacteria that the sharpshooters carried was sometimes specific to grapevines and other times specific to olive trees or citrus orchards.

They had a menacing exterior, the upper parts of their head and back stippled with ivory and yellowish spots, complemented by translucent wings with reddish veins. They were as scary looking as an Orc from *Lord of the Rings,* so it was fortunate they weren't any larger, or people would take cover when they saw them coming.

The sharpshooter was especially effective at tapping into a grape vine's main stem and sucking up the nutrients from the xylem, or water conduction system of the vine. They used a stylus, a needle-like straw, to tap in and suck up the water. This interruption to water flow was not, by itself, deadly to the grape vine. It's what the sharpshooter coughed up from its foregut that caused the vine to die – the bacteria called Xylella Fastidiosa.

When the sharpshooter passed Xylella Fastidiosa into the water conduction system of the vine, the bacteria colonized and flourished, enabling it to conquer and kill the vine in two to three years. The disease process was named after the governmental scientist who discovered it in the 1890s, Newton Pierce. The grape growers referred to it as Pierce's Disease.

As a result of the sharpshooter being the number one vector of Xylella Fastidiosa,

California grape growers and the state government had spent millions of dollars researching and tackling the sharpshooters with education, insecticides and habitat control.

The sharpshooters the migrant workers were netting in the greenhouses were especially deadly because they had been feeding on Xylella Fastidiosa-infected grapevines for a week. They were expected to be one hundred percent incubated with a potent strain of the bacteria, which had been colonized and perfected in the laboratory that a company named 'Metaxas' had purchased a year ago and recently sold.

It wasn't difficult for the Metaxas scientists to weaponize Xylella Fastidiosa by incubating the specific strain for grapes, creating a virulent strain that thrived specifically on grapevines.

The scientists cultured the bacteria in the Metaxas lab then transported it by car to the greenhouses where it was mixed in plastic spray bottles with lukewarm water, and sprayed on the vines to inoculate them. It took only a week for the inoculation to take hold, then the workers removed a plastic barrier dividing the two greenhouses and let the sharpshooters fly into the bacteria-laden vines to become infected with the potent strain.

It had been approximately twenty years since the last naturally occurring sharpshooter outbreak, which exploded only when all the key ingredients for an outbreak came together in nature. The outdoor conditions had to be ideal for the bacteria to thrive, the sharpshooters to be in abundance, and the habitat to be near the vineyards.

Interestingly, naturally occurring bacteria-infected sharpshooters thrived in a nursery environment on ornamentals and bushes like oleander plants. Transportation of nursery plants from Mexico to Redding, California along the Interstate 5 corridor, which coincidentally was the main corridor for the movement of drugs, was the main source of sharpshooter infestation from south to north.

That type of sporadic outbreak could be controlled largely through insecticide application by the nurseries. However, since the pest had been beaten back so effectively and the insecticide was so expensive, the grape growers had dropped the neonicotinoid from the mix of sprays they routinely applied.

The effectiveness of the insecticide was still in question for many who used it because the sharpshooter eggs that were deposited by the female within the plant survived the spray and sharpshooter nymphs emerged during their next hatching cycle. In southern California, the sharpshooters were capable of producing two generations per year, one during the winter and one in late summer.

Fortunately for the mission at hand, the glassy-winged sharpshooter fed on dormant vines in the winter months, depositing eggs and vectoring Xylella Fastidiosa into the older, woody tissues of the vine, so that the new hatch of sharpshooters in the spring also would pick up the bacteria and vector it to more vines. It was the bacteria that kept on giving through the life cycle of the sharpshooter.

An infestation of sharpshooters could devastate hundreds of acres of grapevines, and they periodically had done so in California. For over a century, grape growers, the University of California and the California state government had battled the insects. For a three-billion-dollar industry that included both table grapes and wine grapes, Xylella Fastidiosa spread by the sharpshooter was the most expensive cause of grape loss.

The Mexicans gently loaded hundreds of burlap gunny sacks and quart-size jars full of bacteria-carrying sharpshooters into the white trucks and laid them in stacked cages for air flow. They didn't want the sharpshooters to suffocate on their eight-hour drive to northern California. The trucks were designed with excellent ventilation systems that would oxygenate the sharpshooters during the ride. There would even be a Mexican in the back of each truck with the sharpshooters to rotate the gunny sacks and keep them fluffed up so the sharpshooters wouldn't be crushed by the weight on top of them.

Some of the trucks also carried four-wheelers that would allow the Mexicans to access the center of many of the vineyards to spread the sharpshooters. Carrying them on foot would take too much time for the substantial area they needed to cover.

Over a million sharpshooters were being netted in the greenhouses for loading onto the trucks and ultimate dispersion into the vineyards. The temporary greenhouses would be disassembled and loaded onto other trucks for removal after the sharpshooters were gone. The entire operation was hidden in the woods of Temecula Valley, an affluent area located between San Diego and Los Angeles, and ironically, the original source of a sharpshooter infestation that moved from orchards to vineyards.

The trucks would drive eight hours to Sonoma and Napa counties in northern California to time their release for roughly midnight.

The white trucks were owned by Temecula Valley Trucking, which used to be imprinted on their sides but, for this operation, had been painted over by the hired Mexicans. The owner of Temecula Valley Trucking, a shell corporation named Metaxas in the Cayman Islands, had entered into a verbal agreement to sell the company before the end of the year to King Transport, a national transportation firm headquartered in Minneapolis.

Metaxas had orchestrated the purchase of Temecula Valley Trucking only a few years ago for the express purpose of hatching and transporting sharpshooters. It now needed to divest itself of all the assets to free up cash for operational expenses associated with its current mission underway.

Most of the Mexicans doing the sharpshooter roundup were not trucking company employees. Only the truck drivers were. The sharpshooter collectors were locals who worked in the orchards and had been recruited for this task by a small group of men who had visited the orchards, promising to pay cash up front. The Mexicans were being compensated generously for their work, earning much needed cash before Christmas. They didn't understand *why* they were catching sharpshooters and spreading them in grape vineyards, but they knew it wasn't legal.

The entire California sharpshooter infestation would be completed in 24 hours. And since it was a warm December, the sharpshooters would be quite active, devastating the vines as they sucked the nutrients from the stems and deposited both their sharpshooter eggs and Xylella Fastidiosa bacteria deep into the vine stem. What they didn't damage in the dormant vines, their eggs would damage in the spring when they hatched and moved on, vectoring the bacteria.

The first biological war on food in California had begun.

***

CHAPTER 2

The Ex

Minneapolis, Minnesota

Day One

Blaire Starr was the maid of honor for her older sister, Jackie Starr. Jackie had just married Brent Cahill in a Lutheran ceremony at Jackie's childhood church, Trinity Lutheran Church, in Edina, Minnesota, a suburb of Minneapolis.

It was a cold December day and the wedding party and guests had arrived at the cozy Minikahda Country Club for the reception. They were greeted by a large fire in the expansive entrance and two smaller fires in the bar and reception room. The women gathered around the fireplaces in their formal dresses, while the men fetched cocktails and the wait staff delivered champagne.

Reed Cahill had delivered a few glasses of champagne to the beautiful women himself, then decided it was more efficient to bring a bottle and pour for the women as he introduced himself. He was the best man for his older brother, Brent.

Gradually, the guests made their way into the reception hall where there were tables of eight set for dinner. The wedding party was the only table with name placards and was thoughtfully located near the fireplace. Even though the club was 'old school' stuffy with dark wood paneling, tonight it was the perfect venue of glowing warmth in contrast to the frigid outdoors.

After everyone was seated with the beverage of their choice, it was time for a few short toasts. Brent and Jackie had made it clear that they didn't care for a marathon of toasts. They had been to some weddings recently where there was a call for toasts, and it turned into amateur night at the toastmaster club down at the Hyuck Hall in Podunk. It was a blight on the festivities.

Reed genuinely admired his older brother, Brent. He wanted to make Brent's wedding celebration the best it could be by being his wingman from the groom's dinner through the reception.

Reed had sandy blonde hair that was as messy as Brent's brown hair. He was tall, tan and gorgeous, having arrived a few days ago from his home in Australia. He owned a winery and 500 acre estate in the Margaret River wine region of Western Australia. He was sober and at the top of his game tonight. His partying days of overindulgence at weddings were long gone. At the age of 31, he held himself to a higher standard, being an entrepreneur.

Reed had attended college at the University of California in Davis, where he majored in viticulture and enology. He was drawn to agriculture and wine-making, so he knew from his first year in the department that his goal was to own and run a winery. His pride and joy, named the 'Margaret River Winery,' was still just a fledging winery compared to other, older wineries in the region, but his sales were robust, and he was expanding. Unlike the other Australian vintners, Reed had contacts in the United States for his distribution and he was developing a brisk overseas market on which he intended to capitalize.

Brent and Reed were actually half-brothers, but they were as close as full brothers could be. Brent's father, Darin, had died suddenly when Brent was a baby. His mother, Carrie, raised Brent alone for a year before meeting Reed's father, Brian, and they married within six months of meeting. Soon after, she was pregnant with Reed, who was three years younger than Brent. Brian raised Brent as his own son and never once made Brent feel like a stepson. It was a testament to Brian's love. Love and generosity defined their father, a characteristic he nurtured in his sons. Brent and Reed learned early in life that a big heart was more valued in their home than any athletic feat or financial fortune.

Jackie's father, Al Starr, a retired teacher and football coach, delivered a short, sentimental toast, in Jackie and Brent's honor. He was truly fond of Brent and welcomed him to the family. Al handed the microphone to Reed, who stood and took a moment to gaze at the small wedding party. Public speaking was easy for him, as he was on his feet in front of his winery employees every day. All the women in the room were grateful for an excuse to stare at him, whether it was at his winery or at a wedding reception.

"Ladies and Gentlemen, it's my pleasure to toast my older brother and his beautiful bride on their wedding day. First, I'd like to make this toast in memory of Darin, Brent's father, God rest his soul. I understand he was an exemplary, kind hearted human being, who incidentally had good taste in women, right mom? We know he is with us today in spirit. To Darin." Reed raised his glass, and they all drank. He continued.

"The second half of my toast is to 'love.' The minute I heard Brent describe Jackie over the phone, I knew he was in love. He just couldn't stop himself from going on and on about her. I was walking through my vineyards checking the grapes while listening, and I realized he had been talking for 15 minutes straight about her. It dawned on me that my older brother had fallen in love. I started asking him pointed questions about her, and Brent said he could see himself spending the rest of his life with her."

"I said, 'Brent, it sounds obvious to me that you love her, so man up and pop the question!' I think he did shortly after that."

Everyone laughed.

"When I first met Jackie (a few days ago, mind you), it was obvious why Brent wanted to marry her. I immediately concluded that Brent married up! I was astonished that a woman of her beauty and intellect could even fall for my brother, who must have grown up a lot since I beat him at every game imaginable all those years ago. Jackie will bring more grace and beauty to our family to complement our mom's grace and beauty.

Brent, you've been the best brother a man could ask for. I wish you and Jackie all the happiness in the world, and I'm excited as hell to host you and Jackie at my winery on your honeymoon! Here's to Brent and Jackie!" Reed raised his glass again and everyone drank.

He was ready to pass the torch to Blaire Starr, Jackie's younger sister and maid of honor, but she wasn't there.

Usually, Blaire viewed a bridesmaid's duties as drudgery. Especially if she was the maid of honor because it involved giving a toast. Tonight, however, she was feeling light and giddy because it was her older sister's wedding, and Blaire was thrilled for her. Jackie was in love with Brent, and Blaire had known they would marry from the moment she had heard Jackie talk about him.

Blaire had planned to give her toast immediately after Reed, but a young man in the back of the dining room caught her eye. He was wearing jeans and a navy sweater, his thick beige parka unzipped. He was staring at Blaire. *Oh shit, what is Tyler doing here?* She thought.

She had dropped Tyler a month ago after he got drunk and pressured her for sex. He had whined at her initial refusal, and when she said 'no' a second time, explaining that she wanted to be with him when they were both sober, he had launched into a tirade and started breaking things in her apartment. She had called 911, but he left before the police had arrived. She called him the next day and broke if off. They had been dating only about six weeks, and she hadn't seen him since.

She excused herself quickly during Reed's toast and weaved among the guests to the exit. She didn't want Tyler entering the reception hall, especially if he had been drinking. She couldn't tell from a distance, but as she drew nearer, she could see he had a flushed face and his eyes were bloodshot. Her fear was confirmed.

Blaire walked straight past him and down a hallway where the restrooms were located. He followed her, as she knew he would. As soon as they turned a corner and were a reasonably safe distance from anyone overhearing, she stopped and faced him, struggling to keep a neutral face.

"Tyler, what on earth are you doing here? How did you even find me?"

He blinked hard, but kept a smile on his face. "I missed you, Blaire. I saw your photos on Facebook. The entire wedding is already posted. I wanted to apologize for the way I acted at your place...I don't know what came over me."

Shit. Note to self. Unfriend Tyler on Facebook. "Apology accepted, Tyler. That's big of you to drive all the way over here. Thanks. I need to get back to Jackie's reception. It's my turn to give the maid of honor toast."

His face contorted. "Wait. That's it? You're leaving? You're not even inviting me in? What the fuck, Blaire?!" Tyler must have been drunker than Blaire had realized. She could see that look of rage returning to his eyes that he had had when he had broken the lamp at her apartment.

"Tyler, it's my sister's wedding reception. Can you cut me a break here? I have family duties to fulfill. We can catch up tomorrow. Maybe you should go home, huh?"

She tried to give him a pleasant look, but suspected it came off as phony. She paused briefly, deciding whether to walk back into the reception, trusting he would show himself out, or to walk him to the door herself. Better safe than sorry.

"Come on, Tyler, I'll walk you to the door." She held out her hand and made a move toward the door.

"Bullshit," he spat. "You're not giving me the boot! You go in and give your damn toast then come out here and talk to me. I deserve more than just being shown to the door. After all, we dated for like two months, even though you wouldn't have sex with me!" Tyler emphasized the word 'sex' in his drunken slur loudly enough that Blaire was sure people heard it.

"It's true that we dated, Tyler. But we're not dating any longer, and I'm not going to have sex with you. It would be best if you moved on to someone else. Someone who *will* have sex with you." Blaire was trying her best to keep her voice level to coax him out of the building, but she felt like she was losing control of the situation. His lips were snarling, and he was shaking his head.

"Fuck you, Blaire! You BITCH!" He grabbed her by her upper arms and threw her against the wall. She was pinned. Blaire screamed as he lowered his head and smashed his mouth against hers. His teeth cut into her lips, while she violently tried to free her arms.

There was a blur of commotion before she realized that a man had put his arm around Tyler's neck from behind and had Tyler's right arm bent around his back in an unbreakable hold. Tyler was pulled off of her in one quick motion, as she watched his body being spun around and his face being smashed into the opposite wall. She saw the unmistakable back of Reed Cahill manhandling Tyler.

After he smashed Tyler's face into the wall, Reed walked Tyler to the exit and out into the cold night air. There were already a few taxi cabs lined up for the guests so Reed opened the back door of the first one in line and stuffed Tyler in. Reed shut the door then spoke to the driver through the passenger window.

"Take him wherever he wants to go. Here's fifty dollars. That should cover it."

"Thanks. I think," said the driver and he rolled up the window.

Reed walked back into the foyer and down the hallway where Blaire was standing, obviously shaken. Her lip was bleeding, and her freckled cheeks were aflame. She was so fired up that her auburn hair almost glowed red. Reed took one look at her and put his arms around her. He could tell when a woman was rattled, and Blaire was definitely rattled. He guessed that this was the first time she had found herself 'not in control' of a man. He didn't blame her. That creep would have done harm to her if someone hadn't intervened.

"There," he said as he smoothed her hair. "You're alright."

He could feel her trembling through his tuxedo. She was wearing a skimpy sleeveless golden dress with deep green dye in it, giving him the impression of a princess in a fairy tale. She looked ethereal, like she had just materialized from a mist. With her long, curly auburn hair, he realized he had never seen a woman quite like her. As he held her, he suddenly realized how real she was, and that he liked holding her. He felt like he could stand in that spot holding her all night. He was proud that she had needed him, despite the circumstances.

Blaire felt a thousand emotions at once. The first was embarrassment. *How could she have made a scene at her sister's wedding reception?* Blaire never made scenes. She was demure, poised and smart. She never sought the limelight or called attention to herself. Yet, here she was, in the arms of *Reed*, of all men, shaken to her core over a throwaway boyfriend, who she thought she had dropped a month ago!

She was fearful, too. *Had Tyler just assaulted her?* Her lip stung where he had cut it with his teeth, and she was sure she had red marks on her upper arms where he had grabbed her. That was the first time in her life she had been physically forced by a man, and she was damned thankful that Reed had appeared to peel Tyler off her. She didn't know how to control the fear that was coursing through her body. She was scared, and it was *real.*

Reed's hug supported her weight. She didn't trust herself to stand on her own, her knees feeling like they could buckle at any second. She wasn't crying, but she could feel herself involuntarily shaking. Maybe Reed would know what to do next because she didn't. She was glued to him, soaking up all his warmth and strength. And she was confused, even though logic told her she didn't have anything to be afraid of any longer.

"Reed, I'm so sorry," she said, her voice shaking.

"Blaire, there's no need to apologize. You didn't do anything wrong. It wasn't your fault."

"I can't believe that happened, Reed. Nothing like that has ever happened to me before. Men have always been so polite to me. It's a 'trust thing', you know?"

"I know, Blaire. I know." He kept stroking the back of her head because he didn't know what else to do. He was going with his instincts and doing what came naturally.

"Thank you, Reed," she said politely, but found herself thinking it felt *really* good.

They stood hugging for another few minutes. Blaire felt like there was no other place in the world she was supposed to be at that moment. And she had never felt so secure in a man's arms. When her breathing had returned to normal, she realized that her heart was still pounding. Not out of lingering fear, though. Out of attraction.

As her senses recovered from Tyler's assault, they rebounded on full alert in Reed's arms. How confounding! She was suddenly aware that her arms were around his neck, and her body was melded against his. Her braless breasts were mashed up against his chest, and she could feel the warmth of his body to the core of her being.

"Whoa. Umm," she said self-consciously as she broke away.

"Are you better now, Blaire?" he asked genuinely, keeping his hands on her elbows to support her.

She looked up into his eyes and felt a magnetic pull. She was trying to decipher if his eyes were copper colored or hazel. The lighting was dim in the club foyer, emanating from the fireplace and bouncing off the dark wood-paneled walls, but she had never had such difficulty discerning eye color. She had the sensation of swimming. It was as if his eyes were a mysterious coppery-hazel liquid that was swirling around while he looked at her. *I'm looking into a bowl of tiramisu gelato,* she thought. *I have to get ahold of myself.*

Reed was worried for Blaire. When she looked up at him with those stunning emerald eyes, he noticed she was off-balance. Her eyes didn't have the same sharp, snappy stare he had noticed over the last two days during the groom's dinner and wedding. He saw a softness and vulnerability that he never would have guessed existed in her confident body. She was revealing her raw emotion to him and he felt responsible for protecting her. He wouldn't let her down.

"Blaire, let's walk over to the bar and get something soothing that will take the edge off, huh?"

"Yeah, that sounds good. I have to get in shape to deliver my maid of honor toast," she said. She leaned into him as he guided her over to the warm bar area. There were a few wedding guests buying a cocktail for their dinner table, but Blaire and Reed were soon alone.

They sat on a lavender settee in front of the gas fireplace with two glasses of champagne. It was warm and cozy, and just what Blaire needed. Reed snuggled up close to her and put his arm over the back of the settee. She soaked up his proximity. He gently clinked his glass against hers, and they sipped. Blaire's hand trembled as she raised and lowered her glass. They both noticed it at the same time, which unnerved her even more.

"God, my hand is shaking," she said and handed him the glass. He readjusted and set both glasses on the dark, wooden coffee table in front of them.

"That's understandable," he said. "Put your hands in mine." He rested the backs of his hands on top of her lap, and she lay her hands in his. He rhythmically massaged the back of her hands with his thumbs, attempting to get her back in shape for her maid of honor toast.

Electricity raced up Blaire's spine. A word bubble appeared in her mind that said "swoon." She had never said that word aloud and had no idea why it was front and center in her brain. *Am I swooning? Is it from Reed's touch?*

An audible sigh escaped her lips and her entire body relaxed. She looked at Reed. Again with the swirling hazel eyes that had glints of copper running circles around her dizzy mind. *Reed is casting a spell on me,* she thought. She leaned in closer to him and found herself tilting up her chin toward his mouth. Her gaze moved to his mouth, where she discovered his lips were red and succulent looking.

Reed raised her hand to his mouth and kissed it gently. "I think you're recovering now," he said. He held her gaze after he kissed her hand, enjoying a comfortable silence between them.

Blaire felt another electric jolt go from her hand to her heart. She watched as he touched her hand to his cheek, surprised that she was the recipient of this old-fashioned gesture. Tonight was turning into a lot of 'firsts' for her.

"Umm." she heard herself moan. She didn't recognize her own voice. It emitted a huskiness that had never been present. The stars were rearranging themselves for Blaire and Reed when the spell was suddenly broken by Blaire's sister, Jackie, who was now standing over her.

"There you are, Blaire! What have you been doing for the last twenty minutes? We expected you to give your toast, but they're serving dinner now," said Jackie. Jackie looked beautiful in her wedding dress, her brown hair pulled back and her perfectly sculpted Scottish body accentuated by the slimming style of her dress.

Blaire was jerked out of her reverie, withdrawing her hand from Reed's. She reluctantly stood and followed Jackie. "Ah. Something weird happened with my ex-boyfriend. He showed up, and Reed helped me get rid of him. No big deal, Sis. Let's get back to the table. I'll give my toast after dinner."

"Well that *is* strange! Nothing goes the way you think it will on your wedding day, Blaire. Remember that! Thank you for getting rid of that loser, Reed," said Jackie. Despite the days' twists and turns, she maintained a positive attitude.

"All in a day's work," he said modestly. The three of them made their way back to the wedding party table. They enjoyed their dinners, and afterward, Blaire gave her heartfelt toast to Jackie and Brent.

***